Brother to the Blood

Mike Champagne

DEDICATION

For my sister, Rochelle, who always loved books.

CONTENTS

ACKNOWLEDGMENTS

With special thanks to Rea Rosno, Mary Bloom, and Kathleen Moore for their editorial support in producing this book.

PROLOGUE

They were still there!..I still don't know what to do with them. What do you do when the impossible presents itself to you as reality? I had gone into my safe for several documents regarding Crayden's endowment, and there they were. The envelope with the thumb drive, the transcript, and the two artifacts—in the back. Out of the way...but never off my mind...

CHAPTER 1

I had forgotten the anonymity of the city. I had also forgotten its edge and its pressure. Being Dean of Men at Ardmore College had disarmed me. I'd grown used to the Midwest. Even though I was born in New York and had lived there the first twelve years of my life, twenty-five years at Ardmore had made me a hick! I was, in fact, the worst kind of hick—I was an exile dreaming of homecoming. I don't even know what the romance with New York was all about. I only knew I was a man in love with a memory of home, and nothing could keep me from returning.

Barbara knew this. The kids were grown. They were off to find whatever adventures they could. It was time for us to do what we liked. "What we liked"—it was a phrase that chilled my blood. I was *doing* what I liked. The problem was, it wasn't *where* I liked. I had this terrible pull to return to my boyhood. I talked about evenings at the theater, concerts in the Park,—brunches in bistros near the Natural History Museum, but that was all a smoke screen! It was more like being a salmon and feeling this almost biological need to move uptown to spawn! However, at fifty-six retirement was still out of the question. We couldn't just pull up stakes and retire to the city. We needed something to live on—an adjunct professorship—anything to tide us over until pensions and investments were ready to harvest. I wasn't expecting much, but I couldn't resist this relentless aching to return. Résumés were sent out.

Crayden surprised me. The cream-colored envelope arrived less than two weeks after the first wave of résumés had been sent. Most of them, no doubt, were still sitting on desks somewhere unopened by secretaries and assistants to be added to the piles of other applicants. Crayden was my Alma Mater. Perhaps that was why they answered. It had been nearly forty-four years, but I remembered Crayden as if I had just closed the huge oak door that fronted West End Avenue. It had always been a trendy school. A haven for liberal, well-heeled New Yorkers to shelter their children from the flinty atmosphere of the public schools. The tuition was obscenely high, but all the "best" families sent their kids there, and my parents, eager to live up to that epithet and able to pay, sent me.

The School looked like a Victorian fever-dream—a huge Nineteenth Century brick building with its terra cotta gothic ornamentation. Turrets topped its façade and inside it was a welter of stained glass and carved oak. It filled the block and had a small courtyard in its center that nobody ever used. Hollywood couldn't have done it better. I remember feeling overwhelmed my first day. I was only five! I think I cried most of the day. But to its credit, Crayden enfolded me. In the first year I grew to love the old library. After school it became my haven while I waited to be picked up by Mother.

It was a gallery-sized room with two ornate cast-iron staircases at either end leading to the mezzanine level. It smelled of must and steam heat and books. I remember the comforting hiss of the old radiators on cold winter's days as I curled up with several picture books behind the stacks in a corner at the back of the upper level. Mr. Parnell, the librarian, was very tolerant of "the little ones" as he called us. "Let them browse! Let them browse!" he moaned to the student aids who only wanted to collect the wayward books and go home.

"Time, Master Holliman!" Parnell would bark at me as my Mother's arrival neared. I would collect my books and bring them down to his desk. "Let's see—castles, witches, magic. *Someone* has an imagination! *Someone* loves his books!" He would laugh that peculiar dry laugh of his and add the books to the return cart.

Mother would sweep me into a cab and off to supper at Pino's. Most of our "suppers" were there. Mother didn't cook. Mother had a "career". We lived our lives in a constant swirl of schedules, "catching up with each other" at Pino's or "touching base" at the deli for breakfast. On rare Sundays, if she didn't have a client meeting or a brunch, Mother would take me for "a turn around the park" followed by a movie. Those were very special events.

Dad was a journalist. I remember him gone mostly. His returns were excuses for staying up far too late. He was like Superman or Zorro—I couldn't decide which. He was full of stories about "the world". He was always on the edge of some war zone or in the middle of a city devastated by earthquake. Everywhere he went, huge events were always happening, and he was sent in to "inform the public". He was very important. Mother and I would listen as he talked and talked and filled his glass. As the evening drew on, the stories became more and more vivid. Mother's eyes shone with excitement. He was her hero too. Finally Dad would take a long breath, fill his glass, and look at Mother with a sense of ceremony.

"Well," he'd intone, "What about you, Mary? Still advancing the Culture? What new literary geniuses have you discovered this year?"

Mother was an editor. Her clients were mostly second-string authors— mystery writers, pulp fiction. She always blushed when he asked this and shrugged her shoulders.

"Oh, you know, Chris. The usual cast of characters. Hacks and whores— but they sell."

"Not at all! Not at all! Without you they couldn't survive! You made them who they are, and they know it!" Dad would always say this with just the right emphasis. I think he really meant it although he always said exactly the same thing. "Butchie, your Mother is a very important woman! You want to be proud of that!"

I knew that. I *was* proud of her. I *worshipped* him. They were both important people! It *all* seemed so important. It must have been. When I was in fifth grade, they divorced.

I stayed with Mother, of course. Dad couldn't possibly take me around the world. I couldn't figure it out—what I did wrong. Nothing was ever said to me about it. One morning Mother told me on the way to school.

"Brad, your father and I think it would be better if we lived apart." She kept walking without looking down at me. Her brows were knitted, and she stared straight ahead and seemed to be unable to look to the left or right.

"I thought you did," I said after a moment.

"That's different," she explained. "Your father was on assignment often, but he always came home. He lived with us when he was home."

"He won't come home anymore?" I asked.

"Of course, he will! He'll see you! He'll see you just like before. He-he just won't be staying at the apartment anymore."

"Oh." It was all I could think to say. It was the only conversation we ever had about it.

I remember Mother "maintaining". That's what she called it. She maintained calm. She maintained her career. She maintained our lifestyle. She maintained me. There was very little difference in my life. I saw my dad just as often. They were just as cordial together, and our late-night suppers went on exactly as before whenever Dad breezed into town. But there was something about the way Mother wandered around the apartment restlessly—as if she were searching for something. *I* maintained my composure.

I was eleven. I didn't know why I felt so angry and so restless. It was as if I caught it from Mother. The old library no longer seemed so engaging, and after-school sports had little attraction for me, so I explored Crayden from its towers to the dungeon. At least it seemed a dungeon to me. The great cellar was supported by huge arched walls dividing the basement into many smaller rooms. Old desks and forgotten file cabinets were stacked and left in rows to molder. Obsolete lab equipment from ancient chemistry classes made part of the basement look a great deal like Frankenstein's lab in the old movie. I pretended I was Victor Frankenstein plugging his patchwork cadaver into the electrical storm and watching it twitch. I was engaged in just this mental movie and shouting "It's alive! It's alive!" when Santiago came around the back of one of the arches and dropped his mop and bucket in surprise. I screamed bloody murder! I was nearly out of my skin.

"You're not s-supposed to be there! Y-you scared me! You son-of-a bitch! You liar! You!—" I let fly at the startled man with all my fury. I flailed my fists at him until he pinned my arms, and I dissolved into helpless tears.

Speaking half in Spanish, half in English he got me to stop crying and led me whimpering to a little room way at the back of the basement where a huge old cast-iron furnace thrummed along. There was a dilapidated club chair with newspaper stuffed under the cushion to even it out. He left me there as he went to a small room separated from the rest of the basement with a wooden partition in which there was a small door. This, I came to learn, was Santiago's "room". It was where he lived. There was a cot and a tiny makeshift kitchen. There was a small window that allowed the meager light in from the courtyard well-grate.

Santiago returned with two steaming cups of liquid.

"Here, you drink." He said passing a cup to me. The liquid smelled strangely herbal, but not unpleasant. "Maté—I put plenty sugar. You drink. You feel good."

I sipped the strange brew. The sugar gave the unfamiliar flavor enough sweetness to appease me. After a few moments I felt wonderful. All the tension I had been holding in was gone. I settled into the chair and enjoyed the heat from the furnace.

"Is good, eh? I make every day this time. You drink my maté and you live long, like Santiago, eh?"

I looked at him. He was small—not more than an inch or so taller than me—and brown like mahogany. His face looked carved from wood. High cheekbones and two shining dark eyes set deep. His hair was iron gray, cut short and almost bristly. Although he sat and stood straight, his legs were so short that he looked almost simian. His long powerful arms and shoulders seemed out of proportion to the rest of his body. It was impossible to tell how old he was—especially for an eleven-year-old.

"Do you live here?" I asked. I didn't recall ever seeing him before. I thought perhaps I had stumbled on some strange stowaway or maybe the 'Phantom of Crayden'! *"That was it,"* I thought! *"He lurks in the secret passages, and no one knows about him but me!"*

"Janitor. I clean. I fix. Is me, Santiago." He pointed to a nametag pinned to his shirt. My fantasy was shattered, but I didn't care. The maté and the heat from the furnace had softened me up so much nothing seemed disappointing. Before I could stop myself, everything came pouring out of me: Mother and Dad's divorce, how it felt like I was a guest at home—how important everybody else was and how unimportant I was. I felt royally sorry for myself, and the more I talked about it, the more I wanted to talk. Santiago just sat and sipped his maté. He nodded his head now and then to show he was listening, and I told him everything that was in my eleven-year-old head. When I was just about emptied of thoughts, he stood up and took my cup.

"You go now. Is time. Tomorrow you come. Same time. I make you maté." He stood and waited for me to get up. I wanted to say something more. "Enough for now. You go."

Mother was waiting. We went out to dinner, and I listened to her day. She never asked about school especially since the divorce, but tonight it didn't seem to matter. I looked at her as she talked. For the first time I noticed the almost manic flow of words and the set of her mouth. She was driving it all away with her words. Everything she felt about Dad, about me, even—she was keeping it all out by focusing on her list of activities, her occupation. For the first time I could see how afraid she was. I could tell how hard she was holding on to—everything. When I went to bed, I kissed her good night, something I hadn't done for a long time. She was reading some galleys, and she looked up startled at first, then her expression cleared, and she put her hand to my face.

"Why thank you, sir!" she cooed. Then the moment was gone. "Now, off you go. School tomorrow. I'll be a little late—client meeting. See you about 5:30, OK?"

I was asleep almost as soon as I buried myself under the comforter.

The next day and for some time following it became a ritual. I would find Santiago by the old furnace. He always had a cup of steaming maté waiting. At first I did all the talking. He would always listen seriously, pensively. He would nod and grunt acknowledgement. He never offered advice or lectured, but he let me know by his attendance that he cared. Whatever ridiculous notions I might proffer, he never contradicted or tried to teach. He weighed what I had to say as if I were the greatest sage he'd ever met. Then he would tell the stories.

They were better than anything in the library! Battle and blood sacrifice...Honor wrapped in magic and violence. They were old stories, he said. From long ago. Stories of "when the Gods returned".

"The Gods are strange," He said. "No one can know what they think! A man must sacrifice—give his blood. Pray! Sometimes the Gods, they bring good—sometimes evil. A man can only hope..."

I sat transfixed. The time went too fast. Always Santiago seemed to know when Mother arrived and was waiting.

In sixth grade Mother died. It was a cerebral hemorrhage. I was sitting with Santiago as usual. He finished another story, then suddenly he stood up and looked at me.

"You go, now. Someone is here."

"You promised to tell me about the potion. I love that one!"

"I will not see you a long time, I think. You will be a good man. I See you—tall—in good clothes. You will live good." With that he took my cup and went back to his little room.

When I got upstairs, Mrs. Carmody, our neighbor, was at the office. Her eyes were red, and there was a haunted look on her face. I knew right away.

Dad arrived the next day from Istanbul. He was jet-lagged and gray from the trip. When he saw me he scooped me up. I could smell the liquor on him.

"Well, old man, it's *us* now. We'll figure it out! We'll figure it out!"

It all seems like a whirlwind in my mind. The funeral, the closing of our apartment, the flight to Atlanta. I never mourned her. I tried to say goodbye at the funeral parlor. She lay in an open casket in her white silk blouse and pearls, but she wasn't there! I didn't know where she had gone, but there was no trace of her in the corpse she left behind. It was this "vacancy" that bothered me the most. Her body without her inside it was like a glove without a hand in it. I recognized the "fabric" but the familiar shape had gone, leaving something shapeless and somehow foreign.

Dad had a sister in Atlanta. I went to live with Aunt Jean. There was a "perfectly good public school", which I attended. I saw Dad off and on as before. Aunt Jean gave the best performance of affection I'd ever seen as long as Dad was around. When he left, she ignored me mostly. I stayed with her through high school, and when I left for college, it was with mutual relief.

In college I felt free for the first time. I cultivated friends without getting too close. I was popular without taking on a load of intimacies. What surprised me most was that people genuinely seemed to listen to me. I was full of myself, and I took every opportunity to sound off about everything. I wrote for the campus newspaper; I debated on the debating team; I ran for class office.—I was everywhere, and I loved it!

"You don't want to date me, Holliman. You'd have to really talk *to* me."

That was the first thing Barbara ever said to me. She was standing at the back of the student union hall, the most striking girl I'd ever seen. I went right up to her, introduced myself, and asked her out to the campus cinema project. She just stood there challenging me to answer.

"I talk to everybody," I offered lamely, not expected the opening shot.

"Yup, you're articulate. Downright eloquent, but I don't feel like being an audience for you like everyone else. You date me, Holliman, and you're going to have a two-way conversation. You start 'holding forth' on some earth-shattering topic, I'm picking up the first available guy and leaving you flat. Understood?"

"...Ok."

That was it. I was hooked. We talked all afternoon. We never did make it to the obscure French Film listed on the brochure. We talked through dinner. We even talked making love. It was the first time I had ever discussed my real feelings with anyone since I was eleven years old. She was easy to listen to. Direct but warm, provocative and intelligent. She was my first love. She still is.

"Accept it," was all she said when the letter from Crayden arrived.

"I haven't even interviewed. They might not want me."

"They will."

***

We had no trouble selling the house. It was in a good neighborhood, and the market was tight. It sold two days after we listed it, and within the month we were a middle-aged pair of empty-nesters bound for a new life in the Big Apple.

The interview had been held at the Plaza over tea! Cameron Delaney presiding! Cameron Delaney—Christ!—he was chairman of the Board of Governors when I was a student at Crayden! He was still tall and imperial. The man had to be at least ninety, and you'd never know it! A robust 70 would be the obvious guess. He went on for quite a while about the "principles" of education and the importance of leadership. I listened. When he was done, I picked up the cue and launched into my spiel about tradition and a "thorough grounding" in the classics. I said all the right things, I guess.

I was to be "Headmaster" at Crayden. The former Headmaster had retired, and they said my extensive experience and the fact that I was an alumnus exactly fitted me for the position. The salary wasn't exactly generous, but the proceeds from the house bought us a modest co-op with three bedrooms (in case the kids came for a visit) close to the school, and we had what we needed.

It was early July and hot in that sticky, close way New York can have when the air doesn't move enough. The air conditioner was already complaining at this time of the morning. The apartment was so full of boxes and furniture, I could barely make my way to the coffeemaker in the morning. I hated leaving all the unpacking that first day to Barbara, but I was needed at the school to meet the faculty and tour the building.

"Just go! I'll leave plenty for you to unpack when you get home!" Barbara seemed glad to get rid of me, and, I had to admit, I was excited to begin my duties as "headmaster".

West End Avenue looked almost exactly the same. The old pre-war apartment buildings still hung their forbidding facades over the avenue, and, with the exception of a few sleek high-rises, I could almost close my eyes and imagine being five again and being taken for my first day at Crayden. Pino's was gone. The building was there but it was completely changed. It was now a sleek, glassed-in health club. I stood in front of it for a few minutes imagining it the way it had been. I don't know what I would have done if it were actually still there.—Of course I knew what I'd do! I'd go in, find "our" table, and wait for Mother...I'd say goodbye. I pushed the thought away.

As I approached the building, I was amazed at how unchanged it all was. I went in through the Great Oak Door and up through the main staircase with its stained-glass window on the landing. I rounded the top of the staircase and went through the vaulted door with the brass plaque marked "Headmaster".

"Dr. Holliman, welcome to Crayden! I'm Sally Boyce." She was a youngish woman, though not as young as she advertised. I guessed about forty going on thirty-five. She was trim and neat without being fussy about it. Her desk was piled with mail and documents, and the outer office had the chaotic look of deep transition. A thriving philodendron was artfully draped over the forward corner of the desk next to a cardboard cup of cold coffee. She led me to my office with its gigantic carved partner's desk... It was the same desk that had been there years ago when I was a student here. There were gargoyles on each corner and deep bas-relief columns all around. It was a perfect relic of Victorian excess, highly polished and righteously placed in the middle of the room on a moldering Turkish carpet. Behind it was a high-backed tufted leather chair that looked like an instrument of torture. Behind the chair was the massive stone fireplace with its faux gas logs.

"Pretty grim, huh? If you haven't guessed, we never throw anything away at Crayden."

"I was a student here—years ago." I added. The room was as gloomy as I remembered it.

"I've left the curriculum schedule on your desk. Faculty meeting at 11:00—'get acquainted'—they're all curious. You can expect some serious sucking up."

"I'll make it easy on them."

"I hope not!" she said with a devil in her eye, "Keep them tap-dancing for a while. You'll find out who you can trust."

"...Can I trust you?" I asked with a deadpan.

"I'll always give you the straight goods—if you want it." She looked at me with a distinct sense of challenge.

I looked at her, and there was a sense of urgency behind her elaborate casualness. I got the feeling there was something she needed to tell me. "...Give me your best shot."

She stood back for a moment surveying me, then she took a deep breath and launched. "We're dying on the vine. Enrollments were down 15% last year. Another 10% this year. Tuitions haven't covered expenses for the last four years. We've been running on our endowment, and that's running out. You're the last hope. If Crayden doesn't enter the current century pronto, I figure this time two years from now, this office will make a dandy co-op for some young shave-tail banker or lawyer."

It took me a minute to let it sink in. I whistled a low note and drew a breath. "You don't kid around. Why didn't the Board of Governors—"

"They didn't tell you any of this, huh? That bunch of fossils wouldn't know reality if it bit them in the ass! Look, Dr. Holliman, you don't know me, and you can fire me if you want to, but somebody has to see what's going on around here! Except for mine, we don't have computers.—Do you know any other school today without a computer? We don't have a book in the library with copyright date later than 1960! There's no sports program. Half the faculty is ready for the morgue, and the other half is sending out résumés like flyers for a lost dog. The building hasn't had serious upgrading since 1926! Who's gonna send their kid into a time capsule for an education? The bloody Board of Governors thinks that Crayden's reputation for the classics will carry the day. Well, let me tell you, the word out there in the Real World is that Crayden is a relic. You better know these things before you get started just in case you want to move on."

"I see..." I sat heavily in the leather chair, the psychological wind knocked out of me.

"Do you?"

"Huh?" I asked a little dazed by her torrent of information.

"Do you want to move on—now that I've told you?"

"Is that why you told me? To scare me off?"

"No! I just had to tell you. It's not fair of them to sucker you like that. I'm right, you know. All the bills and all the checks come right across my desk. I know where all the bodies are buried around here, and it's just...stupid to let all this go to waste out of sheer inertia! OK, I'm just a secretary. I don't have a 'Dr.' in front of my name, but every other West Side School is turning students away. Parents volunteer hours of their high-priced, tish-wa-toodle free time just to get their kids into them. I've been here eight years, and I've never seen a single volunteer in all that time.

"Dr. Trask was just as bad as the Board of Governors. He thought it was undignified to expect parents to get involved in the school. I mean, get real! I'm telling you we're dying here."

I looked at her for a long moment. She lowered her eyes for the first time in uncertainty, but just for a second. She looked back up at me.

"I'll pack up my desk. You'll probably want to hire your own Executive Assistant. I just thought you should know." She began to walk away.

"You want to show me around?"

She turned back and looked at me. "What do you want to see?"

"Everything." I said.

We started with the books. She was right. For several years Crayden had been drawing on the principal of its rapidly shrinking endowment fund. There had been no new pledges for at least five years. Enrollments had dropped, especially in the lowest grades—an ominous sign for a private school. The curriculum for the New Year looked good, but when I looked at the faculty roster, I noticed "Allardyce Nichols" listed as senior instructor in Latin and Greek.

"'Dicey' Nickles! Good God, he was teaching Latin and Greek when I was here, and he was a thousand years old then!"

"He's 86. Deaf as a post. He assigns four pages of translation per class and then goes to sleep. If you discount the new hires, your average faculty age is 66. Don't get me wrong; aside from your friend 'Dicey,' most of the staff is still top notch in spite of their ages. At seventy Rosemary Quinn can still keep the fifth graders dancing a jig, and they love her. But how long can she last?"

"What about the new teachers?" I asked with faint hope.

"Losers and left-overs." She answered without a scrap of mercy in her tone. "Salaries were frozen five years ago by the Board. The only teachers who want to come here, couldn't get hired anywhere else. Once in a while someone comes along with talent, but they usually leave. Nobody wants to teach in the middle of a wake."

"Jesus!...Isn't there any good news?"

"Yeah, the roof leaks."

We covered every inch of the building. The slate roof did leak, but it was holding.

"Epifanio knows how to fix slate. He's been here forever—long before me. We're lucky to have him." We were in one of the turrets looking down on the main roof. It was obvious that some new slates had been carefully laid in certain areas. With their sharp edges and darker color they contrasted with the deteriorating, crumbling slates around them. It was clear that the roof was less than five years away from complete replacement in spite of the repairs.

"Epifanio?" I asked absently.

"The Janitor. He lives in the building."

"Jesus! Are we still doing that?...We had a live-in custodian when I was a kid here!"

"Oh, Yeah! Nothing changes at Crayden! We hire crews for the major cleaning, but when something needs fixing, Epifanio is the only one who can keep this museum working."

"C'mon, I want to see the classrooms"

Floor by floor we explored Crayden. The Old Library was exactly the same! I had the feeling that if I went up into the mezzanine I would find myself hunched over a picture book back in the stacks. I half expected to hear Parnell moaning to the Student Aids, "Let them browse! Let them browse!"

The little courtyard with its overgrown, untouched garden still sat in the middle of the surrounding building.

The old gymnasium with its varnished floor was still lined with trophy cases. The trophies, however, stopped in 1976, the year the Board stopped regular sports programs held on premises. Our students went to Cathedral for their "team experience". The Board found it could get off much more cheaply by paying the other school for the use of their facilities and staff rather than maintaining our own.

I managed to push nostalgia aside enough to actually look at the physical plant. The classrooms were huge and airy. The halls were wide, and there was a feeling of solid security about the entire place. What Sally referred to as its "museum" quality was actually one of Crayden's enduring assets. I knew lots of parents who would respond very favorably to the thought of their children held in Crayden's ageless embrace. As we went on with the tour, I began to feel there was hope.

When we got to the basement, it was as if nothing had been touched since I left. The same file cabinets stood in the same rows deep in the basement catacombs. There was the same old lab equipment gathering dust on tables. As we rounded the corner, I recognized the furnace. It was still in service—an old coal burner converted to oil. There by its side was a distant cousin of the old chair I remember when I last sat there with Santiago. I imagined its current occupant sitting there in winter reading the paper during a quiet moment, and I wondered if any other student had found his way down here since my adventures four decades ago.

By the time we got to the "Get Acquainted" meeting, I had a game plan. As we entered, a chorus of expectant faces was peering around stuffed chair-backs at us. The Board of Governors stood behind the service table stirring their coffees almost in unison. Their faces betrayed nothing of the nervousness their clinking spoons reflected.

"Ladies and Gentlemen," I said as I entered the room taking a clipboard with notes Sally had written out of her hands, "I'm Brad Holliman. We have a lot of work to do!"

It was more of a shakeup than the Board had in mind. Once I launched into my view of things (thanks to Sally's intervention,) one by one they took seats and looked grim. The faculty, however, did just the opposite. As I suggested that we refresh the curriculum this year by trading our strengths with neighboring halls for some of their expertise, I saw tired eyes brighten. Basically what I proposed was that we offer our strongest suit, a grounding in the classics, for some of the flashier elements offered by the other schools—Shakespeare for computer training, Aristotle for dance and drama. They began to stand up. I hadn't the slightest idea of how I would do this, or even *if* I could, but their dawning enthusiasm gave me the courage of the damned.

CHAPTER 2

I worked twelve to fifteen hours a day for the next two months. Barbara began referring to herself as a "Crayden Widow". I turned the faculty loose on the other schools. They turned out to be a pretty effective sales staff! By September, we had four computer lab classes not to mention an on-site Phys Ed program. Allardyce Nichols was my best move! The vision of him I had from my childhood was very different after that first meeting in the staff room. Nichols was a quiet, gentle old man with a childlike enthusiasm for any fact or word he could glean from a conversation that might, however distantly, refer to the Classics! He was full of references, ideas, quotations, anecdotes, and obscure historical references, which he joyfully shared whether you were interested or not. You couldn't help but love the man's ageless delight. It was infectious. I couldn't possibly let him go; I knew it would certainly kill him.

So I did what Corporate America would do—I promoted him! I made him an "Emeritus" faculty member complete with a small pension in return for his lecturing once a month on Latin and Greek studies and helping in the planning of the classics curriculum! I told him that his experience was far too great to waste in the classroom. Crayden needed him to fill a more administrative position! Damned if the old boy didn't rise to the bait. All that summer he mapped out a fantastic curriculum for the new Latin and Greek teacher, Brother William from St. Barnabus, down the street. Brother William could actually *speak* Ancient Latin and Greek —the benefits of completing his novitiate in Rome and playing Center at Loyola.—He doubled as Phys Ed teacher. In return, St. Barnabus used our gym free of charge for their students. We saved on salary, they saved on gym rental.

Rosemary Quinn came to my office quietly—almost guiltily—one afternoon. She was tentative, almost shy about something she wanted to propose. "I don't know if you would want this, Dr. Holliman..." she began. She awkwardly blurted out that she had started in New York as an actress, years ago. She giggled nervously, then caught herself. A sick mother shortened her ambitions, and she came to Crayden as a teacher to support the both of them. Apparently "Mother's Illness" stretched out until the old lady died in her nineties only a year ago. Rosemary grew silent for a moment as though the fact of her mother's death was something she was only now fully realizing.

"...I find I have more time on my hands than I'm used to. I've maintained my interest in theater, but now I think I could...could broaden my activities in that area."

She proposed teaching some classes in "theater appreciation"—after school. Encouraged by my attention, she grew bolder.

"...And I think I could manage a play...for each class, of course! Something classical—but New Classics, in keeping with our new approach! And there's this wonderful program the city is sponsoring..."

The meeting lasted an hour. She did all the talking. By the time she was done I was exhausted by the possibilities.

"Why don't we start with the classes and see how much time you have for the other options?"

She looked at me flushed and excited. "You just wait and see, Dr. Holliman! New York is the place to be for theater! These children are going to feast on the incredible cultural banquet this city has to offer!"

With that she straightened herself up and marched out of my office. Later we began to notice a change her style of dressing. From the starched "Crayden" look she had always exhibited, she began to wear "New York Black" all the time. Sally pointed it out to me. In her old age, Miss Quinn was going Bohemian! She used her theater connections to get us hooked up to a New York City Outreach program offering "Arts Counseling" for very little money. Basically, for a few hundred dollars a week we had a steady stream of out-of-work artists to teach music, dance, acting, and—whatever. All I had to do was to find the "few hundred" dollars.

Word got out quickly, and educators from around the area began calling me and suggesting "lunch." They were curious, and I used that curiosity to worm my way into their offices and their curricula. I maintained eye contact and talked as fast and compellingly as I could. By the time our lunches were done, I had conned most of them into trading classes or faculty for some of that famous 'Crayden Mystique'. "Think of it," I trilled, "You give us just a little of your faculty's time, and we lend the Crayden name to your class roster. Shakespeare, taught at Crayden! Greek and Latin at Crayden! History at Crayden Hall! You can add at least $500.00 per year to your tuition without it costing you a cent!"

We had four new enrollments. Our class schedule looked like a timetable for Penn Station, but things were moving. While the faculty and I bartered and sold everything we could think of, Sally was printing up new brochures and writing letters to drum up money from every old, well-heeled Alumnus listed in our files as still living. A small stream of checks was beginning to flow. Enough to keep us from going to the Endowment for more funds to finance this change. I had instructed each member of the faculty to phone every parent of every child in their classes and ask them what they'd be volunteering for this fall. They were to offer a short list of after school duties or a specific dollar amount that would "buy them off" for the fall semester. We raised nearly $20,000 out of that ploy. We bought some new books to add to the library!

In the midst of all this madness the Board of Governors were in my office nearly every day. Their gentle protests were becoming increasingly strident until, just before the doors were about to open for the fall, Cameron Delaney marched into my office towering with outrage.

"Dr. Holliman, I have just had a phone call from Julian Reynolds. He tells me you've been calling him yourself and begging for money!"

"That's quite true, Mr. Delaney. Julian Reynolds is probably the richest living alumnus in Crayden's history. He's on the Board of several museums in the city, and he's renowned for his philanthropic activities. I thought he might like to throw a little money *our* way."

"Julian Reynolds and I have a long history!"

"I'm counting on that. We can use the influence."

"Don't be flip with me, Dr. Holliman! Do you have any idea how embarrassing it is for me to get a phone call from someone like Julian asking if Crayden is in trouble?"

"We *are* in trouble. We've committed ourselves to a total overhaul of our classes. I've pushed through a substantial number of changes, and those changes are going to cost. By the way, if you or any of the other board members would like to write a check or two..."

The old man flushed dark red. "We've made a terrible mistake here! It's quite clear to us that you have no real appreciation for the dignity of the Crayden name. We feel that you have thrown this institution into utter chaos, and that your actions here these past two months may have compromised our ability to continue educating young minds. We think that it's time you tendered your resignation."

"No, sir. I will not resign! I'm here, and I'm staying!"

"Then I have no other alternative. You are dismissed!"

"No, Mr. Delaney, I am not dismissed! I pulled up stakes and relocated on your promise of employment. I have a contract—for three years. You signed it yourself, and, according to my lawyer, you are personally liable. Since the school year has yet to start, you have nothing on which to base any charge of incompetence. I'm reasonably certain I can stretch out any formal protest you might make in court for the full three years, but that would be very expensive for you and for Crayden, and it would only hasten the school's rapid decline. I don't think you want that. We are going to take this moldering ruin and turn it back into a vital institution of learning! What I suggest is that you get out of my way, and watch what happens!"

I was bluffing about the lawyer, but it set him back. Delaney wasn't used to being pushed back, and, like all bullies, he was half as fierce as he wanted me to believe.

"We'll see about that, Dr. Holliman! We'll just see!"

"Yes, we will!" I shot back, "Now, if there's something else..?"

The old man turned almost purple and turned on his heel. He didn't exactly slam the door on his way out but he did shut it solidly. Ten seconds later Sally slipped through the door with silent disbelief on her face. I heard the outer door close with the same finality.

"You creamed him!" Sally exulted. "I thought he was going to have a stroke! He's going to fight you, you know!"

"Let him! I'm going to help him in spite of himself. By the time he's ready to fire me, we'll know if all this is going to work."

"It'll work!—It has to! You look tired."

I didn't enjoy my little triumph. In spite of his B-movie superciliousness, I liked Delaney. He wasn't stupid, just frightened of change. Weren't we all? The changes we were making must have looked disastrous to him. Nothing we had done since I arrived was part of the "Crayden Style". We were behaving like pushcart peddlers rather than educators. In his view, we must have looked like barbarians at the gates. Crayden's precious serenity was about to be shattered.

"Well, tomorrow we open the doors to the future! Hey, you want to slip across the street for a beer? I'm buying!"

"No thanks, Sally. I have some work to catch up on, then I'm going home. Barbara's probably ready to divorce me."

"Rain check, then. See you tomorrow! It'll be great!" Sally slipped out, and I knew I was alone. I heard her leave for home a few minutes later and the building went quiet. I was aware of being the only person in the place.

I couldn't resist the urge to walk the building. It was a kind of final tour. The old Crayden I had known as a child was over. Tomorrow was the New Crayden—whatever that was!

I started at the top in the North turret. The roof was still holding for now. The halls were clean. Classroom doors stood open for the onslaught in the morning. I slipped into the library. Ms. Dennis, the librarian, had stacked twelve cartons of new books by her desk for processing onto the shelves. Not a minute too soon, I thought. Two new computers had been installed by the file desk. They were connected to the Internet. Two computers weren't enough for a library of this size, but they were a promise of things to come, one I hoped I could keep. In the gym the trophy cases had been dusted and the old trophies polished. All the storage had been moved to the basement, and the locker rooms were ready to receive their first students since the seventies. I hoped the plumbing would hold! I ended in the basement. Aside from the items from the gym, it hadn't been touched. For the moment I saw myself playing Dr. Frankenstein...

"It's Alive!" I muttered. "It's Alive!"

There was a metallic crash, and I nearly fainted. I jump-turned as I caught sight of a figure in the half-light standing in one of the arches.

"Jesus Christ!" I let out involuntarily. "Who's there?"

"Ay, no one is here! School closed. You go out!" The figure gestured to the stairs but stayed silhouetted against the dark arch. I could only make out the shape of a small man, slightly stooped with a mop in his hand.

"I'm sorry!—You must be Epifanio. I'm Dr. Holliman, the Headmaster. I was just—checking on things." There was no answer. "Epifanio?"

"Sí. I am here."

There was a hesitation in the voice. He must be frightened, I thought. He probably thought he was alone too.

"I'm sorry if I scared you! I didn't realize you were here."

"I am here."

"...Thank you for all your hard work. The school looks wonderful. I'm sorry I haven't been down sooner than this to meet you, but we've been under the gun trying to put a new curriculum together...you understand?"

"Sí, I understand. I go now."

"No, wait. I—" The figure dodged behind the arch and disappeared.

"Epifanio?...Epifanio!" I moved to the arch where the figure had been but there was no trace. I remembered the furnace room and decided to find him. He wasn't there. It was as if he had vanished. "Epifanio?"...No answer. It was unsettling and a little annoying, but I thought about Barbara and turned to leave. As I turned, the figure was right behind me. I sucked in a shocked breath in my surprise. I nearly ran into him.

"My God! I—" I stopped in mid-sentence. In the dim light I thought I was hallucinating. The heavy shoulders and shock of iron-gray hair, the black gleaming eyes and the mahogany skin...

"—Uh...I'm sorry. I thought you were...gone."

"I am still here."

"You, uh, startled me..." He stood there silently waiting. For a long moment we said nothing.

"You need me."

"Huh?" I managed breaking my obvious stare.

"You need me—for work."

"No! I just wondered where you went. I-I'm going now. Tomorrow we get started!"

"Sí."

"Uh, good night, and thank you again for all your hard work! Everything looks splendid! Good night." I turned to leave. I was blathering, and I knew it.

I had almost reached the stairs when I heard him say in a flat and even tone, "I am right..."

I stopped and turned back to him, "...I beg your pardon."

"I am right," he said again, "You live well. You are dressed in fine clothes."

I was facing him but it took a full minute for his words to penetrate. I must have misunderstood! There were similarities, but that isn't what he meant; that couldn't be what he said.

"You will take some maté?" he invited.

"...Yes..." was all I could manage. I followed him back to the furnace room. He gestured to the chair, and I sat silently while he went to the makeshift kitchen for the maté. In a few moments he returned silently with two steaming cups. He sat on an upturned crate close by the chair, and we both stared into our cups.

"You know me, now?" he asked calmly. "I know you. You are the Angry Young Lord."

I drew a long sip of the maté, not knowing what to say and swallowed. The warm liquid seemed to penetrate me. I could feel its warming effects.

"You make the school good. I hear everyone talk. It is good."

"They told me you were called 'Epifanio'."

"It is the name they give me. Santiago—Epifanio Santiago." As a child it never occurred to me that he had a first name. Santiago was the only name I knew him by.

"I-I wasn't expecting to find you! I mean, it's been –a long time! I can't believe you're here after—after all these years! I thought"—I stopped myself before I became a complete boor. I had intended to say, 'I thought you were dead.' Instead I managed, "You—you look the same!"

His whole face curled into a wrinkled smile revealing yellowed teeth. His eyes danced deep in their sockets, and he let out a barely audible wheezing laugh.

"I am not so pretty, I think. To a child everyone is old!"

I laughed in spite of myself. It was true. I surveyed his face. "Seventy-five, maybe eighty," I thought. He still seemed strong, capable. His hands were large and rough. The hair was perhaps a little grayer than I remembered, the face a little more weathered. His shoulders were still broad and muscular if slightly stooped. All this passed across my mind while we shared the laugh. It occurred to me that I was assessing him. I was a little ashamed of it, but I was responsible now. Crayden was my bailiwick. I was responsible for everyone who worked here, including him. We fell silent for a moment. I was more comfortable, and I looked up at him.

"This is a hard job—taking care of this old building. Why haven't you retired?"

He shrugged his shoulders and searched into space with his eyes, "Where do I go? This is my place. I clean. I fix. This is where Santiago lives."

"Are you...comfortable here?" I motioned to the Dickensian accommodations of the boiler room. It was like a cave. Santiago's little room behind the partition with its hotplate and tiny palette bed was shameful.

"I live good. I have food, a bed...I have work. The Gods smile on me."

"But don't you have some place besides this?"

"I go to the park and sit in the sun. I live good. Santiago is good. I work for you, yes? It will be well."

"The grateful prisoner," I thought. I couldn't believe so little had changed for him in the years since my childhood.

"You should go home. Tomorrow will be well. Santiago can See it."

He rose and beckoned for my empty cup. I handed it to him.

"I've thought about you often."

"It is well. You go now. Tomorrow there is much to do."

He took both cups and disappeared behind the rough partition. I could hear water running as he washed them. I slipped away feeling the same as I did when I was eleven, and Mother was waiting upstairs for me.

CHAPTER 3

The morning exploded with noise. Crayden's sanctum sanctorum was invaded by the "Student Body". The halls were full of children laughing and talking excitedly, catching up with each other after a summer away. But there was more than a little excitement. Word that the gym was being used again had them all wondering, and there was talk about music classes and Theater! Halfway through the week the "Artist-Consultants" began to arrive, and Crayden was host for the first time to front-line, hard-core, under-employed performing artists. The City Cultural Affairs Office sent their liaison to set up the programs and confer with our staff. Rosemary Quinn threw herself into the role of Grande Dame of the Theater. She planned field trips to obscure Off-Off Broadway Theaters and recited liberally from Shakespeare at every turn. She looked twenty years younger, and the students loved her even more.

The entire staff was in a giddy state of confusion for the entire week. The visiting classes from the other schools and the gym classes with St. Barnabus kept everyone off balance. Tempers flared occasionally, but there was a real feeling of comradery in the staff room. Gradually, however, the new routine became the norm. The staff found itself moving at a much faster pace than they had been used to. I was aware that most of my staff were near or past retirement age. I knew I was asking a lot, and I worried about their stamina. After the first month, Orrington Smith, the chemistry teacher, resigned. He blustered into my office and announced that, if he was required to do twice the work, he should be entitled to twice the pay. He was one of the youngest on staff, a mere "slip of a lad" at forty-seven. I pleaded with him for time. I promised that if our "experiment" succeeded, staff raises would be my first priority. As he left my office in a huff, I had an inspiration. I went out to Sally's desk.

"Sally, you have the number of the City EPA?"

"Environmental Protection Agency? It's in the yellow pages."

"Would you call them for me? I want to speak to the head guy; tell him we have an emergency at Crayden."

"Oh, my God! What happened?" Sally stood up at her desk alarmed.

"Just get him on the phone, and put me through."

Ten minutes later Sally buzzed me, "George Gonzalez, Director of the EPA, is on the line, Dr. Holliman. Hold please, Mr. Gonzalez—here you are."

"Dr. Holliman, this is George Gonzalez. What's the problem?"

"I need a chemist, Mr. Gonzalez. Right away."

"A chemist? Well, if you could tell me the nature of the problem, I could send a unit over right away. Is it a water problem?"

"That's interesting. And these units, are they all busy?"

"We maintain teams to cover emergencies whenever they happen."

"That means that you have people on call—waiting, is that right?"

"Look, Dr. Holliman, I need to know what the problem is if I'm going to be able to help."

"OK," I said, "I need a chemist or chemists to teach four classes a day three days a week, and I need them right away."

There was a long pause at the other end. "Dr. Holliman, I don't have time for jokes."

"Let me ask you, Mr. Gonzalez, these 'units' you talk about, are they housed someplace centrally or are they stationed around the city?"

I talked a blue streak. I got Gonzalez to take a lunch with me. He was nice enough, but shrewd—a real politician. I explained that what I was suggesting was something that would make him look very good politically—he was doing his job and contributing the development of education in the city. I finally talked Gonzalez into housing a unit at Crayden. They could use our lab and dispatch directly from Crayden in return for twelve hours of teaching time from the "unit" as long as they weren't on active call. In addition we paid the chemists on a per-hour basis for the hours they taught. St Barnabus and Collegiate asked to share classes with us. Somehow the New York Times caught wind of the whole affair (no doubt from Gonzalez's office), and there was a feature article in the Living Section, "An Old Dog Learns New Tricks".

Crayden was featured as the leader in a new wave of "Educational Initiatives to revitalize education." Ah, publicity! We got twenty-three new enrollments the week following the article, and Dow Chemical offered us a grant to enlarge our math and science staff. I was on a roll! I was a hero! I was on Cameron Delaney's most wanted list! He made himself prominent in the article being careful not to indicate any discord between us, but I could feel him maneuvering. He was watching and just waiting for something—anything to go wrong.

I was watching everything. Doing everything. I kept notes on every nook and cranny of the school and everything that went on. I was having fun! I was happy in the way of a child. I was totally self-absorbed in my own doings and completely unconscious of anyone else on a real level. Barbara chose to ignore my obsession, hoping, I think, that it would burn itself out. I was a hero. I was the guy who saved Crayden! I couldn't help but bask in my own glory. I was totally unprepared for what would happen next.

CHAPTER 4

It was Friday. The faculty was anxious to hurry home for some well-earned rest. By 5:00 p.m. the last of the "late students" had gone, and everyone was headed for the exits. I was finishing up a personal letter to Julian Reynolds to thank him for his gift of $5000. I was grateful for it, but I couldn't help thinking that Reynolds could just as easily have given 5 million if he so chose. I didn't doubt that Delaney had gotten to him about my request for financial assistance. The five grand was a way of acknowledging Crayden while stiffing me. *"So what!"* I thought. We were up and running, and we'd stay that way. In the meantime, I knew just what I was going to do with this money.

"Don't you have a home?" Sally was standing in my doorway with her coat on. She and Barbara had become fast friends, first on the phone, and later they had met for lunch—without me.

"I have one or two loose ends to tie up, and then I'm gone!" I didn't look up from the screen.

"I'm calling Barbara. If you're not home in exactly one hour, I'm going to tell her to divorce you!"

"Tell her she can have custody of the cat."

"It's your funeral. As for me, I'm going to dinner, a movie, and the local pub. Some guy might get very lucky tonight."

"You wild creature—have fun. See you Monday."

She left, and the letter was done. It was 6:00 p.m. Crayden was locked and quiet. I headed for the boiler room. Santiago had been nagging at the back of my mind since our reunion in the basement the day before the semester started. His living conditions haunted me, and I was concerned about his welfare. It occurred to me that I was probably the only person at Crayden who even gave him a thought. Santiago was a dweller in that anonymity only a city like New York can afford. No one saw him. No one thought about him. Did he really exist at all? He was getting on. That dismal cell of his in the boiler room was just too depressing for me to forget. I needed to do something for my old friend. I wanted to talk to him—find out what he needed. I don't know what it was exactly, but I was aware that finding him again was like making a connection to Mother and those long-lost years. When I got there, he was sitting in his old club chair sipping his maté. On a small table was another steaming cup. Waiting for me.

"You take maté?"

"Thank you."

"You sit."

I took the maté and sat on a wobbly stool next to him. It was the same as it had been years ago. He seemed to know exactly when I would arrive. We both sat quietly for a moment. As before, the maté made me feel warm and calm. It gave off a strong herbal aroma —not really tea, but pleasant.

"Santiago, we're going to give you a raise, a substantial one, if I can wangle it from the Board—and a pension."

"...It is well." The old man sipped and stared ahead neither sad nor happy. He just seemed patiently waiting.

"And I'd like to—improve your space, that is, if you don't mind. Nothing too big—a little kitchen perhaps and general upgrade of the space where you live—nothing more than you're comfortable with."

"...It is well."

I was expecting a reaction. I was sure the old man would protest anything that he might perceive as a threat to his job. I was ready with all the calming words and phrases. I wanted to confront his anxieties head on and allay them—except there were none. He sat impassively and accepted my proposal without a flicker of objection. It took me off guard, but I had launched now, and I had to complete my mission.

"...Good. Now, it would help to get an idea of when you took over from your predecessor."

"Que?" The old man turned to me with his brow knotted in a question.

"Uh...the one who was before you—when did you take over from him? What year? Do you remember?"

"I am here."

"Of course, you're here! You're the only one we have on staff, but before you. The one who did this job before you."

The old man turned forward again and took a long sip of the maté. "No. Only I am here. Santiago."

"No, you see, I have to be able to tell them how long you've been here. They'll ask that, and I—"

"I know what you ask me." The low even tone in the old man's voice cut through my straining to communicate. "You want to know how long I work. How long I am here, yes?"

"Yes! It's just to show them that you've earned the consideration because of how long you've been with us."

"I am here from before."

"...Before. Before whom? Before me? Yes, I know that—"

"Before them. Before this place. Before all." The old man looked at the walls around him and gestured to the air around him. "You understand?" He looked at me with an air of finality and faced forward again holding his maté close to his face.

"Santiago ...Do you know when this school was built?"

"Si. I am here."

"1878, Santiago. The school is here a century and a quarter..."

"I tell you. You are the only one I tell. You are the Angry Young Lord."

"'Angry Young Lord'?—"

"My Priest-Father sees this. He sees you. 'Long time, Tlaloc!' he tells me. Tlaloc, is my name. Not Santiago! Not Epifanio! 'Tlaloc, you will be alone. That is the price to save you, Tlaloc. No one can know this. You can never marry. Never make children. The Gods say this. And you may not say to anyone what has happened or who you are. Nor can you tell them of any of this. An Angry Young Lord will come one day. To him you will tell all. He will make you free. You must wait for him.'—I have waited. I will tell you now."

CHAPTER 5

He rose and disappeared behind the partition. I heard him moving things. After a few moments he emerged with an old burlap sack in his hands. He reached in and gave me a small leather case. It was cracked and very dry. Inside was a miniature portrait of a young woman. The picture was painted on an oval of ivory, very faded with a fine gold filigree frame around it. The image was very finely painted. The young woman was slender and dark and very handsome. She was dressed in the style of the Eighteenth Century, staring straight and soberly at the viewer. Her hair was arranged elaborately on her head. She looked to be perhaps twenty or twenty-five. Her shoulders were held straight and square, and her eyes were large and liquid and had a haunted look, like someone very sad or lost. The likeness was small and faded. It was a curious thing for him to show me. I handed it back to him. He looked at me and waited for me to say something.

"Who is she?"

"Someone...I know." The old man gave out one long "AY..." and cried for a moment. Tears rolled down his cheeks, and then he pulled the sadness back inside and wiped his eyes with the back of his leathery hand.

"Santiago—"

"I—I am sorry. I don't think of this for a long time!..."

He inhaled sharply and contained his grief.

"I do a great wrong! The Gods punish me! My Priest-Father's words whip me from long ago. I do a great wrong...I do not listen...I forget the Gods." He was rocking in anguish back and forth. I had never seen him like this. After a moment he straightened up, searching in the air around him for thoughts, for words that seemed too difficult to find. Finally he sat down beside me clutching the sack, and he sighed before he began to speak:

> "My father is Priest. He cannot marry. No Priest can marry. They must be clean. Free of the world! But at night there is a woman—my mother. Many Priests have such. My mother is wife to Quexa, a farmer. My Priest-Father wants her. He calls her to him. Quexa, he knows of my mother and my Priest-Father. But my Priest-Father is powerful. He is Seer to the King. He Sees what no other man can see. Quexa dares not do anything. Say anything! When I come, my Priest-Father tells Quexa, 'Send Tlaloc to the calmecac, to be Priest. He must have the blood!'—It is a school. All the sons of the Top Men go there. At five years they take you. No more you see your Mother, your brothers, your sisters. No more your father. So Quexa must spend all—everything for me to go. He is poor, but he cannot do less if the Priest-Father says it. I think he is glad when I go.

> "Once there, the Priest-Father comes for me. The teachers cannot say no. He is the biggest Priest—the greatest one. He takes me to the forest. He teaches me himself.

> "'These teachers,' he says, 'They know the law. They know the Songs and dances and prayers. But they do not hear the Gods. They cannot feel the earth! They do not know the plants or what they do. They cannot See. I do this. I know these things. You *will know* this.'

> "Then he takes me. Shows me. 'This earth is full of secrets. It heals us—feeds us, but in the end it takes us back.' Then every day he shows me, 'This plant heals the head of strange thoughts. This takes the pain away—this stops the chancre of the body...' Then he takes me to a special grove where the tallest trees are. In the shade there, he picks a humble weed. Small. Nothing a man would see as important. 'This plant gives the Sight, but you may not take from it now. Not until I am gone. I am He Who Must See. I am the only one who knows this plant. It is given to me by the one before me and so on back to the beginning of our people. To chew the plant you must be wise. To See is not always to know. You cannot take it more than once in the moon's cycle, or it brings death.' Many plants he shows me, but two he gives and tells me to keep always with me. 'Take the seed. Grow. This one you take to live, and this

one lets you See. Do not take them both together or it will change you.' I do not understand, but I listen. I remember. I am becoming a Warrior-Priest, a Healer, a Seer, a Giver of Blood. I am the son of my Priest-Father. Each day as he shows me, he does me honor.

"When I am a young man, it is a time of hunger. Nothing grows. One day he says to me, 'The Gods are thirsty, they must drink deep or we will all starve.' There are no captives. For a long time no one fights with us because we are so strong. When our warriors go to the slave tribes, only the weak and the old greet them. The cowards hide in the forest. The Gods do not drink the blood of the coward.

"To feed the Gods, one must come from our own houses. Every house must take one man or woman or child and bring to the stone. Many send a slave, but the poor must send their own. It is a great power for the house to give one up. It is a great power for the one who is consumed. He smells of blood, my Priest-Father, from the killings. Many killings. Quexa now sees his chance to be rid of me and have revenge on my Priest-Father for taking his woman. He sends my name as one for the stone, but he is stupid in his revenge. My Priest-Father sees the names of all who are sacrificed. When he sees my name, he is angry with Quexa and my mother. He calls them to the temple in front of the other Priests. My mother is afraid. She cannot speak. Only the men can speak. My Priest-Father praises Quexa. 'This is a great power,' My Priest-Father tells him. To give up a grown son! And one so promising! You must be held in high honor.'

"'Thanks, Great Lord,' says Quexa curling up his lips in a hateful smile. 'Though I go hungry for Tlaloc to be a holy one, still I am eager to please the Gods! Take him! Take him now, if it please the Gods! I would do anything, everything to make the Gods laugh for joy!' My Priest-Father tells me this as we are walking in the forest.

"My Priest-Father shakes his head wisely in approval. 'It is well, farmer. You give up a great future to honor the Gods. Your delight is a power to your house. You have greater lands. But you should think carefully. Can you give this one so full of *promise? Can you throw away all you have spent to have him trained for the Priesthood?' My Priest-Father gives him room to change his hatred.*

"'Anything! Everything! Take him, Great Lord. I make this gift with a happy heart!'

"The other Priests bow and speak their approval, then my Priest-Father speaks again. 'Are you sure, Farmer? Anything? Everything? This most excellent boy?' Once again he gives Quexa a chance to take back his words.

"'I deny the Gods nothing that is mine.' Quexa is joyful to take me from my Priest-Father.

"'Then,' says my Priest-Father, 'You do not deny the Gods an even greater sacrifice, Farmer? Is your honor so strong?' Sensing the threat, Quexa does not back down.

"'Anything, Great Lord. Take my wife as well, she is a beauty. If her blood pleases the Gods, so be it. She is the next greatest treasure I have, or failing that ...take my blood. I follow my son on the stone if that is what the God's desire.'

"He thinks my Priest-Father is stopped now. He has offered even his own blood, but my Priest-Father knows it is not truly in honor, but in hatred. My Priest-Father is not done.

"'You do your house honor, farmer, but I think the Gods want that much of you another time. As for your grown son, that is a worthy gift...but his blood is already pledged as a Priest. What is already given, cannot be given again. Do you have another at home?'

"Quexa is shaking with rage now. He sees what my Priest-Father is doing. 'It is only a small one!' Says Quexa. 'Barely three or four weeks. The Gods do not want such a poor gift.'

"'This man is most high in honor!' Shouts my Priest-Father. 'He gives the blood of his newest child to the Gods. Here truly is a pious man!' Quexa is trapped. The baby is his only child with my mother, but he cannot now say no.

"To me the Priest-Father says, 'He gives up my son as his own, does he? This pains him. Far worse than giving up his own life!'

"'I go to the stone, if that is what the Gods want,' I said thinking of the poor thing given up so coldly.

"'I do not allow it! I See! The Gods make a strange path for you. I do not understand it, but I See it. You are the Memory! I See you—far away and long after this place. I cannot tell why.'

"He is proud, but he never says this to me. 'Between us there is always a space,' he says. I learn everything he teaches. I learn the forest, the plants. I heal, I pray, but I am not to use the Sight. Only my Priest-Father. He is the Seer. Only he may See the way.

"Then the Gods come. Riding great deer and shining in silver. From the rising of the sun, they come. With them they bring thunder and lightning. The people are afraid. Even the King is afraid. He calls my Priest-Father for the omens. His runners tell of the Gods' coming. In houses on the water and once they come, they burn them by the shore. The King tells our slaves, the Tlaxcala, who owe us blood from many battles, to keep them away. They fight out of fear of us, but the Gods come anyway. The Tlaxacala are beaten down by the powerful Gods, and soon they not only give in but point the way to us. My Priest-Father warns the King, 'These Gods are hungry. We are not ready for them. We must give them blood to drink to calm them.'

"The King sends these Hungry Gods rich gifts to calm them. He tells them we are not worthy and to please stay away. But still the Gods come. Many of our slave tribes join the Hungry Gods. The King makes blood sacrifice every day. He is beyond reason. My Priest-Father tells me that soon it is too late. He tells the King to wait and watch. 'Maybe the Gods come to test us.'

"But the King cannot wait any longer. His fear draws him to the thing he dreads. He takes all the Top Men to meet these Hungry Gods as they come upon our city. He bids us welcome them. I see this. I stand with the other young Priests in a great ceremony along the Great Way. I hear the King speak:

"'We see your coming a long time. We wait. You are tired, oh Great Gods, and you must rest. A palace is being prepared. All we have is yours. Come, and feast with us. We show you all we make to honor you.'

"The Chief God walks to the King with hands held out. My Priest-Father stands between and stops his touching of the King. The Chief God's men raise their weapons. My Priest-Father does not let him pass. But the King does not allow this. 'Stand aside, Seer. This is our God. We are his slaves. If he wishes to touch me, I am only his property.'

"And this is how it goes. The King, my Priest-Father, and all the Top Men take the Gods to the center of the city and give them the King's father's own palace as his own. Food is given to them with great ceremony and drink of all kinds. When the King and the Top Men make to leave, the Chief God does not let them. 'You must now stay with me,' he says. 'I am in need of you as a sign to your people of your good faith. Here you reside with me, and here you stay my pleasure.' The King bows. My Priest-Father, the King, and many others are taken from the temple and brought to place guarded by the Gods' men. They are thrown in darkness and kept there for days.

"The people are in confusion and fear.

"As a young Priest, I am permitted the honor of gathering food for the God's great Deer to eat. Some days later the Chief God and some of his men leave the city. We hear later that he goes to battle another God by the shore. It is all very strange!

"In his place he leaves a Lesser God. A strange God with hair like light and eyes of the sky who seems mad. The chief is very afraid of this one, so he orders a great feast for everyone. The entire city is to prepare for when the Chief God will return. The King gives the Lesser God the highest place above himself and all the Top Men. A great feast! The King tells my Priest-Father they must go to the temple. The Gods must drink deep. The Lesser God is led with his men to the temple. There my Priest-Father offers up Quexa's baby. But before he can let the Gods drink, the Lesser God stops his hand. He is angry. He speaks harsh words, my Priest-Father and the others do not

41

understand, but he knows from the sound that there is great trouble.

"The Lesser God calls the thunder, and many of the Top Men fall dead. One of the God's men pushes my Priest-Father, and the baby falls down the long stairs. Her blood is wasted. The King and the last of the Top Men, my Priest-Father with them, are brought back to the dark room and thrown inside.

"In the dark my Priest-Father chews the plant that gives Sight. He sees what before is not clear. 'These are not Gods! The stories are wrong! Given down to us by Seers who do not see all things as they are. These are men—Silver Men. Their coming is not a celebration, it is a death—a death of all we are!' He tells the King this. In the dark he tells him of his vision, but the King will not listen. 'All is well!' says the King. But my Priest-Father knows. He sees what is coming!

"He escapes, my Priest-Father. When the Silver Men bring food to all, my Priest-Father pulls one in and pushes through the door. The Silver Men are in confusion. My Priest-Father is fast, and he knows the city. He escapes to the canals and waits for night.

"In the night he creeps back to the city and asks where all the remaining generals are. All is in confusion. The people hide inside their houses. 'It is the end of the world!' one man says to him. My Priest-Father does not want to tell him, 'Yes, it is.'

"'Not yet,' my Priest-Father says. 'Show me our warriors. I am the Seer. I see what we must do.' The man tells him where the warriors and generals are hiding.

"They are gone, the generals, to the small temple on the outside of the city. There are not enough Silver Men to keep all the city in their hands. The generals go there to decide what must be done. But without the King they are without a plan, without a fight. How could one fight the Gods?

"'These are not Gods!' my Priest-Father tells them. 'These are men, like us! They do not come to bring us heaven. Do you see the image of their God? A man impaled on a tree! This they

leave in our temples. They pray to this Dead Man. What kind of Gods could they be? They come to take everything from us. The old Seers are wrong. Their Sight is not clear. These are only men in silver, not Gods! The great deer are only animals, and the thunder they carry is not from heaven. We must fight! They bleed like us. Their blood can be shed to feed the true Gods. We must do this. They have laid hands on the highmost ones of us. We must fight them! For this they must die!'

"The generals are doubtful. Finally, my Priest-Father tells them, 'We die. Many! Many die. In the end we lose. I do not know how long, but sooner if we do not. Everything is gone now if we do not stand!'

"The King's brother Cuitláhuac, stands with my Priest-Father. 'Stand!' he shouts. 'Stand, and die for the Gods, not these Silver Men. They are not so many as we. Go out to the city this night. Wake every warrior in your calpuli. Tell them to bring their weapons, their axes, stones—everything to fight! Destroy the bridges on the roads that lead away. Cut them off! And then we cut them down!'

"The Top Men find themselves. They go out and rouse the whole city. Warriors come armed and ready to wait for dawn.

"Just then the Chief of the Silver Men returns. He is angry with the Lesser Chief. He speaks to the King and tells him that there must not be fighting.

"At dawn a great attack is made. The True Gods drink much of our blood. At first we think that the Silver Men cannot be harmed. Our arrows make no difference. But then one warrior shoots true, and an arrow pierces the face of a Silver Man, and he cries out and falls. The entire force goes silent at this. It is the moment when they know my Priest-Father's Sight is true. Then they give out a great cry and fight like wild animals. The Silver Men make thunder and keep them away, but more of the Silver Men begin to fall.

"The Chief of Silver Men brings the King out, and the battle grows silent as the warriors see him.

43

"'What are you doing?' cries the King. These are our Gods! Would you have them bring us all down forever? I am your King. Lay down your weapons. Kneel and beg the Gods to let you live. Kneel, I say! It is a new day. Our Gods come home. We dare not anger them!'

"My Priest-Father is on a wall above them with a force of warriors. He sees the warriors begin to doubt. He feels the confusion coming back. He takes a stone from his pouch and puts it into his sling. He throws it at the King. It hits him hard, and the King stumbles. The Silver Men take him away bleeding. A great cheer goes up, and the confusion among the warriors is gone! The battle goes on much worse all that day. The true Gods feast on blood as never before.

"Two nights later the King is brought out to us dead. The Silver Men leave him by night dirty and caked with dried blood on the square by a temple. We take his body up, and we sacrifice to the thought of what he is as King. He is too eager to believe. The fear makes him foolish.

"We fight. We die. The Silver Men make thunder, and many of us give up our blood. Others take up their weapons and their places. Finally, the Chief of the Silver Men takes his men out on one of the roads away to escape. There are many of them still. They have a bridge—only one. All the Silver Men have to cross before they can move it up to cross the next breach in the road where the canal flows through. By dawn they are not gone still. We fall on them, and many are killed. Our warriors taste blood just as the Gods! They fight like demons!

"We drive them out! There is joy in the city!—but grief as well. The Silver Men break our temples—take our gold—burn our houses. The King is dead of the stone my Priest-Father throws. This is a great wrong! My Priest-Father knows he must pay with his blood at some time soon."

***

The old man sat back in his seat clutching his empty cup of maté tightly. His eyes closed as if in pain, and his head bowed with the weight of the images in his head.

If this was senile dementia, I thought, this was one for the books!

"This...story—" I began.

"I tell you—before. Not all. Enough for a small boy, but not all. Only *you* I tell. Never anyone else. Others I may teach of our Gods, the dances the prayers to make the sacrifices. But no one I tell about me, Tlaloc, and the time I have."

"Santiago—"

He pulled a metal bowl-shaped object from the sack. It was dented and black with soot and tarnish. At first I could not see it clearly in the dim light by the furnace.

"You take. This I give, so you will know."

I took the metal bowl and examined it. He handed it to me in such an absent fashion as though it were nothing more than a bit of junk taken from a trash heap, but the thing itself in my hands nearly jumped at me. It was a helmet. It had a round dome, somewhat dented, with a large crest running front-to-back where it met the upturned ridge of the brim which swept up both in front and in back. I had seen the shape a hundred times in the movies. It was a Spanish helmet, 16th Century in style. Scraps of leather lacing were still attached on the inside but dried almost to dust. These crumbs of leather fell out with each turn of the helmet. I sat turning the helmet, searching for something to say— something to restore a sense of normality. 'Warriors, Kings, Silver Men, False Gods'—what was I being drawn into?

"You go now. Take this thing. It is yours. Also what I tell you—it is yours. When I give it, it is gone from me."

The old man rose. He took my cup and went behind his partition into the darkness of his tiny room. I couldn't rise at first. I was still absorbing it all. Finally, I got up and went upstairs to the office. I found a shopping bag under Sally's desk. I slipped the helmet into it, and I walked out into the cold, late fall night.

It must have been close to 1:00 a.m. The foot traffic was light. When I got home, Barbara was asleep. I sank heavily into a chair without taking off my coat, and I fell asleep.

CHAPTER 6

"Wake up, Holliman! If you think you're getting out of going sofa shopping with me, you're sadly mistaken. C'mon, it's Saturday Morning!"

"Fell asleep in the chair again, huh?"

Barbara handed me a cup. "Mmhm. I'm beginning to think you're trying to avoid me. You look lousy!"

I sipped the hot coffee and scrunched down into the chair. My back ached, and I had the edge of a sinus headache forming. In a flood, last night's strangeness flowed back into my mind. Did I dream the whole thing?

"Don't get comfortable! We're going sofa shopping. I'll give you one-hour. ABC has a sale out in Queens. And take your bag to the study." Barbara tossed the shopping bag with the helmet over toward the chair. I nearly jumped out of the seat! It was real! I didn't dream last night—it really happened?

"What's the matter?"

"....Huh?"

"What's the matter? You jumped like you'd been bitten. What's wrong?"

"...Uh...You just surprised me. I'm not awake yet."

"What's in the bag?" Barbara picked up the bag and pulled out the helmet. "Where did you get this?"

"...Someone gave it to me."

"Who?"

"Somebody at school. The—the custodian."

"How did the janitor get it?"

"...Off a dead Conquistador, if I believe what he told me last night."

"What!"

"...I just don't know what to do about it..." She knew I wanted her confidence.

"Do about what?"

Barbara settled into the sofa holding the helmet, bowl up. I sipped my coffee slowly and told her about last night's episode with Santiago. I felt somehow guilty—that I was breaking a deep confidence, but this was a new one on me. Barbara was the only one I *could* talk to who wouldn't think I was a fool even listening to the old man's ravings.

"The Angry Young Lord, huh?" she mused as she turned the helmet over in her hands. "You know, this looks real."

"The thing is, he doesn't sound senile. His story was wonderfully full of detail. It wasn't like the wandering of a mind losing touch. And he still fulfills his duties at the school."

"He's probably been telling those stories for years to school boys who wander into the basement. He's just gotten to the point where he believes them himself."

"But what do I do about it? If his mind is going, I can't keep him on, but if I turn him in..."

"An old man—no family...big city—not a great prospect, is it?"

"No. And he's a—friend! That old man got me through a helluva time when my parents divorced. I owe him something!"

"Then don't tell anyone."

"I have a responsibility here! I can't just ignore him!"

"Brad, you're not ignoring him, you're protecting him! You said he still fulfills his duties. What're a few fantasies between friends? Let him imagine whatever he wants!"

"For how long? How long before he becomes a danger to himself—or the children? If it is dementia of some kind, he could become disoriented one day—burn the place down. I can't let that happen."

"You're getting a little carried away with yourself aren't you, Holliman? If he's been there so long, who knows how long he's been harboring this delusion—if that's what it is. Just keep an eye on him. Quietly. If you think he's losing it, *then* you blow the whistle. It seems to me what you have here is just a lonely old man full of memories and stories that have gotten all mixed up together. All he probably needs is someone to talk to. If he was such a friend to you as a kid, you be a friend to him now. Listen to his stories, and do what you planned. Fix up his space, and get him that pension. That way, if you do have to let him go, he'll have something to show for all the time he's worked....I can't believe they let him work like that all these years and live in the basement for so little!"

Barbara's practical take on the previous night put things in perspective. She was right. Santiago hadn't hurt anyone. I felt better about the whole episode. I would be the friend Barbara described. I'd help Santiago get his raise and his pension and, if necessary, I'd see to it that he had some place to go if he had to leave. I downed my coffee and showered. The weekend passed in pursuit of a sofa and some leisure time—the first in weeks.

***

"Where's the employment file for Epifanio Santiago?"

Monday was half over, and, aside from a fistfight during intra-mural soccer between two of the girls on the fifth grade team, everything was humming along. I had decided to waste no time in documenting the case for Santiago's pension. I didn't want the old man to be forgotten any longer.

"In the v-drive under 'Staff'." Sally was annoyed. She was always annoyed on Mondays. It was her "hell" day. All the administrative details landed on her desk on Monday mornings, and she was overwhelmed well into mid-week.

"No, Prior to this year. I'm looking for his last raise."

"I archive everything at the end of the school year and put it on data base. The disks are in my drawer—but you won't find any raises. I go back about eight years, and I can tell you, he hasn't gotten a raise since I've been here."

"What about before that?" I asked, thinking that, if I were going to give Santiago the kind of raise he deserved, I'd have to justify it with his past history. The man had lived in the basement of Crayden for forty years, underpaid and without complaint. Crayden owed him!

"Before me, there was only paper. I brought in the computers."

"Those files would be...?"

"In the basement. There are rows of them down there. Start on the north side of the basement. Those are the newest. As the cabinets go south, they go back by year. You want me to go look?" The offer was only half-hearted. The phone was ringing constantly, and she was keeping up all the petition letters to Alumni single-handedly.

"Naw!" I said trying to be nonchalant. "I'll go find it myself. You've got enough to do."

Sally turned back to her desk piled with correspondence and reports. The phone was ringing insistently, and she picked it up instinctively as she opened the mail. "Good morning, Crayden..."

I found the cabinets easily. I had passed them dozens of times. I don't think Sally knew just how familiar I was with the terrain. I checked back a full twelve years. Santiago's record was there. There had been no raises in that year, so I moved south systematically year by year, looking for a raise. Finally, fifteen years previous there had been listed a "cost-of–living increase" for the princely amount of $1.50 per hour based upon a forty-hour workweek. "Could they spare it?" I heard myself say out loud. It seemed that the administration before Trask had been just as tight. Out of curiosity, I started looking back to track Crayden's munificence to Santiago. No raises until almost ten years further back. Dr. Blackson's group had given him a fifty cents per hour raise in 1972. Before that was Dr. Dittmor. "Ditzie" was in charge when I went to Crayden. No raises. I had the information I needed, and I was about to pull the folders and leave, but I decided—out of curiosity, to find out just when Santiago came to Crayden.

I went south along the cabinets. In each year, there was a sheet for Santiago—1960...1957...1953...1947.........1930? That had to be wrong! I went back even further. 1928...25...18...12...1900! These cabinets were oak. The paper in them was a deep yellow around the edges. Everything was hand-written, There was the name "Epiphanio Santiago, laborer, wages 5 dollars per week and lodging" Further back I found the financial records in moldering ledgers bound in leather that was falling off the spines. A "Santiago" appeared in the ledger column marked "dustman" for 1890. I checked and rechecked the years I skipped. I calculated that he couldn't have started much earlier than 1930, and that was assuming he was a teenager at the time!

Then I noticed the first ledger, 1878. It was sitting on its own shelf like a little deteriorating God.

Crayden was founded as a school by Dr. Samuel Crayden in his family's home in 1832. It was little more than a large farmhouse in an upper West Side that was then a scattering of pig farms and hardscrabble vegetable lots. "The Quality" sent their children because of Dr. Crayden's fine moral character and reputation as a man of learning. Besides, it was deemed "healthful" to have their children attending school "up in the country", away from the noise and bustle of the center of the "city" which was then around present-day 14th Street. As the city exploded with population and construction, the city had raced up to Dr. Crayden's "country" farm and swallowed it up. By 1876 he had done so well that he had the farmhouse dismantled, and the present building was begun. Samuel Crayden died six months before the "new building" was completed in 1878, and the Board passed the running of the school on to a Rev, Leyland Case. I found the listing of the "faculty"—Twenty young clerics hired by Case himself, and in a margin I found something that made my temples sweat. In a tight, precise hand, Case had written a note, I think to justify what he felt was a gross extravagance:

"Retained, the Indian named 'Epifany' as per the wishes of our founder, until said laborer can no longer work."

I checked and rechecked the ledgers. There was nothing to indicate that anyone besides "Epifanio Santiago" had ever worked at Crayden as "dustman," "laborer" or anything else. My head was spinning. What the hell was going on here? It was nearly 4:00 p.m. I had been down here for hours without realizing it. I quickly stuffed everything back into the files and returned to the office empty handed.

"Where have you been?"

"Uh...sorry. I uh...got sidetracked." I was aware of Sally's annoyance, but my mind was all around the files in the basement. The whole experience was making me feel queasy. The rational glow from Barbara's analysis of the weekend had vanished, and I was back to feeling like I'd fallen through the looking-glass. I knew there had to be something—some simple explanation. Perhaps there was another "Epifanio Santiago"— before the man I knew in the basement. That had to be it! Somehow, the changeover just wasn't recorded!

"The phone's been ringing off the hook for you! Rosemary Quinn needs approval for a field trip to the Pearl Theater for her class. Brother William wants your call on starting a basketball league with Collegiate and St. Barnabus—God, that man is gorgeous! If he weren't a Priest, I'd screw him to the wall! Delaney wants a meeting to discuss the building fund. Apparently some of the alumni have a scheme in the works to raise money for the full renovation of the building. Imagine—a new roof! What will they think of next? Watch out for Delaney, though. This smacks of something up his sleeve, if you ask me. Oh—A Dr. Soldani from the Met called, he wouldn't leave any particulars but begged that you'd call him as soon as possible. And Barbara wants you to call her right away. *Now* can I get back to being overworked and underpaid?"

"Hm?? Sure, Sally." I passed into my office and sat at the desk absently. Sally followed me slightly puzzled.

"...Did you find what you were looking for?" Sally was standing at my door with a pile of opened correspondence prioritized for me to go through. She placed it on my desk in front of me. I just sat there in thought not really hearing her.

"Hm? I'm sorry?"

"Did you find his last raise?"

"Uh...Yeah, I did. 1972, $1.50, cost of living."

"Twenty-eight years without a raise? They ought to be boiled in oil! What are you going to give him?"

"...Uh...Whatever the current union rate is for janitorial services, I guess, and a pension..."

"He could use it! Who knows how much longer he'll be able to work. When he's gone, we're really going to feel it! Don't forget to call Barbara..."

She retreated to the outer office leaving me with the correspondence. I was just staring into space, I guess, when the phone rang again.

Sally called to me through the door, "It's Barbara! Hold on, Barbara, I'll put you through. He just got back. You want to pick up?"

I picked up the phone still in a fog of my own thoughts.

"Brad?"

"Yeah, hi, what's up?"

"Did you get a call from a Dr. Soldani from the Met?

"Uh...yeah, Sally gave me the message. You know about him?"

"Oh! That's my fault! I'm sorry, Brad."

"For what?"

"I did something I probably shouldn't have!"

"What?"

"I took that helmet into the Met this morning. I asked to see the curator for Arms and Armor, and they passed me on to this guy, Soldani. I wanted to see if that thing was anything...special."

"What did he tell you?"

"That's just it. He didn't *tell* me anything. He asked me a million questions! He wanted to know where I got it. *How* I got it! Brad, he acted as if he were going to have me arrested!"

"What?"

"I told him that it had been given to us, and he demanded to know by whom! He kept saying that it was a criminal act to receive stolen artifacts!"

"Did you tell him about Santiago?"

"No! I wasn't going to tell that little weasel anything. Especially after he threatened to impound the helmet!"

"Impound the helmet?"

"I finally had it with all his insinuations, and I demanded that he show me proof that the helmet was listed as stolen from any collections."

"What did he say to that?"

"The little creep began to backpedal! That's when I knew he was just yanking my chain. I picked up the helmet and put it back in the bag and was ready to walk out. Then he changed his tune! He couldn't say enough, do enough! 'Oh, Mrs. Holliman, you understand we have a responsibility to protect antiquities. If you only knew the number of dishonest collectors who try to sell off stolen property!' I was about ready to slap him!"

"Did he tell you anything about the helmet?"

"Nothing you could go to the bank with. He said that the piece would have to be studied and, if possible, a provenance would need to be prepared—just to prove that it was not listed as stolen property anywhere. We went back and forth about that once more, but he did tell me that at first glance it was a—wait a minute—I wrote it down—a Morion. That's a 16th Century fighting helmet. Very common. Apparently they were like regular issue because they were easily manufactured and strong. The brim offered good visibility and protection. Most common soldiers of the period had them. Basically they're two pieces of metal riveted together."

"So what was all the fuss about?"

"That's what I asked him! 'You're ready to have me picked up by Interpol for what amounts to Sixteenth Century Army Surplus?' I started to walk away again, and he jumped between me and the door. 'Mrs. Holliman! Why not leave the helmet with me, and let me examine it for you! There will be no charge, of course, and in a few days you can pick it up as long as everything checks out.' I told him 'No thanks!' I wasn't going to let him near it. I knew damn well we'd never get it back again!"

"You still have it?"

"Of course I do! But he did let me in on the reason he wanted to keep it for a closer look. He pointed out that the helmet was engraved and plated in silver. Probably manufactured and embellished in Italy, which means it belonged to someone of wealth. And then he pointed to a crest—I noticed it before—He said that the crest could be significant, but he would have to research before he could be sure. I told him I'd have to check with you. Unfortunately I had already told him who you were and that you were the Headmaster at Crayden. I knew he'd be calling you! I'm sorry, Brad. I was just trying to help."

"That's all right. If I can handle 400 rambunctious children I can handle some curator from the Met. I'll call him."

"Is everything all right with the old man? He hasn't burned down the school or anything?"

"...Uh...fine. I haven't even seen him."

"You sound strained. What's the matter?"

"...Nothing. I'll tell you about it tonight, OK?"

"OK, but don't let Soldani anywhere near the helmet. I don't trust him!"

"I won't. See you tonight."

I called Soldani. He was so accommodating over the phone, I felt like I'd had a two-hour massage. Finally, I told him that I would consider a closer examination of the helmet after I had done my own research on the piece. He didn't want to let me off the line, but he knew he couldn't hold me. I told him I'd call in a few days and arrange something.

The next two hours were swallowed up by Crayden's closing for the day. Late parents trooped around with their usual concerns. After-school programs got into high gear. The entire building shook with activity and noise. Parents, faculty and students paraded in and out of the office. Sally had three student aids, and it still looked like a fire sale at Macy's. I did my best to fend off the mob, but I know I must have seemed like a zombie. I couldn't pull my head out of those files in the basement. –"The Indian named Epiphany..."

***

"Brad, it's impossible!"

It was the first night I could remember in months when we had supper at home. Barbara was torturing a head of broccoli with a paring knife while I got a chicken ready to roast. I needed her company to sort out the events of the day. Cooking together had always been our way of connecting.

"You know, I read somewhere about the famous Centenarians of the Andes. These were people claiming to be 100—120—150 years old. Not one, but a whole clutch of people living in the mountains. When researchers did some closer checking, most of them were just lying about their ages. The records suggested that they were most likely no more than 70 to 90 years old, but it gave them a little attention and quite a lot of publicity! There were a few cases, I think, where it turned out that some of them had the same names as parents or grandparents, and because records were so poorly kept, it looked as if they were these incredible ages...until, of course, the missing entries were found in church records or elsewhere. I'll bet that's what happened!"

"But, why would he do it, Barbara? What reason could he have for carrying on such an elaborate charade? He's a quiet, simple old man! I don't think he's talked to anyone but me since the year began. And what about the helmet? Your friend, Soldani, seemed pretty interested. How does that come into it?"

"If it's authentic—He could have gotten it anywhere. Maybe he found it. Maybe it's something handed down to him from members of his tribe! You know, that could be it!—A kind of tribal memory thing! Oh, Brad! This could be a story passed on from one generation to another! What you could be listening to is a first-person, eye-witness verbal recounting of the Fall of the Aztecs carefully passed on from one generation to the next!"

"...You think so? I mean the story is remarkably vivid. He tells in the first person, and he insists he was there!"

"I've read about this!"

Barbara stood pacing as she talked. As she worked out the logic in her mind, she was getting excited. So was I. It was neat! It explained everything. Santiago wasn't losing it—he was sharing it!

"In many cultures stories are reenacted in dance...in song...in story form!" It was like Barbara was onto the magician's trick, and she had to follow it through. "The story-teller becomes the main character. Every detail is assimilated as a personal experience in order to preserve the accuracy of the detail. There seems to be some religious or ritual element in it for him. What was it he called you—'the Angry Young Lord'? Somehow you've become the next in line—the one to inherit the story! If he has no family. Who else would he have to pass on the tradition? Didn't he say he was giving you the story and the helmet? Don't you see? The helmet is like a talisman. It's the vessel for the memory. In taking it, you've become the Keeper of the Flame!"

"I wish you could have seen him! His face! He was so full of emotion... so deep into the memory—if that's what you can call it! It's pretty Goddamn compelling!"

"It's really very touching. If the man had had a son, he'd probably be the one who would inherit the memory. It's quite an honor the old man's given you. He making you privy to information which has probably never been heard outside his tribe!"

"It's so strange, Barbara. He said I was the one to set him free. It made the hair on the back of my neck stand on end! I'd begun to think—well you know!"

"Brad, he's someone you attach a great deal of emotional value to. And then there's the natural human desire to want to believe the impossible. The primitive, gut-instinct to want to make natural boundaries disappear."

"...You're pretty smart, you know that?"

"If you don't put that chicken in the oven I'm going to turn into an axe-murderess! I'm hungry!"

A few glasses of wine and dinner put everything back into its appropriate box. Barbara's unfailing logic and tough brand of kindness gave me a perspective that the months-long marathon I'd been on hadn't allowed me to maintain. I had been running on adrenaline most days, fending off disaster and, in general, making it up as I went along at Crayden. This Strange Interlude with Santiago was just the kind of straw that could snap me. Barbara seemed to know.

"But, Barbara, what do I do with this, information? If it is some kind of inside scoop on a major historical event, shouldn't it be preserved, somehow?"

"Are you going to go and talk to him again?"

"...I think he needs me to listen."

"Why don't you record him?"

"Whatever this story of his is to him, it's...personal. Intimate. It's clear he's giving me something he considers sacred. I feel awkward sharing it with you. I can't ask him to let me record his deepest spiritual life."

"He's kept a lonely vigil, Brad. He wants to be heard. That's why he's telling it to you. If you take it down, you validate him—his mission. You show him that the memory will be kept—at least in the way you can keep it. I think it will mean more than any raise or pension."

"He's got to get that pension in case something happens to him. Without that, he'll wind up in a home somewhere helpless and forgotten."

"Not with you around!   Now, look, 'Angry Young Lord' how about spreading some of that deep concern my way. Do you have any idea how long it's been that I've had you all to myself, conscious and still awake enough to be of some use?"

For the moment—perhaps the last moment—everything was back to normal. For one night I forgot about Crayden. I forgot about Santiago—the helmet...I forgot about everything. It was just Barbara and me like that first night years ago when we skipped the film festival and went right to bed. I slept my last quiet night like a King!

***

"Um—Dr. Holliman! A pleasure!"

Emilio Soldani was a greasy little man. As he extended his hand to me, I could see the dirty fingernails and the dandruff on the collar of his baggy suit. His hair was combed back slick, and his glasses rode low on the bridge of his nose. He peered over them at me looking a little like an unkempt vulture. His fixed smile had no warmth in it, and I knew he wanted something before we began the conversation.   There was something urgent in his manner that he couldn't cover.

"I believe I said I'd call in a few days. As you can see, things are a little chaotic here at Crayden."

"I know! I know! Um—Forgive me for barging in like this. I made a terrible impression on your wife. Um—I apologize for that! It was stupid of me! I have to plead social incompetence! Um—I'm not much of a public relations man, I guess. The Met keeps me in the back room most of the time. I have the expertise, but no charm apparently. If your wife hadn't pressed to see someone right away, I'm sure they would have sent her to one of our more—um—engaging people!"

"Well, she did say—"

"Um—The bottom line is, I *have* to see that helmet again!"

Soldani dropped his head and stared at the floor like a schoolboy who's just been sent to detention. He shifted on his feet and clammed up. Finally he looked up at me over his glasses. One greasy strand of hair fell gracelessly across his forehead. I was beginning to feel a little sorry for him.

"May I ask why it's so—urgent?"

"I think it might be important."

"Uh huh...Can you give me some idea what makes it important."

"No.—I don't know. Um—That is, not until I really examine the piece."

I didn't have the time for this visit. I had a morning appointment with Nick Parrino, head of our EPA unit. I liked Nick. He made himself part of Crayden without getting in the way. He did most of the teaching for the "unit," and I think he was enjoying it. We were supposed to work out the schedule for the second semester. I had to give him the required curriculum, and I was hoping his natural enthusiasm for the kids would kick in with some "extras"—a "Chem. Club," for instance, after School! I thought I might con him into it. Soldani was sputtering along about "documentation" and "indications". Finally I interrupted.

"My wife told me you were ready to impound the helmet."

"Um—No, no, no! That is, I was just trying to keep her there—so-so I could take a closer look. I was afraid she'd walk out, and I'd never see the artifact again! Um—you see that happens all too often! People get scared or they think they have something of value, and they're off to sell it to some private collector for a fortune...if it's really worth anything...that is. Dr. Holliman, it was stupid! I'm really sorry! I couldn't have impounded anything! I'm not much more than a glorified clerk! I catalog the collection. Occasionally—very—occasionally I get to evaluate new acquisitions or re-run a provenance check of something we don't have all the information on. If you could just let me see it. You can watch me. I could do it here!"

That seemed possible, but I didn't quite trust him either. Barbara's evaluation of him may have been off in some ways, but there was something just too desperate about him.

"You know, it's just a helmet..."

"In all likelihood, yes! Yes! Absolutely! It's just I would like to check some of its...features. It appears to have been the helmet of a nobleman. If it is, um—well, then it might be possible to identify the individual and tie the piece into its period....I could write a paper! If it's anything worthy of note, of course..."

That was it! The little shit wanted to "land a big one" in the academic world! There was something about Santiago's helmet that made him hot to get his hands on it. He saw something about it that would further his career! Sally was at the door with a cup of coffee. She barged right in to help me end this little audience with Soldani, and I was grateful.

"Your ten-o'clock is here. Milk, no sugar, right?"

"Thank you, Sally. I'm afraid I have another appointment Dr. Soldani. I'll tell you what. You call on Friday, same time, and I'll try to arrange something."

"Isn't it here?

"...I mean call on Friday, and I'll see. That's my best offer. Take it or leave it! Sally, ask Nick to come in, will you?"

"But that's the end of the week! If you could just—"

"Friday."

"...Friday. Good! Thank you, I'll call. Please don't forget."

"I won't."

"Um—yes. Thank you! I'll see you then." Soldani's eyes quickly searched the office in hopes of seeing the helmet as he reluctantly headed for the door. He collided with Nick Parrino at the doorway. He turned and left abruptly without saying a word.

CHAPTER 7

"Outside the city the Silver Men wait to return, this time with others who are our slaves. These others hate us from a long time ago. They do anything to see us broken. The King's brother is made the new King. The Top Men that are left make a new council. My Priest-Father is the Seer still but death and confusion hang in the air. The world is turned inside-out.

"My Priest-Father comes and finds me. I am with the warriors in the marketplace. Many are celebrating. 'Bury the dead!' my Priest-Father shouts at them. 'Repair your weapons! This fight is only the first!'

"These are young men like me. They think my Priest-Father is wrong to take away their victory so soon. But they put down their drinks and begin to gather the bodies. All goes quiet in the hot sun, and my Priest-Father pushes me into a small hut by the side of the market. The bodies of a woman with her dead child gather flies in the corner. My Priest-Father does not look at them. In the dim light of the hut he grabs me with his eyes.

"'You do not die. I See it! I know what I must do!' His eyes are strange. I am afraid to speak. He is wild and deep in his mind. He hands me a gourd filled with a liquid. 'Drink!' he says. This I do. He reaches into his pouch and pulls out the leaves of the plant that gives sight. 'Chew!' he says.

"'But, Holy One, I am not permitted—'

"'Chew! Swallow the spit! Do not ask questions!'

"He reaches again into his pouch and takes out the simple weed I see from before. It is dried to a husk, and it hangs with seeds. He takes a pod and puts it in my hand. 'These are the seeds.

Raise them. When it blooms drink from the leaves. Let the seeds come and keep them. Plant and grow and drink. This keeps you strong.' He takes another thing, a root, dried and dead and puts into my hand. 'This is the root of the plant that gives Sight. It lives under trees where the sun does not see it. This root grows and makes the plant. The leaves you chew and swallow the spit. Take it no more than once in a moon's passing or it brings death. Remember that to See is not always to Know! Now I give them both to you. Now you take them together. Now you are changed!' He turns from me, and he cries. I do not see this before...ever.

"Then he tells me the price for being saved. I may not take a woman. I may never make children. I must live alone. I weep at what he tells me. I am afraid. 'Let me die,' I cry. 'What good to live like this? What does it profit the Gods?'

"My Priest-Father is very angry. He raises his club and strikes me hard. I fall and bleed from the place where he hits me.

"'Fool! It is not for you to decide. It is the will of the Gods. They show me, and I show you. You are the Memory—and something more. You live with what is left of us. You tell. You teach. You heal. You are the hope and the vine to all we are. It is not for you to decide!' He takes the seeds and the root from my hand and pushes them down into my own pouch. 'Chew! Swallow the spit! See what comes. Then you know!' It is bitter. My Priest-Father is sweating and looking wild. Inside the hut, the heat and the flies and the smell fill my head. After a moment, all goes dark. I fall to the ground.

"When I wake it is night. No one is around. The bodies are gone from the hut, and the moon rises over the empty market. Only the lizards move in the shadows. My Priest-Father is gone.... 'But I have not Seen,' I think. 'My Priest-Father is wrong. There is nothing.' I peek out, afraid to see the Silver Men, but no one is there. I look around and walk in the shadows. Everywhere, there is no one! When I come to the great square, I do not believe my eyes! The forest is everywhere! A great jungle is swallowing the city. Vines cover even the great temple, and nowhere is there movement. Only the night sounds of the forest and the scamperings of little

animals and slithery things in the dark. I am so afraid. 'Father!' I call not too loud for the Silver Men to hear me. 'Father!...Someone! Where is everyone? Who answers me? Who hears me?' Still there are only the night sounds and the whispers in the leaves. I grow bolder. 'Father!' I shout much louder. 'Father, come and get me! Who is there? I am here...I AM HERE!' The last I shout from my soul. I am afraid now as I see more of the city in ruin and overrun with vines and trees. How can this be? What can have happened as I slept? Behind me a great cat creeps up silently. I can feel him watching me. If I turn too soon he springs, I think. Slowly I pull my knife and prepare myself. I turn to face him—and he is gone. I drop my guard, and I hear him spring at me from behind. His claws dig deep into my shoulder, and I drop and roll to the side. The great cat falls off me and turns to finish me off. I look him in the eye and say, 'Come cat; kill if you can, or I will kill you. One of us will give our blood to the Gods tonight.' Then the great cat stops. He rises from his crouch and stands to see me. He comes to me and rubs his head against my leg, while in his throat he makes the whirring sound. I reach down to touch him, and he turns on his back to show me his belly...it is eaten away by maggots! He is made hollow with rot. The smell is more than I can bear, and the sight makes me scream!

"*I wake in the hut. My Priest-Father crouches in the corner staring at me.*

"'*You sleep. You dream. Tell me what you See.'*

"*I tell him my dream.*

"*He looks at me; then he holds me to him. ' The city, the jungle, and the great cat. Now you know; the Gods are true! It will be!'*

"'*Is this the Sight? What does it mean?'*

"*He says close to my ear, 'It is our nation many—many years away. You are alone because you are the last...the long last. The great cat is Death. For you he shows his belly. He does not strike the final blow.'*

> *"I break his hold on me, and I run into the darkness. Around me is the moaning of the wounded city. I run until I cannot breathe. I fall to the ground and sleep. This time no dreams come..."*

The old man closed his eyes and inhaled deeply. I switched off the digital recorder Barbara had bought me. It was a neat little thing. Simple to operate. Everything was digitally recorded and could be downloaded to a computer. She told me it was her contribution to the welfare of Crayden.

"Do you want to stop?"

"A moment. These things I see again, they are like sand in my eyes. I am so young. I cannot know what I See."

"Why don't I come back and—"

The old man motioned with his hand, and I sat again. He bowed his head low as if entering under the canopy of memory. He breathed deeply several times and then began again. I turned the recorder back on and watched as he rocked back and forth, "remembering" what he could not possibly have seen:

> *"We chase them, the Silver Men. The new chief, Cuitlahuac, sends a great force. I am among these. The Silver Men run to Tlaxcala. There they are making more join them from the tribes. We fight expecting to wipe them out. But the Chief of the Silver Men is strong and hungry still. He has raised many against us among the slave tribes. They are strong with memory of our warriors and hatred of us. Our force is no match in open battle, and we lose great rivers of blood. I am wounded here."*

The old man lifted his shirt to show his side. There were long, parallel scars running across his midsection almost from the naval around to his back. Even now they looked mortal. It looked as if the flesh on his side had been raked deeply by something sharp and jagged. He drew the shirt back down and continued:

> *"We are pushed back, and we come back to the city broken and grieving for our failure. I am drawn along on a litter. There is great pain and fever. I do not remember the time then, but my*

Priest-Father comes with a cup. It is the only thing I see. He makes me drink, and then he puts the healing leaves on my side. I sleep. I sleep for days, and when I wake up, I am whole. Many are not. Many die, and now there is a sickness in the city.

"*First a few, then more, then many—many are sick with the fever that brings marks upon the skin. Some live, but many are dead or dying. 'It is the revenge of the Gods!' some are saying. Some believe that the old chief was right. These Silver Men are the True Gods. The doubt is like a cat come sneaking back into our minds. Whole families lie dying with the strange sickness, and still we must watch and prepare to defend the city.*

"*Word comes that the Silver Men have gathered more against us and are coming. They move down the river, conquering every city and village. Most surrender, but at Iztapalapan the cacique resists. The army of the Silver Men falls upon the city, and it is destroyed. The temples are pulled down, and the Man Upon the Tree is raised upon the ruined altars. All who live there are killed. This so frightens the other cities that they not only surrender, but join the army of the Silver Men as it drinks our blood without stopping. Some from our own city in dread leave by dead of night to join them. Quexa is among these. In the night, he leaves the body of my mother, dead from the sickness, and escapes through the canals. But I know I am not done with him! This I See in a dream.*

"'*Get up, Tlaloc! You are needed. Cuitlahuac is dead from the sickness.' I hear this with fear and a sinking inside. Two Kings dead, and the city in pieces around us. This surely is the end. 'The city needs you.' My Priest-Father is looking old and used up. He kicks me on my feet and makes me rise from the bed where I lie. 'Get up! You are well enough. You are not dead. You do not die. There is a meeting of the council. You are called.'*

"'*But I am only a young Priest. I have no place in the council. I have no voice among the Top Men!'*

"'*So many are dead or sick that one as young as you now has a place. Hurry. We must decide a new chief. The Silver Men are all around us. They have cut off the water troughs to the city. They are preparing an attack. We must decide!'*

"I rush with my Priest-Father to the Temple of Huizilopochtli, ruined by the Silver Men. There is what's left of the Top Men. The old Chief's nephew Calmecac is made the new King. Calmecac is a warrior! The decision is agreed with great shouts and clamor.

"'We do not live as slaves! These Silver Men do not see our power yet! Raise the cry. Prepare the arrows and axes! We fight until the Gods drink all our blood and the earth swallows us up—We do not fall!'

"A scream of rage comes from my throat at these words. It is as if Calmecac can see my heart—all our hearts. With this, Calmecac cuts a sacred wound in his loins and lets blood spill to the earth. He binds himself, and my Priest-Father brings in a captive, a Silver Man! All fall silent except for the man himself. He is weak. He cries out and wails in a strange tongue we do not understand. He is pleading with us as two warriors stretch him out on the stone. In one cut my Priest-Father has his hand inside his chest. He pulls the heart free. It beats! The Gods are still with us! The omens are right.

"My Priest-Father gives the heart to Calmecac who must eat. In turn, each of the Top Men eat from the heart of the squealing man. I too eat. It is my first, and I am proud. After that, the body is cut, and each man takes his portion. This enemy will be honored by the families of the remaining Top Men far more than he deserves!

"That night I am with my Priest-Father. Calmecac asks him to See what will come in the days to follow. He is gathering the leaves of the plant.

"'You already chew the leaves. You cannot take the plant again.'

"'I have done so twice already. I must do so again. The King must know what will come.'

"I now know why the Priest-Father is looking old. It is the

poison from the plant working on him.

"'You tell me that more than once in the time of the moon brings death.'

"'Everything brings death. It is a power; this is a death I can know. I have time. It is slow, this death. I will have time to See for the King. When I am gone, it is you. I pass your name to the King. You are Seer after me.'

"I am silent while the Priest-Father prepares the leaves. It is close to the end of our time together, and we both know this.

"'Do you remember the plants I have told you?'

"'All,' I say to him. 'I have them all in my mind.'

"'And do you know the prayers and stories of the Gods? The Dances? The rites? The times and manner of giving blood?'

"'These too I have.'

"'It is well. I am satisfied with you.' The Priest-Father stands before me and sees into my eyes. In his eyes I see the Gods. He takes my shoulders in his hands. 'You are my blood even though it is wrong for me. Yet for me it is not so wrong as it is for you, Tlaloc. You must give up any thought of wife and child. The road you take is very long. I cannot see its end. I can only see the place where it bends out of sight.'

The old man was exhausted. I could tell that the emotional charge of the story was wearing him down. I turned off the recorder.

"It's late." I said softly. Tomorrow—the next day. We have time."

"It is well...you are not angry with me?" The old man sat looking straight ahead without turning to look at me.

"Angry? Why would I be angry? It's a fascinating story." I was busy slipping the recorder back into its case.

"The blood...it is ugly to you, yes?"

"This was a long time ago, Santiago. A world ago. It's not for me to say what was good or bad. It's what was. I'm honored you chose to share it with me."

"We eat the captive—you know this?" He had turned for the first time to study me. I could feel him waiting for my judgement.

"I understand. Why was it done?"

"It is a power! A captive taken gives his blood to the Gods, but his spirit stays with us in his flesh. We eat, and we are him. He is us. His power is in us, and we are like the Gods! The Priests of the Silver Men kill us for this. They call it 'savage.' They say we are without God. But it is not true. The heart I eat—that man is more than he was. He is with the Gods; he is with me then...He is with me now. All he is—I am. He breathes with me. His blood is my blood. As I live, he lives! That one is living in me now!"

"Hm...like Communion," I said drawing on my vestigial Catholicism. I had never been religious. Aunt Jean sent me to church. She insisted for my Mother's sake although I could tell she resented doing it. They taught me. It didn't stick except for the basic theory.

"Yes! Yes! You know this? I say this to the holy men a long time after. They think I am like them. They give me the name Santiago, but I am not theirs. I am mine! I am my people. They send me out. They call me 'savage,' but I eat only the flesh of men, not of the Gods! I kill only captives. I do not impale my God on a tree! What kind of men are these? Who are they to say savage! Who are they to send me away from the people? These are mine! It is me they come to when they are sick. When they wish to See! Who are they?"

It was the first time I had seen him so agitated. He had been calm telling Tlaloc's story, but this last part seemed like a fresh wound. Something personal. He held my arm and held his face close to mine when he spit this out. I pulled back as gently as I could. He seemed to come back to himself. This was a side to this story-telling that made me uneasy. There was something manic in his intensity, and I began to wonder again if this wasn't some part of a dementia that was evolving in the old man's mind.

"The Priest-Father is right. You make me free. I feel the power of the

Gods again! It is so long...But everything is as he tells me. It is well! It is well! There is much I must do!"

Santiago got up from his chair and wandered, deep inside himself, back to his little room. The interview was over without any further fanfare. It disturbed me to see him so distracted. I sat for a moment looking after him, wondering what I should do.

CHAPTER 8

"Before you talk the paint off the wall—you got me!"

Nick was an hour early for our appointment

"Come again?" I said taken off balance.

"Look, I've been working for the city for twenty years, and I hate it! Being here is the first time I've had any fun since I got out of graduate school. It's a pay cut—Mona's gonna kill me, but I'm in. If you want an old, used-up biochemist, a little out of shape and not quite up on the latest developments—put me on the faculty roster for next year."

I was flabbergasted. Nick was a Pied Piper with the students. He had the sixth grade investigating the probability of cloning a mammoth, and the eighth grade was tracing human migration through new developments in mitochondrial DNA. This was college-level theory, and they were sailing through the concepts faster than he could teach them.

"You know I can't raise salaries until enrollments show a significant rise."

"Now you sound like the Mayor. Look, you want me or not?"

"Yeah, I want you! Are you sure you want to give up your cushy job in the 'public sector'?"

"These kids get you thinking. I'm learning as much as they are, and I feel ten years younger—Of course compared to the rest of your faculty, I *am* ten years younger...What do you say? I can take early retirement. With the embarrassing pittance you call a salary and my pension, Mona and I can do fine until full retirement. I want to do it."

"Is the rest of the unit going to resent your quitting?"

"Naw! These guys are all Young Turks. I'm the only old man in the bunch. They still think they're going to light up the world. I'm more interested in lighting up a few faces day to day. In fact, I bet I can get 'em to do a few field trips with the kids. Kendricks is a pretty fair marine biologist, and Thompson knows geophysics—he could take them on a 'tour' of the faults of Manhattan. There's one right under City Hall, did you know that?"

"Jeez, and I was wondering if I could con you into helping out with the science club after school!" I reached out and shook his hand. This was like a gift. "Coffee?"

"Sure."

I poured two cups from the coffee carafe on my desk. We sat quietly for a minute.

"Why biochemistry, Nick? What got you into that?"

"I was going to do research! That was my goal in college, anyway. Pop wanted a Dr. in the family, and he got one, but not the kind he understood."

"So, it's *Dr.* Parrino?"

"PhD, not MD! I did two years of Medical, but I couldn't face being a physician! All that 'fee for service' reminded me of Pop's grocery store— that's what he did, ran a corner grocery—forty-five years! He retired at seventy and had a coronary two weeks later."

"PhD is going to look very good on next year's brochure!"

"Don't get carried away! I've got no teaching experience except for what I've done here, and I'm not certified."

"We'll get you certified! A few courses—you'll clean up like a new potato!"

"You're a silver-tongued devil, you know that?"

We were comfortable together. I liked that. Sally and I were a team, but Nick was a kindred spirit. We were easy together, and that was a relief from the constant tension Crayden had become. I loved the energy, but it wasn't easy being the "buck stop" constantly. I was looking forward to having someone around who didn't always need something from me.

"You know I was thinking about things 'medical' recently..."

"Yeah, huh...Well, don't tell me about your aches and pains! Two years of medical school twenty-five years ago doesn't qualify me to diagnose a headache!"

"No, it's nothing like that. I was...I was wondering, just how long *is* life— I mean really!"

"This a philosophical question or just straight 'nuts and bolts' medicine?"

"Nuts and bolts. How long can we really live? Say, under ideal conditions."

"I don't know...There's lots of ideas about human longevity. If you look at the records, about a hundred and ten years seems to be the limit. Our cells age. After about a hundred divisions they run out of juice. Then you get individuals like that old French woman who lived over a hundred and twenty-two years. There are unofficial instances of people living ten or fifteen years longer than *that*. Current research suggests there may be a gene for aging. Some researchers think there'll come a day when we can manipulate the lifespan through DNA. Why the interest in longevity?"

"Nothing really. I was just curious, I guess."

"It's an intriguing topic. I was just looking at a paper on the some experiments they've been trying on fruit flies and flatworms. In some cases they've been able to triple the normal lifespan by altering certain genes."

"Just what we need—a bunch of senior fruit flies hanging around forever!"

"Well, one day they'll do it. Whether they should or not—that's the real issue. Just look around you. Would you really *want* to live over two hundred years in New York? Can you imagine what rents would be in about a hundred and fifty years? Let alone crime! There was a story on NY1 this morning about somebody breaking into the birdhouse in Central

Park and making off with about twenty rare birds. Birds, for Christ's sake. They'll steal anything!"

We talked for about half an hour, and then Sally came in to remind me I had a meeting with the Board of Governors about the proposed renovations to the building. Nick had agreed to start officially in the fall, but he would continue with the current classes without any mention of our deal until he had everything in place on his end. He had a feeling the EPA would replace him too soon if they knew he was planning to quit in the summer. My own job at Crayden was taken for the same reasons. We had a lot in common.

"I beg your pardon, Dr. Holliman, am I interrupting you?"

Cameron Delaney barged right into the office as if he were King. His perfunctory show of manners barely covered his contempt of me, but I didn't let it disturb me. With him was a young man with a sharp suit and a cardboard roll under his arm."

"Not at all, Mr. Delaney. I believe our appointment is for now, and Dr. Parrino and I are finished. Thanks, Nick, we'll settle the details later."

"Details? Is this something the Board should know about, Dr. Holliman? I'm always interested in anything that you might be doing at Crayden—especially *before* the fact."

"I know you are. See you later, Nick. We'll talk in a few days…"

"Better you than me!" Nick whispered to me as he left. I turned, and the young man in the sharp suit had opened the tube and was pulling drawings out and arranging them on my desk.

"This is Martin Olsen from Spencer and Chase. He's their Restoration Expert. He's made some drawings of the architectural changes for the building, and I thought I owed you the courtesy of viewing them before they were put into place."

"Architectural Changes? I thought Crayden was Landmarked. I don't believe we can make any changes, Mr. Delaney.

"Not to the outside of the building, you're right, but we have a free hand inside the structure. We've retained Spencer and Chase because they were the firm who actually built Crayden. They have all the original specifications and drawings. It's quite remarkable!"

"I'm sure it is! Just what changes is the 'Board' proposing to the *inside* of Crayden."

"Nothing that would alter its intrinsic character, I can assure you! *Some* of us are dedicated to the tradition of Crayden in *all* its facets. Mr. Olsen...?" Delaney swept his hand out to the young man in the sharp suit, and he took the cue like an overeager little chorus boy.

"Basically what we've drawn up is an interpretation of the original plan of the building. Mostly it involves a massive updating of the infrastructure, wiring, heating, water supply, and the like,—and, of course, the roof has to be completely replaced...but I like to think that we've made some additions for Crayden's future."

"Those being...?" I asked in as neutral a tone as I could manage.

"Well, the most striking is the pool!"

"Pool?" I asked. Why are you adding a pool? We have so many other needs. We don't have a swim team, nor, for that matter, does any comparable school on the West Side."

"That's another triumph of your very own, Dr. Holliman."

"I'm afraid I don't follow, Mr. Delaney. How is the addition of a pool at Crayden related to anything I've done so far?"

"It's directly a result of your efforts with Julian Reynolds. Julian has his—'notions' about things. After your letters and a brief discussion with the Board, he's decided to foot the bill for the entire restoration of the building. He had only one stipulation—the addition of an Olympic-sized swimming pool in the basement of the building. Julian was a swimmer at Princeton. He came quite close to Olympic status. Julian's always felt that if he had discovered swimming a few years sooner—say, those years he spent at Crayden—he'd have made the Olympic Team. Apparently, he wants to provide that opportunity for some other 'Julian-in-the-making' who might be attending Crayden today."

"He wants to install a pool because an individual student might one day make the Olympic Team? Did you discuss this with him?"

"Oh, yes. I encouraged him! Julian will provide everything else that we need, but we must have a pool installed. He considers it a memorial to his own youth."

"Mr. Olsen, I'm sure you know that such massive changes to a structure over a hundred years old—"

"Will be handled with the utmost care! I'm very good at my job, Dr. Holliman. We'll be in and out in two years or less!"

Since he didn't dare dismiss me, it seemed that Delaney had come up with another plan. He would "renovate" me out of the picture. So, his latest gambit was a pool to neutralize me.

"I've taken the liberty of getting Collegiate's approval for a sharing of their new building for a period of time while we wait for our own building to be completed. I assured Julian that with your emphasis on change and updating Crayden's image, this would fit in perfectly with your plans for us." Delaney couldn't help looking smug as he stood next to Olsen with his plans pinned to a board and his youthful certainty pinned to his posture.

"...I see. And our new offerings? Computers, the arts, sports...?"

"We might have to 'trim' some of your 'enhancements' to our curriculum. Of course, you would still be Headmaster of Crayden, but our class schedule would have to be held to its 'core' of classics and required subjects."

"In other words, everything I have done would be erased for at least one full year..."

"Possibly two...."

"I see. By then my contract would be up"

"We all have to sacrifice for progress, don't we, and Crayden will benefit from an entirely new infrastructure and a stunning pool!"

"My plans are very complete, Dr. Holliman! Crayden will be the envy of every private school in New York! Solar power on the roof, a complete fiber optic system, high-tech windows, the most efficient heating and cooling system available...Mr. Reynolds himself has approved of every last detail. Construction will be under my personal direction and will start immediately following the current school year." Olsen was oblivious to the little battle raging between Delaney and me.

"...Is it necessary to disrupt the entire building?"

"As you pointed out, Dr. Holliman, this is an old structure. We will do most of the heavy deconstruction and retrofitting during the summer months, but the excavation for the pool will have to continue during the following year."

"Then we could theoretically use our classrooms in the fall."

"No problem! We're a private firm. We can move much faster than the city in its public schools. But—the pool, as I said, will require us to shut down most of Crayden's essential systems."

"Could you finish that the following summer?"

"That would be much too expensive, Dr. Holliman!" Delaney interrupted. "We can't impose on Julian's fantastic generosity."

"I'm afraid extending the construction period would double the costs. In any event, the contracts have been signed. Everything is in place." The young man was rolling up the plans he had stretched out before me, which I had barely reviewed.

"What do you mean?"

"Mr. Reynolds has contracted Spencer and Chase. The Board has approved. No changes can be made without penalties being imposed."

"I see. Thank you, Mr. Olsen. You've been very informative."

"...Well, gentlemen...You'll be seeing quite a lot of me. I'll be in and out of Crayden nearly every day in the coming months with my team. I assure you, Dr. Holliman, we will not disturb any of your classes..."

"...I'm sure you'll be very circumspect." I had locked eyes with Delaney, and he knew he had me.

"I'll just leave the two of you to discuss...whatever you need to do for preparation. Have a nice day."

"Please confer our gratitude to Julian Reynolds again, won't you, Mr. Olsen?" Delaney kept his eyes on me.

"Oh, I don't see Mr. Reynolds, I'm afraid. Everything is done through his Foundation. I'll send an e-mail. I believe he reads those." With that, Olsen left us squared off in my office.

"...Mr. Delaney, I never intended—"

"No, I'm sure you didn't! Just as I'm sure you didn't intend to save Crayden by destroying every ounce of decorum and dignity we had built up over the years! You've turned this place into a circus side show,—students from—everywhere disrupting our time-tested approach to learning. Arts programs with no relation to the arts they purport to champion. News stories, TV articles, and an atmosphere of total chaos, all at your instigation."

"You really hate me, don't you, Mr. Delancy?"

"I *dislike* you, Dr. Holliman. Quite a lot. You misrepresented yourself at our initial interview, and you've done nothing but grandstand since you arrived. When I was young, a man presented himself for what he was, not what he thought people wanted to see. I –'we'—took you on to carry on the traditions of Crayden, not make a mockery of everything we have loved. If it were possible to get rid of you, I wouldn't hesitate for a second! Does that settle the issue in your mind?"

"...Yes, I guess it does! Believe me, that disturbs me—"

"Oh, please, Dr. Holliman—"

"Will you, for Christ's sake, let me finish? My God, you're an insufferable old bore! I'm sorry if that offends you, but you're acting like petulant child. Things aren't going your way, and so it spells the End of Everything!...What is wrong with you? Surely you knew we were close to shutting down! I refuse to believe you didn't know that Crayden was dying on the vine!"

"We weren't dying on the vine!"

"The hell you weren't—and you knew it! A shrinking enrollment and a diminishing endowment can only mean one thing for a private school like Crayden. What did you think I was going to do? Preside over its funeral?"

"I thought you'd be pleased! Change!—isn't that what you're always proposing. Well, now you have all the change you can handle."

"Umhm, so you think tearing apart the entire building will stop progress!"

"I would do anything to rid us of you, Dr. Holliman. You are the embodiment of everything I despise about this media-obsessed, public-focused, electronic morass of a world we find ourselves in. Honor, dignity, learning a grasp of the classics—"

"Is everything we're teaching! Nothing has changed those values, but our style has to reflect the world in which our children live! There's a lot about the current day I hate too! Don't forget I'm part of the 'Old Crayden' myself, but I've got to get us through this transition period if I'm going secure a future for this institution. We want the same thing! Can't you see that? The only thing we differ on is the style I've chosen."

"Your carnival approach to education is hardly progress, Dr. Holliman! You have pushed us into a position of looking like pushcart peddlers and hucksters. I know Crayden needs to—keep up, but we can do it with dignity. That's a quality you don't seem to possess!"

At least it was out now between us. Delaney and I were face to face with all the resentments on the table. I knew I'd never win him over, but I was hoping to defuse the situation to some degree. He leveled his best insults regarding my "style". He fumed and attacked everything I had done. He refused to acknowledge any of the developments since my start as anything but a herald of disaster...including this proposed reconstruction of Crayden itself. He was an old man under siege by changes he couldn't embrace, and all I could do was let him vent it all. He did. When he left, I knew he was exhausted, but I thought I detected at least a hint of respect. I had the feeling that by standing my ground and really listening to his tirade, I had weathered the front of his fury. I had the distinct impression that things would be less confrontational.

The "changes" at Crayden that were coming put me on a runaway train, but I wasn't going to be erased by them. I was determined. I had to find a way to keep us in place as a working institution. The physical changes could work *for* us as long as we remained open and functioning in our own plant. But how?

CHAPTER 9

"The Silver Men attack many times. They build their water-houses and sweep the lake. No one can leave by water. The sickness is everywhere, and the people are more afraid than ever. As a Top Man, I must go house to house and rouse the warriors.

"'Fight!' I tell them. 'Fight, or all we are is gone!' But they are spent. I force them, but there is no spirit in them to push the Silver Men away. Every day word comes back that more slave tribes join them to destroy us. Calmecac keeps us at the walls. The Silver Men are afraid of him, but it is only for a breath more. A force is gathering for another push against us, and we all know it is finished.

"My Priest-Father calls me to his pallet. He is soon to die. Already his lower limbs are cold, and the poison from the plant makes his breath shallow. His skin is grey, but his eyes blaze when I enter.

"'Tlaloc! Tlaloc, you come now.' He hands me his holding skin. 'This is now yours. Inside are the ceremonial knife and the leaves from the plant that gives sight. You take my place. Long, long may you carry the word! Remember, my son, what you see, what you feel. Tell the people. Don't let them forget who they are! Heal them. See for them. Keep the dances and the stories. Hold the Gods inside your head, that the people know what you know of us. You are going into a distant place. I am staying here forever. I say now to you, you are my son! I will pay the Gods for this, but I am glad. It is enough for me, this time. But you drink deeper of time than anyone knows among us. Use this, Tlaloc. You are the life we have left!'

"He rolls to his side and slips into the earth. He gives his last blood. Two women who are watching wail in fright and run from the room. They see the End in sight, and they are afraid. I hear a great noise outside in the street. It is as if the whole city is in pain, and I think this cannot be for the Priest-Father! No one knows yet. What is happening? I rush out to see Calmecac. He is in his feathers and armor on the royal war boat. He is leaving to do final battle and die. The boat slips toward the lake with all warriors paddling fast. Calmecac stands at the front with his axe ready to swing. Two of the water-houses make for him. Calmecac tells the men to row for shore, so that they can make a stand in a better place, but the water-houses are on him. With ropes they snare the war boat, and the Silver Men take him! He is swinging his axe, but there are too many. It is over. A great number of warriors come for the city. They are on us! I am taken and bound. All the Top Men are taken. Houses are burning. The books! All the books are burning. Women are screaming. Children are crying."

The old man shook and held his hands to his head. His face was a mask of horror as he relived the Fall of the Empire. Tears flowed down the furrows in his brown cheeks, and he rocked back and forth in abject mourning. I couldn't help but kneel and put my arms over his shoulders. I rocked with him as if he were a small child and murmured the senseless comforts I once murmured to my own children.

"Shh!...It's over now....over. That is gone. The time is gone. Now you are safe. It was long time ago, and all those people are gone. It's a memory— a dream...Shh! now..."

Slowly the old man let go of all the anguish within him. His body unclenched, and he gained control of himself.

"...You...have the last? This fall of Calmecac?...The burning?..."

I reached for my digital recorder. It was still running, and the tiny green light was on.

"Yes. I have it. I got it all."

"It is well....These things I do not see for ...long time. I do not feel them.

...Now I feel. That day I give my blood. That day we all give our blood—But Tlaloc does not die."

"What does Tlaloc do?"

"I run! I see the Silver Men have taken more than they can count, and I run! Like a coward I run into the jungle and hide! The city burns around me. My people are dying,,...and I hide myself deep in the dark and watch it burn. All. Everything. I hear them scream. In the flames on the temple of the Sun, I see the Man Upon the Tree being raised where once my Priest-Father pours the warm blood of captives out to the Gods. This dead God with the bowed head rises above the power of all my people, and now I know I am alone. I hide in shame from myself."

The old man bowed his head and was silent for a long time. I didn't know what to do. I wanted to leave, but I was afraid to miss something—some part of the story on file. Finally, he lifted his head, and –he was smiling! His dark eyes burned with absolute joy! He opened his mouth full of yellow teeth and laughed almost without sound. He laughed with growing intensity, and he stood. He began to sing and beat his hands on his knees to the rhythm of music in his head. His song picked up in volume and pace, and he began to dance around me and the chair on which I was sitting.

"Santiago?—Santiago!..." He did not answer. He continued the strange dance and threw himself into the spirit of it with such intensity that I was afraid he would hurt himself. I kept the recorder on and watched and listened, and he built to a crescendo, and then he stopped abruptly with one final slap of his palms to his knees."

"It is well! I am free. I am free of this I say! I give it to you. All! I am Free! I must give blood!"

Santiago pulled a pocketknife from his worn trousers and, in one motion, he opened it and laced a two-inch cut on his left forearm.

"No!" I tried to stop him, but the old man was quick. The blood poured from his arm. I reached for him and grabbed the arm, but he pulled away and resumed dancing. Blood spattered around the floor and over both of us. Finally I grabbed him and forced him to the chair holding the arm and trying to clamp off the flow of blood."

"Why you stop me? I am with the Gods! I give the blood. The Gods see me again! Tlaloc is a man, again!"

"Be quiet!" I barked. I grabbed my handkerchief and made a tourniquet. The bleeding stopped almost immediately, but the gash in his arm was still open and fresh. I knew if I released the handkerchief, he would lose more blood. "Come on, I'm taking you to the emergency room!"

"No! I don't need doctors—medicine. It is well! All is well! I give the Gods what they do not have, and they are pleased!"

"Stand still! Keep your arm up." I tied off the handkerchief, and I sat the old man down in his chair. I was weak in the knees at seeing so much blood. How was I going to get him over to Roosevelt Hospital? He would never make it that far. Losing that much blood he was bound to collapse..."Come, on. I'll get a cab. Move slowly...!"

"NO!" The old man pulled away from me entirely, and anger welled up in him. "You understanding nothing I tell you! You hear but you do not listen! Tlaloc does not die! *I* do not die! The blood is what I give. It is to be free! Blood is what I owe...what I do not pay for long time! Now I pay. Tomorrow I pay also! I pay the Gods because you come. You are what my Priest-Father Sees. The Gods live! They do not die! All this time— long time—they wait for me!"

"Santiago, please, you're—you're not making sense. You've lost too much blood. I have to get you to a doctor!"

"No doctors! I do not need. Look! See! The blood is what I give!" The old man unraveled my handkerchief and held up his arm to me. Miraculously the wound had stopped bleeding. He must have missed the blood vessels. It was beyond luck. I sat in relief, my whole body shaking. Santiago threw the handkerchief at me. "Why do you not hear me? I am what I tell you! I do what I must do! I do this for all my people. I am the last to know these things. The last to See! But you are blind! Even when I tell you, you do not see! Go. You do not see! You cannot. Leave me to pray. Leave me to sing!

The old man began to dance and chant in a tongue I had never heard. His energy was manic, but I was too spent to do any more. I stumbled out of the basement in my blood-spattered suit, clutching the handkerchief soaked in Santiago's blood.

CHAPTER 10

"Pedro de Alvarado!" Soldani was standing in my office door. It was the middle of a busy Wednesday. I had a meeting with the Board of Governors in twenty minutes—my third in two weeks,—and I had four teachers out sick. The door had simply opened, and he stood there saying only the name.

"...I beg your pardon?"

"Pedro de Alvarado—That's the crest—on the morion—the helmet!"

"Dr. Soldani, I don't want to be rude, but how did you get past Sally?"

"Uh...I'm sorry. I—uh...she wasn't at her desk, and I took the chance that you might be in. And...you are!"

"Not for long, I'm afraid. I have a meeting very shortly, and we're covering for—"

"Dr. Holliman, I won't take your time! I just—I wanted to know if you might have the helmet...here. I did some research on the crest. I sketched it from memory from seeing it in my office, and I—I did some hunting, and what I found could be extraordinary! You see, so few identifiable personal artifacts have survived. I have to be sure that my memory of the crest was correct, and, of course, there's a great deal of testing of the artifact itself and—uh—"

"I don't have it here." I had to cut him short. The truth is, I had forgotten all about Soldani. It had been four days since my hair-raising experience with Santiago. I had gone back the following morning and that night as well. I looked for him every day. I couldn't find him.

Nobody had seen him, and yet his work was done. It was clear to me that he was avoiding me. I was worried. Barbara shared my concern. The violence of that night and the new element of self-mutilation convinced us both that Santiago was deteriorating. I had to find him. I had to make sure he was all right, and I had to do something for him—about him.

"When do you think I might see it? It's very important! You don't understand how important a find like the helmet might be! Pedro De Alvarado was a first lieutenant to Hernan Cortes—the conqueror of Aztec Mexico! He was a ruthless adventurer, savage even by Cortes' standards, and he was instrumental in the slaughter of the Aztecs and their ultimate subjugation...He's a very important historical figure! That helmet was his!—At least I *think* it was! It's a direct link to a major historical event!"

I couldn't tell him what I'd been through. I couldn't tell anyone—not unless I had to! I owed the old man some loyalty for his long ago kindness. I couldn't allow myself to believe that this sudden aberration was anything more than a kind of tribal expression of release. It had to be that. Just as the account of Tlaloc was a tribal memory passed down from father to son. Barbara was right. The recipient of the story absorbed it as his own life—made it live again. Once passed on, the teller was freed of his burden. Santiago was showing me his relief! He was free, and now the burden was mine!

"I'll call you just as soon as I have the time to let you come in and examine the helmet. Now, if you don't mind—"

"I do! I do mind! I'm sorry, Dr. Holliman, but this is much too important to brush aside! Finding an artifact of this importance is just not something you can dismiss so easily!"

Soldani stood between me and the door, looking nervous and self-righteous all at the same time. His rumpled suit and disheveled hair made him look like an outraged crow. He was adamantly refusing to be shown out.

"I've come here to—to claim sponsorship—if you will. I will take full responsibility for the provenance and the research! It will cost you nothing! All I insist upon is the right to document the helmet in my own name! You can impose any restrictions on the piece. I'll sign any affidavits. Think of the prestige a find of this nature could mean to your school? I mean, an educator such as yourself, instrumental in bringing such a find to light! It would be amazing what this could do for your standing!"

I found myself listening in spite of myself. God knows I had done everything I could to bring Crayden into the limelight—and to get the funding we needed...

"I—I know I've made a terrible impression on you and your wife, Dr. Holliman. Please, please forgive me! I'm a charmless man, consumed with my profession. A 'geek,' that's what they call people like me. I have no personal life—not one *you'd* consider worth much, anyway. I see almost no one. I spend all my time pouring over manuscripts and dusty artifacts in the basement of the Met. I don't think anyone there even knows my first name. A find like this—Dr. Holliman, if you have any sense of history, this is monumental! I—I won't deny that I want to connect myself to it. It would be the making of my career. H-However, if you object to my involvement...I can put you in contact with someone else—"

"Dr. Soldani...please..." I was more than a little ashamed of myself. Just a second ago I was thinking about what he had said about the "prestige" of the find and what it could do for Crayden, and here this pathetic, desperate pedant was willing to throw aside his own ambitions for the sake of bringing the helmet to light. "I really do have a pressing meeting. I promise I will call you tomorrow morning, and we can discuss what to do about the helmet. How's that?"

"You will call? Tomorrow? What time?"

I picked up a pad of "stickies" from my desk and made a note. "9:30 call Dr. Soldani at the Met."

"Uh—212-555-6762—that's my direct line."

"Got it. Tomorrow morning, I promise."

"9:30?"

"Yes! 9:30."

"...Wonderful. Very good! Thank you! Thank you, Dr. Holliman! That's very generous of you. Thank you so much!"

"Dr. Soldani, my meeting...?"

"Oh, yes, yes! Absolutely. Thank you. I'll let myself out! 9:30. That's wonderful. Wonderful!"

"Is something wrong?" Sally stood in the doorway to the office. Soldani's head whipped around in surprise.

"No, no, no! Nothing at all! That's tremendous! Wonderful. Thank you, Dr.!"

Soldani stood undecided and confused for a moment, and then he sprang for the door pushing Sally against the jam as he ran out.

"Ow!" Sally bumped her head against the jam, but I could tell she wasn't seriously hurt. "Boy, what a nut-job!"

"You OK?"

"Yeah. What did he want?"

"...Salvation."

"Huh? I was in the Ladies room—I didn't see him come in. "

"It's OK, I handled it. Is the Board here? Did they hear any of this?"

"They stopped downstairs in the Library. Delaney's got that jerk from the Spencer and Clark with him. You know, the one that looks like he needs an enema!"

"I'll join them in the library."

"Good luck!"

CHAPTER 11

"Hasn't anyone seen him?" Barbara was torturing her salad with a fork. Maffei's was busy. It was always busy, but for a neighborhood place, it wasn't a bad restaurant. We elected to eat out at least twice a week, because if I stayed home, I would inevitably work on paperwork for Crayden. After the Board meeting, I didn't have much appetite. The battle with the Delaney and the mystery of Santiago's disappearance were weighing on my mind.

"Nobody! I've gone down to his digs almost every day at different times, and he's never there. I've waited for him in the evenings—nothing! I'm worried about what he might do to himself."

"I had to throw that suit away. The cleaners couldn't get out the blood...C'mon, Brad, he's been with the school for a long time. Even if he is losing touch with reality, there's never been any indication of trouble before. He'll come back."

"That's just it, Barbara, he's not gone! I can feel it! He's hiding! His work is always done. The school goes on just as always, but he stays out of sight. I can't have a student finding him somewhere full of blood and—dancing around! Right now, you and I are the only ones who know about this. At some point *I* have to *do* something. I should have done something right from the start when he started this crazy business!"

"You didn't want him losing his home or his income. You couldn't know how far it would go!"

"You think Delaney would care about that? Hell, this whole situation is tailor-made for him to use to get rid of me! Do you know what I'd look like to the community, if they knew I harbored an unbalanced, possibly violent man in a school full of children? Why did I even entertain these ridiculous stories?"

"You were honoring an old friend! One who needed your attention—one who needs you now! Brad, nothing has happened! An old man told you an ancient tribal story. He passed a priceless relic on to you. He trusts you! It's still all right. He'll come back. He'll seek you out—I know he will. When he does, you'll decide calmly and honestly what to do."

"I don't like the other scenarios I have in my head! Suppose he starts all the 'Angry Young Lord' shit with one of the students? How do I explain that?"

"Deal with what you *have* not what you *anticipate*! Until you find him, this is all pointless worry! I know you're worried about Santiago. You're worried about the school. You're worried about the Board. Jesus, Brad, what are you going to do, have a stroke over this? Is that what we came to New York for? Because, if it is, I'm going back! This isn't worth it!"

"...All right. You're right, it's not even known by anyone but us. When he surfaces, I'll get him some help—something."

"...Eat your salad." Barbara watched me for a few minutes while I picked at my salad. The waiter brought the entreé, and we sat in silence for a while. Neither of us showed much interest in food. "What about what's-his-face?"

"Hm?"

"What's-his-face—the greasy bean-pole who tried to glom onto the helmet. You said he came in to see you."

"Soldani."

"If you ask me, *he's* the one who should be locked up. Now there's an 'axe-murderer' if I ever saw one. He always looks like he needs a bath!"

"I have to call him. I promised him I'd set up a firm time to let him examine the helmet."

"I thought we agreed he wouldn't have anything to do with it! Brad, that man was ready to try to steal that object right out of my hands! You can't trust him with it!"

"He was...different from that. What you saw was career desperation. The guy works in the basement of the Met. All he wants is a little recognition, but he was willing to throw it away, if that's what it takes to get the helmet out to be examined."

"Yeah, I'll bet he'd say anything to get his hands on it!"

"I'm not going to let him take it out of my office."

"You're going to let him see it? I can't believe you'd do that! Brad! That guy just wants to get his hands on the helmet. He'll tell you anything— He doesn't care! He wants the helmet!"

"He's not going to get it. If I let him examine the thing, it will be with me present, and it goes nowhere else! Barbara, he's an expert. He thinks the helmet belonged to some officer with Cortez. Pedro something or other. He says the find of the helmet could be a major coup for the school."

"So you're going to turn it over to someplace, if it's what the grease ball says it is? You don't think Santiago will care about that?"

"I'm not going to 'give' it to anyone! Not without being sure everything is kosher all around!"

"He gave you that helmet and his story as a trust. Whatever his frame of mind, he looks upon you as someone very important in his world, Brad."

"Don't you think I know that? I—I don't know what I'm going to do about it right now—not until I know that he's not going to hurt himself or someone else. I've got to find him first. Then I'll decide what to do..."

CHAPTER 12

"All is gone! Everything burned! Warriors are dead...everywhere. Everywhere there is blood and burning...."

The cup of maté was sitting on my desk steaming as I walked into the office. The school was empty—had been for hours. I had worked with Sally for the last two hours calling each Board member and detailing all the reasons why Crayden could not be closed or moved for now. I thought some of them agreed, but none of them were committing to anything. It was maddening, and I finally sent Sally home. I wanted to write follow-up letters to each Board member. As I came into my office, Santiago was waiting for me. It had been twelve days since the bloodletting in the basement. He sat in a darkened corner of the room, his black eyes shining with anticipation. He sipped his cup and watched me. I stopped for a moment, afraid to scare him off. Measuring the opportunity, I went to the desk and took up the cup, sipped it, and stood looking at him.

"Are you all right?"

He stood immediately and approached. He was smiling—joyfully!

"Sí! Sí! All is well! I pray. I work. See, Santiago is well!" He pulled back his shirtsleeve, revealing the cut he had inflicted upon himself. There was nothing left but a faint red welt. "You drink...I tell. All is well."

I sat silently. Only the shaded desk light lit the huge office, leaving the rest of the room in deep shadow. He was fervent without the mania he had shown in our last meeting. He seemed controlled, and I needed a chance to think about what to do with him.

"Everywhere there is blood and burning. The Silver Men push

all to the plaza by the great temple. In shame I come from the jungle and the dark. I hide inside the bravery of the other warriors. I am among the living, but I feel dead. Many—many are killed as we are pushed to the plaza. Any warrior who dares to look at the Silver Men in the eyes is killed, and his carcass is thrown onto the piles of others. Women and children are there and old ones. The city cries as it burns."

"I am bound to a stick across my back. I cannot move my arms. My head is forced down, so that I can look up only with work. The Silver Men carry our idols to the plaza. Those of gold they keep. Those of stone and clay they break. The holy pictures and books are piled high and one lights them. When the flames grow, the women wail. We are all sure we are to be killed, but when? When is this awful thing done? The Silver Men cheer and look up. I stretch my back to see. Above us on the Great Temple the Man Upon the Tree stands high. The Chief of the Silver Men stands before us and says strange words we don't understand. A woman stands with him and tells us what he says. She is one of us!

"The warriors see her. They hear her words and growl like dogs that a woman of us is standing with the Silver Men. Some warriors, those who growl, are struck to the ground until there is silence. The Chief of the Silver Men speaks again, and the woman tells us, we belong to another tribe, the tribe of Silver Men. We are theirs, but first we are to be made the children of the Man Upon the Tree. He is the God who made us. It is He who decides our fate.

"Then we are taken to the pens where our animals are kept. There we are to be held like pigs until the Man Upon the Tree takes our blood. The warriors are kept apart in small groups, so that we cannot fight. We are tied to sticks or together, so that we cannot run. We wait to be taken to the temple to give our blood. It is what we expect. We prepare...but it is slow to happen!

"Men of Cloth come. Men without weapons. Only a few. They take us one at a time. They say words; they pour water on our heads. Once this is done, Silver Men take us away. We think

this is the time for blood to flow. I am kept by a Cloth Man.

"'Padre,' he calls himself. He asks me how I am called. This I understand from his way. 'Tlaloc,' I tell him. He nods but he cannot say it right. I look at my stick. He sees my hands bloody, and he understands that I do not want to be tied when my blood is taken. He speaks to a Silver Man who shouts at him, but he does not change. He says more words, and the angry Silver Man cuts my ropes. My arms fall; the feeling is long gone from them. Slowly they wake.

"Padre says many words to me. I do not understand him, but I can see that he does not want my blood. This is wrong! I am a warrior! A warrior can choose to be slave or to give his blood. I choose blood! I tell him this! I tell him, 'I am Tlaloc, Priest, son of the Priest-Father, High Seer to the King. I am taken into the Top Men. I do not serve another! I give my blood! Strike the blow! Give the Man Upon the Tree my blood! I go to the earth with many others. Let your God drink deep from me. I do not care!'

"He is silent. He listens, but he says nothing. Long time. Then he points to the Man Upon the Tree on the Great Temple, and he whispers to me, 'Jesus!'

"'Jesus,' I say back. So this is the Man Upon the Tree. 'Jesus!' I cry, 'Take my blood! I am Tlaloc, and I am ready!' I grab a knife from the hand of a Silver man and strike myself in the chest. Here."

The old man opened his shirt and pointed to a two-inch scar right-of-center on his chest.

"The Silver Man takes a stone, and hits me on the head. I go down to darkness."

The old man was silent for a moment, watching me to see if I understood. I could feel his need to be understood, but I was afraid to incite the kind of agitation I had seen him fall into before.

"...But Tlaloc doesn't die?"

"No," he continued:

> "I do not die. The Priest-Father is right; again the great cat shows me his belly. I cannot not die there. Days I am in darkness. Then I wake. I see Padre by me. He puts cold water on me and says words low and fast. I do not know how I am alive.

> "When he sees me open my eyes, Padre comes close. 'Jesus,' he whispers, and he puts his hand on my head, and that is when I see that he prays. He lifts a cup and says, 'Agua.' I drink, and I know my people die, but I do not. The Man Upon the Tree does not want my blood. My Gods claim it first. It is to keep me with my people. What is left? I am He who must 'See' for them. I must heal them. I am the Memory of my Priest-Father. This I know."

He stopped. We both sat in silence for a while.

"...Santiago, where have you been?"

"I am here. I know you look for me. I come now."

"Why did you wait all this time? You know I was worried."

"Sí, I know. But Santiago must have time to 'See.' I take the plant. I See. It is well."

"What do you see?"

The strangest look came over his face. It was a mixture of joy and sadness both, so hard to describe. His eyes brimmed with tears, but he remained calm. When he came back to himself, he spoke low and steady.

"I am yours. From you I am born this time. The Gods see me. What you do is right. I follow. I do. Your people are my people. Your enemies are my enemies. I serve the Gods; I serve you."

"You can't hide from me like that! I need to know where you are!"

"Sí, always. I am with you. I am here. If you say my name, I come."

"I was terrified for you! All that blood—I thought you were dying."

The old man laughed his peculiar wheezing laugh. "The cat still shows me his belly. I give only my blood. To my Gods."

"What if you had died? How would I explain? I don't know if you understand, but as Headmaster here, I'm responsible for everything that happens in these walls. Something like that—"

"You do not see again! Santiago does not show you this again. I am yours. I work. I do. This I promise—on the Gods!"

It was a promise simple and profound. I don't know why I accepted it so readily, but his contrition was so complete, so full, it defeated my anxieties. I capitulated. I didn't realize the responsibility this carried for me.

CHAPTER 13

"Did you hear about that kid from Spencer and Chase?" Sally was standing in the doorway of my office with a cardboard cup of steaming coffee. It was Monday, and school hadn't opened yet.

"Huh?...What?" I was deep in a letter I was drafting.

"That kid...Olsen! It was on the news this morning before I left. They said he was missing. Nobody's seen him since last week. Lives with his mother. Poor thing is beside herself. They actually showed her on TV begging anyone who saw him to call the police."

"Olsen—the 'Restoration Expert'?"

"That's him. He disappeared last week—right after he was here I think."

"...Really..."

"No wonder we haven't seen him. He came a few times with a small crew of engineers right after you met with him, and as near as I can make out he went 'poof'! Didn't he say he'd be around a lot?"

"Yeah...I wonder what happened."

"Who knows?...You want anything before I open the doors?"

"Uh...No. I'll call Spencer and Chase when they open up. It's too early for them. I need to know what's going to happen to our project."

"Maybe this is good. Maybe they won't be able to start."

"I doubt that. They're a big firm. They'll send someone...I think."

Sally went back to her office. The letter I was drafting was to Julian Reynolds. Maybe this was the time to talk to him directly.

***

Nick and Mona liked good food and music. It was a perfect night for Barbara and me. The four of us were good company. Before dinner was over, Barbara and Mona were friends in that way that experienced women have once they've passed the competitive years. Nick and I were already comfortable with each other. I had invited them to dinner in celebration of Nick's acceptance of the position at Crayden. The food and wine made conversation easy.

"I still don't know what you want me to teach!" Nick was smiling, but his question was right to the point.

"Chemistry mostly, maybe a little biology—if you're up to it."

"Hey, Holliman! For *one* night you can forget Crayden! We invited Mona and Nick out to celebrate. You got your chemist! Now for Christ's sakes, let's not talk shop all night!"

"She's right. I'm sorry, Nick, Mona! Glad to have you with us!"

"Nick's like a kid! All he talks about is his students!" Mona was a well-kept woman. She tended to carry some weight, but she dressed well, and she always looked perfect. I could tell Barbara felt a little overshadowed, but she never let Mona see it.

"It's the 'Craydenitis'! Once a man has it, there's no hope! Brad's absolutely consumed by Crayden! Ever since we came here, every waking minute it's Crayden, Crayden, Crayden!"

"He *is* the Headmaster. I guess he's got a right to obsess a little. Didn't Nick tell me something about you going here when you were a kid?"

"That's right. I'm an alumnus. I was in school at Crayden for seven years before...I moved away." I poured myself another glass of wine, and for a moment the conversation lulled.

"The Board's been on his tail right from the start. That old bastard Delaney'd have Brad's head, if he could figure a way to keep Crayden going without him. Instead he's having the place torn down."

"What! What do you mean torn down?" Nick was alarmed.

"Take it easy! Crayden is not being torn down. The Board got a huge grant for a complete retrofit. They're planning on starting after the current semester." I shot Barbara a warning look, which she didn't see.

"Right, and they want to shelve everything Brad's done! Shove all the kids into another school—shrink the classes back to nothing!" I loved Barbara's absorption of my battles as her own. I could see Nick's concern.

"You're safe! Got to have chemistry! Right now, everything's up in the air. The plans are drawn up, but their expert architect has gone missing. Anyway, nothing's happening until we finish our transition plans. I wasn't planning on saying anything to the faculty until everything was set up."

"Sorry..." Barbara looked a little sheepish when she remembered that Nick worked for Crayden now. "It's Delaney. He wants to turn the clock back to 1957!"

"Delaney's OK. He's an *old* man with strong opinions. I kind of admire his open disdain of my methods. He doesn't pretend, and he doesn't take prisoners! He's willing to turn everything upside-down just to get rid of me."

"Sometimes a good fight keeps you going!" I thought Nick might have something there.

"I certainly seemed to keep Delaney's blood moving."

"I'll drink to his blood!" Barbara lifted her glass, and we all toasted.

"Delaney's Blood!"

"Here! Here!"

"So what's going to happen?" Nick was seriously interested.

"Nothing right now. I think they're re-grouping. The guy they had drew up all the plans. With him gone, they have to review everything and assign someone new. As for Delaney, he just—he just wants things the way they were. Don't we all? I mean, let's face it, aren't we all old enough to want some things to not change. I admit it; I do! I can think of lots of things I wish had never changed—Eisenhower, the taste of milk when it came in bottles with the cream on top, drive-in movies, Marilyn Monroe *before* she was a sick kind of icon, Woolworths, Nedicks hot dogs! Nobody asked me, and they all changed! I didn't want it, but they changed anyway. It leaves you feeling a little left behind. It doesn't matter about all the good things right now—all the *better* things we have. They're never as good as what you knew as a kid. They couldn't be. You were young, and they were part of it. If they're gone, where does that leave you? Delaney doesn't bother me. I think I've become the object for all his discomfort with 'modern times.' If I'm honest with myself, I want a lot of the same things he does, but I have to be practical enough to take on what we need and forget about what I might want."

"So what happened to the guy they had? The architect?" I could tell Nick was still trying to assess how the changes at Crayden might affect him.

"Who knows? This is New York. Anything can happen. They asked us about him. He was at Crayden just before he disappeared, but nobody really saw him. I guess they're checking around. Anyway nothing's happening right now. Delaney is going to have to wait to nail my ass."

"At least Santiago seems to be better!" Barbara tossed off the comment without thinking. Immediately after she realized what she said and hid her eyes in her wine glass.

"Santiago? Who's Santiago?" Nick had turned the question to me. I tried to make light of it.

"Oh...just the janitor. He's been with Crayden longer than—than anyone. He really should retire..."

"I don't think I've ever seen him."

"He stays pretty much out of sight. He's kept that museum going for a long time, but he's just...just...old. He should retire. I've been trying to find a way to pension him off. The Board would probably just fire him, especially once the building is begun, but I can't bring myself to do that."

"You said he was 'better'; is he sick?"

Barbara gave me a quick guilty glance and went back to her drink.

"No, no not really. You have to understand, he's been the janitor at Crayden since I was a student there. He's long past the age when he should be working, and...and he's been a little erratic lately."

"...In what way?" Nick focused on me, and I shifted in my seat. I was sure he could sense my discomfort.

"Just uh...strain, I think. My shaking up Crayden this year has made his job a lot harder, and he's getting up there in years. I want to maneuver a good pension for him before the Board gets around to dumping him without the consideration he should have."

Nick looked at me for a minute. "Jeez, he *must* be up there! You and I are about the same age; that puts him at eighty-ish at least! And he still takes care of the whole building?"

"We contract in the big jobs and the seasonal cleaning, but, yeah, it's pretty much Santiago for the day-to-day."

Nick gave a long low whistle. "They don't make 'em like that anymore! I wouldn't want to take care of that heap at *my* age, never mind eighty!"

I tried to be nonchalant. "He's pretty remarkable, all right. Look, Nick, don't mention any of this to anyone, will you? I need a little time to inform our colleagues of the changes, and I don't want Santiago to hear anything. He's been a friend of mine for a long time."

CHAPTER 14

"Padre teaches. I learn. All around the city is destroyed. What they cannot steal or destroy or kill, they make nothing! How we speak, how we live, what we think—it is the dust they kick with their feet! The Cloth Men try. They pray—much praying, but they do not stop the Silver Men. They talk at us. Always! They tell us of Jesus. The tell us of love, but there is no love in them!

"They take the little ones from the calmecacs and make them speak like them, see like them. Our warriors are made slaves. They are poorer than farmers, less than women. Any warrior who holds up his head dies. There is no more talking then. Only one word can you say, 'Sí.'

"At night the women weep. Those who are young are passed to the Silver Men and broken too. They give up themselves to the touches of the Silver Men. They bear their children, work for them. In time, to be the woman of a Silver Man is more than to be a warrior's woman. So low are our men that they no longer see themselves at all. They are like air. They are like clear water. They cast no shadow on the earth.

"All this time I work for Padre. In the temple of the Man Upon the Tree. This he calls 'church'. Padre learns my words—slowly. He is not so smart as me, but I never say this. I learn the ways of 'church'. I serve on his altar when he gives church to the Silver Men. I make the motions. I seem like the good son. I know his words, and I teach him mine, but I do not say more than what I want him to know. I do not tell him the things told me by the Priest-Father. I do not tell him again who I am. Better that he sees me as one among the many. Not smart, not important. All this time Padre tells me of Jesus, the Man Upon the Tree. He is a poor man's God. No warrior. A worker of magic and tricks. This, Padre tells me with pride! When it is time for Him to strike back, He shows His weakness. His own people in shame nail Him to a tree and ask for a thief in his place. A thief to replace a weak and poor God. To myself I cheer for the thief and hate the weak and sorrowful Man Upon the Tree. Jesus should die! He is weak! But these things I do not say.

"I work and say little. Finally Padre tells me it is time. He takes me; he gives me a name.

"'I have a name,' I say, but he says that Tlaloc is a savage name, not fit for one with a new soul. 'What is this soul,' I ask. He tells me it is the spirit within. 'How is it that this is new when it has been within since my birth?' Padre laughs and talks about the loveless love of the Man Upon the Tree, more foolishness of Jesus! Baptism he calls it. I am called Epifanio—Epifanio and Santiago. But I am Tlaloc, Priest and Warrior, son of the Priest-Father, Seer to the King! I am one of the Top Men! I am Seer now! This I want to spit into his face, but I do not. I must not die. I must stay close to my people. I must be there for them.

"This I do. At night outside the ruined city I see them—some one time, some another. They come for healing first. This I do from the plants, 'But never,' I tell them, 'Say to the Silver Men or Padre what we do. They kill us all. They make us disappear.' The people are quiet. By night they come to me. I heal them. I sing to them quietly to chase away the demons and the darkness.

"Soon they come more for the songs and dances. They want to remember what we are. We give our blood when we can, and sometimes, when there is a need, I take the plant and See for them. When there is a change among the Silver Men that frightens the people, I See. I tell them what to do and not do—to stay away from their knives and fists. I tell them how to stay alive. They come more and more, and I am soon the Keeper of the Old Ways. I am The One Who Knows.

"This day Padre tells me now I am ready to eat the flesh of the Man Upon the Tree. It is a great honor he says to take the Flesh and Blood of Jesus. I think, 'This I know!' Tlaloc has eaten the heart of his enemy still warm from his chest. I have taken my portion from the sacrifice! Can it be that we are really the same? Have I been wrong about their way? This Jesus, the Man Upon the Tree, is he not then the sacrifice for all? Just as the heart of my enemy, does not the power of Jesus come to those that eat of him?'

"I ask this of Padre.

"'Yes, Epifanio! This is the Truth! He is the sacrifice, and every time we eat his flesh and drink his blood we have the Power! He is with us always!' His face is like a torch! He laughs and prays and tells me I am a True Believer. He holds me like his son—but I am not sure of this. It is well enough with Padre, but something feels wrong. He takes me to church and has me kneel. He kneels and prays as I have never seen him! He cries! I do not know why, but I cry with him because I feel I must. He rises and takes a cup from the altar. This cup I have seen a thousand times. He says words I have always heard but never understood, and he tells me to open my mouth. He says, 'This is His Body. Take and eat!'—But it is only a dry crust of bread! He gives me the cup and says, 'This is His blood! Drink!'...but it is only wine. Not a good wine. When he turns away, I spit the mess into my hand and hide it in my shirt. I am not wrong. Their ways, the ways of this Jesus are a lie. A trick of the mind. They do not eat his flesh or drink his blood. They have no power. They have no truth.

"I say nothing. Padre weeps like a woman for joy. If it pleases him, I weep. What do I care? I am with my people."

***

I turned off the digital recorder. Santiago stood from the chair in the shadows of my office with a questioning look.

"There is more. Much more!"

He had found me alone in my office. He'd brought the maté, sat and pushed the digital recorder toward me without a word. It didn't matter that I was working on yet more letters to the Board trying to make them see that Delaney's plan to move us while the building was completely renovated would likely kill our chances to survive. The vote was coming up, and I was worried. How could I explain to them that this multi-million dollar makeover was nothing more than Delany's attempt to maintain control over the school? If I said that, it would look like I was simply trying to hang onto the job. Delaney had been right, hadn't I petitioned Julian for money? Wasn't I the one who said that if we didn't modernize, we'd die? How could I now claim that this wonderful endowment was being used as a means to neutralize the changes in our curriculum? Christ, it sounded ridiculous to *me*! I sat back in my chair and tried to squeeze away the tension headache that was growing between my eyes.

The phone rang and jarred me from myself. It was Soldani. I had dodged him for over two weeks, and he was incensed. I knew I was wrong.

"Dr. Soldani! How nice—"

"For God's sake, Holliman! I've been calling you for over two weeks! You promised me! You told me I'd get a chance to examine the morion and write a full documentation!"

"What I told you, Dr., is that I would try to find a time for you to look at it again. I never promised more than that." I had been playing him. Soldani was too erratic—too damn sweaty for the prize for me to trust him.

"I—I uh, Dr. Holliman!" The man spluttered on the other end of the phone. His confrontational manner crumbled the moment I pushed back. I knew he wanted to kill me, and I couldn't blame him. There were just too many uncomfortable questions surrounding the helmet for me to let him trumpet the find to the public.

I looked at Santiago standing patiently in the darkened corner. His eyes blazed dark and waiting even in so little light. I didn't want him exposed to the Board. I didn't want his...tribal story to become a curiosity, or worse, I couldn't bear to see the old man bundled off to some "home" because he told about a distant past as if he himself had lived it.

"Right now, Dr., I have an entire school to run and a Board of Governors to answer to. I can't drop my responsibilities to satisfy your curiosity about an old helmet!"

"But, uh, Dr. Holliman, I told you! This could be very important! Not just to me! It could be important for you! For your school!"

"I'm not discounting that! I just don't have time right now!"

"Well—all right! All right! Just—don't let anyone else see it! You understand, don't you? I mean, if it is what I believe it is—someone could just...jump on it and—and take it away! Can't you tell me anything about it? About how you got it? Please!"

This was the one thing, I couldn't tell him. "Dr. Soldani, I will call you at *my* earliest convenience about the morion. Is that clear? Please don't call me or contact me again until I call *you*. I hope I make myself clear!"

"Oh but—"

I hung up the phone. The mental image of him on the cover of *Archeology Today* in his baggy, shiny suit with his unkempt, oily hair and slipping glasses holding the helmet, slipped past my mind. It wasn't pretty.

Santiago was watching me. There was a difference in him now. He "attended" me, it seemed. It was not like before. Now he came in with an air of—deference. Yes, that was it! His attitude toward me had changed from one of distant dignity and mystery to this vague obsequiousness. It made me uncomfortable. I wanted things as they were. This new attitude made me feel as though I were "over" him in some powerful and unapproachable position.

"Santiago...It's late."

"I go." He turned to leave.

"These memories you give me...These memories of Tlaloc..."

"Sí...."

"...Why do you give them to me?"

"You are the Angry Young Lord. The Priest-Father Sees you...long ago. He tells me. I tell only you."

"How do you know that *I* am "The Angry Young Lord?" Perhaps someone else, some other man is this person you must tell."

"Is you. I See. I am Seer now. It is why you come. Even you do not know why you come. But you come, and the Gods see Tlaloc! The Gods see you. Now I am yours."

"What do you want me to do with them? These memories you give—what must happen to them?"

He looked at me and cocked his head to the side. A smile grew from his face, and his eyes danced like hot coals. "They are yours. You will know. You will know."

This was making my head ache even more. He turned to leave once more.

"You haven't been 'giving the blood'...have you?" The image of his stabbing himself in the arm was never far from my mind.

"...This you do not see again." He would not turn to face me.

"I know you promised, but I need to know!" I took his arm and pushed the sleeve back. There were no new wounds. I was relieved. "I'm sorry. I don't want you to—to hurt yourself."

"I am not hurt." The old man turned to look at me. "You bleed—more than me."

"...What?"

"I See. I See you bleed."

"...What are you talking about?"

"They come. Bring papers. Make changes. I see. They do not hurt you. That does not happen."

He turned and slipped out of the office without another word. I went after him, but when I got to the outer doorway, the hall was empty. There was no sound but the clicking of steam pipes. I went back to my office for the Tylenol.

***

I had put it in my drawer the night Santiago had cut himself. I was so shaken by the experience that I must have shoved it in the drawer and forgotten all about it, but there it was. I was in a meeting with Nick—to sign his contract. When I opened the drawer to pull out a contract copy, the bloodstained handkerchief fell onto the floor. We both stopped and stared at it for a moment.

Nick gave a low quiet whistle and picked it up. "Now I know what happened to your last chemistry teacher!"

I took the handkerchief and shoved it into my pocket. "Scissors! I cut myself a while ago!—I should have thrown this out. I guess I forgot."

"Try again..." Nick just looked at me knowing I was lying. I never was very good at lying.

"It's really nothing. Let's get your contract signed, so I can own your soul for the next three years."

"Sure..." Nick pulled back and began to sign the contract copies. As I watched him, I wondered. Could I trust him with all this—Santiago, the story, the helmet, the bloodletting? He was new, it really wasn't his responsibility.

"I'm going to enjoy having you here. I mean, you'll be about the only faculty member I don't have to 'parent'. Aside from Sally, there's really nobody else to have a beer with."

He finished signing the copies and shook my hand. "I'm looking forward to it." He had stood and was poised to leave, but hung there for a moment. I knew he was waiting for me to say something.

I measured him for a moment. "Have you got a moment?"...

I told him.

Not every detail, but the broad strokes—The "memories", the morion, the disturbing bloodletting—he listened without raising an eyebrow. When I was done, he sat back and thought for a moment.

"Just you and Barbara know about all this?"

"I owe him! He was more important to me as a kid than I ever realized then. I don't want him humiliated or institutionalized. He's physically vital! He does the work without complaint. What's so damned frustrating is that he seems so competent, but these stories—these memories are so real to him! Christ, he *lives* them! I have the sound files. It's all so—real, it's hard for me *not* to believe it all happened to him! Then there's that Goddamn helmet!"

"Has he hurt himself since that first time?"

"No, he promised me he wouldn't do that again. But...he's so strange now. It's not like before. Suddenly *I'm* his father. He's been reborn in some strange way, and now he haunts me like some kind of weird shadow. He seems to sense when I'm alone, and he's always there!"

"You could tell him to leave you alone. That you don't want to hear any more of these memories of his."

"I could...Look, Nick, I don't want to hurt him. He seems to need to tell this story. As Barbara says, I seem to be the new carrier of this tribal memory—or whatever it is. If you could see the urgency in him, the intensity....I-I don't want to crap out on him. When I was a kid, he was there for me."

Nick sat back and thought for a moment. "...Can I have that bloody handkerchief?"

"Uh...why?"

"I'll bring it back."

"Why do you want it?"

"...I could run a few tests. Blood tells its own story..."

"We're kind of crossing a line here, aren't we?"

"Yeah, but it would tell you more about his general health. It might help you to help him."

"I feel like a spy!"

"If it's the way you say it is, it sounds like the old guy's placed himself in your hands."

"You won't mention this to anyone, will you? Not Mona—no one! I want all this kept in strict confidence until I can figure out what to do about him."

"Not a word." He felt solid to me. It was good to have someone besides Barbara to confide in about all this. I wanted desperately to let down to someone, and now I had.

"Find out what you can." I gave Nick the handkerchief, and he left. For a moment I felt some relief, but there was still that vague anxiety at the back of my skull, like an itch where you can't scratch it.

CHAPTER 15

"So, you're telling me I'm killing Crayden..." Julian Reynolds nailed me with his steely gray eyes. He was a heavy old man. He walked with a cane and moved slowly, but his mind was as sharp as a blade. It cut straight to the point.

"If the pool happens—a complete renovation of the building... we're forced to move to another school, we have to cut back for...oh, two years, maybe three. By then..."

"No momentum. All the juice will be out of the battery, and you'll be an orphaned ex-Headmaster with Cam Delaney barking at your heels. That about describe it?"

"That's pretty much it."

"Spencer and Chase are probably the oldest and the worst bunch of grifters in the business. They can suck the ink right off a dollar! The contract is set. I take out the pool, they still get paid for it. What makes you think you're worth it?"

"Mr. Reynolds—"

"Jesus Christ, call me Julian. Don't make me feel any older than I already am with all this formal bullshit. Cam drives me crazy with that. He was always a pisser when it came to 'formality'." He derisively over-pronounced the last word. "Cheeeerist! He was a tight-ass as a kid, and he still is! I could renege—tear up the check...!" He peered at me over his rimless glasses.

"...You won't do that."

"Yeah?...Why not, sonny?"

"...You'd still have to pay..."

He began to chuckle. "Umhm! Nice. You listen...you took a hell of a chance coming to me. Cam Delaney and I go back to the Flood! I could pick up that phone right now and get him on the line and tip him to this little confab you arranged. I wonder what he'd say. He and that sorry-ass Board of Governors would be sharpening their knives on your foreskin! Assuming you got one, of course...'Holliman', what is that, German?"

"...Yes."

"...You a Hebe?" The old man was staring right at me. There was more than a challenge in the question.

"...Yes, I guess I am."

"You 'guess'?"

"My father was Jewish. My mother was a Catholic. We didn't practice *any* faith when I was growing up."

"...Uh, huh..." Reynolds surveyed me pushing his glasses back up over his broad nose. He chuckled again and finally broke into a full laugh. He extended his hand as he spoke, "Well, Holliman, meet Rabinowitz, Moishe Rabinowitz, son of Chaim Rabinowitz, a 'Rag and Bone' man from down on Hester Street." He was laughing heartily as he pumped my arm. "Ha, ha, ha! What's the matter, boy, you look confused!"

"I—I had no idea—"

"Naw! Nobody figures me for a Jew. Back in my day that was about the worst thing you could be next to a nigger or a woman. Pop didn't want me shut out of the 'advantages' he never got. He sent me here, to Crayden with all the rich Goyim. Money he had—tons of it. Rags and bones went to scrap metal and salvage. When World War I came around, he had 'materiel', and he knew how to get more of it whenever the government needed it. But he was always a Hebe! How could he hide it? He had the beard, the accent—worst of all, he had the Faith, that 'God of our Fathers—Moving Mountains' kind of Faith. It was his comfort, I guess, but it was his curse just the same. He knew it! He didn't want me to, so 'Rabinowitz' turned into Reynolds and 'Moishe'—Goddamn

'Julian'! I don't know how he did it, but he got a fine, upstanding Anglican couple to front as my 'Aunt Sally and Uncle Joe'. Crayden was restricted, of course. Then he sent me uptown to rub elbows with the 'old money' while he grubbed for shekels in the garbage and the rubbish. Joe Delaney tolerated me—barely...until I showed him I knew something, but Mrs. Delaney—she was a peach! She tried to be a real mother for me. When she died, I cried for a month! I saw my old man whenever I could. My God, I admired that man! You know, he saw the Depression coming—knew it would happen! He got out just before the whole thing collapsed, and he was sitting on a pile of cash while everybody else was jumping from windows. What a time that was! You weren't even born then!..Cam's old man shot himself."

"What?" He was rolling now, in the way of old men desperate to impart their stories before it was too late. I couldn't and didn't want to stop him.

"Oh, yeah! We were in college—Princeton. A telegram came when we were just about to take midterms in our sophomore year. Joe Delaney pumped a 38 into his brain when he found out the banking firm *his* pop had started—with a little help from J.P. Morgan himself—was about to go under. Cam left Princeton. Went home to pick up the pieces. He sold everything they had and hung onto his father's firm. It took him twenty-five years to restore it. Then, just when it looked like the Delaneys were about to see better times, a bigger bank came along and swallowed Cam's little firm whole and spat him out onto the street. Don't get me wrong, Cam's not broke, but he never made back the kind of money his old man had seen. Cam does all right—a few good investments over the years, and he had Crayden to take up his time. You don't want to lose all that pretty money...do you?"

"No, sir, I don't!"

Reynolds laughed out loud. "Christ! An Honest Man! Ha, ha!"

"I thought you could use some coffee." Sally burst in. I could tell she was too curious to stay out of the office. She was carrying a tray with carafe of coffee, cups and a plate of some non-descript pastries. She put it down on the old partner's desk and turned to us both. "How do you like it?"

"Pretty good from where I'm sitting!" Reynolds gave Sally an appreciative ogle.

"Be careful what you say! I'm old enough to be your...niece." Sally tossed her comment back as she poured out two steaming cups of coffee. She brought Julian's over to him. "What do you like in it?"

"Black...It's been a long time since I've had a 'niece' to spend money on."

"Are you harassing me?" Sally challenged him playfully. I could tell they were both amused.

"Is it working? It's been too Goddamn long, I'm not sure I remember how it goes."

"Nothing wrong with your memory. Just don't get your blood pressure up!"

"There's a pill for that. There's a pill for a lot of things these days." Julian laughed at his own joke—so did Sally.

"Yeah, well suppose you take one or the other, and we'll just see how you feel later! You fellas want anything else before I go?"

"No thanks, Sally. Oh, did the Board respond to my proposal for Santiago's raise?"

"Not yet. I just sent it out two days ago. Call if you need me!" Sally slipped back into the outer office. Her flirt with Julian must have convinced her that everything was all right so far.

Julian watched her leave. "Now that's a good looking woman! Even twenty years ago, I'd have chased her down and covered her with money! No...shit...don't get old—you won't like it! Who's this Santiago?"

"Hm? Oh, we have a janitor. He stays on premises. He's overdue for a raise, maybe a pension.

"We had a 'resident custodian' when Cam and I were students here. Scared the hell out of us! We hardly saw him, but we made up all kinds of stories. I remember seeing him once. Short, dark—piercing eyes! Anytime you were somewhere you weren't supposed to be, he seemed to find you! 'Injun Joe' we used to call him. I think he was a Mexican or something. Jesus, I haven't thought about him in years!"

His description sucked the air from my lungs for a moment; then I recovered, "Uh...Yes, well, this one is getting on. He's been with us—a long time. It's time we did a little something for him."

Reynolds looked at me for a long moment. He sipped his coffee, and the air fell silent between us. I felt skewered like a rotisserie chicken.

"OK, ...It'll cost me, but I'll put a hold on the pool for...three years. —I'll tell Cam it's a cash flow problem or some such crap. He won't believe it, but, hell, it's my money! You know, when you get so Goddamn old, just about the only thing that's any fun anymore is making people dance to your tune *if* you can afford it, and, Sonny, I can afford it!"

I thanked him profusely, but he waved away the gratitude.

"Sure, sure! Just put a plaque over the pool and keep it shined up real good. *I* won't see it, but maybe somebody will."

"The day the pool opens, you'll fire the starting pistol for the first meet!"

"Nope. —I'd be happy to oblige you, but six months—a year, maybe—that's about all I got left, and, as far as I'm concerned, a shiny plaque is about all the immortality I'm gonna get."

"I'm sure—"

"Hold the bullshit, sonny! An old man knows. I'm pretty nearly finished. Bad heart, bad kidneys—bad intentions. Crayden's my last philanthropy... Ah—you get what you give! I never believed in all that afterlife crap. I lived my life in the 'here and now'! I did what I wanted, and I had a good time! That's about all you get, if you're lucky. I had mine! Put up the plaque—'The Moishe Rabinowitz memorial pool'. Ha, ha! Won't that just get their garters in a twist! Ha, ha, ha." Reynolds laughed deeply, and I found myself sharing his fun. We shook hands, and the old man hauled himself out of the chair with difficulty. I walked him to the door. "I'll have the changes put in place. Good luck, sonny, give 'em hell!" He walked through the door, and I knew I might not be seeing him again. After a few moments Sally came in.

"Well? What happened? Will he kill the pool? C'mon! I've been dying out there for an hour!"

"Nope."

"Shit! He can't do that! That can't—"

"But he will delay it for three years! Full renovation but no disruptions to regular classes. We're clear!"

"Yeeehaa! So much for Cameron Delaney and the Board of Governors! This is great! I'll call Barbara; this calls for a celebration! What's the matter? You don't seem so excited."

"Oh, I am. I am...I'm just curious..."

"What do you mean? He agreed, didn't he? He won't go back on the deal?"

"No...I don't think so. He asked me if I thought I was worth it..."

"Don't ask pointless questions! C'mon, get your coat, turn off the lights, and don't let the door hit you in the ass! We are going out!"

Sally tugged me by the arm and shoved me through the door into an evening of alcohol and congratulations. My mind kept returning to Julian's description of "Injun Joe".

"Scared the hell out of us!" he had said. I knew he was scaring the hell out of me!

CHAPTER 16

Word spread like wildfire. Crayden had gotten a huge endowment from the Reynolds Foundation—A complete restoration of the old building and an Olympic-Sized pool…"at a later date"—in its vast basement. I looked at the pasted smile on Cameron Delaney's lips in the newspaper pictures as he took the check from Julian. Even in print he could barely disguise his defeat. I had arranged the ceremony in a nearby hotel. Julian was distant—almost formal, but, as he passed by me on the way to the podium, and without halting his slow progress, he winked at me from his "upstage" eye. No one saw it but me, and I wouldn't give it away with even a nod. I simply looked at him as he looked at me. We knew. We had our secret.

As Julian finished his speech, he called Delaney to the podium and handed him the oversized check. Delaney stood stiffly and took the check with all of the grace of a cigar-store Indian. The old man was trying to sort out his hatred of me from his love of Crayden. I could tell that he was glad that his beloved Crayden would get the much-needed re-fit, but he still had me, and that rankled him. I tried to approach him and make peace, but the press and the reception kept us from making that connection. I drank too much, and before I realized it, I was struggling not to slur my words.

"OK, Holliman. You've had a good time. Time to go home." Barbara maneuvered me to the door without anyone noticing. We were out in the night air before anyone saw the Headmaster close to being plastered. The cold sobered me up, and by the time the cab reached our apartment, I was reasonably myself.

It was late. Against her wishes, I dropped Barbara at home and went over to the school in my tuxedo to pull some files I needed to study before the morning. As I entered the inner office, the small desk lamp was on, and a cup of maté sat steaming on the blotter. Santiago stood in silhouette against the windows. I could feel him watching me enter. It was unsettling the way he could anticipate my arrival, yet, somehow, I knew he'd be there waiting for me.

"...It is well," he said evenly his voice almost veiled like the dark in which he stood.

"Yes," I answered, "It is very well!"

"I come, I dance for you." He stayed in the shadows waiting for me to agree. I didn't want a long session with him tonight, but I was in an expansive mood, and I hadn't seen him for several days.

After the Reynolds foundation had called formally to "inform" me of Mr. Reynolds' decision to grant such a large sum to Crayden, I had been lost in the planning of a formal ceremony. The Foundation left the preparation up to us entirely. I wanted the press for two reasons: I wanted another high-profile positive story about Crayden to keep us before the public for the sake of enrollments, and I wanted Julian's last hurrah to have some fanfare. I believed I was the only person with whom he had shared his physical decline. I was sure that Delaney had no idea. The way he had spoken to Julian at the banquet made it clear that he expected his old friend to continue on indefinitely. I don't think he saw how slowly Julian moved or how much it cost him in physical exertion just to mount the steps to the speaker's platform. I saw it. I saw the heavy way he sat and the subtle ways he conserved his energies during the evening. He listened more than spoke. He sat all the time, and when he rose to speak, he was very brief, preferring to seem modest rather than reveal his exhaustion. His visit to me must have been a huge drain on him. It all seemed so obvious to me now, knowing what I did, and, yet, no one else seemed to notice. I admired how Julian managed to fool everyone, but, then, he had fooled a lot of people all his life.

"Dance? You have no memories to give me tonight?"

"You make a victory. I must dance. The Gods laugh, and so I must dance." As he spoke, he emerged from the shadows.

"Santiago, what is all this?" The old man was stripped to the waist. His face and body were painted or tattooed in a blue gray array of figures, half picture, half like writing. Around his waist was a band bearing a fringe of brightly colored bird feathers. His hair was knotted at the back, and more feathers had been applied in a line across his crown looking like the crest of bird.

"You come. Take the maté. Come!" He was pulling on my arm, and I was mesmerized by his strange appearance. "I make a place. You come." I grabbed the cup of maté and followed him down the rear staircase to the basement. In the center of the main room the floor had been cleared. Santiago had drawn chalk-stylized figures of snakes and birds and strange looking men, which I took to be his Gods themselves, in a kind of circle around the area. Pictographs lined the circle, and candles lit the room. Santiago seemed to move more quickly than usual. His eyes had a strange liquid cast in the candlelight that shot living shadows against the crumbling brick walls.

"Drink! Offer the prize to the Gods!"

I raised the cup in a kind of salute and drank the maté down.

"It is well... Before we have a war. When we win a fight. When the crops are good. When we escape death. We dance. Your battle is my battle. I make this place as I make the places for my people when they come. You drink the maté. You see. You know what I do for the Gods."

The old man walked to the center of the circle and called out in a language I didn't recognize. It was not Spanish, that I was sure of. Though I had never heard it, I was sure it must be the language of his tribe.

"It is well. I am ready to dance the thanks to the Gods. They give us a victory. You have a prize. The Gods must have their dance."

It might have been the liquor along with the heat in the basement, but I was feeling light-headed. I sat on broken school chair. A sudden warmth overtook me, and I had a feeling of great well-being—a kind of peace.

The old man moved in and out of the shadows with surprising agility and grace. As he moved, he sang a strange but haunting "song"—half chant half moan. It mounted in rhythm and intensity until the old man seemed to leap from corner to corner in the room. I watched him, realizing that I was witnessing something very few had ever seen. The warmth that I felt melted the strangeness of the scene. What was happening seemed perfectly right. It was deeply fitting in a way I had never experienced before. Now I couldn't describe the dance accurately. It was wild but hypnotic, and the song was like a call from something deep inside myself, although I had no idea what the words were saying. When he finished, he stood for a moment in the darkness beyond the light of the surrounding candles, and I could hear him breathing. At first I thought he was catching his breath, but then I realized he was crying. Sobbing quietly in the dark.

"Santiago?"

The old man raised his hand for me to stay where I was, and I complied. I sensed that this was a moment he could not share. He struggled to regain himself, and then he turned to me.

"I give this to the Gods for you. You go. The Gods see you now. The Gods know you now. They protect you. I am happy you know this. You go. You will sleep well."

I left. His odd words, the dance, everything that had happened since I entered my office—should have unsettled me, but I had this deep feeling of contentment. Nothing seemed more important that getting home and sleeping. When I came in, Barbara was waiting up.

"Brad?...Are you OK? What took you so long? I was worried!"

"Nothing to worry about. I'm fine. Very tired. Let's get some sleep.

"Where are the files?"

"Huh?...I—I'll look at them in the morning. Right now, I just want to sleep. C'mon." Barbara followed me into the bedroom looking concerned. I slipped out of my tux and slipped into bed, and I was out before my head even hit the pillow.

CHAPTER 17

"What do you think they were looking for, sir?" The young police officer stood in front of the open door to my office. He had been questioning me for twenty minutes, and all I could think about was last night—Santiago's strange dance, my curious mood. Were the two things linked, I wondered.

"I don't know officer—uh—Hidalgo. I was here briefly last night. Everything was fine. I can't imagine who would have done this!"

Sally was brewing a fresh pot of coffee and monitoring the entire interview. She was always very protective of me, but, for now, she was quiet. Her office was intact. The rest of the building—as far as we could determine—was untouched. It was just my office. Furniture was overturned; every book was pulled from the bookcase, and my desk was emptied of its contents. The room had been ransacked!

"I want you to do something for me, sir. Without touching anything, I'd like you to look around the room—check out every detail, and see if you can tell if anything is missing."

"I've already told you; there's nothing to steal! There is a safe, but no money, nothing of any significant value..." I stopped for a minute as the morion came to mind!

"...Yes sir? Did you notice something?" Hidalgo straightened when I paused and was ready to take notes.

"Uh...no. No, I—I was just a little overwhelmed by—by the mess! It'll take me days to put everything back where it belongs!" I lied. The morion! That was the only thing of any value in the office, but no one knew it was there! I had hidden it in the foot cabinet at the back of the kneehole in the old partners' desk. I had discovered the cabinet shortly after I took over the office in the fall when I had dropped some change. As I crawled under the desk after the last quarter, I had brushed a carving in what I though was the back panel of the desk and the cabinet door popped open with a quiet click. Behind the panel were two deeply set shelves just the right size to hide a good stock of liquor bottles. This, of course, was the original purpose of the hidden cabinet. I suspected that many antique desks of this size and proportion had been constructed with this handy feature, but there was no evidence of it ever having been used for that. It was empty, just a curious convenience to find in an old Headmaster's desk.

"If you wouldn't mind, sir. Just look around one more time and check as thoroughly as possible. You might find something you forgot is missing."

I moved as casually as I could, so as not to signal my sudden apprehension. I didn't want him to know about it. I didn't want to explain the helmet to anyone, let alone this young policeman. As soon as its existence became a public matter, what was I to say about it? How could I avoid it's connection to Santiago, the stories, and the entire absurd position in which I had put myself by maintaining an aging custodian in the early—or late—stages of senile dementia? I'd be a sitting duck for Cameron Delaney and the Board of Governors. As I rounded the desk pretending to look all around, I glanced under the desk, but the kneehole was a dark cavern in the gloomy office, and I couldn't tell if the cabinet had been opened or not. I took a pencil out of my pocket and pretended to make notes. Suddenly I dropped the pencil right by the back of the desk near the kneehole. "Damn!" I voiced in fake frustration, and I knelt down to pick up the pencil. I peered at the back of the kneehole, and there I could discern that the panel was in place! If the burglar was looking for it, he had missed it!

"Is everything all right, sir?" the young officer stepped into the room.

"Fine! Just picking up my pencil. I don't see that anything is missing, officer! I've looked at everything. There doesn't seem to be anything gone!" I hoisted myself up on my feet and stared at him with the innocent eyes of the half-liar.

"Any particular students who might have it in for you, sir?"

"Vandalism, you mean? No! I can't think of any serious behavioral problems at all. What about you, Sally? Any of our students likely to have done this?"

"I can think of a few in the Upper School I'd like to string up by their ankles, but that's just because they're teenagers."

"There's nobody who has it in for Dr. Holliman? Someone who would want to trash his office for revenge?"

"Just his wife, for overwork and neglect, but she'd get him at home personally rather than take it out on his office."

"Uh huh..." the young policeman was writing.

"Hey! That's a joke! Look, why would somebody tear up his office and not mine? *I'm* the one the students deal with most of the time. It would make more sense if they went through my office."

"Yeah, sure, but I have to note everything, ma'am."

"'Ma'am?'" Sally blurted out.

"Uh—It's part of the investigation." The young officer reddened knowing he'd embarrassed Sally.

"Listen, cutie, do I look like a 'ma'am' to you?" Sally challenged

"No, ma'am, uh miss—sorry! If there's nothing missing, Dr. Holliman, aside from my report, is there anything you want done?"

"Such as?"

"We could do a thorough investigation, fingerprint the place, that sort of thing."

"Is that really necessary? This is the beginning of a school week. The building is full of students. I don't want school disrupted over nothing more than a possible prank. It isn't good publicity for the school."

"That's your call, sir. I will file my report, and if you find anything at all missing, you'll need to call it in immediately!"

"Absolutely." I was relieved, but Sally was still stewing.

"'Ma'am', huh? I guess I've gotten to that stage where hotties like you think of me as an older woman."

The young cop closed his book and tucked his pencil into his uniform looking at Sally.

"We're taught to treat everyone with respect, m-miss, but that doesn't mean we don't appreciate the people we meet." It was obvious the young cop was flirting, and Sally brightened up immediately.

"That so? I suppose I am too old for you. Too bad."

"I like older women. They're more—interesting. My last girlfriend was a few years older than me. We got along real well."

"What happened to her, then?"

"She left me for a younger guy."

"You're good, cutie! You got the touch! OK, I guess I'll have to let you off the hook!"

"Gee, that's too bad. I was going to ask you out for dinner."

"How old are you, handsome?"

"Twenty-eight."

Sally studied the young cop for a minute and then made her decision. "...You know where Marley's is in the Village?"

"Sure!"

"I'll be there tonight about 7:30. If you show up, we can talk about the 'older-woman/younger-man' thing."

The young cop took out his pad and made a note. "7:30...Marley's with..."

"Sally."

"With Sally. See you then...Sally." The cop left the office.

"Aren't we pushing the age limit here?" I asked her.

"I work in education, don't I?"

"Just make sure to get a note from his mother."

"Married people are so damn smug? How come you didn't want him to fingerprint and all that?"

"What are they going to find? Everything is here. There's no real damage, just a mess."

"Who would do this? Why? Is there something I should know?" Sally's intuition about me was getting as good as Barbara's. I had to be careful not to let on what my real motives were. I hadn't told her about the helmet. She had never seen it, nor did she know anything about Soldani other than he was a sweaty, obnoxious little man who wanted something from me. The only people who knew about it were Soldani, Barbara, Nick, me, and Santiago, of course. I desperately wanted to keep it that way. I wondered if he were desperate enough to try to come here and steal it.

"Yeah, how long will it take me to put all this crap back where it belongs?" I started picking up books and lining them up in the bookshelves.

"The exercise will do you good! Nick Parrino called. He said he needs to see you. I told him you were free for lunch. That all right?"

"Yeah, great, by then I might have my desk back together. Ask him to meet me at Cherry's on the corner. I'll need to get away from all this dust by then." I sneezed deeply.

"Gesundheit! Have fun!" Sally closed the door, and I dropped the books I was pretending to work on. I went over to the desk and popped the kneehole panel. It clicked open, and there in the dark recess I could see the morion still on the top shelf. It hadn't been touched.

I crawled back out from the desk, sat down and dialed Soldani's direct line. The receiver clicked, and I heard Soldani's voice"

"Dr. Soldani here…"

"Dr. Soldani, this is Dr. Holliman at Crayden. I—"

"Uh—I'm not here right now. Leave a message. Beep." No answer. I wasn't going to discuss this on an answering machine, so I hung up. I determined I'd call later and let Soldani know about our little break-in. I was planning to tell him that the morion had been stolen, and that I was sorry, but he wouldn't be able to study the piece. I knew that would provoke him to either reveal his guilt or quit his constant pestering to see it. I could produce a police report if he doubted me. If it was gone—it was gone! If he *were* guilty of the break-in, I had the perfect excuse for telling him to drop dead. I was feeling very clever, very "in control". I had dodged Delaney's architectural bullet, and now I would be rid of Soldani. All I had to do now was take care of Santiago.

CHAPTER 18

"I don't know if it's anything. There's obviously something wrong with the sample...or my analysis. I haven't done this for quite a while, you know."

"I'm confused! What are you talking about?"

"That blood sample you gave me. I did a complete work-up..."

"What did you find out?"

"Well, I don't where to begin, I mean, it's completely anomalous to anything I've seen before." Nick was unusually intense. I wasn't used to this side of him.

"Can I take your order?" The waitress was as bored, and Nick was excited.

"Uh, turkey club on rye with mayo, coffee. Nick?"

"Huh...Uh...Uh...Nothing. Uh, coffee, that's it." The waitress left.

"Ok, what do you mean?"

"I've spent the last two weeks checking and re-checking my results—on that bloody handkerchief of yours..."

"And?"

"And, it's the damnedest thing! For instance, ethnicity...Amerindian. Except that there is absolutely no European trace. Absolutely pure. You see, just about all of the South American tribes demonstrate traces of a European coefficient in the blood. Centuries of interbreeding—there *are* no absolutely pure bloodlines. But the real surprise is the nearly full complement of telomeres. There's been practically no degradation, and the cells show an unbelievable amount of telomerase—well, they're just not normal."

"Wait a minute. You've lost me. Telomeres, telomerase—speak plain English."

"Well—How do I explain it? In every cell of the body, including blood cells, you have chromosomes—strings of genes. Some of the genes determine sex, eye color, height, all of the physical characteristics of the organism, but on the end of every chromosome there are bits of repeating genetic information that control replication—the replacement of that cell. We call these bits of information "telomeres". Each time the cell replicates, the telomeres shorten. When the telomeres degrade too much, the cell can no longer divide. It dies. We don't know everything about the overall aging of the body, but the degradation of telomeres seems to have a direct effect on the length of the life of an individual cell. In an older person the telomeres show a greatly shortened length throughout the body. Not in the blood in that handkerchief! The telomeres were intact. As far as I could determine, the blood could have come from a newborn, not a man of eighty! And then there's the presence of an unbelievable level of telomerase."

"Now you've lost me again. Slow down." My head was spinning, but I thought I had gotten most of it.

"Telomerase. It's an enzyme released by telomeres that can aid in the repair and replacement of lost genetic material. We find it in cancer cells. Cancer cells don't age or die like normal cells. They survive and replicate unchecked as the cancer grows, because of this enzyme."

"...Then he has cancer. He's sick."

"Not unless his whole body *is* a cancer. The level of telomerase indicates that it must be present throughout the body—in every system—at every level of cell growth, but that's impossible. At least, I think it is...I don't know, I'm out of practice! I must have screwed up the tests! Plus, there's an incredible number of antibodies in the blood—disease-fighting elements. I checked my results, but it doesn't make sense. None of it."

"It must be something like that. Cancer. He's old, he may have had it for a long time.

"I'm out of my depth here. Something's off. The results I got just aren't possible. Either I blew it or the sample is tainted somehow. Only..."

"Only what?..."

"I was really careful. The tests don't indicate adulteration of the sample. The results are just...weird!"

This was beginning to sound like science fiction. That sticky fear of events running headlong out of control came flooding back.

"...I-I just don't—what do we do? I mean, is he sick? Does he need a doctor? What are we looking at here?"

"I don't know. According to you he seems to be losing touch, but he's still physically sound. He does his work, right?"

"...He danced for me."

"Come again?"

"...After the grant banquet. He danced for me! Nick, it was beyond strange, but at the time it seemed perfectly natural. I sat there sipping maté, and I watched him leaping and singing like—like a young buck. He told me he was dancing for the Gods in thanks for our victory. I don't know, all I felt was 'This is cool!' you know? I haven't even told Barbara about it yet. I'm so used to his odd behavior and the stories that—that this seemed perfectly normal! He painted himself, made a space in the basement, he even wore feathers, and he sang in a language I've never heard before. It was eerie, but I felt I understood what it was all about. Afterward he cried. Cried like a baby. He said he was all right, and then told me to go home and sleep."

"When you speak to him, does he ramble? You know, is he incapable of staying on subject."

"No! He's clear as a bell and focused. It's almost frightening how focused he is on the stories. That's what I thought he wanted after the banquet, to have me record more of the stories. But, then, he only wanted to dance. When we talk about real events, he knows what I'm talking about. If I leave instructions for something to be done—he does it! I can't—I can't find the dementia outside the stories, or memories, or whatever the hell they are!"

Nick sat back. Our orders arrived, and we lapsed into silence. I chewed on my sandwich without being aware of its taste. Nick sipped on his coffee. For the moment we were both lost in our own thoughts. Finally Nick sat up.

"The maté! You say he always brings you a cup of it when you record. Can you get me a sample?"

"You think that has something to do with it?"

"It might! It could! What's in it? Do you know?"

"It-it's just some South American herbal tea. He gave it to me when I was a kid! There's nothing in it!"

"How do you know what's in it?"

"He wouldn't give drugs to a kid. Not to me! If there's one thing Santiago is, it's loyal to me!"

"What's loyalty got to do with it? In some cultures children are given large doses of drugs to alter their consciousness—to heal them, to drive out spirits. Can you honestly say that Santiago is incapable of that kind of behavior?"

"...OK, I'll get some. If it'll help, I'll get some....Nick, I don't want people to know about this."

"I know. Right now, I wouldn't know what to tell them anyway."

"....Do you think he has cancer?"

"...I don't know. I don't have any answers here...just lots and lots of questions."

CHAPTER 19

"I am the favored of Padre. He loves me as his son, he says. He loves me as his God loves his children. But I know. This God gives the blood of his son not to other Gods but to the weakest and greediest men. What kind of a God is this? What kind of 'love' is this? Yet, he is kind, Padre. He gives me food. He teaches. He keeps me from the Silver Men who are many.

"Others come now—farmers who want land, and they bring Dark Ones to work it. We did not know that anyone could be lower than us. But These 'Dark Ones' are treated even worse than we are. The sellers of things come with goods from the land of the Silver Men. The women come, 'European Women', Padre calls them, and our women are thrown from the beds of these beasts and made to work in the kitchens and the fields. Their bastard children, half like their fathers, are treated like work animals. They fetch and carry and watch their half-brothers pampered and petted and given the first place above them. Their proud blood is shamed!

"I see it. Some of the people are the same, but some are not. In so little time they forget the Gods! They forget that we are Kings of the land and all around. They are bowed and broken, and they pray to the Man Upon the Tree! They beg Him for help; they ask Him for their food! Some stay strong. Inside they are still what we are.

"I am with these people. I tell them. I teach. I sing, dance—See when they need it. Because I know this Man Upon the Tree and his ways, I hide our Gods inside this church. I take His fiestas and make them our own. His Top Men become names

for our ancient Gods. His sacrifices I use to cover our own rites and ways. This way I can speak with my people in the open, and Padre and the Silver Men do not know what we do. I keep the Gods alive in them by night. By day, I bow with Padre to his weak and hopeless God. I watch for my time.

"Padre is getting old. He does not see well with is eyes. He does not know I am as I was, but others begin to look at me, to see I am strong still even though I try to be invisible. Padre's love for me is blind also, and he does not hear them when they say I am strange. Then one day I am helping with the Church when a Top Man of the Silver Men comes. Whenever one of these comes, we know it is trouble. He calls to Padre who stops the giving of Church and comes. Behind this Top Man in the shadows of the place are eyes, sharp and searching. They seek after me. A face comes forward into a shaft of light from the window; it is Quexa!

"He is old now, but he is alive! He is bound to this important one, but all that is nothing in this moment. Quexa sees me! A smile cold and hard comes to his mouth. I am held by his eyes. Padre returns to Church, and I follow, but I know. Quexa means to harm me if he can. I must be ready!

"It is a few days. I serve Padre, and I watch. At night I keep the Gods for the people, but I warn them that there is trouble. I tell them to keep the Church like a mask to hide behind. 'Never take it off to show our face.' I tell them that there is one with us who hates. 'One comes to bring us great harm. This Quexa who comes with a Top Man wants my blood, and he takes the blood of many as well. Do not speak with him. Turn your backs when he is near.' This they do. For them I am the Healer, the Teacher, the Seer. They do not yet see me different.

"I am walking in the square. Padre wants a few chickens for the church garden. I look in the market. As always, I talk with the people. We give each other the secret signs and words to say, 'We are one in the old ways.' Then Quexa comes. He is behind me and calls my name.

"'Tlaloc...Tlaloc! I see you are still a bastard with a Priest to

watch over you!'

"'No Quexa,' I say, 'I am still a Priest with a bastard to watch! We see you, but we do not look upon you. You give yourself to these beasts like a dog that needs feeding! We know you. Be careful. The Gods are thirsty, and you have no other children to offer to them.'

"'Look at him!" Quexa shouts in our language, 'His face like a burning monkey! Look how low he is now! Your Seer, your Priest, buys chickens for his Padre. To this you come? To this you come for Truth? He is as beaten as we all are! He is nothing! He cannot hide behind a Priest anymore! We do not need him! The old ways are done! They are gone! He keeps you with him for his own power! There is nothing left! Look around you. The temples are pulled down. There is no King! There are no Top Men left among us! The Old Gods are dead! He takes you where you die too!'

"The people do not move. They are afraid. All around are Silver Men. At any moment they come and take us away. I nod, and some pass in front of Quexa and make a wall of people. Quexa shouts louder, but they are on him, and he is quiet now. They swallow him up in the market as if he is not there. The Silver Men do not see what we do. My people take Quexa to the forest and stay with him. I bring Padre his chickens. I am the good son as always. I stay quiet and serve and watch until night. When Padre sleeps, I am gone.

"Deep in the forest we make a temple. It is small like the temples of our old fathers before we are so great—long before we are so beaten. Here, the Silver Men do not go. They are afraid of the forest. We are not. Here there is the writing. Here there is the place to give blood. Many, many nights I give blood for the people. Many nights they give blood. This night we will give Quexa's blood. This night the Gods drink deep.

"When I come, he sees me.

"'Use your knife, Tlaloc! Take my blood! It is the last blood you take! I give you to them! They know your name. They

know who you are. The one I serve knows everything I know. I tell him about the bastard Warrior-Priest. You are one with bad magic. One who does not change. I tell them you are close to the King—you make war on them! I tell them you still give the blood!'

"It is a small thing to die, Quexa. Once you say to my Priest-Father you wish to give "everything, anything" to please the Gods. Tonight you give everything. The Gods are thirsty!'

"Then take my blood; I don't care. I am old. But know that when I am not with him in the morning, my master knows it is you who does this. He goes to Padre, and you are undone. You are all undone! Go on, take it! Take my blood. It is your own you are giving!'

"In one quick slice, I open him. I reach inside and grab the heart and pull. It comes to me even as his last words are in his mouth. His eyes widen, and he slips into the earth. I hold the heart high, but it is a poor omen. The heart does not beat. The blood is barely warm. I cut the dead thing in pieces, and we eat knowing it cannot bring good. Quexa is with us now. Whatever good he has, we have, but it does not make me strong. I sing. I pray. I dance and take the plant to See, but the vision is not clear. The body is carved, and we devour it all, not for strength, but to hide it from the Silver Men. In the dawn, nothing of Quexa remains, but our stomachs are full of dread and hating. Without words we go back, each to his master, slaves again for a day we do not know.

"When I come back, the Important One is there with two more Silver Men. Padre is waiting for me."

"'Where is the one called Quexa?" Padre asks. 'These men are very powerful! They say you are no Catholic! They say you are a savage Priest dancing naked in the night and serving your Old Gods. They say you teach the young the old ways, that you give the lie to everything I teach you!'

"'Padre!' I answer, 'I serve you! I do not know of these things. Someone lies! Someone hates. Santiago is your child. You *make him! He is yours. There is only love in him for you and for God!'*

"'They say it is not true!' Padre comes forward. He cannot hide his anger. 'They say Tlaloc is Seer to the King.'

"'How can I be Seer to the King? There is no more King.'

"'They say you are a Top Man now. Is this true? They say—' He sees my shirt is brown with dry blood. I do not have time to change. 'What is this?'

"The Important One grabs my shirt and smells.

"'Blood!' he spits and motions for the others to smell the cloth. 'It is blood. The savage has killed!'

"'No!' I say, 'It is a chicken I kill for you, Padre. One from the market. It is for your table!' I make myself low and cowering. I cry like a frightened woman to make them believe. I catch Padre's robe and hold tight.

"'Where is Quexa?' the Important One says looking down at me with death in his eyes.

"'I do not know this Quexa! Why do you ask me? I rise to serve Padre. I kill a chicken, and then I come to bring in water! Save me, Padre! Do not let them kill me!'

"I have my knife in my belt under my shirt. If I cannot make them believe, I know I use it. The Important One pulls my hair to lift my face and puts a knife to my neck. I am ready with my hand by my knife.

"'Hold! This is a place of God! This is a child of God! If you take his life, God will turn his face from you!' Padre puts himself between me and the Important One's knife. He does not know I am ready to fight and ready to die.

"'Quexa is missing. He tells me of this one, a mighty Priest and one who fought us from the walls years ago. This one, he said, keeps the Savage Gods for the rest. He takes them into the

forest, and there they do Satan's work!'

"'Look at him! He has served me and our God all the years since we saved him! How can he be such a one! If the savages resist us, it is you—what you do to them that makes them afraid to believe!'

"'Step aside, Padre. This one is mine!'

"'No! This one is God's!' Padre pulls me to my feet and looks into my eyes. 'Santiago, tell them—no, show them! Show them the chicken you have killed, and I will send them away.'

"'Yes!' I cry pretending that such a slaughtered chicken is just outside the door. I know my way now. I must take them to the door, and, if I can, I must run! I must run to the forest. They will not follow me there. They will never find me there! I bow low allowing me to gain my knife unseen by the Silver Men. I motion for them to follow me, and I back toward the door. Every muscle of my body aches from the night's dancing. My head is thick, and I do not know if I can run, but I must try! The Priest-Father tells me I must go on, and so I do! My head is heavy with the plant, but I must move like the great cat! I bow and bow again. I come closer to the door. The Important One's men are on me; they are ready for anything. 'Through here. By the chicken pens. There is a block. Come. Come!' I sound eager to prove myself, but the door is my only thought.

"When we get to the door, I have my knife waiting to taste their blood. I lean back for strength and step forward in one quick motion launching the knife. It takes the eye from the nearest Silver Man. He screams in agony, and blood gouts from the place where the eye is no longer. The second one feints to the right and tries me, but I am faster. I draw my knife across the front of his throat, and he falls.

"Only the Important One is left. Seeing me spill his men's blood is too much. He stands frozen with his mouth unable to speak. Then he screams. Loud and long, he screams like a woman in pain. It is all the time I need. I am at the door.

"Padre calls, 'Santiago!' and I turn. Padre moves in front of the doorway. 'Santiago, don't do this! Pray with me! Give your soul to Jesus!'

"'I give my soul, long ago, Padre! Now I give my blood! I give my blood and the blood of my enemy!'

"'Am I your enemy?' he asks tearing his robe and baring his chest to my blade.

"'You take my Gods and give me this Weakling who does not stand for Himself or His people! You put Him in our temples! You burn our books, rape our women, make slaves of our children...You take away my name, and you want me to love you! Tell me, Padre, what do you *say? Are you my enemy?' I look deep in his eyes, and he knows the truth. He covers himself and lowers his eyes as he stands aside. I am through the door and running as fast as I can. I am gone"*

His voice was hoarse with emotion, and it trailed off with the last line.

It had been three days since my office had been trashed. I had stayed to finish sorting and cleaning it up, and the time got away from me. I had stepped into the bathroom for only a moment, and when I emerged, there on my desk was the steaming cup of maté. Santiago stood waiting. Without a word I had taken the digital recorder from my desk and put in a new memory stick. He said nothing until he saw the light go on, and then he had begun. I made sure to leave some of the maté at the bottom of the cup remembering what Nick had asked, but Santiago had not taken his eyes off me. There was no opportunity to pour off some of the liquid into a container. I was fixated on the cup. I nervously shifted my eyes from Santiago to the cup and back again. I must have done that dozens of times as the old man told his memory. Now that he was done, my eyes were glued on the cup sitting on my desk. It was hopeless. I knew I couldn't sneak—I looked up, and he was gone! He had left the cup! He had never done that before, not in all the times I could remember. It was as if he had known, and he was obliging us.

I rose quickly and went to the outer office. He was not there either. The door to the hallway was ajar slightly, and I went into the hall to listen. There was no sound except the reassuring clicking of the old steam radiators. There was no creak on a stair or distant footfall to suggest that Santiago was anywhere near.

I returned to my office feeling like a thief and stashed the digital recorder back in the desk. I grabbed my coat and the cup with the remaining maté and headed out into the night with my guilty prize.

CHAPTER 20

"...Police found the mutilated body of a Caucasian man on the Upper West Side last night. The body was found by a homeless man behind the garbage containers at the rear of D'Agostino's on Broadway. So far no one has come forward to identify the corpse. Police estimate that the man was killed several days ago. City Hall rejected another bid by the Teachers' Union to shift control of the city's classrooms back into teachers' hands..."

I was sitting at the table trying to make sense of the sheaf of papers the Reynolds Foundation had sent regarding Julian's grant. I hadn't seen him again since the banquet, and I knew why. I couldn't help wondering if he had told Cameron Delaney about his condition. Barbara was poking at a few strips of low-sodium bacon as they sizzled in the frying pan. Breakfast was the only meal she really enjoyed cooking. It was her habit to listen to the news and lay out a small banquet, which I rarely ate. After 30 years of marriage, she never grew tired of this ritual.

"That's less than two blocks from the school! That could have been you stuffed behind some garbage cans! What time did you get in last night?"

"Uh...I don't know. 1:00—1:30, I guess. There are plenty of people out at that hour. This is New York! I'm careful. Besides, Santiago's still finding me with his 'memories'."

"Don't go in, and he won't find you! You spend too much time there as it is. I'm getting real tired of TV dinners alone in front of the TV, Holliman!...What kind of things is he telling you?"

"More of the same. Now it's more about Tlaloc and the Church. You know, trouble with the Priests and the suppression of the people. It's interesting stuff! Strange, but interesting."

"Is he all right, otherwise?"

"'Otherwise?' Yeah, for him, I guess...I-I just wonder if I should just end this whole thing. —Take him to a doctor...do something!...I don't know."

"You know what'll happen."

"Of course I do, Barbara!" I snapped at her, and she looked at me for a moment. I hadn't told her about much lately—not about the dance or the blood Nick analyzed or the sample of the maté I had cribbed last night. I was feeling like I had already compromised the old man, but wasn't I compromising myself with all this cloak and dagger? I had lied to the police, or at least not told them about the morion. I was going way out on a limb to protect an old man's delusional memories...if that's what they were! Christ, Delaney would love to find out any of this. He'd fry my ass in butter!

"What?" She knew something was eating me. I knew I'd have to tell her sooner or later, so I told her...

"It's the idea of it, Barbara! I run a school! I'm harboring a possibly dying old man who exhibits strange behavior where there are children! This is getting serious. How long? How long before this delusion begins to show itself at the wrong time? Suppose some kid runs into him half naked with feathers in his hair. One word of that, and Santiago goes to the funny farm, and Delaney hands me my walking papers."

"...Do you really think he's dying?"

"I don't know what to think! If you had seen him dance—it was incredible! How a man that age can move like that! Nick says the blood is abnormal, like it's a cancer, but not a cancer—whatever that means! Even he doesn't know what to make of it. He's hoping to find some answers in the maté, but, in the meantime, I don't know what to do!"

We sipped our coffee in a brief silence. The platter of bacon and eggs sat untouched in front of us.

"...What about his family?"

"What?"

"His family. He must have someone. Maybe this is a good time to contact them and let them know about his condition."

"There's nothing in his records about a family. He's never said anything about relatives except for the characters in this story."

"Have you ever asked him?" It was obvious, and I had completely discounted the possibility. I was so intrigued with Santiago's storytelling that I had accepted my own idea of him. Why couldn't he have a family somewhere? Did I really think he had lived in the Crayden basement for 40 years without contact with anyone from the outside? Did that make any sense?

It was a new possibility, and it offered the prospect of an exit from this maze of growing anxiety in which I was rapidly losing myself. I left for the office thinking that maybe there was still an escape hatch.

***

When I got to the office, I tried Soldani again. If he were the one who tore my office apart, I knew I'd hear it in his voice. I heard Soldani's voice again in the familiar message. I hung up and buzzed Sally on the intercom.

"If you're not dead or dying, this better be good!" Sally was having a rough morning. We had our understanding. I ran the school, but she ran the office. During school hours, she had a free hand to deal with students, teachers, parents and staff. She cut through paper work faster than I ever saw anyone else do it. At the end of the day she went home. Of course, if any real problems came up, she would happily dump them at my door, but there never seemed to be any that she couldn't handle. She supported me completely; keeping her was the best decision I had made at Crayden.

"I just wanted to know if the guy from the museum called me. You know, that Soldani guy."

"Nope. No messages. Rosemary Quinn wants permission to take the fifth grade to see *Aida*, and the outlet by my desk is shorted out—no computer for me today!"

"Run an extension cord...Give Rosemary the parent forms and my blessing—How much are the tickets, anyway."

"$55 per student!"

"Ah, the cost of culture! ...I'll tell Santiago about the outlet...If he's around," I muttered to myself.

CHAPTER 21

"I am in the forest long. I do not go back to the city because the Silver Men look for me. This I hear from those who come—who seek me out. They are the last of our warriors, those who slip the laws of the Silver Men by night. They make their way. They find me, and with me they stay. Others come at night, a few in need. They are afraid. I am not in the city among them to lead them with these 'Spanish'. It is the name they call themselves. We call them the Silver Men as we first do. But now...it is different. Now we know their name.

"We are like a small tribe, these warriors and I. Some of them have women, children. We talk of the Time of Greatness and of the powerful Gods, but the Gods do not see us. Living is poor. We hunt our food. Plant what we can. People come, and we tell the stories. I dance and heal. Those who come make us a secret. But they are very few. Time is hard on us. These warriors grow old. They lose their strength. They forget. Only I am able to tell the stories any more.

"Finally of the old warriors, One looks at me, and he says the thing I know all are thinking, 'It is true. You are a strange thing! See how we grow weak, but you are the same.' In the water of a puddle after a rain, he points at my picture. Even though I know it is true, I look. I am as I am. I feel my arms, my legs. They are strong, and my eyes see; my ears hear. I remember—everything! I see the face of the Priest-Father. I hear his voice in my head. I see the face of my mother as if I am only a day from her arms! All is as clear as it is now.

"The warriors' women begin to move away from me in small

ways. They do not bring food to my bowl or look at my face. They tell the children to stay away. They back away from me if they see me. All do the same. When the need comes for healing and the stories and the dances, they sit away from me and keep silent. I am now both more and less than I was. One by one the old warriors die. The women die also in time. The children are grown and their children also. All see me with wide eyes. This life is hard. At the fires at night they whisper together and look across their shoulders at me. They leave...one by one...in darkness for fear I may curse them. They go back to the 'Spanish' for an easier way. In time I am alone. No one comes. The forest falls silent, and the only sounds are the sounds of the dying of the city in my head. The sounds of the Fall of my people.

"I let the time surround me. 'I need no one,' I tell myself. I scratch my living from the forest. Spiders and lizards keep me company. The forest only whispers to me. I am growing like a wild thing waiting for the trap. I pray to the Gods, but they do not see me. I give my blood, and it sinks in the ground and goes away. I take the plant for Sight, but my dreams are empty except for the cat. In dreams he lies down by my fire and rolls on his back to show me his terrible belly. His voice rolls soft and sleepy in his throat, and I stroke his head. I wake wet and hot with my heart beating behind my eyes.

"...I know I must go back.

"One day I know it is the time. I travel along the paths around the city. As I get close, I can smell the city. It is a different smell than I remember.

"As I am close, I change my way. Gone are the feathers and weapons. I remember how it is with Padre, so I make myself a simple man in torn cloth. I enter the city. Gone are the temples! In their place are the churches of the Spanish. It is a market day, but not such as I see before! Music plays—music strange to me—loud, angry. Hundreds talk and argue over the prices of things, but not in our language. Everywhere the Spanish is in their mouths. The place is a mess of stalls without order or reason, and I see in the stalls the women dressed in woven

colors that are foreign. Their hair is different, and they are loud and without modesty. There are foreigners there too. There are the Dark Ones with strange eyes. Among them are the Spanish. They and their women walk like lords. I see only few of the Silver Men we fought. A few only! Why do the people not kill them? Why do they not push them out?

"I walk. The Calpuli are no more. The white houses limed with plaster and painted with the symbols of our language are gone. There is garbage everywhere. This we would not have before! This is an offense to the Gods! Instead, huts of palm, dried gray in the sun, are all there is. The grand houses of the Top Men are vanished. Different houses are there now and buildings I do not recognize. The wide plazas and roads are there still, but this is not the city I know! These are not the people I know. In some I can see the warriors of the Time of Greatness, but these wear no feathers or shells. They do not walk with strength or carry clubs and spears. I see many who are us, but not us. I see the blood of the Spanish. They are things made by the Spanish. Not our children, not theirs. Loosened, lost things with no Gods and no ground to put their feet.

"No one sees me—not the Spanish and not the people! There is no one who knows me. I am in the forest too long. All I know are gone, and those around me see only a hole in the air. My heart is bursting with blood. I want to shout, "It is I, Tlaloc, son of the Priest-Father, Seer to the King. I am come to take you back to yourselves! Come, and see me, and rise from this poor spirit...But I must see before I speak. I must know what the people are now.

"I walk for hours, and all I see is strange. Finally One comes to me and searches my face with his eyes. He is old and shaking. His mouth is open like a child, and I think he is crazy. Then he speaks to me.

"'Old Father, do not kill me! I am one you heal many—many years ago. My father brings me to the forest. We think you are a story, but my father hopes. I am sick, and they say I am to die.' He speaks to me in pieces of our language mixed with the Spanish. His voice is dusty. 'They say you are the One Who

Heals from the Time of Greatness. They say you know the plants and the prayers, and my father brings me to you. You heal me! You give me new life, and my father weeps. He dances with you, and you tell the stories and sing the songs. I remember this! I remember your face!'

"'...I am he,' I say to him, and he embraces me.

"'They say you belong to the Gods. They say you stand in your own spot, and the river moves around you. Now I see it is true! I was a small child. Now I am old, older than most men become. I know this is your doing. You stand still in the river. The Gods are great! I am here to serve you ...Come inside my miserable home. Tell my children and their children the stories! They do not know them. They do not pray. Only me! Only I pray to the Old Gods. See! I give the blood at harvest!' He shows me his arms where he cuts. Thin arms with flesh barely hanging there.

"I hold him and whisper, 'I am here, my son. Take me to your home away from all this noise.'

"His home is small and cramped but clean. He takes my hand, murmuring in the mixed scraps of our tongue that he knows. The words swirl around me, but my eyes are full of this strange people we are now. Some faces, those of us as we are, and some mixed and not of us. The Spanish words fly through the air, and I hear only pieces of our tongue quickly covered by hands over mouths.

"In the house I see too many people in such a small place. It is near mid-day, and they are gathered for food. A strong woman with gray hair is handing out flat bread pieces with red paste to each from a central stone. She hands to each silently. It is not enough for all, but she gives each a share from old to the youngest.

"As I enter the door led by the old man, all stand.

"'Father!' says the gray-haired woman in the same poor mix of our own tongue. 'Who have you brought? You know it is mealtime, and there is little to go around. Pardon, stranger,' she says to me in the Spanish, 'But my father wanders and does things we do not understand. He is very old, and his mind is weakening. We do not have food to give you.'

"'Silence, daughter!' snaps the old man, and he slaps her as hard as he can. She takes the blow with a surprised yelp, and all in the little house suck in air. 'You do not know who is here! You do not speak to the Old Father this way! This is the One Who Heals! This is the Old Father from the forest come among us! I see him again before I die, and look! He is the same as he is when I am a child. The very same! The Old Gods are great! They bring him to me, and I bring him to you! Lower your eyes, and give him food. Make a place for him! He is come among us, and we are honored. Please, Old Father, sit. My miserable home and wretched family are yours if you have us.'

"All lower their eyes, but they look sideways at each other. Little ones are pulled from the center, and the woman with downcast eyes points to a place where I sit. She gives me a flat stone with two small breads with paste—her own and the last child's. All are silent. I take the stone and hand the child its bread. 'Children have bread to grow strong,' I say in our language, and she is surprised. I break the last bread in half and give one half to the gray-haired woman. 'An obedient daughter pleases the Gods. This kindness is great to them and to me. I am thankful.'

"She takes the bread from my hand and looks at me with questioning eyes. All are silent as we eat. The old one says, 'You do not believe, but it is true! This is the Old Father, the one my father takes me to after the Time of Greatness. He lives! He is here!' These remain silent. They do not look at me but at each other with sidelong glances.

"Finally, the woman speaks again in the mix of our language. 'I am Chicahua, daughter of this man. We are a poor family as you see. Pardon my rudeness. I see you are one of us. This is still my father's house. If he brings you here, we are happy to have you.'

"'You speak the language. Everywhere I hear the Spanish. Why do you not speak it too?'

"'Outside this house. My father teaches us to speak the language among ourselves from the time I can remember. Our blood is pure. Here we speak the language, and here we live the old ways. I am his daughter. These are my sons and these, their sons, and these their sons. All have mothers of the tribe. But these young bloods do not find women to marry. They are of age, but the girls are not pure. If I do not find them wives, our line ends here.'

"'Then you must go outside the city. Surely there must be some—'

"'We cannot leave without permission. The Spanish lords want us all here. They say we owe them, and we cannot leave. Those beyond are lost to us. We work for the Spanish. At first they make us slaves, and then they tell us that is wrong. Next they pay us for our work, but not enough to live. They say we must pay them for teaching and protection. Protection! They work us like dogs. Give us nothing! Take everything. All of our family lives here. The women sell what they can make in the marketplace. We work in the houses of the Spanish and in the fields. The men work in the mines by day and labor at night. Many die, and the Spanish grow fat. It is so for many, but most are not like us. Pure blood. Our neighbors laugh at us. They call us lost and strange. The Priests come and want to make marriages for my grandsons. I smile and say, "When the time comes, Father" but they are not fooled. They tell me, "God does not care about blood, and a young man must have a bride to avoid sinning." Sinning! What do they know! It is a sin to abandon your parents and grandparents! It is a sin to forget who you are. My grandsons will have pure brides! This I will do!'

"'I believe you, Chicahua, daughter of this old one. I believe you do all you say. But...do you believe your father?'

"'He is a good man. A good father. He does not beat me except what you see today, and he teaches the young ones what he

knows of us. It is from him we know what we know.'

"'And what is it you know, good daughter?'

"'That once we are great. That our people have other Gods besides the ones they teach us. There is a God for War, and one for rain, for the sun...for all in this world. He tells us that these Spanish come pretending to be the Serpent God. They rise over us like a wave and bring us low. They bury our city in their lust for gold. They soil our blood and take our souls. We know how to give the blood. At times when the Spanish Fathers don't see, we make sacrifice. We give our blood—as much as we can to keep them alive. Some day they come and strike these Spanish!'

"'And do you believe your father about me?' I ask again.

"She hesitates. I know she worries she says too much already. Who am I? Can she trust me? What is her poor old father doing with this strange man? Why bring him here? 'I believe my father sees the Old Father when he is a child. This my mother tells us as well when we are young. I believe he sees his face in you.'

"It is a good answer! She says yes, without saying yes. She doubts without insulting. It is an answer worthy of the people. 'I wish you are with us when the people despair from the attacks of the Silver Men! Your tongue is careful and powerful. With it you can talk to the Gods, and they hear you!'

"'They do not hear us now! My Grandsons are to make bastards with the mixed girls they find here. We are to sink like the rest, I think.'

"'No, daughter, this I do not let happen. As I am the Old Father, I find proper maidens for these warrior sons. Let their blood awake us all and drive out these foreigners!'

"All around me laugh. I am surprised at the suddenness of it. I am struck dumb, and they laugh harder.

"'Be quiet!' She shouts, and they all fall silent but their eyes look laughing yet. 'Do not be hurt by this. We hear these same words from my father every day! It is as if you hear it with us. It is his constant word. *Drive them out! We wish it, but first we drive out hunger who sits with us every day. First we drive out the staring of our neighbors who hate us for living in pride of our blood! First we drive out the lash!'* With this she pulls the tallest of the youths in front of me. *She lifts his shirt, and there are the deep marks of the whip carved into his flesh as deep as the bone! 'See this one! He breathes bad since this happens. He looks at a girl—A Spanish girl, and she looks back. For this they beat him until he is nearly dead. They give him to me to bury, but I do not let him die. He lives, but he cannot work. To breathe hurts him, and he does not look up from the dirt any longer. There are many young ones like him.'*

"'Get me hot water,' I tell her. I sit the youth on a low stool in front of me, and I place my hands on his back where the scars are deepest. I feel the places where the bones are broken and healed to the lungs beneath. This is why he breathes so shallow. 'My son, I must bring you great pain, but I can make you well. Do you want this?' The youth looks up slowly. His lidded eyes search my face, and he nods slowly. 'Turn away!' I shout to those in the room. 'Turn away, and seek strength in the Old Gods! I have come among you to help. Turn, and pray for your lives!'

"They turn slowly. When all eyes are away from us, I reach with my fingers around the bones in his back, and I rip quickly at the places I can feel the joining. I move his bones within his flesh. I feel the tearing inside. The youth is white in the face, and his eyes roll back in his head, but he does not scream out. The woman comes with the hot water, and I point to a cup. This she fills, and I put the leaves of the plant which blocks pain in the water until it goes green. This I make the young warrior drink. He does, and he sleeps instantly. I tell the woman to cover him and all to pray and give him peace until a night and morning have passed, and he is come back to them. All fall silent. Many go out to work. I stay. The old woman stays. Her ancient father stays. We watch to see the youth sleep like dead..."

***

"...There is something you want?"   Santiago had interrupted his narrative, and it took me a moment to realize.

"Hm? What? Ah...yes, yes the plug near Sally's desk is out again."

"I fix." He sat there boring into me with his eyes. I had left the recorder on.

"Oh!" I fumbled with the recorder and shut it off. There was a strangely awkward pause between us. Santiago didn't move. He sat there just looking at me. "Uh...what...what happened to the young man?"

"He wakes. Three days. Longer than I think. He rises. Hungry..." He deliberately said as little as possible, watching me and seeming to be waiting for something.

"That's quite a story! The family must have been amazed!"

"Yes...there is much I can do. I know what the plants can give. There is much."

"That would be a wonderful thing, wouldn't it? A cure for injuries like that? Who wouldn't think it was wonderful?"

"Some. Some do not believe. Some do not hear the Gods. Some do not know any God but the tools in their hands. They do not know the God who sits upon their heart and tells their hands what to do. They do not hear his voice; they hear only the empty sound of the tool. To them it is the tool and not the God which is wonderful."

There was more than an accusation in this. He knew what I had done with the maté in the cup he left. I could feel it. He was chastising me. Challenging me. "Santiago..." I began my justification.

"The Gods work inside me." He interrupted. "They work inside you. Guide you. What you do is their work. What I do is their work. If I tell you the boy rises hungry, strong—better than he is before, do you see that it is the Gods in my hands who guide me?"

"Of course! Divine inspiration—miracles! There are stories of miracles throughout history—"

"Not a story! What *I* see! What *I* do!" He was on his feet grasping my arms with his face pushed close to mine. His eyes were nailing me down to my chair.

"Santiago, all these things you tell me—I know you believe them, see them as if you were there—"

"I am there! It is me, Tlaloc! Not Santiago! Not this man you see who cleans and fixes. I See for you! Dance for you! I show you all I am. It is *you* only who knows me now. It is only *you* who sees me!"

"I know you believe you are Tlaloc, son of a great Priest who lived long ago..."

"He lives now! I live! See this flesh. It is the same. I am the same. With these eyes I see! All!" He released me and calmed for a moment. He sat holding me with his eyes.

"...My blood speaks to you. What does it say?"

"What?"

"My blood. It is changed. Not like other men. What does it say to you? I give it to you so that you can know."

"...You know about the test? I—we only wanted to help—"

"What does it say?" His eyes blazed with righteous anger.

"Nick says it seems to be like a cancer. It's not normal. I'm concerned for—"

"Not sickness. Time. Long Time is in my blood. It holds me. I do not slip into the earth. I am what is left. I am here to tell. You are here to listen. It is the work of the Gods. I cannot change it, and you cannot. When I say everything, it is done."

"How can I believe all this? Santiago, the things you tell me—"

"Then you listen..." His voice was quiet but intense and deeply sad. "When I am done, we are done. I am a shadow again."

"Santiago, you're my friend—"

"You are my new father, but you do not know me! You are my freedom, but you do not want to understand! You do not trust!" He was deeply stricken, and I felt the depth of the betrayal he felt.

"Santiago, what you expect of me…it can't be real!"

"What is 'real?' Only what you know? Only what you see? Is this the only 'real' you know? That is a small life!"

"I know you believe—"

"What? What do *you* believe? Nothing! You do not believe in the Man Upon the Tree…"

"…I. I have respect for God…"

"But you do not believe! All that happens, all you are…The Gods make! They bring you to me. They put us as one! You come because They bring you! The Priest-Father sees you long ago! He tells me, and you are here! That is real!…I am yours—that is real! This skin,"—He grabbed my hand and put it on his shoulder, "This is real! I tell you what these eyes have seen. What these ears have heard. That is real!" His desperate face was close to mine, and I could smell the maté on his breath.

Slowly he backed away. He sat back down and turned the switch on the recorder as he did so. I didn't move as he did this or for a long time after as he continued his story:

CHAPTER 22

"He rises hungry, this young warrior. But he is more than before. It is just before the men return from the fields and the women from market on the third day. Chicahua and the ancient father are there. I know the rest talk about pushing me out. I am a liar to them. 'The boy is dying. See how he sleeps. This one is no Healer. He stays for food and that is all!' They do not have to say this for me to hear it. It is in their eyes and the way they hold their bodies when they see me. I am a stray dog to be driven from the door.

"'Food, Grandmother! I am so hungry. So hungry!' He stretches standing on his feet as straight as a tree. His body is leaner, taller! His eyes look to the sky as he stretches, and he smiles. Chicahua looks at me and cannot speak. Her joy makes her dumb. The Ancient Father laughs and dances and prays in the old language.

"'I breathe! I breathe full! There is no pain. And I can stand full. Look! I can reach the ceiling! I can touch the floor. I am strong! I am...hungry! Please, Grandmother, I must eat!' She looks to me, and I nod. She goes to the cooking place and makes a plate of red paste and bread. He eats and begs for more. This he does again and again until all the food is gone. He is eating the last when the men begin to arrive. As they enter muttering their dissatisfaction with me to each other, they fall silent, and they watch this boy devouring the last of their supper. They pile up in the door as each enters unable to believe what they see.

"'The Old Father! The One Who Heals from the Time of Greatness! I tell you! I tell you! Look at you! What do you say now, eh? What do you have to say now?' The old man was shaking in his triumph, and the young warrior stands and grins at the family, the red paste still on his mouth.

"'I eat everything,' the young warrior realizes. He is embarrassed by his actions. 'I am hungry. So hungry! I do not think of any of you! Do not worry! I can make this right!' The young warrior pushes past the silent family and runs out the door. When he is gone, it is as if each finds his breath again. Questions pour around the room 'How is this possible? Is this some trick? This is some black magic! Something is not right, and look, now he is gone, and we all starve tonight!' They are unable to believe what they see. Like you they cannot let go of their doubt of me. Chicahua is the only voice of truth. She makes them be silent. She tells them what she sees. She offers that the old man is at least part right. I am a Healer. I am a great enough Healer to bring back this boy. They can see that. They cannot deny what they see!

"'They argue. They talk. No one can agree. No one believes. Then the young warrior returns. He carries a young pig still wiggling.

"'See what I have! It is from the one that beat me. I went to him and showed him I was healed. Strong! I am strong enough to beat him dead for what he does to me. He screams, "You cannot have my daughter, Mestizo!" I tell him, "I do not want your ugly daughter! I want to give you what you give me!" He is afraid of me. He calls for his men, but no one is near. I go there at a time I know he is alone. He pleads for his life. I tell him, "Give me three pigs from your pens. One to eat and two to breed. You can keep your daughter, and I do not kill you! But say something to anyone, and I do kill you! Tell me what you choose!" He agrees. Here, Grandmother! Tonight we eat like men! Tomorrow we have pigs in our own pens to make us rich!'

"'You are foolish!' the boy's father says. 'He is Spanish. He has power; we have none!'

"'We have me!' the young warrior says. 'He says nothing, or I do kill him. He knows this. He keeps his life, his daughter, and his silence, and we keep his pigs! Grandmother, why are you standing there? The family is hungry!'

***

"It is this way with the family—They are afraid of me. They do not know what to say. Now I am a thing they cannot move from among them. Now the young warrior is married. A pure girl is found across the city. Her family hides its blood, but I find her for Chicahua and the young warrior. He leads others, warriors of the blood. They plague the Spanish. They take what is needed. They fight by night, in sly ways. They take what the Spanish have not counted, cannot see. The spirit of the people is come again!

"Again I tell the stories and dance. I tell of the Time of Greatness and the Silver Men, so the family knows from me, who Sees. The Old Man sits by me waiting for his time to end. One night he slips into the earth in the quiet of the moon, and I say the prayer for him that I say for the Priest-Father. I weep as I do not for many years.

"The family grows in spirit. Soon their pens are full of piglets. What is taken from the Spanish is left in places for the poorest to find. All around are lifted by these mysterious gifts. The world is better for the people, but the family keeps its quiet, and the Young Warrior and his men keep their ways secret and subtle.

"One day a woman comes to Chicahua with her daughter who is soon to die. She is wasting away and nothing helps. The woman is wild in her grief. She pleads with Chicahua to do what she did for the young warrior. She does not know it is me who heals. I am a distant uncle. The family keeps me quiet so that neighbors do not know of me. They are afraid of too many eyes.

"Chicahua listens and looks at me at times when the woman does not see. Her eyes ask. I nod and say, 'Woman, leave this one with Chicahua. She needs to see what is possible. Go, and come back when the moon is full again. This one is either healed or gone in that time.'

"'She is my only child! She cannot die! Please, say she does not die!'

"'Go!' I tell her, 'It is not for us to say. Chicahua does what she can.'

"The mother goes, and the old woman thanks me. The girl's mother is the daughter of an old friend. The child is weak since birth. She is not pure blood, but the mother is.

"I tell Chicahua to give the girl a sleeping drink I make. I do not want the girl to see what I do. She is to think it is Chicahua who helps her if any help can be given. This Chicahua does, and the girl is deep inside herself when I see her. She is near the time of womanhood, but small as a young child. Her bones do not grow, and her blood is thin. Her breath is sour with a rot from inside. I see this. There is a plant, but I must go into the forest. I must find it, and it is not near us.

"I am gone days, looking for the plant. While I look, Chicahua is afraid. The mother comes daily asking for her daughter. She does not see Chicahua doing anything. Chicahua pretends. She makes a liquid from corn and water and gives it to the girl whenever the mother comes. Finally the mother snatches the cup from Chicahua one day and tastes the 'medicine'. The woman is wild with anger. 'Liar!' she calls Chicahua. She tells the old woman that she goes to the Spanish to tell them how she is lied to by the old woman. She tells them about the young warrior and how he is gone at night some times when things happen in the city. Finally Chicahua tells her. She tells her it is the uncle who heals. She tells her I am gone for plants to make the healing. For a while the mother is quiet, but soon she is angry again. 'Where is he, this strange uncle? Why does he take so long? See how my daughter suffers!'

"When I am back and the mother jumps at me, she does not leave. She waits with her daughter. I cure her now, or she tells the Spanish everything. She tells the Spanish I leave the city without permission. Chicahua is pale with worry for the family. I tell the woman to be silent and sit. I prepare the plant along with root of another I know brings strength to the body. The girl needs both to be healed. She is on the edge of slipping into the earth. The medicine either heals her or pushes her into the earth. I do not tell the woman this. I know she cannot hear this.

"The girl takes the plant and chews the root. She sweats and shakes. She sleeps. She cries out. The mother sits with her watching her and warning me. I can do nothing more but pray. I also dance and give the blood. The woman is there when I do this, and she is afraid. The family is grown used to this, but she is not. She screams at me that I am a demon, a thing from Hell. She does not know the old belief except as distant rhymes and childhood stories.

"'My daughter dies — you die! You all die! I tell everyone what you do. The Spanish kill for less than this. This is a place of lies and black magic!'

"'Silence, you ungrateful thing!' I say to her. 'The girl suffers from the bad mix of blood within her. It is you who do this! If she dies, it is you who kills her! Now, silence, or I kill you before you can leave!' Her eyes grow big. The men of the family move toward her to hold her, but I tell them to leave her. She is quiet now, and I pray in the old language.

"The night hours pass, and the girl sleeps quiet now. The mother too sleeps.

"With the sun the girl wakens. She calls to her mother, and the mother cannot believe what she sees. The girl's eyes are clear, open—she is free of pain. Chicahua brings her a thin soup and the girl eats all. The mother stares at her daughter eating. She has not seen her take food so well for many weeks. 'Her face is alive! And, see, she takes food!' She turns to me with a face of fear and doubt. 'What are you? What are you that can do this? Not even the Spanish doctor could help her. How can you?'

"'He is a Healer, this uncle. From far away. He comes when my old father dies.' Chicahua is frightened, but I know that this woman's doubt must be made still.

"'Woman, do you want your child to live or not? Why do you question me? What do you want?'

"'You—you speak strange names and cut yourself. You pour your blood on the earth! You are a demon!'

"'Then take this one with you. In three days she will die, if that is what you want.'

"'No! She is my only child! Why are you so hard?'

"'You tell me I am a demon, but I heal your child. You ask this one for help then threaten to let the Spanish kill her. Woman, you have no thanks in you! Only fear and suspicion! Take this one with you, and prepare to bury her. I am done with you!'

"'No! Forgive! I am a stupid woman! I am only afraid to lose this child. I have no other! Take pity! Finish what you do! Please! I want only to know how you do this wonder.'

"'I do nothing! I follow the old ways. See what it does! It is our Gods who heal her. It is to them I pray, not this weak Jesus who hangs on a tree! Pray to them, woman, if you want this one to live!'

"'Show me! I pray! Whatever you say, I do!'

"I see she is desperate now. She wants only to save this girl and keep the healing, but the door of her mind is open. '...Do nothing. Say nothing. She stays here until the full moon, and she walks home on her own. You keep silent and bring food for her, so the family is not burdened. Go now, and let her sleep. Tonight you come with food and clean clothes. Then we begin the learning.'

"The woman leaves spitting blessings and apologies. Chicahua is angry with herself, 'I am a foolish old woman! I have no strength. I shake my house with my own fear. If this one talks, my house falls. She is the daughter of a friend. I do not know she is like this!'

"In the full moon the girl walks home. She is strong enough to need no more medicine. She is a quiet thing, but her eyes are bright, and I see the rot is gone. She lives a good life now. The mother brings gifts of cloth and food to me. I give them to the family. She covers me with praises like wet blankets. Like Chicahua, I do not trust this one. I know her tongue runs like water. I tell her to go home and be silent, but I know she is not. I tell Chicahua it is wise to move the family.

"There is talk within the family that night. The young warrior wants to kill the woman and be done with it, but I tell him that others already know. The family must leave. If word gets to the Spanish, they die. I tell him to lead his family into the forest. Find a place deep, and stay to yourselves. There is much arguing, and it tires me to see how little they trust me yet. Only Chicahua stands with me. Finally it is decided that the Young Warrior will take all those born in his time and younger to the forest. There are several strong youths, their wives, children, mostly young ones. The older ones howl with anger at them and me. I am breaking the family. I am making their house weak. I am taking them over, and who am I to tell them how it is! They say I want their house and goods. They say I want to push them out and take all they have.

"Finally Chicahua speaks, 'This one comes and shows us healing like we never see. He shows us the Time of Greatness through his eyes. Eyes, I think, which see it for themselves. My old father is right! This one is the Healer from the Time of Greatness. Some power of the Old Gods sends him to us. Our young men push back at the Spanish. Our family prospers; we have pigs in our pens. Even the Mixed-Bloods hold their heads up more than before. I do this to us, not this one. I tell the mother it is he who heals, and she tells another. I think this one is right. Send the young away! Let them live without our fear. Time is either our friend or our enemy. This is what I say, and I am the one here who decides! Go with your women and children. It breaks my heart more than I can say to see our little ones away from our arms. We do not have our young men, but we live! The best of us is safe! This I say!'

"The young are sent away with great sorrow in the family. The young warrior vows to return each changing of the moon to help the family and bring word of those that leave. Love is given to them by all, and anger is held for me and what I do to them.

"I know I must go. The elders do not want me. Only Chicahua. I leave early before the sun comes. I find a place in the forest I have not seen for many years! I have wandered looking for the plant that gives sight, and in this spot I find it in abundance. There is a stone shoulder coming out from the earth that I

remember. *This is the very place the Priest-Father takes me when he shows me the plant long ago! It is a sign from the Gods. I drop to the ground and give thanks. I give the blood. Much blood. I take the plant. I dream...*

"*I am in the city with the family in the house. All are there. Chicahua beckons me to sit at the table. She places before me a small mountain of tortillas and paste and begs me to eat. All the family watches. I know they are hungry but they wait for me to eat. I know I must. As I take the first bite, I hear the banging on the door. I know it is the Spanish, and I make to rise and fight them, but Chicahua holds me to the seat. She holds her fingers to her lips for me to be silent, and she goes to the door. She turns before she opens looking at the family. She opens the door.*

"*It is the cat! The horrible beast with the rotted belly. He springs upon her devouring her in seconds. He turns on the family biting and gnashing with his fangs and ripping with his claws. He eats! He eats without stopping. I am rooted to the chair. I cannot move as the cat devastates those around me. The old and young alike, he devours them all. Not one is left. When he is done he comes to me making the whirring sound in his throat, rubbing his head against my arm. He rolls on his back to show me his hollow undersides. It is more than I can bear. I run from the house out into the street. The cat springs to the door with his head poking out looking at me. He roars once at the moon, and then he walks away into the city. It is as if nothing has happened. I go back to see if there are any I can help, but there is not one. He has eaten everyone, every soul. All that is left is the small mountain of tortillas made by Chicahua and the red paste. I go to the table, and I see that the meal is untouched, but there is one difference. The red paste is blood.*

"*When I wake, the moon is high. I am wet with sweat and forest damp. My arms still trickle blood from the cuts I make, but I see. I know that I live still. I live beyond this family. If I stay, I take everything they have. They all die. This I know. If I am there, the great cat comes for them all in one turning of the moon. If I want them to live, I must leave them.*

"More. I think it is for me to leave all my people. If I stay, I think the cat will ravage them all. This family is only a part of the whole. The only feast I can give them is blood.

"At the camp the young warrior is distraught when I tell him.

"'You come to us and teach and heal. You make me whole again, and now you leave? What power is in this? We do not know the old ways! Why do you come if it is to kill our family and leave us with nothing?'

"'I do not leave you with nothing! You come with me into the forest. You are the one I teach. For one moon I teach you the plants and the stories. I give you as much as you can hold in one moon, and then I must go. It is not safe for you to have me here. It is not safe!'

"'We can meet the danger! We are strong! The Spanish cannot come here. They are afraid of the forest, and we know the ways!'

"'It is not the Spanish! The Great Cat comes. The Jaguar eating everything in its path. It eats everyone—but me. To me he shows his belly still. He comes for you.'

"'Old Father, what have I now? Who is to guide us if you are gone?'

"'The Gods are all we have. They are strong still. It is they who show me this way. You are young as I am when my father leaves me. I do not lead well, but you do! You are the one to lead them, help them live. You are the one to give the people the old ways, not me.'

"'How am I to give them the old ways? I do not know them! I cannot know them in one moon!'

"'One moon is the time we have, boy! Be silent with the reasons why this cannot be done. Listen. Take all you can from me. It is all you have when I am gone. Come! Make your goodbyes to your cousins and their women. Kiss the children. This is the moon of your life. We cannot waste it!'

"He is a quick student. He draws in everything I say, and he remembers! I give him the names and stories of the Gods: Tonatiuh, the sun God; Metzli, the moon; Xolotl, the evening star, and Xipa Totec who gives us the plants and brings spring change; Tlatecuhtli, of the earth, and Texcatlipoca, God of night and destiny. So many I tell him and their stories and the dances and sacrifices they like. I tell him to beware Huizilopochtli, God of War. It is he who brings us where we are. Appease him, but do not build your temple to him. He leads us against the Spanish, and see what it does! We are warriors, but we are also beaten. We cannot rise if all our men slip into the ground. Now is the time to worship Tocí, Goddess of childbirth. Make the people strong. Grow warriors, so that in time we are great again!

"'Teach the club and the spear. Show the young how we fight, that pleases Huizilopochtli, but do not let him lead you. Keep to the earth and your women and children. Grow!' I show him the plants—many plants. These he does not learn so well. He does not have a great gift for this. I push at him. This plant for the wind, this plant for wounds and burns. This is for eyes when they grow dim. The bark of this tree cures a rot that comes from inside. This root gives strength, but dig it only in the wet months or it dies out. So much! I try to teach him the plants for Seeing. The mushrooms and the slime of the frog that brings the dreams. I give him the plant, but when he wakes, he shivers and cries like a girl. I tell him how to See in dreams and to think before he tells the meaning, but he cannot take this. He refuses this. It is his fear that holds him back, and I know that the people will not have a Seer. Learn the plants and this animal, and know what they do. Learn! Remember! That one tries. That one learns! This he agrees to, and I take this as hope.

"The moon passes, and we return to the camp. There is greeting and joy from all. The children laugh, and a feast is made. The Young Warrior comes back a Man among men. The other young men see the difference, and they talk to him in a new way. The women prepare him the best meal and put him at the front of the feast. His woman makes him a headdress of blue feathers and gives him this honor to wear. I know I am seeing a

new King! It is too soon, but I know this. I feel this, and when they dance and sing, I slip away.

"I leave without more tears and questions. I leave this young King, and I now look for my own way. I sleep in the forest in a place where the water is cool and the moss is deep. I sleep long. I see the white wings of great birds. They are carrying me far away. They take me some place I do not see before among a people I do not know. They are not a tribe. They are not us. I am with them, but they do not see me. They do not speak to me. I am a shadow among them.

"It is a dream I do not understand, but I know it is for me. In the morning I gather what I can of seeds and leaves and the plants of the forest. I do not know where I am going, but I know it is important that I take these things. I head to the ocean, far away from the family and my people. I leave them before the Great Cat comes to take them all."

CHAPTER 23

"It was unidentifiable. My buddy in the toxicology lab couldn't identify any of the compounds in the liquid. High levels of anti-oxidants—that's about it. He was able to determine that it wasn't a narcotic. I don't think you have anything to worry about. It doesn't seem harmful in any way."

"...He was clear about it, you know, that *he* was this Tlaloc."

"C'mon, Brad, maybe it's dementia or maybe it's just religion. He still relates on a real level. He does his job. Nobody sees him but you. Lighten up!"

"I couldn't tell him I believed him!"

"Drama. That's all it is. The very young and the very old are full of drama! Dreams and fantasy keep you moving even when you don't have the power to act. It gets the juices flowing!"

"Except according to your frigging blood test he's this 'newborn' old man with endless telomeres, or whatever the hell you call 'em!"

"Forget the blood test! It has to be an error! I'm sorry I ever did it!"

"Wait a minute! You were intrigued. I know you were! Why this sudden blasé attitude?"

"The blood wasn't fresh. It could have been tainted. Who knows? The results had to be wrong."

"...He was devastated. Absolutely shattered. He said once he had finished his story, we were through. Jesus Christ, what am I dealing with here?"

"You knew this was coming. Everything he's done up to now indicates this identification with the young Warrior-Priest in the stories. Why does his disappointment surprise you? Sounds like he's at the end of it. The Warrior-Priest going off into the sunset. He was expecting a bigger response. I think Barbara was right. This is some tribal memory thing. If he were with his tribe, there probably would have been some ceremony—a passing of the torch. He had to live it completely to tell it. He wanted you to live it too. You're his heir, and you're not buying. What he's been giving you may be an unbroken line of memory going back to the conquest of Mexico. Hell, what an historical trove of information! You know, you might have something in those files that historians will find really interesting...if they can somehow be verified."

"Y-you don't think he's dying or about to go completely insane?"

"Naw! I'm a scientist, Brad. When your results defy logic you have to go back to basic laws. People don't live five hundred years. We both know that. I must have screwed it up."

"You said you double-checked your results."

"Yeah, I did. That doesn't mean I can't be wrong? Jesus, Brad, you need a vacation! He's just an old Indian with a great story to tell. Forget the damn test—It's impossible to determine anything from it. I never should have suggested it. Man, your history with him has you out on the ledge! C'mon back in here, boy, before you fall off, and carry me with you!"

"...I guess it's everything going on. All this tension with Delaney and the Board. The pressure of pulling Crayden back from the abyss...I guess I do need to get a little perspective."

"You need time off! Do you gamble?"

"Hm?"

"Do you gamble? You know, dice, blackjack, that sort of thing?"

"Uh...not really. Never had much time for that sort of thing."

"Well, you do now. Mona and I are going to the Sun this weekend for a little R&R. Why don't you and Barbara come along? We'll double date! The girls'll love it, and for a couple of days you'll be out of here! What do you say?"

"...Ok. Sure, why not? A weekend is just long enough to lose Crayden's entire endowment!"

"Cool, can I use some of that too?"

"Why not. It'll be a double trial. Maybe we'll even get adjoining cells."

Sally knocked on the door. She entered in an uncharacteristically subdued way. She had come to think of Nick as part of the "inside" establishment, and she liked him. I couldn't understand this sudden formality.

"We're going to—where?"

"The Sun. A little drinking and a little gambling."

"There's someone here from the NYPD to see you. Is your meeting over?" Sally looked at the two of us, and she seemed a little stunned.

"Uh, yeah, we're done. It was—someone from the police department?"

"He says he's investigating the murder of that grease ball from the Museum. You know, that Soldani guy?"

"What?"

"He asked me how well you knew him. I told him I didn't know. I didn't give him any information." Sally stood in front of the door waiting for instructions.

I couldn't think for a minute. Soldani? Murdered? Who the hell would go after a nervous little bookworm like him? What could he have done? Oh, my God!... My mind went to all the phone calls I had been making to him. Of course, they were here!

"Nick." He got up without any further word between us. "Have him come in."

"Them. There are two of 'em." Sally followed Nick out, and two young men in suits entered. One of them came first, and he shook my hand.

"Dr. Holliman, I'm Lieutenant Rifkin, NYPD. This is my colleague Lieutenant Gergan. We're here on an informal inquiry. I hope we're not disturbing you."

"My assistant told me what you're here about. I'm shocked! I don't—what can I do for you? Please, have a seat."

The second young man, Gergan, surveyed the old office a little overwhelmed by its musty formality while Rifkin started right in.

"This'll only take a minute. We're contacting everyone who might know something about Dr. Soldani."

"When did he...when was he killed?"

"Several days ago. His body was found behind a supermarket not too far from here."

"My wife and I heard about that on the radio! That was him?"

"Yes, it was in the news. His office machine has several calls from you. Would you mind telling us how you knew Dr. Soldani?"

"Sure. It was purely professional. Dr. Soldani was—was helping me with some research. I didn't know him well."

"Could he have been coming here to see you?"

"He was here a couple of times, but I wasn't expecting him. We hadn't really begun the research."

"What were you researching?"

"It was an antique helmet. A gift from a friend. He wanted to examine it, but my schedule is very full."

"I see. Your wife was on his calendar. Apparently she saw him some time ago."

"That's right. She originally brought the helmet to him for inspection, then later he came here to talk to me about examining it more closely."

"Umhm. Did you see him at all within the last four to five days?"

"Oh, no, not at all. Crayden keeps me pretty much booked up. I hadn't seen him. I was calling him regarding an appointment."

"I see you had some kind of break-in recently—about five days ago."

"Yes, someone trashed my office. Nothing was taken. I think it was probably students doing a little mischief. Everything is back to normal."

"So you think it was students?"

"That's what it seemed like. I mean, nothing was missing. My books and papers were all over the room, but there wasn't even any damage to speak of. It seemed to me that it was probably a prank."

Rifkin made a final note and closed his notebook. "OK, that's it. Thank you, Dr. Holliman. We'll get back to you if we need to, but I don't think so. Sorry to bother you on a busy day."

"That's fine. No problem at all. Uh, how...how was he killed?

"I can't say. There are some unusual aspects of the crime that we can't discuss with the public."

"Oh. 'Unusual?' Really? If there's anything I can do. This is so terrible! Did he have any family?"

"Not that we know of. Have a good day, sir."

The two men slipped out of the office leaving an empty feeling behind them. I couldn't help but wonder why his body was found clear across town from the Museum in our neighborhood. Could he have been here? Was he the one who rifled my office? Was there a connection? I didn't like the suspicions I harbored. I didn't like the 'unusual' part of Soldani's death. How unusual? The hair on the back of my neck was standing up.

Then I thought about what Nick said. "Go back to basic laws." He was right, I'd allowed my childhood imagination to run away with me. What was I thinking? I was looking at Santiago through the eyes of a desperate, sad ten-year-old. Santiago was an old man. He was my friend. In his loneliness he wanted to give me the memories of his culture, to share something of himself and his people before he died. I was a little ashamed of myself that I couldn't be more accepting of his gift. How would it have hurt me to let him think I believed him? I was so concerned about his pension and his security, but I wasn't really looking at the man. He wasn't demented, he needed human contact, someone to 'see' him, and I had denied him that. What kind of friend was I?

***

The weekend was a tonic! Nick showed me the ropes—roulette, blackjack, craps. I learned that I was a lousy gambler! I put myself on a hundred dollar budget for the weekend. When I lost it, that was to be it. After the first hour—that was it. I went bust on the blackjack table after half-a-dozen hands.

Nick, on the other hand, was amazing! He watched and waited to "to see what the room was like". I couldn't understand what difference it made, but it seemed to work for him. On the first evening he won over five hundred dollars between craps and the roulette wheel. The second day he won over a thousand! It was exciting even though I was mostly watching him play. Barbara loved the slots and won back the hundred I had lost. We went to shows, ate, drank, and laughed about everything.

Barbara and Mona complained about "too much food", but they ate like truck-drivers and acted like schoolgirls together. It was just what Barbara and I both needed. When we got back on Sunday night, we were exhausted and completely relaxed. I resolved the next day to fix the rift between Santiago and myself. I would listen and share with him, and let the old man have his contact without the stupid anxieties I had built up. Nick was right. The story was over. Tlaloc had left the family and gone off on his own. I needed to make Santiago understand that I valued his story and believed it. I needed to give him some kind of validation.

Crayden was on track. I had seen to that. I had time now to give an old friend the attention he deserved. I returned to my office with a real feeling of well-being.

CHAPTER 24

"At the ocean there is a big village. It is a Spanish village. People come and go. There are many Dark Ones chained in the sun being pushed into the water-houses of the Spanish. Some Mixed-Bloods whip them and curse at their slowness. The houses here are pushed all together. Everything smells of close living and rot.

"For a time I watch and listen. I wear clothes I take from a pole near a house at the edge of the village. Soon I am hungry. I know I must eat, but the only place I smell food cooking is one where the Spanish go. I watch them enter. They give something to a man who gives them a measure to eat. I have nothing to give this man, but I must eat.

Then one comes up behind me and says in Spanish, 'Do you want to eat?'

"'Yes,' I say, 'But I have nothing to give for the food.' I see this man before. He is a Mixed-Blood who whips the Dark Ones into the water-house.

"'I buy you food, mestizo, but you work for me, eh? I lose one man. I need another to push the Black ones into the ship. Do you agree?'

"'I work for food...'

"This one feeds me at the place where the Spanish eat. It is much food. More than I eat most times, but I am hungry. Later he takes me to the water-house. He gives me a whip and tells me to come 'below'.

"Inside the water-house there is a place where a tall man cannot stand. For me it is just enough, but the Mixed-Blood must bow or hit his head. He tells me to make the Blacks lie down close to each other. Then I am to take a chain and feed it through a ring at each man's foot. The chain is then tied to a bigger ring on a tree that is part of the water-house. This I must do until there is no space left in this place. I must fill every space with black men tied with chains.

"'Are these to be sacrificed?' I ask.

"The Mixed-Blood grabs my arm and looks me in the eye. 'Watch what you say, mestizo! They throw us both out if they think we are savages!'

"'Why "savage"?' I ask.

"'Don't say anything! Do as you're told!' He hits me hard on the shoulder, and I nearly fall. I kill men who treat me so, but I know he does not know me. He does not know what I can do.

"All that day I lay Black men down in the water-house and chain them. Some are sick. Some are crying. I do not understand their talk, but I see that they cannot live long in this place.

"Finally the Mixed-Blood returns when the water-house is full. He gives me some 'money' and tells me to return tomorrow if I want more. He says I do well, but I do not like what I do.

"'Some of these are dying. Their blood will be wasted. It is better if they are sacrificed.'

"'I tell you not to say this! These Blacks go far away to be sold! It is not your concern if they die or if they live. If you want more money, you come. If not, you can starve. I don't care!'

"With this he pushes me to the door. I feel my anger rise, and I am on him! I have him on the floor with my knife at his chest. He is surprise by my quickness. He is bigger than me, but I am stronger. This he can feel. His eyes go wide, and he begs for his life.

"'I am the Seer of the People. The Healer from The Time of Greatness. If you touch me again, I have your heart in my hand to offer the Gods!'

"'Please! I mean nothing! I tell you to save you! These Spanish put you in chains if they hear you speak this way. They take you far away and sell you! Is this what you want?'

"I let him up. I see in his eyes that this is true. He pulls away, and I think we are done.

"'...Do you want to work tomorrow, Mestizo?' He asks me this, and I am surprised after what I do.

"'...I work, but you do not touch me!'

"'Strong! You are strong for such a small man! Good, you come tomorrow, and I give you more money, but you work hard!'

"I leave. I go to the place where food is sold. I give the 'money' for more food, and I eat as much as I can hold. I find a place in the straw behind a house to sleep. In the morning I rise before the sun. Only a few birds begin to sing. I bathe in the ocean. Only once before as a child have I done this. It is when the Priest-Father takes me with him to a place distant from our city. The ocean he tells me is a place of healing. Its waters taste of Life. Bathing in the ocean cleanses the spirit. I am in need of this, and it is well.

"I come to the water-house before the Mixed-Blood comes. I can smell death from the water-house. Some have died in the night. This I know. I hear others moan and speak in strange words—not Spanish...not my language.

"Finally, he comes.

"'Go below decks,' he tells me. 'Unchain the dead, and throw them in the water.'

"'What about the others?' I ask. 'Many are sick. They need healing. Am I to heal them?'

"He looks at me startled.

"'You can do this? You can heal these?'

"'I tell you yesterday when I nearly cut out your heart that I am a Healer. Do you not believe my words?'

"'Get rid of the dead,' he says, 'Then heal if you can,'

"'I need herbs and plants. Do you let me gather some for this purpose?'

"'Get what you need, Mestizo, but do not show the Spanish this!'

"I clear the water-house of many bodies. Others come to take the empty places. I look around at the black men, and I know some are too far gone to heal. I go around the edges of the village to find plants and herbs. There are many growing that I know. These I take and return to the water-house.

"I make a maté with some herbs, with others I make paste or take the juice—what is needed. I work with many. By night the moaning has stopped. Some sleep, some are silent watching me with surprise. The Mixed-Blood returns and sees what I do.

"'These don't look any better!' he growls at me. 'You waste my time!'

"'Feed them. Tomorrow only a few die. See this for yourself.'

"'Get out! I do not pay you for promises. You do nothing! I do not pay for nothing!'

"'Tomorrow you see this.' I leave him with no 'money,' and so I cannot go to the food place. I find my nest in the straw and sleep hungry that night.

"In the morning I bathe again in the ocean and return early to the water-house, but this day the Mixed-Blood is waiting.

"'What do you do? Say nothing to the Spanish! I come this morning to see for myself. Only one dies this past night. One! Do not let the Spanish see this magic! They cannot know what you do! Come, see the Blacks! See what you do!'

"I come below decks. I am greeted by weak but living men. All

say the same word in their own tongue. It is a greeting, I know.

"'Can you keep them alive?' the Mixed-Blood asks me.

"'If these men want to live, I can,' I tell him. 'But some do not. They are alive now, but they die anyway.'

"'If you work with me, can you keep them alive if they want to live?'

"'Yes,' I tell him.

"'Then you are my man! You are what I need to do this work!'

"'I am hungry,' I say, 'You do not pay me.'

"He reaches into his pouch and pushes a handful of this 'money' into my hands. 'Take! Go, and eat, and come back! I make you rich if you work for me! Go, and eat.'

"I take the money, and I tell him to feed these Dark Ones and give them water, if he wants them to keep living. Then I go and gorge myself again at the food place.

"The Mixed-Blood comes and finds me. He says he wants me to stay on the water-house with him. I am to gather the plants I need for many days. I am to stay on the water-house when it takes these Black men to where they are sold. This he says is my work, to keep as many alive as I can. If I do well, he tells me, he gives me much money.

"Many days I work with the Mixed-Blood. Some of the Dark Ones seek death, and I wait for the cat to find them. I sleep close to them to heal them if I can on the journey. At night an animal comes for some of them, one I do not know. He passes by me. Once he looks at me. He sniffs my body and snorts as though I have a bad smell. He goes for the ones who seek him.

"For the rest—they live. I take them above to the sunshine when we are on the water. I calm them with plants and give them enough food to keep their stomachs from hurting. Fresh water they have, and I see that some begin to look to the horizon ahead.

"We come to cold water and sharp air. I am cold, colder than I have ever felt. My hands shake, and the wind bites my skin. The Mixed-Blood gives me clothes to wear that smell of sweat and says that soon we come to land.

"In two days I see a green place ahead. I smell the land. It is a different smell from the place we leave. As the water-house moves closer, I see a hollow between the trees. There is a village. It is here we make our journey. The water-house comes to a wooden platform over the water, and the Spanish captain orders the Dark Ones to come out. The Mixed-Blood and I take them from 'below'. Some cry and grab my hands. They say words I do not know, but I understand they tell me thanks. I know the word they say so many times is a name they give me. They say this name and take my hand. They cry and give me signs of sorrow. I am consumed with the feeling of betrayal. I give them this place. I am the one who keeps them from the animal. I do not think I help them, but they say this name and take my hand as they leave.

"The Spanish captain follows the parade of black skins in the cold air. They go to a marketplace in the middle of the village. Here other men look at the Dark Ones. They look them in the teeth, eyes, arms and backs. They do not see the Black Ones draw their souls inside themselves. I watch as men from the village speak up in a tongue that is not mine, nor Spanish, nor the tongue of the black men. They call out to a man who stands with the Blacks, one by one the Blacks are taken from the market and disappear. The Mixed-Blood tells me, they are sold. They are gone from us and their other world. They are here now to work for life for these strange men.

"When there are no more Black Ones to sell, the Spanish captain comes to the Mixed-Blood.

"'It is well. Most of these live. They sell for good money,' he says to the Mixed-Blood. He gives the Mixed-Blood a pouch of coins and walks away to the village saying he is thirsty.

"The Mixed-Blood comes to me.

"'Do not tell him what you do, or he sells you. He does not know

about the magic in you. He sells you or kills you perhaps if you speak of this.' Then he reaches into the pouch and pulls out six gold coins. 'Take these! It is more than your kind get anywhere, but say nothing. You stay with me, mestizo, eh? I make you rich!'

"I have nowhere else to go. I stay on the water-house. There is food and water enough. I hide from men. I hide from the Gods.

"Many times I make this journey. Many times the Mixed-Blood gives me the gold for healing. I am fed. I live in the water-house 'below'. Before long I know the words of these black men. They come from a place where the sun is born. At times there are women too and children. I do not like these times. The children slip into the earth very easy! They are too short to see the horizon ahead. I learn to speak with them, but I do not learn their names. I do not want to know them.

"They are warriors, like me. In their land the tribes fight, many are taken and made slaves. This I understand. It is the same for us. We do this, but none of them are sacrificed. Blood is not the Water of Life for their Gods. They do not honor and then eat those they take. Their Gods are also of the earth, like ours. They do not have the cities we have. They do not have the great temples. But they are proud, and their Healers too use plants. Some among them See, though not the ones we have upon the water-house. They see me heal, they see me pray. They ask me to pray for them. They ask me to question, to tell the Gods their names and ask for power to kill the Spanish. We are much alike. I come to see them like my own people.

"It is on one of these journeys when things change for me. We have too many on board. This time there are a good number of women and children. Some of them are whole families, but they are chained apart. They call out to each other at night.

"'Are you still with us, my wife?'

"'Yes, husband I am here. I am still strong. Lele, where are you child?'

"'Mother! I am scared! It is dark, and it smells! I am hungry *too.'*

"'Hush, my child. We live. We are still together. Your father saves us soon.'

"The man is silent when she says this. He stays silent in the dark when the woman promises the child to be saved.

"'Shut up, you!' murmurs another one. 'You get us all killed! That short one, the medicine man, he listens.'

"I do not talk with them at this time. It is in the lonely dark when lizards move inside their stomachs. It is the same with every journey. They learn slowly to trust me, but never with their hearts. By the end of the traveling they beg me for help, for escape...for death. The nights have worn away their doubt of me, and they grab at my heart for some hope for themselves.

"It is these three, the man, the woman, and the small boy, Lele, that tear my heart from my chest finally. I do not know the names of the others, but this boy I know—Lele. He is small and thin, with eyes as round as river stones. He watches me when I pray. He comes to the water-house with worms inside him that eat at his stomach and entrails. I give him a tea to drink that kills the worms. At first he is very sick. He throws out the worms through the mouth and bottom. The tea nearly kills him, but he is free of them now. He is weak but gaining strength. He lives long enough, I think, to be sold away from his mother and father, but I do not know if he will survive that.

"They do not know this. I cannot tell them. At night they whisper to each other of being together at the end of this hard journey. I think of my own people, and I cry in the quiet dark."

CHAPTER 25

"Why you stop?" Santiago was looking at me with annoyance and confusion. I had never done this before, and he was deep in this memory when I turned off the recorder.

"Santiago, what is this? Tlaloc is gone from his people."

"Sí, I am gone. If I stay, the cat will come and devour them all. I must go."

"...But it is over. The Fall...the loss of who they are. Tlaloc is done."

"...No...I am not...done. The Gods see me again. Tlaloc is not done." He reached across and turned the machine back on:

***

"One day, several days before we come to the land again, I see the three on deck. They are not allowed to be together, but they can see each other. It gives them joy to see each other outside the dark 'hold'. They signal to each other and smile and say things with their mouths that their voices do not sound. Pretending to look after the man, I take him aside where others do not hear us. I tell him that in a few days, we come to land, a village. I tell him that there they all are sold to strange men. All are made slaves, and these three will not be together.

"He moans, 'Why do you tell me this? Why do you torture me? Kill me, Healer! Kill my woman and my son! Do it! It is easier for us to die than to be together no more. Do we live through all this to be taken away from each other? No, I cannot bear this! Give me a knife, and I kill myself! Then take this knife and kill the woman and child. This is the only healing you can give us

now! Do it, if you are any man at all!'

"I tell him to be the warrior he is born to be. If he is so willing for the three of them to die together, I can give them a chance. It is a slim chance, and they are likely to slip into the earth, but it is what I can do. He looks at my eyes and slowly nods. I tell him that he is to lead the rest. Some do not follow; some are too weak, but some fight! On the night we find the land, I open the chains that hold them. They must creep to the deck and take the water-house. They must get close to the land and jump into the water and swim to freedom.

"'Lele is weak. He cannot swim far to save himself. You and the woman swim with him if you get free. If you do not, he will die with you. Do you want this?'

"Again he nods.

"'You cannot hide in the village. All like you are slaves. You live only if you stay far away from the strange men in the village. They are a kind of men I do not know, but they are not far from the Spanish. Once you take the water-house, they want to kill all of you. You tell this to the men below. Tell them they cannot stay near these men. They cannot make a bargain with them. They are hunted down if they stay near the village.'

"That night the whispers fly like bats in the dark. Some groan with fear. The women cry. The children cry hearing their mothers cry. It is a soft blanket of sorrow I hear, but I say nothing. None wish this, but none deny it. The weak ones give themselves to the Gods. They know they are the first to die. The next day the man looks to me for speaking.

"I take him aside as before, and we talk.

"'We take the water-house. We fight. We know we die—many or all. It is all we have left. I free my son and woman or die with them!'

"'Tomorrow,' I tell him. 'Tomorrow we come to the land and the village. I slip the chain from you when we are close. You are fast, if you are to succeed. When the water-house is too close to land, other men come to help the Spanish. You are all taken and

killed then. The water is cold! Colder than any water you know. You do not swim long and live. The Gods make your flight short and fast!'

"The next night I watch from the deck. There I see the land slide into eyesight. I see the open space in the trees, and I smell the village though we are still far off. I watch from a dark space between two wooden boxes tied to the deck.

"'What are you doing up here, Mestizo?' The Mixed-Blood startles me. He sees me and comes up behind me. I jump inside my skin, but I make no movement.

"'I come to see the water-house meet the land,' I tell him. 'It is still a wonder for one who does not his whole life travel on the great water.'

"'...This is not your first journey,' he answers 'Why does it interest you now? This is the first time I see you 'above' since you work for me.'

"'This is the first time you see me,' I tell him as I look in his eyes.

"This he does not question. He is uneasy near me. I know this. He leaves me alone most of the time. He talks only when he tells me what I am to do, or he pays me. He does not want to know more than my work. I am glad of this.

"'When the sun comes up, we make more money, eh, Mestizo?'

"He thinks this is what my mind hopes, and I look at him, "It is well." I leave him and go below to do my last work, I think, for him.

"It is time. I know that I must take away the chain, and the Blacks must do what they can. I do not know what is to happen. I have not taken the plant, and I do not want to See. I take my key and quickly remove the chains from the men first, then the women and then the children.

"They are all as silent as the dark. Lele stands with his eyes still as big as river stones looking at me. He does not speak. I see that he gains strength, but he is still very weak. I do not think *he can swim in the cold water and live, but I cannot change what is begun.*

"Quietly the men move up the ladders and creep onto the deck. The Spanish watch the shore sliding closer. They do not look behind them as the Blacks stalk them. The man gives one silent signal, and the men are on the Spanish, clubbing and killing without sound. It is wonderful to watch as the Spanish slip into the earth without making even a whisper. Their mouths are open but no voice escapes. They are too surprised. The man is joyful. The ship is nearly theirs. Then from below I hear a great scream. It is a woman. The man, hearing this, rushes to the sound as do I. He knows it is his woman. The others finish off the rest of the Spanish in silence, while the screaming from below is all any of us can hear.

"When we get there I see it is the Mixed-Blood. He has Lele by the throat with his knife, and the woman screams at him in her language to let the boy go, or she kills him with the iron pike she holds at him. She is a tall woman, strong and has the force of fear for her young behind her eyes.

"The Mixed-Blood sees me, 'Fool! You let these Black Ones go! Now they kill us all. Tell the woman to drop the iron, or I cut the child's throat!'

"'Where do you go then?' I ask him. 'See. The man is here. If the boy is killed they both kill you. You have no way to save yourself! Drop the boy, and she lets you live, I think.'

"'You know them? You know what they say?'

"'I learn their words. I know you must pray to your Jesus. You see him very soon!'

"'You tell them, I let the boy go, but they let me go. I do not kill the boy, if they do not harm me.'

"I tell the woman what he says. She looks at me with fierce eyes. 'I smash him like a melon! I dance on his bones!'

"'Woman,' I say, 'What do you want? Take your boy and go with your man. The Beast of Death waits for you everywhere

you turn. Do you want to meet him here in this dark hold?'

"She looks at me, and then she looks at her man. They have not touched or talked, but they are as one. This I feel. She drops the iron and turns to look at the Mixed-Blood. She holds her hands out to show him she does not harm him. But the Mixed-Blood does not drop the boy. He still has him by the neck. Lele's eyes roll in his head. His body is limp, and I see that he does not live much longer this way.

"'Now tell them to move back. I go to the deck. Tell them if any one of these animals touches me, the boy is no more!'

"'They promise you!' I tell him. 'They do not harm you. Let the boy go. See how he hangs in your arm. He is dying! Let him go!'

"'No! These are animals! I do not trust my life to them or you! You let them go. You are with them. You are an animal! Get out of my way!'

"He makes for the ladder dragging the dying boy with him. The woman grabs the iron and with one smooth move runs on the Mixed-Blood screaming with hate in her throat. The man screams as well. The Mixed-Blood steps quickly to the side, and the woman misses with the iron. She cannot stop her forward run, and her body passes by the Mixed-Blood who pushes his knife in her throat cutting her breath. A great gout of blood flows from the wound, and the tall woman collapses to the floor in a pile of meat and bone. The man springs now. He has a long knife in his hand, but the Mixed-Blood is quick. He pulls the boy up close again between him and the man's waiting blade. He is still moving toward the stairs. The two turn together as in a dance, the man waiting to catch the Mixed-Blood, the Mixed-Blood keeping one eye on the stairs. As they turn, the man moans and wails for the dead woman. He screams for his son. He is ready to spring for the Mixed-Blood and take his chances, but I am first. The Mixed-Blood has turned enough to put me behind him. I take my knife and quickly slip it between the ribs on the left side. I slice sideways at an angle, feeling the blade cut through the muscle and sack holding breath to the point where I know the heart beats. It is *all done in one quick move, and the Mixed-Blood goes limp. He and the boy drop.*

"The man screams with rage. He is on the body of the Mixed-Blood hacking and chopping at it. The blood spatters in sticky sprays all around us and on us. I move to Lele and take him up. I feel at his throat. I can tell that his heart still beats. I lay him down and rub him as I pray to the Gods to let him go a little while longer.

"I take a dipper of water from the water barrel and pour it over the boy. Its coolness makes him stir, and he coughs from the choking. Finally he opens his eyes. His father cries and screams his name.

"'Shut up!' I tell him. 'Look for your wife on the other side of life when you get there. Now, take Lele and swim! The others are gone already, if they are smart. Take him if you have any thoughts of life left. Without you he is dead!'

"The man hears me. He takes my hands gushing out thanks and apologies.

"'Enough!' I say. 'Go! Swim! Stay away from the village if you want the boy to live!'

"The man picks up the boy. Lele is looking at his father now. His round eyes are deep and quiet. He is weak, but he is alive, and there is yet a chance if the father can come to himself and move!

"'Run your knife into my side,' I tell him.

"'...What? No, you are my friend!' He looks at me with horror in his eyes.

"'Run your knife into my side here! If you don't, the men from the village kill me for sure. I do not die! They are to think I fight you! They are to believe me when I tell them that we throw you into the water at sea. They are to think you are dead. Run your knife into my side! Quick!'

"He is confused, then I see the cloud pass from his eyes, and they

understand. In one swift move he cuts me here and climbs the ladder with the boy in his arms. He does not look back.

"I do not see him again. I know this. I do not know if they live. It is well. The pain is great, but I know I live. Before the men from land come, I go to the place where the Mixed-Blood keeps his money. I take this along with my own. I think I need this. I Know I am here in this strange place for a long time."

CHAPTER 26

"It won't work, Dr. Holliman!"

Cameron Delaney as usual had pushed his way past Sally and into my office. His eyes were cold blue and his complexion was flushed.

"...Mr. Delaney, what a surprise." I rose to meet him, but I was smart enough not to hold out my hand.

"Julian Reynolds called me last night. He suggested that, in view of our 'differences', it might be better for Crayden if I tendered my resignation as chairman of Crayden's Board! I assume this was your doing."

"...Uh...No, Mr. Delaney, this is the first I hear of it! I never discussed anything like this with Mr. Reynolds." I was completely taken off guard. My only talk with Reynolds never included removal of Delaney from the Board. I was as shocked as the old man was.

"Well, I'm sorry to disappoint both of you. I won't be resigning from this position! I have enough support to continue no matter what sophomoric maneuvers you might try, but I am disappointed, Dr. Holliman. I thought that you were a more direct individual. I didn't think you'd resort to backstabbing!"

"Mr. Delaney, I had nothing to do with this! There must be some misunderstanding. Mr. Reynolds and I only discussed the delaying of the pool construction. We never talked about removing you, or anything else except making sure that Crayden could continue as planned."

"He was quite definite about it. He suggested that I had allowed my feelings about you to stand in the way of Crayden's best interest. He intimated that unless I resign voluntarily, he would exert whatever pressure he could to have me voted off the Board."

186

"He wouldn't do that! You're old friends. You grew up together!"

Delaney looked at me for a moment, and then a cold smile flashed across his face. He let the moment settle before he continued.

"He told you that, did he? ...I see. It didn't occur to you that he might be looking out for his own interests."

"What? What does he have to gain here at Crayden, Mr. Delaney? What could he possibly want?"

"Everything....everything he can get!" Delaney's eyes were looking above my head searching somewhere I couldn't see.

"Look, obviously I don't know what's going on—"

"For once we agree, Dr. Holliman. You haven't got a clue about Julian. But I do."

"For Christ's sakes, he's a dying man, Mr. Delaney!"

"What!" Delaney stopped cold and focused his full attention on me. I had really spilled the beans, and I wasn't sure what to say. "Oh, for God's sakes, Holliman, what did he tell you?"

"...I wasn't supposed to say anything. I'm a fool to let it slip, and I'm sorry! I didn't want to upset you, but, yes, Mr. Reynolds told me that he has a very limited time left. Six months to a year at most. He told me Crayden would be his last philanthropy."

Delaney dropped his head like he had been bludgeoned. He leaned forward standing with his hands on my desk. His shoulder shook with deep sobs.

"Mr. Reynolds, let me get you a chair—"

Slowly his head rose in a kind of grimace, and I realized he was laughing. Finally, he took in enough air for a deep, full guffaw to escape from deep inside his gut.

After a moment, he composed himself enough to speak, "H-his last philanthropy! Ha, ha, that's amazing! His last and his first! Dr. Holliman, you have been treated to a performance of exquisite perfection. Six months? A year, maybe? The man is *my* age. How long do you think *either* of us might have? Of course he's dying! Everyone's dying! You have to listen for the things Julian *doesn't* say. He's playing you for a fool, which means he's after something—something big enough to bother to play to your sympathies."

"I'm sure Mr. Reynolds has everything he could possibly need—"

"It's not about need! It's not even about the prize! It's about 'winning!' Men like Julian make money as a by-product of their real ambitions. What he's after is 'reprisal'. He wants to 'get even' with everyone, the World...Life! No one can be better, be happier, have more! He has to have the 'most' of everything. Whatever it is! He's been competing with me since I first met him!"

"But...he told me—"

"We grew up together? We did. That's true—well, not strictly speaking 'together'. Julian has never been 'together' with anyone in his life. Julian is with Julian. Everyone else is just a prop."

I knew enough to remain silent. Delaney was not a man to talk about personal issues, and this seemed so totally out of character, that I was literally forced into silence. Finally he spoke.

"...Just exactly what did Julian tell you, Dr. Holliman?"

I didn't know what to say. I mumble something about "Not wanting to violate his confidence any more than I already had."

"Fine. I will respect your misplaced sense of loyalty. Let's start with the truth. Like all good fabulists, I'm sure Julian was careful not to stray too far from the facts. Did he reveal the reasons he came to 'live' with us?"

"Well, he did say something about that, yes."

"He's Jewish. I presume he told you that." I nodded. "Good. That saves quite a bit dancing about. It was New York in the twenties. Julian didn't have a mother. She died on the boat during the crossing; I'm not sure of what. His father was a ruthless, ambitious immigrant. Early on he had amassed quite a fortune right out of the slums. He made most of his money in scrap metal and the like, but he also owned real estate and other holdings. He was quite brilliant with money, but he had no time for Julian. Julian was 'kept' with other families, reputable Jewish families, for pay. He got food, a clean place to stay, and not one scrap of affection or warmth. He was always 'the border'. No one hurt him, but no one cared for him either. At least that's what he told me once after too much beer on a summer night in college.

"My father was 'old money', but he was what they used to call a 'plunger'. He liked speculation. Through most of the twenties, that kind of temperament made lots of money. Times were fat! The firm his father began was flying high, but every now and then, Dad's mercurial style put the business in temporary difficulties, so he'd borrow money from somewhere, anywhere until he could 'fly' his way out of it, and he usually did. A lot of our friends "flew" with Dad. Joe Delaney was quite a miracle man! But this one time he had backed a bond that was no good. We lost big. He couldn't find the kind of money he needed to trade his way back on top. That's when Julian's father came into the picture. Rabinowitz arrived at my father's office just when Dad was contemplating the 'unthinkable'—bankruptcy. He had an offer for Dad, salvation with a string."

"That you take in Julian?"

"'Take in' is good. It describes the transaction, but it was we who were really taken in. Julian arrived bag and baggage at our house. Those haunted brown eyes of his 'took in' the whole situation, and right away Julian knew the deal! He was to become Gentile—Christianized, made acceptable to the Uptown Establishment. We were to play the 'Pygmalion' game with him. In return, Rabinowitz gave Dad the loan he needed to keep the firm afloat. I found out later that the terms of the deal were ruinous. The interest was so high that my father had to harness all his skills just to keep the firm's nose above water. And into the bargain there was Julian, a 'cousin' I was to introduce to my friends, take to school, be a 'companion' to! For the money he lent, Rabinowitz bought my family, Dr. Holliman. We were indentured to Rabinowitz from that day on.

"And Julian was quick to the game! My poor mother fell for his 'Lost Little Boy' act! She fussed over him and squandered her warmth on him as if he were her own son. Julian was like a bottomless pit for her affection. He swallowed it whole, drained her emotionally, and always managed to make her feel as though she wasn't doing enough. He bled her emotionally just the way his father bled Dad for his talent in business. She would fret over him as though he were an ailing child on the verge of death! 'Did Julian do all right in school today, Cam? Does he have any friends? Why doesn't Julian laugh more? Cam, why aren't you nicer to Julian!'

"I tried. I actually tried to make him into the brother I didn't have, but Julian never responded to me that way. I was his 'tour' guide in this new world, and he was a quick study. Mother absolutely adored him! To her dying day she worried about his 'adjustment' to this new life. She compensated for his strange coldness, and told herself it was just his losing his mother so young. She celebrated his every accomplishment as if it were a miracle. When he nearly made the Olympics in swimming, Mother was delirious with it! Her last words were for Julian. He 'couldn't make it' when she was dying, but she didn't mind. She hoped that she had given him at least a little idea of a mother..."

Delaney caught himself for a moment and then looked up.

"I sound like a jealous, bitter old man, don't I? I suppose I am. At first, Dad was cold to Julian, didn't like him at all. It was later that he was taken in by him too. When we were older, he took us to work in the firm. What they call summer internships today. He called it 'showing us the ropes'. Julian was a prodigy. Within two weeks of being in Dad's office, Julian knew the workings of the entire firm. He had the feel of the place almost by intuition. He seemed to know just what Dad was planning in his investment strategies, and he understood what equities were good and which ones were not worth the paper they were printed on. Julian would discuss the markets for hours with my Father while I delivered the mail and chatted up the secretaries! My father was dazzled by his acumen even though he didn't entirely trust him! 'You ought to tear a page from Julian's book, Cam. He's a sharp one! By God, he's got the stuff!'

"He had the 'stuff' all right. When we were at college, the Crash came. Dad had been smarter than most and kept the Firm liquid. Except for his debt to Rabinowitz the Firm was poised to ride out the Depression while other investment houses were closing their doors. Julian told his father about Dad's clever move. All that cash when Cash was King! Rabinowitz swooped down and called his loan. With everything tanking, Rabinowitz was eager to grab a wad of ready cash, and he had determined that the cash in Dad's firm actually belonged to him. I supposed it did. Dad had no choice but to pay. The interest on the original loan had more than repaid the principle, but the terms held the Firm responsible for the entire amount. I think it was then that it finally sank into my Father's mind that Rabinowitz owned him outright. High-flying Joe Delaney was grounded."

Delaney paused for a moment, pinching the bridge of his nose as if he were squeezing away the images.

"So there you are. It's a little Shakespearean, I suppose. Old men's stories often are."

He had left out his father's suicide, if Julian's account was accurate, and I was sure it was. He also left out the part about his taking up the family cross, clearing the debt and restoring the Firm at least partly. I couldn't ask him for confirmation.

"Be very careful, Dr. Holliman. What looks like a helping hand may wind up becoming a slap in the face. But then, I'm the enemy. You have no reason to listen to me. I've taken too much of your time. Good day, Dr. Holliman, and good luck."

Delaney left the office as abruptly as he had arrived. He left me groping for a perspective in this strange contention between him and Julian. Why had Julian asked him to resign? Why could he possibly want that? Moreover, why had Julian painted a picture of fond acquaintance with Delaney, when it was so clear that Delaney was anything but fond of him? It *was* Shakespearean. It seemed like I had been absorbing nothing but the stories of old men. I was losing my grounding in the present at a time when it was becoming increasingly vital that I keep both my feet on the pavement!

CHAPTER 27

He was silent sitting in a corner patiently waiting for me.

The maté sat on my desk as I entered my office. I had been meeting with the architects about the proposed renovation. It was close to 10:30, and I was dead tired.

"Santiago...I'm very tired tonight. Would it be all right if we recorded another time?"

"It is well. Another time. No time. It is what *you* wish."

"I want to hear about Tlaloc; I-I'm just so tired..."

"...You drink the maté. It makes you feel good. I sit with you. I go."

His complete submission to my whim filled me with guilt. I had promised myself to be the friend I should be to him. I promised myself to be patient, to stop fantasizing the ridiculous and just listen; only now I didn't feel like listening. The meeting had knocked the wind out of me. Drawings and charts had been all over the table. Schedules and codes—it was a complete haze in my mind, and I was supposed to keep track of it all!

"It goes well. I see it. I see smiling people. I see you standing with Top Men. The Gods smile on this work."

"That's very comforting, Santiago. Right now I feel like one of those warriors Tlaloc saw sacrificed with his heart ripped out of his chest and his body kicked down the stairs."

"...That is an honor. To be given to the Gods, it is a great power..."

"Of course, I'm sorry! It was a stupid joke! I'm exhausted, and I guess I just don't have much sensitivity to anyone else's life right now. That's why I think we should record you later."

"You drink. You feel better." He held his own cup as he always did waiting for me to begin. It was an old ritual between us, and he was right. There was a kind of comfort in it.

I picked up the cup and sipped deeply. The sugar was more plentiful than usual. I sipped again tasting the sweetness and remembering the old boiler room in the basement. That would change. There would be a new system. Everything would change. Everything I remembered that held me to Crayden was going to disappear. The basement would be transformed into a swimming pool, and Santiago's room...well, that would be swept away too. The maté was stronger than usual tonight. As I sipped, I noticed a distinct under-taste I had never noticed before. It wasn't unpleasant, but it was...different...

***

"English' they call themselves, but this is not their world. They are traders and travelers looking for what they can take from this place. Water-houses, 'ships' they call them, come and go all the time. It is summer, but not the summer of my home. The trees are beaten down and the plants trampled. The smell of animal skins is everywhere. In the storehouses great piles of skins are tied waiting to be sent away. Flies and mosquitos bite, and there is the stink of too many everywhere. Such people! They are loud. They are always angry. Languages I hear that I do not hear before. Once I hear the words of the Blacks from the ship, and I turn to see the man and his boy, but I see no one. There are Blacks in the cellars, in the corners of the houses, in the barns in the working places. They work and sweat and say nothing that anyone hears but me. I know their secret words.

"There are others there too. Strange people who live separate from the rest. They pray to their God in a way I never see. They do not pray to the Man Upon the Tree. They do not believe in this Jesus. These people interest me, but they do not see me.

"Here, too, no one sees me. It is good they do not. I am the only one of my kind. There are men from everywhere, but not like me. Ships come. Some carry Mixed-Bloods; I see them, but I do

not talk to them. For now I must learn this place. I must be far away from my people so that the cat does not find them.

"At first I walk the edges of the village. I see what they are. I watch what they do. One thing I see first—the gold I have—they must not know about. I find a place by a tree with two trunks, and I bury it for safekeeping. It is the God they worship above their Jesus! I see them steal from one another. I hear them lie. I watch them take anything they can when no one looks, but I am silent.

"I do not need gold now. For days I live outside the village in the trees. Two great rivers run on either side of the village. They are too wide to swim, but there are many fish. I hunt. There is enough for me to live. All this while I look for the man and his boy, but I never see them.

"One night I am roasting a fish by a small fire. There is a sound in the trees. Someone is watching. I pretend not to see. I feel him move closer to me. I know he will spring soon, but I am quicker! I jump at the place where he hides, and I land on him. He cries out and struggles. I have my knife at his throat, and I say in my language, 'Move and I spill your blood for the Gods! They drink their fill!'

"The body beneath me goes slack. There is no sound, no movement. I shift my weight and turn him to see what I have caught. It is a boy! Not yet fully grown. His knife is buried deep inside his chest. He falls on it when I jump on him. He is bleeding, and he soon slips into the ground I think.

"Then there is another on me! This one fights like a storm. Arms and legs are everywhere. There are no words. This one has me around the throat with a stick and pulls at my breath. I can feel my spirit trying to fly away, but I do not let that happen. I reach with all my strength behind my head. I feel the shoulders of my attacker, and I push at the spot where it is soft between the neck and the back. I hear the warrior scream in pain and the hold on my throat is gone. Air rushes back into my lungs and my mind comes back to me. I turn grabbing a stone to kill this one, and I lift it high above my head to bring it down and smash the brains out. It is then that I see. This one is a

woman, a girl, young and tall. She fights like a man! She is pounding at my face and head trying to hold back the stone I have raised at her head.

"I hold for a moment, and she kicks with her knee, and the sharp pain between my legs makes me double up on the ground. She also falls back, the pain in her arms still pinching them down. We are both silent, breathing hard side by side on the ground our eyes fixed on each other looking for the next attack.

"The boy coughs blood, and the girl is up shaking him in spite of the pain I know she still feels. I move away enough to be out of her reach still trying to get to my knees.

"'His blood is draining out,' I tell her. 'You must hold it back, or he dies.'

"She says something in yet another language I do not know, but I understand from her saying that she hates me for the wounding of the boy.

"'It is not my fault. He attacks me. Let me show you—' I move toward the boy, but she grabs a stick and is ready to try to kill me all over again. I hold up my hand to show her that I have no weapon. I move slowly to the dying boy. She is watching me with an eye ready to strike.

"I can feel that the boy still has his spirit, but not much longer. I reach around the blade of the knife buried to its hilt in his chest. I press hard on the places where the blood seeps. The boy cries out and his eyes open. She strikes me with the stick, but I do not let go.

"'Stop! See, he lives! Come here and help me if you want him to live!' She does not understand my words, but she seems to know that I do not mean to cause any more harm. I motion for her to come to the boy and help. I put her hands on the places I can feel the blood flowing, and I make her press down. The blood slows and nearly stops. Carefully I look at the wound. The knife has gone deep into the lungs. I must take the knife out without doing more damage.

"Slowly I pull straight back on the knife, and I feel it give in my *hand. I move it out slowly to be sure that nothing else is cut. The girl holds the same places to keep the blood from spilling out any more than we can help. The boy cries out at the pulling of the blade.*

"'Be silent!' I tell him. 'What I do, the Gods must approve, or you will slip into the earth.' He does not understand me, but he is silent now. He is weak but awake. The pain is deep and it tries to pull him into darkness, but I keep talking to him in my language, and he seems to want to listen.

"I put the blade of his knife into the red place in the fire and I blow to make it as hot as I can make it. I cleanse it in the fire on both sides. When the blade is as hot as I can make it, I quickly slip it back into the wound. The meat of his chest sizzles, and the boy cries out loud. Suddenly he falls silent. I can see that he has hidden in the darkness where the pain cannot reach him. This is good. I must repeat this action again. The girl watches me and listens to my words. She does not know what I am doing, but she understands that I mean no harm. I motion to her to release the pressure on the boy's chest. I check to see if there is more blood, but there is none. For now he sleeps. By morning he either dies or feels the pain of more life. I pack his swelling wound with a root paste I make from my bag. The paste will stop the wound from going rotten, but the body must decide if it has enough blood left to live. Now he is in the hands of the Gods, and I go back to my fire and the fish I was roasting.

"The fish is still on the stick but has fallen in the dirt outside the fire ring. I brush off the dirt of the forest floor and push the stick back into the ground so that the fish hangs over the flames to finish cooking. All the time the girl watches me with a combination of mistrust and surprise.

"We are both silent, exhausted from our fight and the helping of the boy. The boy sleeps deeply. Soon the fish is cooked, and I pull it from the fire. I put half on a leaf and push it over to the girl. The other half I eat greedily. She takes the fish suddenly and eats all the while watching me. She does not trust that I do not try to kill her again even though it is she who tries to kill me first.

"I sing softly to the Gods and I pray for the boy's life. She does not join me, but she watches my every move. The boy remains deeply breathing on the ground. To appease the Gods I give blood. She makes a noise when I draw the blade on my own flesh, but she does not try to stop me. She watches as I let my blood spill on the ground and continue my praying. She watches also as my cuts begin to close. This she watches most of all. She never sees this before.

"By morning the boy is awake again. He is thirsty, and I give him water to drink. I motion to the girl that I must find food for him if he is to heal further. I go the river and take the small shell animals I see the 'English' take from the rocks around the shore. I open these with my knife and smell. There is life in these! I can smell the ocean water in them and the soft animal inside has the smell of strength and goodness in it. These I bring back in plenty. Some the girl and I feed to the boy. He eats two or three, and we eat the rest. He sleeps again, but now it is a real sleep not a hiding in the darkness from pain. His body has enough blood to stay alive I think, but he must rest a long while.

"After we eat, this tall girl and I sit looking at each other. She talks to me in questions I do not understand, but there is something in the way she says the words that gives me the meaning.

"She looks me up and down, and her words tell me that she sees me as short and ugly. I laugh.

"I look at her. I feel her arm and leg muscles, and I say to her, 'You have the strength of a man, but big as you are, girl, you are not stronger than me!' She is not like the 'English'. She is not like the Spanish, and she is not like any of the ones I see at the village. She is like me, but not like me. She is as tall and handsome, as I am short and ugly, but she is more like me than the Mixed-Bloods I see on the ships.

"In her own words she tells me that the boy is hers—a brother, I guess. They are not from the village of the 'English', but they are from another village somewhere nearby. She and her brother see me and watch me. Her brother thinks I am a demon

197

or something come from the earth to kill them. He waits for me—to kill me. She does not want this, but he is a boy and does not listen.

"I ask her where the village is. I tell her we must take her brother there in a day or two so that he can heal among his own, but she pretends not to understand this. I think she does not want me to know the place of her people.

"In the next day the boy is stronger, but not yet able to stand. He talks to his sister. She tells him what she knows of me. I know she tells him of the healing. She tells him also of the praying I do and the giving of blood. This last I know because she shows him the cutting of my arm and points to the place where now there is no wound. The boy listens with round eyes and says little. He thinks. He is young, but I see in him a deep thinker, one who looks into the things around him to find the reasons for their being. Finally he says something quietly to his sister.

"'Ahh! Hai!' She says sucking in air. I can see she is excited by the boy's words, but I pretend to be sharpening my knife. I do not want them to know that I am understanding some of their words. The boy tells her that I am some kind of magic man. He believes me to be something half spirit, half man come to save them. From that time she is careful with me. She does not show so much doubt, but she is careful still. If the boy is wrong, she wants to be ready for me!

"I make another trip to the river for the shell creatures, and I catch a huge fish. These I bring back and begin to make a fire. The girl stops me and takes over the fire-making. I go to the fish to gut it and make it ready, but she takes the fish from me as well. She says words in her language and motions for me to sit by the boy. I am not sure what she wants, but I can tell she speaks with great respect. I go and sit by the boy and watch her prepare what I have brought. The boy speaks to me. He wishes me to understand that she does only what a woman must do. It is a woman's place to make the food the man has caught.

"We fall into silence as we watch his sister work. Finally, after much thinking, the boy asks me a question. I am not sure at

first, and then he repeats, and the meaning becomes clearer.

"'Are you a lost spirit?' is the question he asks me. 'You are not like our people, but you are not like the ghost skins in the wooden camp. Have you come from beyond life? Your magic is powerful, yet you do not use it against us. What are you?'

"I know this last question. I understand his need to know what stops me from killing both of them.

"I point to his chest, and I lift my arms up to the heavens to show how I pray.

"'A shaman! You are a shaman! A Healer and a spirit-caller!' The boy is very excited. He calls to the girl and says these same words to her. I do not understand what she says back, but the boy moves closer to me, and he looks into my eyes. He looks deep inside my eyes like he is looking through my body into my soul. He is searching me. He does this in a way I do not know in a long time. It is in the way of the Priest-Father and the other teachers long ago. But this is strange in one so young. This looking is hard to bear, but I stand up to it. I must not be weak.

"The boy says words now that I do not understand. His sister looks back at him in surprise and fear, I think. She does not believe his words, this I can tell. She talks to him.

"'No, you are wrong,' she says. 'You do not know that. It is not possible. Such things cannot be in the living world!' I do not know these words when she says them. She tells me this later, when I am among them. The boy is quiet and sure. He says what he says again, and we all fall silent. I am fighting to understand. I know that what he says is somehow important, but I do not know in what way. Not yet."

CHAPTER 28

I wasn't even aware of it happening. I had been sitting there listening with the recorder on. The headache I had been gathering was gone. My fatigue was gone. It was almost midnight. I reached over and turned the switch.

"Santiago, it's late. My wife will worry if I don't return now!"

"It is well. She sleeps, but you go now. You are well?"

"Yes...Yes! I feel—great!" I did feel well. I felt as if I had slept the whole night, but only an hour and a half had passed. I was wide awake. My shoulders were relaxed—that's where tension settled in my body. My mind was at ease, and the meeting was clearly registered in my memory. I remembered the schedules and the stages of renovation, the impact of each stage on the operation of the school and the contingency plans for each possible interruption in the organization of the transformation! It seemed simple. As well, I remembered all of Santiago's story. I paused for a moment and looked at him.

"...Something is wrong?" He asked this in a way that told me he was expecting my question.

"...Where is Tlaloc?..."

"...You do not want to know this question...you do not believe in Tlaloc."

"...I know you believe in him. Believe you *are* him...Where is he?"

"I am here."

"...Here...before the buildings, the people...?"

"Before all. There is forest. The Europeans are few. Ships are all they have. They hunt. They eat only a small part of the land now. They build poor wooden places. They fight. They do not see me, but I see them. They are not much different than the Spanish. I watch them a long time. I wait...a long time."

I absorbed what he said. "Yes, I guess it would be a long time. I have to go."

I turned to leave. Just as I reached the office door I heard him say, "No one stops you. I do not let that happen. Not the thief or the old one."

I stopped in my tracks and turned to him, "What do you mean 'not the thief'?

"They do not stop you. You are the Angry Young Lord. The Gods give me to you. I keep you well."

"Santiago, what do you mean by 'not the thief'? Do you mean Soldani?"

He looked at me with a completely blank face. There was no flicker of emotion.

"I do not know this man."

"The thin man with the glasses from the museum—did you see him?"

"I do not know this man..." The old man pulled himself inside, and he shut me out of his mind. He seemed hurt by my questions. The suspicion I held for the moment was something I didn't want to think about. It was absurd! I reminded myself of what Nick had said "Go back to basic laws." He was *not* Tlaloc. He was an old man. This story was a tribal memory... It had to be. This latest...chapter. This personal narrative was just a way to keep my attention. That's all it could be. I was not going to let my imagination run away with me again! Why was I torturing myself this way? *"Go home,"* I thought. *"Go to bed."*

Santiago got up slowly. The stoic look never left his face, but his eyes were softer now. He had forgiven me; I was sure of that. He was clear. He took my cup. He walked past me to the door and stepped through.

As he did so, he said, "...It is a great power..." and he was gone

***

"He's got to go! He's standing in your way, Holliman! He's going to continue to harass this change as long as he's Chairman of the Board. Do you know what his latest little maneuver is? Goddamn Landmarks! He's petitioning the Landmarks Commission to halt the renovation until they determine that we're in full compliance. Christ, what a pisser! First he's trying to get me to hustle the thing up, and now he doesn't want it! That what you want, Sonny-Jim? I know Cam! He's a tightass son-of-a-bitch, and he won't let go as long as he draws a breath!"

Julian was amazingly animated for a man who expected to die momentarily. He sat behind his huge desk in a new glass and steel tower on 55th street. The entire office was sleek marble and polished wood. It was spare and flooded with light. Julian's eyes were dancing with energy as he discussed Cameron Delaney. He wasn't at all the ponderously moving elderly man I had seen at the presentation ceremony only a few weeks ago. I had come to see Reynolds to stop his push to remove Delaney from the Board.

"Crayden is all he has. We can't take that away from him. You must know that."

"Godammit, this is business!" Julian slammed his pudgy fist on his desk with fury. He stood and glowered at me as his face flushed red. "If you're going to turn into a sentimental little girl on me, I've got no use for you, Holliman!"

"I wasn't aware you were using me, Julian"

"Cute! Understated outrage with just a hint of hurt feelings. For Christ's sakes, Holliman, you got me into this! Well, now I'm in! Checks have been passed—and cashed, and I'm going to make Goddamn sure this little 'gift' of mine goes the right way!"

"And what way is that?"

"Who does he think he is, playing with *me*? I'm not some pushover, soft-centered little academic! He wants to play? Fine! Let's play! I've started putting pressure on that assortment of little toadies he calls his Board. I'll own them before he changes his Goddamn underwear! You're going to be hearing from them very soon. You're going to suggest *strongly* that Cameron Delaney should be voted out as chairman, and then you're going to suggest that you might be able to persuade me to fill in, in a titular way only, as Chairman until a more appropriate choice can be made."

"I don't know that a 'soft-centered little academic' like me can do that, Julian"

"You will if you want to stay as Headmaster at Crayden! I can make a couple of phone calls, and you can be disposed of like yesterday's trash."

"First Mr. Delaney and now you. I seem to have cornered the market in venal old men...I won't make it easy. I have a contract."

"Oh, please do! My lawyers are always hungry. I haven't fed them in a while. You should make a nice hors d'eouvre for 'em!"

"Fine." I got up to leave, weary of watching him rage and gloat. It was a little like watching Mr. Dithers in the comic strips when I was a kid, stomping and fuming at Dagwood Bumstead. It occurred to me as I was getting up that there weren't too many people who even remembered "Blondie." "Whatever you have to do, Julian, I guess you'll do, but I'm not going to join you in destroying Cameron Delaney, whatever your reasons. I wanted to save Crayden. What a crime! What a terrible thing to want to keep a great old school like Crayden going and offering kids what both of us had a chance to get. See you around, Julian. Good to see you feeling better."

"...Hang on, Holliman. Sit back down..."

Reynolds was silent for a moment. He looked at me taking stock of the conversation. He took a deep breath, and I saw his eyes dance brighter than before. Then he simply sat back down at his desk completely calm.

"...Go ahead with everything. I'll leave Cam alone."

"I...don't understand."

"Listen, Sonny-Jim, we made an agreement; we're partners in this little enterprise. The first time we met, you were an eager little 'missionary' trying to pull the rug out from an old bastard who was chewing your ass! You were hungry for the green I was spreading around, that much was obvious, but so is everyone else around me! Flatter the old prick! Stroke him good, and get some goodies out of him! Christ, I own a building full of 'em! Now you come in here and ask me to lay off on the old bastard! You've got a Goddamn conscience! You've got 'principles'. What the hell do I do with that? You're not just sucking up for the money I'm donating, so what good are you to me? I can't control you, and you're not going to roll over for some ready cash....I guess that makes you the right guy for the job."

"...Come again?"

"You want to know why I threatened Cam with removal from the Board."

"All right, you could start there."

"I had to let Cam know, he's not unshakeable. He's got to get on board or we—you and I—might *have* to remove him eventually. Are you prepared for that if it happens?"

"...I'm not comfortable with it."

"I didn't ask you that! Oh, don't look like I just kicked your pet puppy! I don't think there's anything Cam can do that I can't get around, but suppose I'm gone. I have to know that you'll do what it takes to push this thing through."

"Look, Julian, I'm just Headmaster of Crayden—for the next two and half years. I don't have that authority or that influence."

"You do now. I intend to name you the head of the Julian Reynolds Foundation. When I'm gone, you'll be responsible for not only the Crayden project, but a host of other philanthropic associations and endeavors. Most of the stuff runs itself. You won't have much more to do than you do now. Job comes with a $250,000.00 annual salary. Interested?"

"I...I like my current job, Julian."

"Then keep it! No reason you can't! I'm talking about free money, Sonny-Jim. You got something against making six figures for doing practically nothing?"

"It's a very tempting offer."

"Good! Give in to it! It's a satisfying experience. Look, Holliman, I have no kids, no close friends, no...attachments. What I have is this business and the Foundation it supports. The Foundation is all that will carry my name. I'd like to have somebody running it who has some balls. Why not you?"

"...You don't know me that well."

"I just met you! I'll have the papers sent to your office tomorrow. Talk it over with your wife, your shrink, your local bartender—whoever you need to. If I get the papers back, you're on. That square with you?"

This was not the meeting I was expecting to have with Julian. Then nothing since I arrived back in New York was what I was expecting.

I didn't know why, but I kept hearing Santiago's words. "... It is a great power."

CHAPTER 29

"Jesus, Brad it was weird. It was like I was watching myself in an old horror movie."

"Did you see him come in?"

"No! That was spooky. Not a sound. No creaking door. No footsteps. Nothing! I looked up from my lab table, and there he was practically nose-to-nose with me! I think I yelped!"

"He does that with me too! He comes and goes—there's no warning, no movement or sound to let you know he's there. He just is! And when he wants to, he's gone!"

"He didn't say a word! He just sits down and rolls up his sleeve."

"What?"

"He asks me, 'You are doctor?'"

"'Not really—' I started to say."

"'Cut!'"

"You didn't do it, did you?"

"Hold on—I asked him what the problem was, and I told him I wasn't that kind of doctor, but he still sat there.

"'You cut. Here. You see.'

"I told him again, 'Santiago, I'm not a physician—or a surgeon. I don't cut people!' Then he took out his knife and opened it."

"Oh, God..."

"'You want to see. I show you. You see the blood. See the time it holds.' He was just about to stab himself. 'Wait!' I yelled, and he stopped. 'If you want me to take a blood sample, I can do that. 'Take,' he says. So I grabbed a fresh syringe, and I took a good sample"

"...He came to you to give a blood sample?"

"Wait. It gets better—or worse depending on your perspective. After I had taken the sample, he still sat there. 'Cut,' he says, 'I show you what the Gods do.'

"'Santiago, I have the blood, that isn't necessary!'

"'Cut!' he says. 'You cut, you see. Then you know—*he* knows.'"

"What did you do?"

"I knew if I didn't do it, he was going to do it to himself, so I pulled out a clean scalpel, and I made a small, superficial incision on his forearm. I was reaching for the alcohol, and he held my hand. Christ, he's got a grip! Brad...that incision closed up right in front of me! It was just a nick, but enough to allow a trickle of blood. In a matter of seconds the blood clotted and the wound...began to...knit. The tissues were almost visibly repairing!"

"Well,...isn't that what happens?"

"Yes! But not like that! Not that fast! I held him there for half-an-hour, and in that time the incision was only a red line. It was closed! 'Now you see,' he says. 'You tell only him. No one else. He believes you.'"

"Did he seem...manic? Disturbed?"

"Nothing. He calmly walked out. No discussion. No drama. Gone..."

"He didn't say anything else to you?"

"No. Nothing. He picked up a mop and bucket and walked away somewhere. I'm not sure where. I can see why you've been weirded out by him, but I don't think he's dangerous to anyone...This is more than story-telling, Brad. What he showed me—what I saw...is not normal!"

"What did you do with the sample?"

"I'm going to analyze it! That first sample wasn't fresh; it was clearly contaminated. This one is brand new. I took it myself. I'm going to take it to a lab I know. I have a friend who really knows what he's doing. I'm going to find out what's happening here!"

"You can't do that! If there is...something.... If someone else finds out about this —"

"...He's cool! This guy I know—he'll be discreet. I won't tell him anything, I promise! Don't you want to know? Don't you want to find out once and for all about Santiago?"

"...I don't know."

"You don't know? Holliman, you've been agonizing over the old man for months! You've been fantasizing all kinds of crap! Now you have a chance to get some hard facts. Christ, he's giving it to you!"

This was more than I wanted to hear. I had gotten comfortable with our previous plan to humor Santiago, to listen sympathetically, and leave the story unchallenged. I wasn't prepared for this new wrinkle, and Nick's adamant demand that I get "hard facts" put me right back in the hot seat.

"What happens to Santiago?"

"Nothing. Why should something happen to him?..."

"C'mon, Nick. Suppose there is something—"

"That's not going to happen!"

"You said yourself, it wasn't normal the way his flesh healed! Suppose there is something. Something nobody's seen before. How long do you think it'll be before your 'Cool Guy' breaks for the medical journals or the newspapers? How long before Santiago becomes an anomaly—a medical phenomenon—A one-man fountain of youth?"

"You mean 'Tlaloc', don't you?"

"...OK...suppose...just suppose he *is* Tlaloc—"

"Now I know you've lost it!"

"You said it wasn't 'normal'!"

"Jesus Christ, Holliman, it's a far cry from 'not normal' to immortal! Where the hell is your sense of proportion? That's the difference between Science and the Arts. In Science we look for facts—evidence. In the Arts you keep looking for the fucking rainbow! Get off the Yellow-Brick Road! It's leading you nowhere!"

"All right...all right...I know you're right, but what do I do with him...for him—with all the changes that are coming...He can't be here much longer anyway. It'll be hard enough to tell him that his job is over. Now I've got to persuade him to see a doctor—accept some kind of care. There's no family. Barbara suggested I check into that, but we found no one."

"He seems pretty bonded to you. I think he'll do just about anything you ask of him."

"Shit!...Maybe there's something in the Reynolds Foundation that could take care of this..."

"Reynold's Foundation? What have they got to do with this?"

"He offered me the job. Running the Foundation"

"Jeez! Reynolds hired you? What about Crayden?"

"I can stay here. It's mostly oversight and rubber-stamping projects, according to Reynolds. I can stay here and run the school. If I take it."

"Does it pay anything?"

"Yeah! 250K a year! Maybe they have a charity or something that would have a place for Santiago..."

"You need an assistant or anything?" Nick was smiling, but I could tell he was impressed with the offer.

"I haven't talked to Barbara about it yet. I just had a meeting with him this morning. I don't know why, but I'm not sure it's the right thing to do."

"If you don't want it—I'll take it! What are you, nuts? 250K to be a rubber stamp! You need to think about it?"

"He's... a manipulative S.O.B. I don't know if I can trust the offer...but it might be just the position I need to help Santiago."

Asking Santiago to surrender himself to the hands of strangers in a place he had never been before—it was a responsibility I didn't want to accept. In unfamiliar surroundings without the activity of work...how long would he last like that? I guessed I'd better research this Foundation. Maybe I could help him. Maybe not.

CHAPTER 30

"They live small. The land is a spirit for them. They do not give the blood to Huizilopochtli, and they do not know the Serpent. They take no slaves, make no sacrifices. They do not eat the flesh of the enemy and take in his strength. They do not have great temples, and they do not have a great King. It is the women who carry the family. The husband joins her family. The men have powers in council and ceremony and in war. They count their time by Sun and Moon, but they do not know how the heavens move, nor can they write their stories for their children as we. They have healing, but it is small, simple. They die as we from the sicknesses of these Europeans. This group is only a fragment of a once larger one. They sit and tell of the ones gone into the earth. They tell of times from far ago when they are strong; and they sing about the earth and the sun and the moon. Birds they sing of and hunting and the battles they fight. They sing to the spirit of the land, the place they go when they slip into the earth. There is nothing big about them, but they are plain and real. They live from day to day without holding on to anger and greed like the 'English'. They do not live in fear of thirsty Gods who demand their blood as we do, nor do they build great cities to be put in order and kept. Grace lives in their quiet times and the smiles between them. It is a great thing. Each day comes and goes like a breeze, and I am taken in with them!

"The woman and her brother keep me. She is called Anasan, and the boy is Oratamin. The tribe is tall and handsome. To them I am a runt, ugly and strange, but they take me. In time they see me as their own because of the boy and his sister. I am never part of someone. Not with my own and not even with the

Priest-Father. This is more than I know from all my time..."

Without any fanfare he reached into his shirt and took out a small, oval object and placed it into my hands. It was the miniature portrait on ivory I had seen when Santiago had first started this long narrative of Tlaloc. I looked at the faded image in its tiny filigree frame. There was the lovely, dark girl staring sad and silent across the two hundred or so years since the image must have been painted.

"...Santiago, who is this woman? Is this Anasan?" He looked at me with hollow, haunted eyes and said nothing for a long moment.

"*...The boy Oratamin has the Sight. Not so much as my Priest-Father or me when we chew the plant, but he has it without the plant. His Sight is not so clear or so long, but he Sees. The Tribe knows this. He is much valued. He is too young for council, but the elders come to him and ask what comes, and he tells them what he Sees. He saves them many times. He Sees me! He knows a little of what I am, but not all.*

"*'Tlaloc, you teach me. You are from before; you are from now. You have a great power in you. You teach me. I learn from you.'*

"*Anasan hears this. I look to her and she lowers her eyes. 'Why do you look away from me? Am I so ugly?'*

"*'...You are ugly, yes. Small and rough like a toad. But that does not make me look away.'*

"*'I offend you. I wound Oratamin. You are angry with me.'*

"*'You save him, too...you...use a healing I do not understand...You frighten me! I would not keep you, but Oratamin says we must. He has magic...like you. He says we keep you.' She goes back to her work and does not look at me.*

"*'Now you take me and show me your magic! You are with us. We make it so. You are one of the Tribe. I am young; I have much to learn from you.'*

"*I take him to the woods, but there are very few plants like the ones I know. Some I recognize. These I tell him. I show him a moss to keep the rot from a wound. There is a plant to make the heart beat stronger when it is weak. There are some that grow in the warm months that are close to those I know. These I teach also. 'Dry these and keep. In winter you use them until they grow again.' From my seeds I plant, including the plant that gives Sight. This grows but only in summer when it is warm, and only in certain places. This I tell him can kill him if he uses more than once during the cycle of the moon. I take him to a place away from the Tribe, and I tell him to chew and swallow the spit. This he does. He falls, and I think I kill him. He does not move. I cannot feel him breathe, but my touch tells me he is like dead, but not dead. He is this way for four days. In that time Anasan finds us.*

"What do you do to him!' she screams. 'You kill him when he takes you to us and gives you our home?'

"No!' I answer. 'I give him what he asks for. He takes the plant that gives Sight. He does this because he wants it! I do not make him!'

"You do not stop him either, you ugly toad! He has the Sight! He does not need your plants! You kill him!'

"She is on me with her knife drawn. She kills me if she can. We fight like animals. I do not want to kill her, but I know I can. She moves like a great cat. She is deadly if I am not awake watching her. Then Oratamin comes awake.

"Stop, Anasan! Stop what you do! I have Seen...much! More than I see before. Tlaloc is a Traveler. We are his rest. You more than me, but you must not fight him!'

"She leaves off me and stands away breathing deeply of hatred and killing in her heart.

"He takes you from us! He brings you here; you are dead upon the ground. What am I to think?'

"Am I dead? Am I harmed?'

"You are dead! I know what I see!'

"I am between Life and Death. I am where I fly above the ground and days and nights. I see ahead and behind. What I see saves us...All but you, Tlaloc. You are the Traveler. With us you rest, but you go ahead...far.'

"It is my curse. I carry many with me, but I am alone.' This I say but Oratamin laughs. He takes my hand and says like he is a careless child, 'Not for now! Not alone for now! I see what you do not! One like you in blue feathers, smelling of old blood comes. He says it cannot be, but I see what is. This one, Anasan, is your rest. This one gives you a space within her.'

"Stupid boy! I give this one nothing! I do not like him! He is a toad, and he brings us great harm!'

"He saves us! What he shows me saves us. You give him everything. I see this! Tlaloc knows what he cannot know, feels what he cannot feel. With you Tlaloc knows what a man can know. It gives him everything and takes everything from him. Tlaloc, rest! Be at peace while you can.'

"You make no sense. What he does to you makes you foolish! I kill him for it!'

"You do not kill him. Even now you are wondering. Even now, your heart thinks of the toad and changes. Can you feel it?'

"I am done with you both!' Anasan leaves us, and Oratamin laughs, and he dances! I know this dance! It is the dance I show you when you have a prize! This I do not show him, but he knows! I watch. I hear the tongue of my people! The prayers true and real! When he is done, he sleeps again, but now it is the sleep of the weary. When he wakes, he knows nothing of this. He is as before..."

...As he trailed off I could see him thinking of this scene. Pondering it. I waited a few minutes, but he remained silent.

Finally I spoke, "Then this is Anasan? The Indian Girl. This is her picture?"

"You keep. Is yours now. One comes for you. You go." He stood and heaved a long sigh. As he went back to his "room"—the room which would probably not be there much longer, I switched off the recorder...

CHAPTER 31

"...I came to give you this." Delaney stood at my desk, tall and stiff as he always did in that old-soldier posture of his.

"What is this, Mr. Delaney?"

"It's my resignation as Chairman of the Board of Governors of Crayden. I've sent duplicates to the rest of the Board. Effective immediately, I believe *you* will be filling that post."

"What? What are you talking about?"

"The rest of the Governors drafted and signed a petition asking me to resign. It was delivered to me this morning. They nominated you as my successor. I assume you accept—gladly. Now you have a free hand to finish—-what you have begun. It appears I underestimated you, Dr. Holliman."

"Mr. Delaney, I had no knowledge of this! I would never approach them behind your back— never ask them to do anything of the sort!"

"I would have come during business hours...but I wanted time to verify...the document. I polled every member. Each one used the same phrase— 'new blood'. It was as if they were quoting from a single source. I called your home. Your wife told me I'd find you still in your office. Dedication. That is your strongest...virtue."

"Mr. Delaney—"

"Dr. Holliman, you've won. Allow me the grace of bowing out with some dignity."

"I didn't do this, Mr. Delaney. I would not do this!"

"I know it wasn't you, Dr. Holliman. This has Julian's fingerprints all over it. Blind, bully-boy tactics—that's *his* style. The distinguished men who have helped me all these years on the Board might have resisted in younger years, but now they're old and...tired. I over-taxed them with this little fight of ours. I should have known better...I understand you have signed on as Executive Director of the Reynolds Foundation. Congratulations."

"How did you...? It's a titular position. I am first, and foremost the Headmaster of Crayden!"

"How fortunate for you. Be careful."

Delaney let himself out. His posture was as erect as ever, but this subdued demeanor was something I had never seen in him. As he left, I wondered if I would be seeing him again.

***

"*She watches....*"

"Jesus Christ! Santiago...I'm really not ready for this now!" I had just returned from a Board Meeting. That group of senior gentlemen was quiet and receptive but completely cowed. There was no dialogue. At the end of the meeting, two of them had slipped me their resignations. I didn't know what to do about that. I felt like a barbarian at the gates.

"Time is small. I finish soon. I give everything to you." The maté was on my desk. I had not noticed it.

"I'm just not in the mood! I have to meet my wife—"

"I am not long. Take the maté—"

"I don't want the maté! Santiago, I want to go home to my wife."

"It is well to go home to your woman. You sit...drink. I am not long..."

I realized that he wasn't budging. He sat in the corner where he often did, half in the dark. In exasperation I dropped my notes and papers and sat at the desk. He waited, watching me. Finally I grabbed the cup of maté and sipped pointedly...He waited again...I pulled out the recorder and pressed the button:

"...She stays away from us. From Oratamin and me. She leaves us when we are together. Within the circle of our tribe, she is proud and respectful.

"With the boy, it is questions always. He listens and thinks. The council does not know of me, only that the wise boy and the girl keep me. I show him the healing, and he heals. Things they do not see before. Many are helped. The boy learns fast. He uses the plants I show, but he does not take the plant that gives Sight. I tell him I give it to him, but he says, 'No.' He does not remember the dance or the tongue of my people in his mouth, but he knows he does not want the plant. 'I see without this plant. You know this, Tlaloc. When I look into you, I see you are not the same as other men. I feel it. Yet, you are good.' I wish for him to take the plant. I long to hear my language again, but I do not make him. He is not of my people. It is wrong for me to give it to him before.

"Anasan watches all these things. She sees her brother healing. She sees me telling him. She is like the cat in my dreams. Watching me. Wanting to take my life. One night I can feel her nearby. She is waiting for me to sleep. I wait and pretend to sleep. She is quiet. She comes into the lodge. She is quiet as the cat. I wait a long time. Finally she leaps at me with her knife drawn!

"'Die, you ugly toad! I do not want you! I do not take you! Die now!'

"I catch her as she falls on me. I roll over and pin her to the ground. The knife drops from her hand, and she is under me spitting fire with her eyes. 'You make Oratamin your thing. He is not a brother any more. He is your tool! You take him over with bad magic! You cannot have me!'

"'I do not want you, woman!' I tell her. 'He comes to me for the knowledge; I do not make him! Take him! I do not walk with him again. I leave! I live away from here!'

"'Liar! You know he follows you! You make him follow you. You try to make me—feel for you!'

"'I make no magic! I cast no power over him—or you! I tell you, I do not want you! You are a tall, angry stick! Go from me! I do not look at you!'

"'I see you! Crouching in corners, watching me. I know you look at me! You are not one of us! You are a spirit catcher! A shaman. A thing alone!'

"When she says this, I move away from her. Even without her knife she draws my blood. 'Then kill me! Take your blade— strike! End this long time alone...I will not fight. It is a kindness you do' I turn my back to her and wait for the blow.

"I can hear her breath. She reaches for her knife and picks it up. I close my eyes and wait. I think she is the cat come for me at last. I am gone from my people. I am with these plain ones. Tlaloc has no reason to stay on the earth.

"Then I feel her. Her hand is on my back. She unwinds me from myself and stretches me out. Her hands soothe me, caress me. Her eyes are changed.

"'Take my life! I am a warrior!'

"'Be quiet, you ugly toad...I am taking your life' This she says in a voice so quiet and gentle. She takes away my skins and covering, and she mounts me. I am never with a woman. I see. I know. But the Priest-Father tells me, 'Tlaloc you can never marry. Never make children!' I do not. Tlaloc keeps alone. This...woman is the first...the only one who comes to me. We are like two lizards with no end...no beginning. I am lost in her. When the sun comes, I know she is right. She takes my life."

CHAPTER 32

"There was no Goddamn choice! He's cozy with the Governor, for Christ's sakes! He went all the way to the Governor to pull strings!"

I stood in front of Julian's big desk. Delaney's resignation had been on my mind for the past four days, ever since the old man had come to my office that evening to hand it to me personally. In the intervening days, most of the Board of Governors had resigned.

"Crayden is in violation of its charter. There is no sitting Chairman, and the Board is nearly liquidated. That was a choice, Julian!"

"They voted *you* the Chairman, Goddammit! Take the fucking chair, and you'll be in compliance!"

"I can't take the Chair! I'm Headmaster of Crayden; it's a conflict of interest. If I take the chair, I'd have to resign my position."

"So resign! You make enough now. You don't need the job!"

"I want the job! I want to see Crayden through this whole thing. I want to see it back up on top the way it was when you were a kid and when I was. I want to see Delaney proud of what we did...not go to his funeral brought about by my displacing him."

"I told you it might come to this! Didn't I! Christ, Jesus, Sonny-Jim, if I'd known this Goddamn philanthropy would be such a pain in the ass, I'd have thrown you out of my office the first day!"

"Well, you didn't! Crayden needs a Chairman. I'm here as the Director of the Reynolds Foundation to advise you that you'd better find a way of getting Delaney and his cronies back, or the whole place goes into the toilet. That's not much of 'legacy', is it?"

"I'm not knuckling under to Cameron Delaney! He's not going to control this!"

"Crayden is all he has."

"Christ, what a candy-ass you are!"

"You hired me as Director of the Reynolds Foundation. I assume you wanted me to give the Foundation at least the appearance of a 'heart'!"

"'Heart'?! What the hell do you think I do all day? Cry? Sit around here with my thumb up my ass? This is a 'Going Concern', Sonny-Jim. While you're having your coffee, I make more money than you'll see in a year! I'm not playing tag with Cam Delaney!"

"At least call him on the phone! Ask him to reconsider!"

"I already did that!"

"Wh-what?—What did he say?"

"He told me to shove it up my ass! Actually, I think he said, 'in view of our "maneuvering" he felt it was best if he "acquiesced" to our wishes!' He wouldn't say 'shit' if his mouth was full!"

"...Nobody wants to be on the Board of a sinking old private school. Even if we are reviving it. There's no money in it. It's a dead end. Delaney and those old men were the only ones who cared enough to be on the Board!"

"...I'll handle it...."

"—How will you handle it?"

"I'll handle it! Now get out of here, Holliman! I don't have any more time for this shit! You just run your Goddamn school! Go!"

Back at Crayden Sally was waiting at the office. She told me that Spencer and Chase were back. They were "all over the building", according to her, re-taking measurements and re-calculating everything.

"Well, at least there's some activity going on. I was beginning to think everything would fall through."

"I don't like it."

"What don't you like?"

"This bunch is different than the first ones. That little Olsen guy with the sharp lapels—He was on a mission. He was 'making changes'! These guys are different. They're not looking at the same things."

"Well, what do you mean?"

"...I don't know. But I heard one of 'em say, 'Yeah, we can go up plenty, if we want to.' What do you think *that* means?"

"...That's probably just—who knows? Right now, I just want to get the Board back in operation and get *our* operation back to normal!"

"Speaking of 'normal', Dr. Nichols is in your office. He wants to 'go over' the curricula."

"Oh, God!"

"He's 'very excited' about some new ideas!"

"Couldn't you tell him I died?"

"Give him half an hour. I'll come in and save you with a 'contributor meeting'. That'll get you off the hook."

CHAPTER 33

"I am now not Tlaloc, Warrior-Priest. I give up all the Priest-Father tells me! The Gods do not see me now! I do what I know I cannot. I take a woman. I give up my people. I give myself to Anasan. I am her ugly toad, and she loves me. I do not know how this is. She is tall and strong and good to see. I am short, and those who see us laugh. I hear them in the village. 'Anasan, where is your dog? Is he sniffing around the woods with your brother? Does he come when you call him?' All the women laugh. 'He is so small! You need two of him to make a man!'...She does not listen. She stands taller when she is next to me, and she looks at the others as if to say, 'This one is worth all of you!' The boy is right. She is my rest. I never have a time like this. I never know this feeling before. I am a man like other men.

"Every day I teach. Oratamin knows much of what I know. He says nothing of Anasan and me. He accepts. He watches me, and he looks like one who does not share a secret. At night I leave him, and I go to Anasan's lodge. It is forbidden, but I am like a starving man. I do not care that the Gods do not see me! I do not listen to the words of my Priest-Father. I block them out. Only I hear Anasan's voice, feel her body close. It is the only thing I want. It is all I think about except when I teach the boy. We are careful that others do not see this. I have found life. No one chases me; no one tells me what I must do. It is all to me.

"In time Anasan comes to me. I am with Oratamin by the fire after we eat. 'Your child is in me.' She put my hand on her belly. I do not know what to feel. Now I hear the Priest-

Father, 'You can never marry, never make children.' I am afraid. I am also filled with surprise.

"'How can this be? How is this possible?'

"'How? You can ask this? Is this not what men and women do? What we do? You are a strange little toad!' She laughs, but it is not angry laughter. She laughs like one happy to give a gift. I see her, and I am destroyed with feeling. I hold her. 'Tlaloc! You will squeeze the child out of me!' I let her go at once afraid and confused. She laughs at my stupidity. I laugh. We laugh together until my tears come.

"Oratamin waits. He does not laugh, and he does not frown. He waits. Finally Anasan says to him, 'Brother, you are not proud? Our family grows. One day soon you take a wife, and she gives you a child too. What is in your mind? You say nothing. It is you who tells me my feelings for this one change. It is you who say this.'

"'I do not remember this... But I know this child.'

"'How can you know this child? It is a long time away yet. You cannot know this child!'

"'She is a special child. She carries Tlaloc's Gods within her.'

"'Stupid boy! All children carry the seed of their fathers! Besides this one is a warrior. A boy. A woman knows!'

"'No. She comes. Half a Traveler. The fury of his Gods rides in her. Do not ask how I know this. I See it!'

"I hear him. I am afraid. I am afraid for Anasan and for this child. What terrible thing do I do? I do not want Anasan to see me thinking. I say I am going to find a plant for the growing of the child. I make myself look proud and happy. Anasan laughs, and says, 'Look at my toad! He cannot keep still by the fire. He must find the magic for our son to be strong.' I leave camp and go into the woods. There I shake and weep and say the prayers of shame. I give the blood—so much blood to the Gods. I cut deep and let it come. Let the cat come, I do not care! I grow cold, but I do not die. My blood seeps into the

ground and is lost. I chew the plant. My sleep is deep...and black. No dreams come. The Gods do not see me, nor do they hear me. I am lost to them.

"In the morning I am stiff and cold. I wake feeling hollow. I return to the lodge. Anasan sleeps, and I wait for the sun..."

For once I wasn't exhausted or working late. Santiago waited for Sally to leave, and he came in with the cups and waited for me to nod. He seemed calm although sad with this part of the story. In this pause I had to ask him—

"Santiago, why does Tlaloc have this in his story? There are none of his people. He no longer fights against the Silver Men. What is the purpose?"

He looked at me confused for a moment, searching for the words.

"...Because...because Tlaloc *is* the people. He is all that remains..."

"There were the others—The young new King of pure blood. The one he teaches in the jungle."

"Yes. He is there and his few. But they are not long. Tlaloc knows this. He leaves them so that the cat will not take them before they leave their footprint in the sand. But they too will be drowned in the blood of the Spanish. It must be. Only Tlaloc is the people now. This he knows. Where he goes, go all the people. With him are the prayers and the dances and the giving of the blood. All the ways that they are."

"...But you say the Gods do not see him...do not hear him?"

"...No...not for now...not with Anasan. He is lost to them. He is lost in her. He does what he must not do, and he is...only a man."

"That is not good?"

"Yes! It is well! It is the time he holds close! It is a time when he doubts the Priest-Father and his vision! Why not take a wife? Why not have children? Why do the Gods deny him this? Why does he carry all with him and wait...for the Angry Young Lord?"

"For me..."

"Sí...for you."

"What happened to Anasan? The woman in the picture is beautiful. Did Tlaloc stay with her?"

Santiago looked at me for a long moment. He lowered his eyes and searched for the words:

> "...The boy comes to the camp. He does not speak. He brings a fat rabbit and builds a fire. He skins the rabbit and hangs it for cooking. When he is done, he comes to me and takes my arms. The marks are still there.

> "'You speak to your Gods'

> "'Yes.'

> "'They do not answer you.'

> "'No...'

> "'They watch you. They wait.'

> "'Then they must wait! I have waited! I have served them across much time! Many places! Now I do not wait! Now I live as man!'

> "'Yes. Now you do. But your journey is much longer. I do not See how long. They wait when Tlaloc learns what he must. They do not answer you. You live with us. Your Sight is clouded even with the plant. Your prayers fall into silence. The blood you give they do not drink. You have this place and this time. Is it enough for Tlaloc?'

> "'Is what enough for Tlaloc?' Anasan has come out. She sees us by the fire and hears this last thing. 'What is enough for Tlaloc? What do you ask of him now, brother?'

> "'I ask nothing of him. It is what he asks of himself. I come because we have no parents, no old ones to demand the gifts or make the ceremony of marriage. What you do must be made right. I am younger than you, but I am the one who must arrange the marriage. This we must do before your belly shows. Before the women talk.'

"'Let them! I am not ashamed. This warrior in me is powerful. This I know!'

"'Tlaloc, you must kill a deer. Bring it to camp, and roast the meat. This you bring to me as a gift. Anasan, you make the corn cake to give to Tlaloc. This is done, and I tell the village you are one. Tlaloc will join the wolf clan.'

"I do not understand this. Any of this, but I know it is important for Anasan and Oratamin. This I do. I kill a deer and roast the meat. Oratamin shows me the ways. Anasan comes with small cakes she makes and gives them to me. If I take them, we are wed.

"'Only this? I ask. 'Is it these small gifts that make one of two?'

"'No,' Oratamin answers, 'It is the giving of yourself that makes you one. Do you give yourself to this woman?'

"'...I have. You know I have. I give everything I am! I do not care what comes...Tlaloc gives all he is to Anasan if she takes him.'

"'And Anasan accepts this one?' Oratamin looks at her deep, knowing she does not see all of me. 'Think, sister, do you accept this one who is not one of us? Do you accept what he is and what he is before, and what he is...later?'

"'He is my own little toad! I see him! I accept him. I take his life to mine.'

"It is done this way, and Oratamin tells the village the news. They do not say anything. None talk against it, but I know it is a surprise. It is not done in the circle as usual, but because Oratamin is a shaman, it goes away without much talking. Tlaloc is now one of the wolf clan. Tlaloc is not alone!"

CHAPTER 34

"...I told him I must have contaminated the sample."

"Christ, Nick, I told you this would happen! You know how you were when I gave you that bloody handkerchief."

"That's why I told him it was contaminated. Look, I gave him just enough of the sample to do one set of tests. He doesn't have any more to check. I was careful about that. Without more he can't check the results. He doesn't know I already did my own set of tests."

Nick and I were having lunch at Maffei's. We needed to be out of earshot and away from Crayden. Maffei's was neutral enough. His "guy" came back with the exact same results as Nick, confirming Nick's original analysis.

"Did he believe you?"

"Yeah. Why wouldn't he? The results are too freaky to be anything but a bad test—or something."

"Or something? What do you mean 'or something'?"

"Of course he had questions: 'Where did I get it? Are you in contact with the donor?'...I told him that the sample was given to me by a friend who asked me to have it checked. More than that I couldn't tell him. He was persistent for a while. But he stopped calling. I'm pretty sure it's done. He's a young lab tech. Not high up enough to have any clout or credibility. If he went to anybody with results like that, they'd laugh him out of the lab. He'd lose his job."

"...You're sure of that? Nick, this is all getting too strange for me to take in! You're telling me that Santiago's blood is that weird cancer-thing you explained before? He's got blood that...that—"

"Doesn't deteriorate. It doesn't degrade. It doesn't age. What's more it's *pure* Amerindian. There is no European coefficient...no mix of anything else. His blood doesn't exist today."

"...So...he *is* Tlaloc? He's a five-hundred year old Indian who witnessed the Fall of the Aztec Empire?"

"No!..I'm telling you that he has a very, very rare blood type with...unusual properties. Something I haven't seen before. Something there are no records of. That's all. The rest of it...his stories? I'm convinced are just that—stories. Use your common sense, Brad!"

"I'm trying to, Nick. I don't know what to think here!"

"...Well, he may have come from a small, isolated group that somehow resisted assimilation."

"He did say that he retreated into the jungle with a group of warriors! They hid from the Spanish."

"That could be it. The stories are the memories of this one small, isolated group. There are examples of isolated tribes deep in the Amazon who have never made contact with Whites. It could be like that. When Cortez showed up, they escaped somehow and stayed away from any contact. I bet there are other survivors of his tribe somewhere in the wilds of Mexico living today. He somehow got separated and got to New York."

"...He told me how he got here."

"All right! There you go! Case closed!"

"As a 'Healer' on a slave ship!"

"Huh?..."

"He left the jungle, all right. He hopped a slaver and got to New York—just after the 'English' took control! He led a slave revolt on board a ship! He stayed with a small group of local Indians. Jesus Christ, he just told me about marrying some Indian girl. I saw her damn picture!"

"No...no, you know that's not true. Somehow this is still a part of the tribal memory."

"What 'tribal memory'?—He's alone! Everything he's been telling me lately is of a man who has been alone for...decades. Living on the fringes of civilization. Wrestling with loneliness and loss. He even talks about losing his faith in his Gods!"

"...Ok...look, suppose you were an old janitor working in a hulk of a building like Crayden. You know you can't hang on forever! The Headmaster was a kid when you were first there years ago. What do you do? You spin a story! You try to fascinate him. Keep him on the hook. Create sympathy! Keep your place as long as you can!"

"Now we're torturing the plot, don't you think?"

"He's got you working to find a pension or some place for him to go! He's been pretty successful, I'd say!"

"So, I'm just the gullible, sentimental old pedagogue!"

"Now who's torturing the plot? You know what they say, 'eliminate the impossible, and whatever is left, however improbable, is the answer'!"

"And the morion and the picture of the Indian girl?..."

"Props. Talismans. Whatever!..."

"What about the rapid healing you witnessed? Even you were spooked by that!"

"Genetic anomaly. Probably having to do with isolation and inbreeding. I know—he tried to reel me in to this story too, but I'm not buying! Brad, there is a scientific explanation for everything you've told me. For everything we've seen. Believe me, I'd love to examine him...if he'd let me! As for the 'memories' he's giving you,...I'm Science, not Lterature!"

"...It's one helluva a story!"

"So, let him tell it. Keep recording it. It obviously makes him feel like you connect with him. It allows him to hold on for a little while longer. Who does it hurt?"

"...You're a very good 'explainer'—you know that?"

"Speaking of holding on for a while longer...what's happening with the building? Am I still gonna have a job next year?"

***

"Santiago?...Santiago?" I had gone down to the boiler room. Spencer and Chase people were still coming in and studying the structure. They came and went. Once in awhile a 'Field Man' would come to my office to say that they would need to do more tests, but they would be sure not to disrupt our class schedule.

"Tests? What tests? What are you testing for?" I asked.

"Everything, sir. We don't want to compromise the existing structure. We need to make sure that whatever we do, it doesn't threaten the original structure."

I couldn't help wonder how a new roof and mechanical upgrades could 'threaten' the original structure, but more than this, I was worried that I had heard nothing more from Julian about our Board.

As I turned to leave, Santiago was right there almost nose-to-nose with me. I think I jumped, and he laughed in that dry, wheezing laugh he had. I flushed with annoyance.

"You do not get used to me. You are the same as when you are a boy. You jump! Then you get angry! Haaaa, haaaa...!"

"Santiago...uh...Ok...Look, I wish you wouldn't do that!"

"You come, sit! I fix..."

"Wait! No, I—"

He disappeared into his room, and I could hear him drawing water and putting in on the ancient gas hotplate.

"I came to find you to tell you I couldn't stay. I have a meeting—"

"With the old, fat one. Sí, I know this. It is not now, yes?"

"Uh...Not right now, no, but I wanted to go home and change. I should freshen up."

"It is a big meeting, yes?"...He was calling out of his room as he rummaged around.

"Yes, a very big meeting. We need a new Board...uh...new leaders to keep the school going."

"...Sí. You keep! This I See. You keep."

"Not without a Board of Governors, Santiago. It's part of our charter. We can't function without one."

He emerged with two steaming cups of maté. The bits of herbs were still floating at the top. He handed one to me.

"You keep...you sit, yes?"

"...Santiago...I don't even have my recorder with me—"

"Here. I get." Apparently he had gone to my office and gotten the recorder. He smiled as if there was nothing odd about this. "You sit." He handed me the small recording device and sat on his old chair. I knew I'd only prolong this if I resisted. I had perhaps an hour before I had to leave to get to Julian for our meeting. I sat and pressed the button:

> *"Tlaloc is filled with this child! With this woman! Never does he know this! Every moment is this thing that happens—this good thing that makes him smile inside. It is warm like a sun. He is always hunting and bringing in food.*
>
> *"'Stop!' says Anasan. 'We cannot eat so much. You give this and this to the old who have no one to hunt for them.'*
>
> *"'I wish to give you...everything! I wish to make you a Top Woman!'*
>
> *"'You make me tired, Tlaloc! I am only at the beginning. I can grow and prepare food! I tell you when we need. You go with Oratamin. Teach! Do what men do! It is a woman's thing to bring a child. For this I do not need you!'*
>
> *"'I am a Healer! I wish to keep you well!'*
>
> *"'I am as well as I need to be! Go away, and do something!' She*

is angry but not really. I see that my feeling is more than she wishes to know. I go to the water where the water-creatures live. Their shells are rough and sharp on the outside, but inside they are smooth and shine like the moon. These I take and open. The animal I eat, and the shell I begin to smooth and polish with the sand. I shape these and make them round like the full moon. I drill small holes, and with thin strands of gut I string them like a line of moons for her. This takes me...many days. It takes me from her, and I do not make her angry again. But in time she looks at me with questions.

"'Oratamin says you do not teach him these few weeks...'

"'He knows much from me. He does not need me so often now. He is soon a man.'

"'This is true. Do you...go to see your Gods?'

"'No. They are silent and do not come to me now.'

"'You do not hunt?'

"'You tell me not to.'

"'No...We do not need....Tlaloc?'

"'Yes?'

"'What? What is it you do? No one sees you. You are gone from people most days. You come at sundown, and we eat and sleep. What takes you away?'

"'I do something. It is what you ask of me.'

"'What? What is it you do?'

"'I cannot tell. It is something I am not ready to share'

"'...No one sees you...'

"'I do not mean for someone to see me...'

"'You are a member of my clan. The Wolf Clan. We have a proud lineage.'

"'It is well. Our little one is born into a strong line.'

"'What you do—is it something a member of the Wolf Clan can do?'

"'Am I a member of the Wolf Clan?'

"'Yes! When we marry, you join my Clan. It is our way.'

"'Then it is something a member of the Wolf Clan can do...'

"'You are an ugly toad, and I do not have you!"

"'Then you do not want this...' I show her the necklace of moons I make. It shines in the firelight, and her eyes dance when she sees it. She reaches for it, and I hold her.

"'Ah!...What is this thing? What do you show me? Is it for me?'

"'I am an ugly toad. I could not make something with beauty in it.'

"She laughs and reaches for the thing. 'Perhaps you are not such a toad. I must see this thing you say you make.'

"She puts it around her neck and admires it. It is not like the beads the others make. I make it in a style of my own people. It catches the fire and shows rainbows in it. She is taken by it. 'I have a man who gives me pieces of the moon! No one else has a man who does this! I am a woman among women. They laugh at my choice, but let one of their men make such a thing! They do not know you heal. They do not know you are a traveler. This Oratamin tells me. But this I wear. Every day. They will have jealous eyes!'

"She is pleased with me. No one is ever pleased with me. I am always a thing between people. I am a rock between my Mother and Quexa and the Priest-Father. I am a rope between my people and their past. I am a wall between the Spanish and my own. I am a knife between the Padre and his Jesus...I am a question between you and your 'sense'."

"Santiago—"

"Do not be sorry. It is as it must be...:

"We live like no other man and woman, I think. Each day she warms me, gives me the sun within my heart. As her belly grows, I grow more impatient to see my son. Three times I chew the plant. The dreams do not come. The Gods remain silent. I do not have the Sight now.

"The council takes Oratamin in as a man. He is the Shaman. He is grown tall and handsome as Anasan. In council he Sees for them, but not in the way my Priest-Father and I See with our people. His Sight is short and full of different paths. It is different than the way I know.

"At night by the lodge fire, he is still Oratamin, the boy—my student. No one knows this is our way. He asks questions still, but now I am not able to tell him what I See. I can tell him only of the plants and healing. I cannot tell him of my people, but when he speaks, it is as if he knows without my telling him.

"'Tlaloc, this child you love already, is her Mother's daughter, but she carries your Gods inside her. She is the greatest joy and the greatest sorrow you know.'

"'I hear this from all who have their children. I know this is true.'

"'For you it is deeper, truer...'

"'I am ready, Oratamin. I wait a long time for this.'

"'No, Tlaloc, you are not ready. You are never ready...But your journey goes on. I am sorry for you.'

"'Do not be sorry! Tlaloc is...happy. It is not a word I use for me, but it is true. I am a man. I am a husband. I am soon a father! The Gods cannot stop this! I have this, and I do not let it go!'

"'...No. I can See that. You do not let it go. Be happy, Tlaloc.'

"This is all he says. The weeks and months pass more slowly than I ever know them! Anasan's belly grows, but there is no child yet. Now I do not want to be far from the lodge.

"'Stop watching me, Tlaloc!' she tells me. I can feel you every day—watching! Go and fish. I have the taste for fish! Find me a big fat one for the fire, and I cook. Go! Watch the fish!'

"This I do. I know from her voice she is not pleased with me at that moment. I know that I am like one in a trance, seeing things that are not. I am gone all day fishing. No one comes with me. The men of the village are not against me, but they are not for me. I am someone, but not of them. They do not talk much with me. Only Oratamin, and he is hunting a deer now. He sees a woman he wants. He makes the gifts to her Mother and Father if they accept him.

"I catch many fish. I am like a man possessed. This one is not fat enough. That one is not big enough. At day's end I have enough to feed many. These I put in a litter and drag them back to the lodge. I know Anasan makes me give them up to those who have none, but she has the pick of these. When I come upon the lodge, the sun is down. It is quiet. There is no fire in the pit. I look for Anasan, but she is not there. I start the fire. I have it burning when Anasan speaks behind me.

"'...I am sorry, Tlaloc!'

"I spin and turn to her. She stands pale but firm. In her arms is a rolled skin. All is quiet, and I have a great feeling of dread,

"'Anasan! You—have...'

"'The child is here...I am sorry!'

"I rise to her. Hold her. I am afraid to look. '...He...is dead?' I am sure that the Gods are punishing me.

"Anasan is weak, but she stands tall. Tears are at the corners of her eyes. 'It is not the son I promised you. It is a girl as Oratamin says...She is here.'

"She pulls back the skin and I see Her. She is not a toad like me! She is handsome like her mother! I quickly pull back the skin and look at her. She is whole, and I am full of wonder. I laugh!

"'You are not angry? You do not have a son. This one is not

what I promise!'

"'She is a tall, angry stick, like her Mother! She calls me toad! She fights like her Mother, and she knows me as her father! I am...grateful! Anasan...I am a man...your man!'

"I make her sit by the fire. I take a fish and begin to cook. She tries to do it, but I do not let her. We feast! It is a night I never know! It is a life I never see! When Anasan and the child sleep, I slip into the forest. Away from all, I make a place and I dance! I dance for all that I see...all that I know...all my people! I give the blood even though the Gods sleep, I give it. I owe it. They let this be. Let them slumber. When they wake, they drink and know that Tlaloc is grateful!"

CHAPTER 35

The faces were all new! Not one of the old Board were there. Delaney and his old, conservative friends were all gone now. Instead, around the conference table in Julian's office were a smart, sharply-tailored group of far younger men. Most of them were in their thirties or forties I guessed. In fact the only "old" face was Julian's.

"Meeting will come to order...." Julian took a seat at the head of the table. "Let's make this short and sweet, fellas! I don't have the time to waste on all this bullshit. That'll be your job. Dr. Holliman here is the Headmaster at Crayden. The old Board voted him the Chair, but he can't take it. Violation of Charter. That's where you all come in. I twisted all your arms to join the Board. I don't give a rat's ass if you care about Crayden or not. You won't be running it. That's what Holliman does! I don't care what the fucking Charter stipulates, none of you will be expected to contribute—money or time. I'll do that. The money part, anyway. The time thing will be mostly Holliman. He makes the decisions about the Goddamn school. You guys are just suits. You come to these short meetings once a month. He tells you what's happening. You vote 'yea,' and go home. In return—I continue doing business with your companies. Everybody straight on that?"

The men all looked at each other. Some muttered assent; most just nodded.

"OK, now I nominate myself as Chairman—all in favor?" All hands went up silently. "All opposed?" No one raised a hand. "Motion carried. Julian Reynolds, sitting Chairman of the Board of Governors. Thanks fellas. You can go now."

One by one they shook my hand and introduced themselves on the way out. It was over in less than ten minutes.

"…Well, what do you think, Sonny-Jim? I got you your Board and an alumnus for a Chairman. You happy now?"

"…All the old Board quit?"

"I told 'em it might be better if they all walked away. There might be some…friction…between the old and the new members. And that wouldn't be good…for anyone."

"Some of those men spent years keeping Crayden afloat."

"Well, now they don't have to. With the Reynolds foundation behind it, Crayden will 'float' just fine. I looked at the books…What you did, helped. Cam must have seen that…Oh, stop looking like I kicked your Goddamn puppy! You don't want those old farts carrying tales back to Cam, do you? A new broom sweeps clean! Now you can get on with what you want to do."

"…I just thought we should show them a little gratitude. For years of service"

"I'll send 'em all a fruitcake!—Jesus Christ, Sonny-Jim you better get over this girlie sentiment of yours. Crayden ain't gonna survive if you get all warm and runny over every SOB that walks by! Cam and his buddies were setting you up for failure. I saved your Goddamn bacon!"

"Yeah…why?"

"What do you mean, 'why'?"

"You don't know me. Not really. Until a few months ago, I was just a query letter asking for money. Now you're 'saving my bacon'. …It's a fair question—Why?"

"Call it payback."

"Payback?—For what? What did I do?"

"Not you!…The Delaneys…I figure I owe them."

"So, you get Mr. Delaney thrown off the Board of an organization he's dedicated himself to?"

"I saved the goddam thing! Whether Cam likes it or not, he was riding it into the ground with that 'Anglican chill' of his. He's so Goddamn rigid he couldn't wipe his own ass! Buck up, Sonny-Jim. Cam Delaney ain't that delicate! If Crayden went down—*that* would kill him...not being thrown off the Board."

"That's a pretty drastic 'favor'!

"Yeah...well, if I have to be the villain, fine! I can take it. You know...when I was young, the Delaney's were the only ones that tried at all to be some kind of a family for me. I can do this...Even if Cam hates me for it."

"...Tell him."

"That was a long time ago. Too late for that. This'll have to do. Now, I'm going home. I got business to do tomorrow."

"See you at the next meeting then. Unless the Foundation needs me for something."

"I'll call you if I want you."

On the way home, I was trying to put the two views these old men had of each other together. They didn't fit.

CHAPTER 36

"Elalie she is called. She is running always. She is her mother again. The same long legs. Tall and good to look at. This pleases me. It is not good for a girl child to look like me, I think. When she is fifteen summers, many young warriors look at her. But she does not look back. She says she is not ready to make the corn cakes for one man.

"Anasan and I watch her grow. She works with the women, planting cheerfully, but when she can, she follows me and Oratamin when we hunt. We know she is there, but we say nothing.

"Finally Oratamin says to me this time, 'Tlaloc, I see a deer over there. I should shoot it?'

"'Yes,' I say, 'We need meat at the camp.' But she does not call out. She says nothing and pretends she is a tree or a rock. Oratamin raises his bow to scare her, and still she says nothing. He does not shoot. He wishes only to flush her out from the woods and admit she follows. Suddenly Oratamin trips on a tree root. The arrow flies, and we hear her scream! We think we kill her. My heart is beating fast as we run to her. She is not dead, but the arrow is through her leg. It is a bad wound. There is much blood. I break the head away and pull the shaft back through the leg. It has not hit the bone. She breathes deeply, but she does not cry out. Oratamin seeks the plants for healing while I push on the place where the arrow goes in. There is a hole with a jagged lip that spits the blood. I know that there is tearing inside. Without thinking, I say the prayer to the Gods a Priest says when he asks their help...and she says

it with me! In my tongue she says the same words! Oratamin returns with the plants to stop the blood and begin healing. He is frantic with what he does. He says again and again, 'It is a mistake! I do not do it willingly. Oratamin is a stupid man! Oratamin is a careless one!'

"I take my hand away to put the healing plants in place—and the bleeding is no more! The jagged lip of the wound stops its spitting and there is only a small run of blood now. Soon that too stops.

"Oratamin looks at me and sits back on his heels. His eyes are strange. I speak to her. I tell her that she is well, and she is not afraid. Soon Elalie's wound is closing.

"She looks at us both and says, 'Father, Uncle do not say this to my Mother! She will beat me for following. She tells me not to hunt with the men. I do not listen. I like to hunt. I know she hunts sometimes! Elalie hunts too! I can hunt as well as a man. Watch me! Watch me, Father. I make you proud! What are you looking at?' She looks down and sees the wound has closed. 'It has stopped now. Can we eat?'

"'Daughter,' I say 'Is it this way before? You do not bleed?'

"'Always! Always, I bleed, Father. I fall, a briar catches my skin, I slip with my knife at cooking, but it does not last. Mother tells me to be careful. I am clumsy.'

"'Your Gods are in her, Tlaloc. She is like you. She heals.'

"I know this is true. I see it. We hunt and Elalie gets three rabbits. She makes so much noise about her success and that Oratamin and I get nothing! She is happy. She sings all the way to the lodge. That night I tell Anasan what happens—what we see.

"'Yes,' she says, 'it is true. She is not sick ever. She is strong like you, and her wounds give little blood. It is a gift of the spirits!'

"'She is you in courage! The first time you see me, you almost kill me!'

"'I do kill you if I can! But you want to save Oratamin. I cannot kill you then! It is lucky for you!'

"'She is her mother's girl!'

"Anasan is silent for a moment. Her back is to me. I feel there is something she wonders. 'You...don't wish...for a son?'

"'I am content with the daughter you give me...It is more than I deserve...'

"'No! No, Tlaloc, deserves a strong son! Many sons! It is I who cannot make them! I am a bad wife!'

"'You take me. You give me...everything...more than I dream. You are a wonder to me!' I fold around her and she is quiet. We sleep.

"That night for the first time I dream again. I dream without the plant...

"Anasan stands by the fire. She is cooking. Elalie is helping her. There is a noise behind the trees. A wolf approaches the fire, his head down and growling low with hunger. He leaps and he is on Anasan. In one move he tears out her throat, and Anasan lies on the ground! Elalie calls out to me. I rise with my knife ready to kill this wolf, but the beast lowers his ears. It is Elalie he wants. He is close to her, and he turns to take her, but she is quick. She jumps upon the wolf's back holding its great head in her arms. She brings the wolf down, and she rolls with it until she is underneath the beast, and she has it with its paws clawing the air. In one quick jerk she twists the beast's head, and there is a hard, 'crack!' The beast is dead.

"I am made of stone...I cannot move! I cannot speak. She comes to herself and sees the blood of the beast and the body of her mother, and she screams.

"I do not know the meaning. I take the dream to Oratamin.

"'You do not want the meaning,' he tells me. 'You are a Seer greater than I. You already know, but you do not want to See. Tlaloc, it is not that your Gods do not see you. You do not see *them.'*

"I am angry. I leave the lodge. I take myself away for days. I do not eat. I pray. I give the blood. I am so far from my people and so long away, I think I lose them. I try to lose them...let them go. I know this is true, but I cannot lose them. I am them. Elalie is part of them as well. It is a part that will not let either of us go! I have cursed her. I know this! I do this to her. Now I know Oratamin's meaning telling me she is the greatest joy and the greatest sorrow. I cannot run from this...

"I go back. Anasan sees me. She does not speak. I sit by the fire; it is nearly dark. She gives me food. Elalie's eyes are big. She waits for words between us, but none come. I eat in silence, and later I sleep with no words between us. I do not know how to say what I know. I cannot say it to her.

"In the night there is shouting. It is far off, and there is the smell of fire! I jump up. Anasan is awake as well. She looks at me with eyes that say, 'Quiet!' We listen. The smell of fire is strong, and it comes from the direction of the English. Suddenly outside the lodge there is a sound. Someone comes close to us. It is not one who hides. This one makes too much noise.

"I go out and tell Anasan to stay inside and watch over Elalie. I hear someone breaking the bushes and running over branches snapping them. It is One in panic. One being chased! Suddenly the brush near me parts, and a big man falls to the ground nearly at my feet. He is a Dark One. He breathes hard, and he bleeds from the side where he has been cut. He cannot speak, but he raises his hands to ask for mercy.

"'Anasan! Anasan, come!' She comes out of the lodge followed by Elalie.

"'Who is that, father? What is happening?' Elalie looks at the Dark One on the ground. 'He is hurt!'

"'Go hide, Elalie! Be invisible, your father and I will take care of this!' Anasan has her knife drawn ready to fight.

"'He is being chased! He asks for help.' I say. 'We drag him to those bushes. We pile branches over him!'

"This we do quickly, and we hear others coming. The smell of them tells us it is the English. They smell bad. They smell like the Spanish! The smell of filth and too many people and fire clings to them. They break the clearing, and there we are pretending to sit at the fire. Anasan stands again with her hand on her knife. I put my hand on hers and calm her. I raise my hand open to these English. There are three. They carry muskets and knives, and they are ready to kill. Their wild eyes search the clearing of the lodge looking for the Dark One. One says something to me. I have not learned this English, but Anasan knows some words. Her people sometimes trade with these. She answers him. He asks something else, and Anasan shakes her head, 'No.' One of them goes into our lodge. We hear him throwing what we have over the ground. He comes out and talks to the others. The first one steps forward to Anasan. It is then that I am ready to kill them all. I see that he means harm. I am ready to spring at him, and he speaks to Anasan in a voice I know is a threat! She whispers to me only, 'No.' She nods to the English. They look to each other, and suddenly they run out of our camp into the dark woods crashing and shouting and still looking for the Dark One. We wait a long time listening. None of us move waiting to see if they come back.

"'What do they tell you?' I ask.

"'They look for the One hidden. The Dark Ones have set fire to their village, killed English! They hunt them. These English do not like us. We stay away from them. They have their world. We have ours. If we keep this One, they come to our world and kill us!'

"'They are gone. We must see what we have with this One.'

"'We kill him and leave him for the English to find. It is the only safe way!'

"'He asks for help. He makes no move to hurt us.'

"'He brings trouble! If we keep him, the English will come, I tell you. We fight these English. They honor nothing! We must be rid of this One!'

"'Very well, but let him go away on his own. We do not need to kill him! We send him out.' I take the branches away from the hiding place. The Dark One is lying in the leaves under the plant. He sleeps from his wounds. He is big. Taller that any man I know. Taller than Oratamin, and he is powerfully made. His skin bears marks of the lash on the back and sides. He bleeds heavily from a cut in his side. This I press to see if it will stop. It does. I pack it with dry moss and use an ointment I make from the plants. I tie clean leaves to hold the dressing, and I make a tea that will soothe the pain. Elalie helps me move him inside the lodge. Anasan does not help. She wants him gone. She watches if the English come back.

"It is still dark when this One wakes up. He sits up with a jump and looks around the lodge. When his eyes fall on me, he falls to the ground on his knees, and he rocks up and down moaning, 'Oh, I am dead!...I am dead!...they kill me and send me to the spirit world!' This he says in the language of the Dark Ones I know from the water-houses. 'It is the very same!'

"I say to him in this same language, 'No, you are not dead, but you will be if you stay here. The English come for you. If they don't kill you, my woman does. She fears you bring death to this lodge!'

"'I am not, dead? But you are Medicine Man! I know you when I am a boy!...Lele...I am Lele! You help my Father and me to escape. That was...many years ago! You are dead now, and so I am dead now too!' He rocks back and forth crying.

"'Don't be foolish! Stop that crying! Are you a man? Did you escape the Water-house to be a woman? Your Father is ashamed of you! I am ashamed of you. I save you—You are mine by right, and I am ashamed to see you like this!'

"He comes to himself and his eyes grow bigger. He comes close to my face and he touches it then he pulls back with fear. 'You are a witch! You are a spirit come to steal my soul!'

"'What does he say?' Elalie asks pulling on my arm. 'How do you know his language? What does he say? Why is he so afraid?'

"'Child, be silent! This one just now escapes death. Do you think he sings for gladness?'

"'He knows you, Father! How is that? Why does he fear you?'

"'Be silent, and let me speak with him!' I turn to Lele, and I take his hand. I put it on the handle of my knife, and holding his hand, I make a cut in my skin. I bleed. 'There! A spirit does not bleed! I am no spirit. This is the lodge of my Woman, Anasan. You come to us from the dark forest with English running after you. You ask for help. We help you, now you must go!'

"The fear leaves his eyes when he sees the blood. He comes closer to me. 'How is this, Medicine Man? How is this that you are the same as when I am a boy? I remember you! You give me new life even in that dark place. You kill the one who kills my Mother. You tell my father to leave and hide. This we do. We live. We are free while others in that place are caught and put in chains. I am long grown. My Father is long dead. How can this be?'

"'You ask this now? The English hunt you! They will kill you if they can. You must run far away from here. You cannot bring death to this lodge!'

"'I will go, but tell me this magic. If you can make this magic, the English cannot touch us—any of us. You are truly more powerful than they!'

"'I have no magic and no power. To a boy everyone is old. I was younger than you know when you see me then. It is a trick of the mind that makes you think I am not changed. I am small and ugly. You remember only that.'

"'Father, what does he say?!' Elalie listens, and I know that she understands some of what we say.

"'He wants only to get away from the English.'

"'He knows you! How does this one know you?'

"I cannot answer her now. I must listen to Lele.

"'I work in the village of the English. My father and I are free. We work for food and a place by the animals in winter. I learn the way of metal from an English who does this. He needs help and cannot buy one like me. I am strong. He says I work for him, and he gives me money. This I do. Sometimes he beats me, but I learn. The money keeps my Father and me free. Some that run from that boat with us still belong to the English. They do not make money. They are owned. We make a plan for them to be free. We set fire to the English houses. We kill the ones that beat us. They catch many of us. Some of us run. This is how I get here.'

"Anasan comes into the lodge. Her eyes dance with fear, 'I hear them! They come back! That one must go now!'

"'They come again,' I tell him. 'If you stay here, we all die.'

"'I owe you my life twice and the life of my Father!' He rises to leave, and I know he is weak.

"'There is a cave on the hill near the river where the river-rocks gather. If you get there, hide. I come to you with medicine and food.'

"'Hurry! I can smell them!' Anasan stands at the opening of the lodge.

"'Pray to your Gods for me, Medicine Man. Your Gods are stronger than any!' He kneels at my feet with his head down.

"'Go!' Anasan grabs him by the arm and pulls him up. She pushes him from the lodge, and he runs into the brush more silently than before. It is only a moment before the English come. They are angrier than before. They ask Anasan more questions, and I am ready to fight. Her eyes tell me to hold my hands. She points away from the clearing, away from the place Lele runs. The leader knocks the pots into the fire with his musket to show his power. They leave."

CHAPTER 37

"It's called Laron Syndrome"

"He's not a dwarf, Nick."

"I know that! I'm pointing out a kind of paradigm! The gene that affects their growth factors also makes them immune to heart disease and diabetes! It's a recent study. It affects a small community of individuals in Ecuador mostly...I saw it in National Geographic, Brad. I didn't make it up! They think these individuals will live a longer-than-average life span due to this anomaly. If they have this, Santiago may be part of a small community with some other anomaly. The point is, there is an example of something outside the expected."

"You think the blood being odd, the rapid healing...that's like this...Laron thing?"

"It fits! I told you, the lack of a European coefficient in Santiago's blood has to demonstrate isolation from the general population of his country. Most likely a small group in a remote area. All the strange behaviors—ancient customs preserved—also through isolation."

"Umhm, and the tele—?"

"Undegraded telomeres. The rapid healing?—proof of a genetic mutation. If you could locate his point of origin, I bet you a year's salary we'd find a small indigenous group with some members exhibiting the same characteristics."

"He's still telling the story of Tlaloc."

"He wants to hang on to his job...and you."

"You know...He finally brought up something I could latch onto. Something historically traceable...Besides Cortez and all that, I mean."

"Really?"

"...I think. He talked about an uprising...of slaves. One of them was a boy he had helped escape with his father from the slave ship. He was involved in setting fire to part of the English settlement and the killing of some whites. I did a little digging. There was a slave uprising in New York...in 1712...It involved about eighty slaves and some freemen."

"...You think he looked it up?"

"It's possible. I don't know. Does it matter at this point?"

***

"Every day for three days I go. Elalie comes with me. We feed him. I heal his wound. Every day she watches us and listens.

"'I cannot go back in the town. They know me. They know I am one of those that burn their houses. That raise our hands to them.'

"'Then you run, Lele. Go far away. There is everywhere to run.'

"'I must free those who fight with me! They are caught. They are to be killed. The English are afraid of us, and so they must keep us in chains or kill us....I have a woman.'

"'Do they kill her too?' Elalie asks, and I am without words when I hear this!'

"'You know what he says? Elalie, speak!' She betrays herself and is caught by her own mouth. Slowly she nods to me.

"'How? How do you know this tongue? You never hear it before. Only when I speak with this one. How do you understand what is said?' I am holding her wrist and she looks at me afraid.

"'...I just know! I listen and I know! Father, you hurt me!'

"'I let go of her, and I pull my fear back inside. She is as I am.

250

She has the gift of tongues. She learns fast and understands. 'What else do you know?'

"I know this one, this Lele, sees you as a child, and now he is a man. He calls you Medicine Man. He thinks you are a witch or a spirit. He is not sure.'

"He is a frightened man. He fears for his woman...for his life— that is all! We must not make more of this than it is.'

"You do not tell me. Why? Why do you not tell me before? Is it something I cannot know?'

"It is not important! What is important is that this one goes away!'

"We are speaking in our own tongue. Lele touches my arm with questions.

"You must go,' I tell him, 'You must run far away if you want to live!'

"I do not go without her! You help me?'

"I have a woman too! This is my child! We are part of her people. I do not risk this for your woman! I hide you. I heal you. Now you are to go. Go alone or with your woman, I do not care!'

"You leave him wounded and alone? You leave him to get here by himself? Father, that is not our way.'

"You do not tell me our way. I tell you! We are done with this one. Come! Lele, I am sorry for your woman, but I am more worried for my own. I pray to my Gods for you. I do not know if they hear me. Go well.'

"We leave him. Elalie is angry all the way back to the lodge. She argues with me and calls me many things. She is ashamed. She thinks I am cruel to let this one help his woman on his own.

"When we come to the camp, I know it is wrong! Pots are everywhere. The fire is out. Inside everything is on the ground, and there is a strong smell of filth and too many people and fire.

—It is the English!

"Now Elalie is silent. The fear swallows her words of anger for me. She looks around the camp and finds nothing. She returns, and I sit with her.

"'We must see Oratamin and the others. They know what happens. We are gone too much from here. Perhaps your mother is in the village.'

"'She does not leave here like this. Father, there is a fight here! You know this! The English come. They take her!'

"'Do not say that! We do not know. Perhaps she fights. Perhaps she runs away! We go now to Oratamin. He tells us what happens.'

"In the village there is confusion. Many English come to them. Women and children are held while the warriors answer many questions. They do not fight for fear that the women and children are harmed.

"'They ask us where the Dark Ones are, but no one knows. No one sees these Dark Ones. We tell them this, and finally they leave us. They show us their angry faces, but I know there is much fear. They tell us the Dark Ones kill some of them, burn their houses, run away. They catch many, but some still run. These they want. They think we have them. I tell them we have no Dark Ones here! They look everywhere. They tear down lodges, look in the rocks and trees. No Dark Ones. Finally they leave us.' Oratamin stands looking at me with eyes that tell me he Sees something.

"'...What?' I ask. 'I know you See. What is it?'

"'They have Anasan. They think you have one of these that run from them. They take her. They hold her! You do have one of these Dark Ones...'

"'I take him back! I give him up! They give her back to me!'

"'No,' he says. 'You take him back, they kill Anasan; they kill you too. You tell them where they find him, they kill Anasan, *they kill you too. We go with you and take him back...they kill us all.'*

"There is some way! I know there is some way! I do not let them kill Anasan!' I am on my knees. I am calling from my spirit. I am reaching for the Gods who do not hear me.

"There is one way...' Oratamin says quietly while I am screaming.

"What! I do this! I cut out my own heart!'

"That may be, but not now. You join the Dark One. Help him find his woman. Go at night. Together you find both women in the English town. Together you fight. You come out, or you do not. That way, I do not See. It is the only way that is not clear to me. That is the only way which does not show itself.'

"I must know!' I beg him.

"Then chew the plant. See for yourself! I am only what I am. You...are the one who chooses blindness...deafness. You must open yourself or trust what I See.'

"He is cold. I know he blames me for Anasan. They all do. Without Anasan, I am apart from them. I feel it. They do not look at me. They go back to themselves picking up the damage of the English around them. The children move away. Only Elalie, Oratamin, and I stand there looking at each other.

"Father, I can go with you! I am a good hunter. We can find Mother and Lele's woman. We can bring them out of the English village!'

"You stay here! I do not risk you too. I have done too much already. I must find Lele, join him. I do not know the English town now, but he does. He knows the ways of it. I do as Oratamin says. I show that I am worthy of these people.'

"Father, I am strong like you!'

"You are my life! The life of your Mother! You do not do this! Oratamin, bind her if you must, but she cannot follow me!'

"'She does not go. The women hold her while you are gone.'

"'You can't hold me!'

"'Daughter, this you must do. If I am to save your Mother, you must listen and obey this one time! There is no time to argue!'

"Oratamin holds her, and I run into the forest looking for Lele. He is only half healed from his wound now. He does not move so fast. I go in the direction of the English. I follow the smell of them. I am closer soon, and I hear someone to my side, stalking me. I feel this one nearly ready to spring, and I call, 'Lele!'...The sounds stop. This one is listening, waiting. I call again, 'Lele, it is me...Medicine Man. I come to help you!' He crashes through the bushes and stumbles into the space where I crouch. I see that his wound is still bringing him pain.

"'Why do you come? You tell me I must go, so I go. Why do you find me?'

"'The English have my wife. They come for her while I am healing you. The only way I can help her is to help you!'

"'You save me again! I pray to my Gods that I die this day. I know that I have no strength to do what I must do. You come. I know we help them. We free them all!'

"'You say more than I think we can do! Look at you. Your wound opens again and bleeds!'

"'Not so much. It is the pain. It is hard to run.'

"'That I can stop.' I fix a tea of plants that grow everywhere there. They take away pain for a long time, but there is a danger in that. Without pain a man does not know if he makes the wound worse. I tell Lele this, and he laughs.'

"'You tell me, Medicine Man, what is worse than the wounds we have right now?' He takes the drink and looks at me, 'I am sorry. I bring you this. I bring you only blood!'

"'I am a Brother to the Blood! It is always my way. My Gods drink it for their Life! Whatever blood I have is theirs...if they *want it. You only give them a chance to see me dance again!'*

"'Then dance well, Medicine Man. We must do a brave thing.'
He tells me that there are two more hiding near the town. The
English have taken many of his people and keep them in a 'jail'.
It is a place that is guarded. Anasan is among them. Lele's two
tell him that tomorrow they are to be judged, then killed. His
friends do nothing. They are too afraid to be caught, but they
watch. They know the ways around the town where the English
do not see.

"'Can they tell us where this 'jail' is? Can you find us a way
there?'

"'Yes. They do not come with us, though. They are afraid.'

"'We do not need them.' We are shown a place in the town. A
stone building. Inside we can hear the Dark Ones. Some call
out. Others cry. They know they are to die soon for the killing
of the English.

"I go close to the stone place. They are kept behind a strong
wall. The doors have thick metal pieces holding them up. Three
English with muskets sit at a table playing at something with
little white bones. They drink from cups. I go back to Lele who
waits hiding behind a wall.

"'Did you see them? Are they alive?'

"'I did not see them, but we must hope. There are three guards.'

"'I will run on them and kill them!' Lele is ready with his hand
on his knife.

"'No! Think. They play at a game. They do not expect anything
except the Sun in the morning. They drink...Wait.'

"'We cannot wait! The time is short. If we do not free them, our
women die. They all die!'

"'I say wait! One of them comes out soon...to piss. This one I
kill. Quiet. No one hears. The others will not know until it is
too long for him to be gone. Another will come looking. That

one we kill also. That leaves one. He is frightened, I think, when his friends do not come back. He comes to the door to look. He is cautious. We must wait again until he thinks he must get more help. When he walks out—then we kill him as well.'

"'What if it is not that way?'

"'Do you know a man who drinks and does not piss?'

"Lele looks at me...and he smiles. He is calm now. I move near to the stone house and wait with the crickets and frogs. It is a while but one guard comes out. He has his musket. He moves to the bushes. When he puts down his musket, I take him with my knife. I cut quick where the wind makes the voice in the throat. There is no sound. Lele and I drag away the body. We cover the ground where the blood was spilled.

"Soon the second comes calling the first. He goes almost to the same place. This one has his musket ready. I cannot let him make that noise. I wait till he calls the name again, and I answer, 'Ha!' He calls again coming in my direction. I answer again, 'Ha!' Lele takes him from behind. He holds the hand on the musket with one arm and breaks the man's neck with the other. Even the crickets do not change their sound.

"So far all is going well.

"We wait. The Third does not come out! He does not look for his companions! 'What do we do?' Lele asks. 'It is not long before the sun comes up. The last man does not come out. We are done! They are all dead!'

"'Not yet! I go and look for this last one. If he shoots at me, you must run hard at him before he can load again. You must kill him quick, and let the others out. All of you must run as fast as you can. The musket will bring many more English.'

"'Wait! I will do this. You have a child, I do not.'

"'You are too big! I am not seen. I know how to be invisible. You are like a mountain! Do as I tell you, and we may yet free our women.'

256

"The moon is down now. It is the darkest it can be. I creep closer to the doorway. I hold my breath and peer through low enough that my head cannot be seen by someone sitting. He has his back to me, the third one. He sits in the chair and he seems to be looking at the playing bones. I wait...Suddenly I see! He is asleep! That is why he does not come out. He sleeps while his companions die! His arm cushions his head and he seems almost awake, but I hear his breathing. Quietly I creep inside. I hear the crying from inside the locked room. It is quieter now. No one calls out. Sadness has grabbed them all I think and stopped their protests. Silently I draw my blade. I creep up upon the third man. In one quick action I grab his head, pull it back and drive the knife straight down deep into his throat. He twitches for a moment and then goes limp. I lower him to the floor and run to the door. I wave to Lele to come!

"Lele is in the door in three huge bounds. He stays quiet and looks with wonder at the third man.

"'Asleep.' I tell him. Lele nods and takes the iron key from the wall. Quietly he turns the key in the lock and instantly there is a wave of moans from beyond the door. Lele pulls the door open quickly and tries to silence them all. Some do so. Others make too much noise. They call out in stupid joy!

"I hear someone call out from beyond the stone house. I know others are coming. 'Quick, run!' Lele shouts. There are many. They run out of the stone house. Lele searches in the dark room and goes in. I follow. In the dim light I try to find Anasan in the confusion of people pushing each other to get through the door. I see her. She lies on the floor in filthy straw. Her leg is hurt and she is struggling to her feet.

"'I knew my toad would find me! The English...they take me. They ask me where the big Dark One is, but I do not tell! I do not tell!'

"'Come!' I shout. 'We must get out!' Many are pushing at the door, fighting each other to get through. I have Anasan by the waist, one arm across my shoulder. I have all her weight on me, and I am pushing at the others, but we cannot get through. Suddenly Lele comes. He pulls several from our way.

"'Go, Medicine Man! Take her out of here!'

"I fly with her! I run as if I have nothing in my arms. I climb the nearest hill in the clearing, and the woods are just beyond. Her leg is broken, but she will live. I have saved her! My heart leaps up. Oratamin was right! This way we both live.

"As I think this, I hear a musket fire. It is close—very close. I wheel around to see. Standing there is the English from our camp, the one who asks the questions of her. He is re-loading his weapon. I know I must be fast. I turn back to the woods. I am running. Anasan is moving her good leg, but she cannot help me at this speed. There is a grove of trees up ahead. I hear the musket fire again, but I do not turn, I do not slow down. I run! I run and run and run. My lungs burn, and my legs beg for rest, but my mind does not let me stop. I run until I am in the village of The People. As I come, I see them run toward us. Oratamin is there. He stares at us. They all see us. Elalie runs toward us calling out.

"'Father! Mother! You are here! You are with us. Mother, you—'

"She stops in her words. She takes Anasan's other arm and helps me lower her to the ground. My lungs are screaming for air, and I cannot talk.

"'Mother?...Mother!...'

"'Leg!'...I manage to say. 'Her leg is broken. She is soon healed. I make this happen....' I am gasping for air. Elalie is searching Anasan; I do not know why.

"'...Dead! She is dead! You bring her home dead!'

"'...What?...No!...She is unconscious...from the pain! She is not dead! She is not—' Then I see there is a wound in her back. A musket ball finds its way to her heart. She is dead as I run with her. Before I get her to her people, to Elalie. She is dead! AAAAHEEEE! AAAAHEEE! NOOOOOO! AAAAHEEEE!'"

CHAPTER 38

"Santiago? Santiago!! Stop!"

I couldn't get the old man up on his feet. He had sunk to his knees, wailing over and over again. He beat his chest and hit his face, splitting his lip. It was a gut-wrenching, soul-deep wail. Tears streamed from his brown face, which was contorted into a mask of pain. He swayed from side to side and continued the mourning of his lost Anasan.

I did my best to hold his hands, but he would free his hands and beat himself over and over again. Blood trickled down his face. One eye was turning blue around the rim. The recorder had flown from my desk and gone I don't know where. All I could do was hold onto him and wait it out.

After what seemed to be an eternity, he slumped into quiet sobbing. I went to the bathroom and wet two handfuls of paper towels and came back to him. One bunch I put on the back of his neck. With the others, I began to wash the blood from his face. All the time I kept murmuring stupid, senseless things like, "It's over now. It's long over! Don't think about it. It's long over..."

Finally...finally, after at least a half-hour of this uncontrollable emotion, he became quiet. His head was bowed, and he stopped swaying. He breathed heavily, exhausted. I was worried that perhaps he would have a stroke or a heart attack, but slowly his breathing slowed. He grabbed at the chair next to him for support, and he pulled himself up into it. He took a paper towel and wiped his face and eyes. He raised his head a little and tentatively searched my face. He seemed afraid to look me in the eye.

"I...am...crazy from this...you know? I could not save her! I could not keep her safe!...the Gods punish me! I know this! They let me take her...then they take her from me! Ay! What do they want? I cannot tell!"

"It was the English Guard. He shot her. You—Tlaloc can't blame himself for that!"

"Yes! The English! This I see. This I know! I know the face of this English! I know what I must do!"

"I think we should stop for now. This has been too much for you, Santiago. All this...memory is doing you no good!"

"Sí—is good! It is good that I tell. Good that I give all to you. It is what I must do!"

"You need to rest—"

"No! No rest! This thing I do, I say! I do not hide it. I do not think I can't hear the Gods, can't see them! I know I can! It is as Oratamin says, I do not *want* to hear them! I close my heart to them, and now they tear it from my chest! They devour it!"

"Santiago, stop it!" He had drawn himself up holding on to my jacket with both fists. He shook with emotion, but he was silent for a moment. I saw him turn his eyes inward again. He let go of my jacket, and he sat back down. He sat forward in his chair and kept talking.

I looked around the room and spotted the recorder. It was still on. The LED was still on showing that it was still running. As he spoke, I retrieved it, and he plunged back into that terrible night:

> "...I know I must go back. I am as our warriors are when they make war on another tribe. I am filled with the spirit of Huitzilopochtli!"

> "Oratamin tries to break my mind. 'You do not feel this alone! I lose a sister! Elalie, a mother! The People lose a brave and generous spirit! Tlaloc, if you are one of us, you must think that what you do is not only for you! It changes the world for all of us!'

> "But I do not listen! I can hear nothing, see nothing but the face of the English and his musket. I say nothing. I go to our lodge

and there I make ready. Elalie follows and Oratamin. The People stay behind. They take up Anasan's body to prepare it for burial.

"I strip to the waist. On my body I paint the symbols of war! In my hair I put the feathers of a hunting bird—the nearest I can find to that I use with my people. I prepare the lodge ground and draw the Gods and demons...And then I dance! I praise Huitzilopochtli in my own tongue and beg his power. I give the blood and pray he drink deep now...and deeper later. Oratamin and Elalie watch me. They say nothing. Elalie watches and listens. Some words. I hear her repeat. The fire glows in her eyes. The sun is moving higher. Inside the lodge, in a skin that I keep that no one knows, I take my Priest knife. It is the one given by the Priest-Father. It is made of the black stone. I have carried it always. Now it lives out its use!

"I run toward the town. Oratamin and Elalie follow behind. Oratamin is afraid I will bring trouble to The People—Elalie is excited...curious, but not afraid. At the edge of the town we stop on the ledge above where I stand with Anasan before...

"Below there are many English. They surround a small number of Dark Ones. I see Lele! He is captured but I do not see the woman. There are about twenty Dark Ones. The English have put up posts in the ground. To each they tie a Dark One. Several pile sticks around them by their feet. An English says some words. Finally two English come with fire. They light the sticks and the Dark Ones burn! They scream! They scream 'til their spirits leave their bodies. The smell of cooking meat comes up to us on the ledge where we stand, and Oratamin empties his stomach in disgust.

"The English only watch as one by one the Dark Ones scream out their life spirits and hang limp and burning on the posts. Soon all are dead...except Lele. He alone stands watching his people burning. I can see that he is spent. His wound is bleeding, but the tea I make still stops the pain. He will not feel the fire, I think.

"But the English have something different for Lele. They think he is the leader. For him they have made something worse. A *great wheel is brought to the clearing. The wheel rides on its side. It turns but does not go anywhere. To this they tie Lele so that he is stretched out between its spokes. When they turn the wheel Lele also turns. Two men come with clubs. They turn Lele, and the two men bring the clubs down on his legs. From where we are, I hear the crack of his bones. They turn him, and again they bring down the clubs this time on his arms. Again I hear the cracking of bones, but Lele does not cry out! I see the English looking at each other. They do not understand why he does not scream in pain. They do not know my medicine. Again and again they turn him and strike, each time bones crack and splinter inside his flesh. He is dazed and the blood runs from him in the splits in his flesh, but he only looks at them. Soon he is nothing but a body with only a bloody mush for arms and legs.*

"Finally an English—my English! gives a word, and one brings the club down on Lele's head. He is gone. The boy with the round eyes like river stones who cried for his parents in the dark hold, the boy I heal of the worms that eat him, who looks at me with thanks when he jumps into the cold water with his father—that boy slips into the earth.

"Twenty-two we see die, that day. These English are like the Spanish. They are the masters! They decide who dies. They make themselves Gods!

"'We go now. You have seen this thing. They are many. We are three.' Oratamin wishes to go.

"'I am one! I seek only one. Oratamin, you go, and take Elalie with you. I wait. At nightfall I take this English. This I do for Anasan!'

"'No. Not Anasan! Not for her! She does not watch you risk everyone to avenge her.'

"'No one sees me! The English will not know of me! I take him and give him to my Old Gods. They have been long without a sacrifice! I do them honor!'

"'You honor only your hatred.'

"'Then go! I do not need you here!'

"I wait the day on that ledge. We watch the English in the town. The bodies of the Dark Ones are taken away. Lele is untied from his wheel and follows the others. Some come, and the place is swept clean of the deaths, but the smell stays. At sundown the town grows quiet. We are on the edge of it. Here there are English warriors. They come and go, but it is not until dark that I see 'my English' come from the stone house. He carries a pipe with him such as the ones I see Oratamin's counsel use. I smell the tobacco burning. He draws the smoke from the long curved stem and sits on a stone looking at the evening.

"I wait until I see his back round and grow soft. I know his thinking is far away on something. I creep closer until I am only a short distance from him. I pick up a small round pebble, and I throw it sharp and hard. It hits him on the back of the head. I see him start and stand to look behind him in the direction of the throw. I crouch behind a rock, and I make no sound.

"Soon he is seated again. Again his shoulders go slack. I throw again and hit him squarely behind the ear. I hear him call out and curse. He stands quickly and looks angrily about. I make myself small and silent. He looks longer now, trying to find who is hitting him. I wait. He waits...looking. At last he thinks his enemy is gone. He sits. He draws on his pipe, but it is out. He takes out a small square box and strikes a spark into the bowl of the pipe, but it does not take. He stands again angry, and he turns to go into the stone house. I pitch another stone at his neck and at the same time throw a larger one into the bushes just beyond the clearing.

"He grabs his neck and turns to hear the second stone landing in the bushes. He curses and runs into the stone house for his musket. In a moment he comes back out heading toward the place where the second stone lands in the bushes. I throw another further in, and I hear him call after it. He is chasing the sound of the stones. As he moves deeper into the woods, I bait him, hitting him with pebbles and tossing the larger stones to draw him away from the town. So I draw him further and

further away by his anger. At last he is far enough off. I must tease away his musket. The town must not hear it fire.

"To do this I creep up behind him. He is wary. I must be silent. If I move too quickly, he will fire, and I will lose the silence. I am careful to make no sound. The pebbles are stopped, and his anger is fading. He sees he has gone far into the woods. He rests his musket in the bend of his arm. This tells me he does not think his enemy is near him now. He looks around thinking he must return. Just as he releases his grip on the place where the musket fires, I jump him. With a large stone I hit him across the top of his head, not to kill him, just to daze him. The musket drops to the ground. I drop and roll and snatch it away from him.

"He shakes off the blow and pulls out his knife. He is a big man, but he is slow. I stand before him watching his eyes. They tell me he comes in to stab me, and I move aside taking his arm and pulling it hard up and in back of him. He screams in pain and drops the knife. I kick it into the bushes and turn quickly for a sapling, which I turn around his ankles to trip him. He is on the ground, and I am on him! He is strong, but I am faster. With a piece of hide from my belt I tie both his hands behind him. He scrambles to his feet to run but I trip him again, and he falls hard doubling over on one foot. He calls out in pain, and though he tries, I see he cannot rise again.

"Now he screams for help. He calls toward the town, but his anger has drawn him so far away, no one can hear him—but me. I crouch in the dust by him and look at him. He spits angry words at me, but I do not even try to understand him.

"He tries to crawl away, but I grab him by his boots and drag him back. He kicks at me, but he does not get me. This we do...many times. He screams and crawls. He kicks. I drag him back. I play with him like a cat with its prey. I want him to feel afraid. I want the blood to pulse and boil inside him. Finally he grows weak...exhausted. Now that I make him as frightened and angry as I can, he is ready.

"I take out my Priest knife. There in the clearing I dance my victory. I say the prayers of thanks and glory, and I show the

Gods the knife. I dance around him offering him to Huitzilopochtli. 'Take him!' I cry. 'Take this blood and drink. Know that we still live if only in me, if only in this act today. We still live, and we give this blood to you!'

"I leap on the exhausted man. I rip open his clothing. I raise the knife and plunge it straight into the chest. I reach in and take the heart and pull it out. It beats! It is a sign! As it beats, I take it to my mouth...and bite!

"'Tlaloc! Tlaloc, what do you do?' Oratamin stands there. He face is open wide with fear. I swallow. The blood drips down my chin as I straddle the body of the English. 'This is sacrilege! This is an evil thing you do!'

"'No, Oratamin! Not to me! This one is a sacrifice to my Gods! This one I give to them. His blood is theirs! The heart I eat to give him a life in me!'

"'There is nothing I see in this that is of men! It is an offense to our kind! It is a great evil, to eat the flesh of another man even one who does a wrong thing! Anasan's spirit curses you for this! She turns from you in the afterlife! You are a demon!'

"'This I must do! This is the way I know! I am what I must be! I cannot be of your kind. I must be my kind!' This I say as I stand holding the heart.

"'Father!' Elalie sees me. She has come upon us, and she stands looking at me. She does not know what to say.

"'Look away from me! Oratamin, take her away from here! This is not for her to see, not for you to see. It is the way of my people! Only I know this. Go! Take her away!'

"Oratamin takes her. When they are gone I finish what I begin. I eat the heart cold. The rest I bury deep in the wood. No one finds this English. Oratamin and his people are not blamed for this. The man is...disappeared. Who knows what is become of him?"

CHAPTER 39

"It's a 'feasibility study'."

"I see—a 'feasibility study' to test the feasibility of what?"

"Mr. Delaney, why are you here?"

"I may no longer be Chairman of the Board of Governors, but I still...care very much about this institution, Dr. Holliman."

He hadn't lost a beat, as I feared he might. Delaney still sat ramrod straight in his chair, and his steely blue eyes still looked directly at me. There was no falter in his military manner. His visit carried a sense of challenge with it.

"Of course, Mr. Delaney. I'm sorry that things worked out as they did."

"You might be."

"I'm sorry? Is there something you're trying to tell me?"

"How's the new Board? Is it...to your liking?"

"I...don't know them. They all joined very recently. We're only had one meeting."

"I see. And Julian, is he giving you a free hand? No—interference?"

"He's...largely uninvolved. We are to meet monthly as per charter. The running of the school is solely in my hands."

"Well, that must be a great relief to you. No one prying into the curriculum, challenging your decisions."

"...Mr. Delaney, what did you come here for? I'm sure it wasn't to check my stress level, so I'm assuming you had something important to tell me."

"Your new Board—were you aware that half of them were Spencer and Chase executives?"

"...The new roster hasn't been presented yet, but no, I didn't know that..."

"None of them, by the way, ever attended Crayden."

"Several of the old Board members weren't Crayden alumni."

"That's true. Sam Holbrook—Dr. Samuel Holbrook and Dr. Marvin Ingersoll were both Princeton men. Educators with long careers in the field."

"I was aware of their credentials."

"Not one of your new Board has any background in Education. In fact, the balance of the Board is all business associates of Julian's—all of whom, I might add, owe the health of their businesses to Julian's various enterprises."

"...I rather guessed that was the case from our first meeting. Not much give and take. Julian had them elect him Chairman, and that was pretty much it."

"And now you yourself are in Julian's employ. Quite a sum of money for a largely figurehead position, don't you think?"

"I'll earn it, Mr. Delaney! I took the position to help direct the philanthropic efforts the Reynolds Foundation is making to Crayden! Julian has made it very clear that he doesn't want to be bothered."

"And how's that going for you? Up to your eyeballs in plans and reports? Overwhelmed with schedules and projected finishes? Hammered by meetings with Spencer and Chase's architectural team and the army of contractors who will soon be 'upgrading' the building?"

"I told you, Mr. Delaney. After Olsen's disappearance, Julian directed Spencer and Chase to redo the entire study under a new team. It's all very new—less than a month. I'm sure that at the next meeting all this is going to fall on my shoulders."

"That will be a burden! Are you sure you can handle all that *and* be Headmaster?"

"It won't be that extensive. The building will have its major mechanicals rejuvenated, and a new roof will be installed—during the summer months. That's all. The plans for the pool will be...delayed until we deem it a more appropriate time."

"Summer is only six weeks away. Aren't you running a little behind if you're going to make that schedule? But wait! You did say it wouldn't be that extensive."

"That's right."

"And the 'feasibility study' is happening now?"

"All over the building, yes! In the last three weeks there have been troupes of engineers surveying the grounds, taking measurement, running tests..."

"And, of course, they've all been reporting their findings to you."

"No, not yet. I'm sure I'll be getting the full results of the study when it's complete."

"Olsen was able to accomplish all of that in under two weeks with the help of, I think, three engineers."

"We don't have him now, Mr. Delaney!"

"Yes, I know that. Very strange, very sad for his mother, I'm sure. What I'm getting at, Dr. Holliman, is—doesn't it seem odd to you that what one architect with a minimal crew was able to accomplish in such a short time is taking a much larger group—from the same firm—a much longer time? If you are the director of the Reynolds Foundation and the individual who will be directing the work done on the building, why haven't they been reporting to you as they go along? Doesn't that seem...a little out of sync?"

"I'm sure I will get a full report at next week's Board Meeting."

"My God, Holliman, you're as dense as a brick! Something's up! It doesn't take this long to work out plans if you've got someone like Julian and his money behind a project. This isn't some public project run by the city's graft machine! This is a privately funded, straightforward re-fit. Julian is playing you for a fool."

"I didn't think you were the type to engage in character assassination, Mr. Delaney."

"I'm sorry you think that of me, Dr. Holliman. It is not my way to idly challenge the ethics of another man behind his back. I can't offer you proof, but I will tell you that I still have a few well-placed friends. There is a rumor in certain circles that Julian's company is planning a new project—something very substantial at Crayden!"

"He can't do that without talking to me."

"That's just it, isn't it? He isn't talking to you. Not much anyway. I didn't want you to solicit him for money, if you will recall. It's best not to wake the bear!"

"Mr. Delaney, we're landmarked! He can't do very much."

"Julian tends to do whatever he wants."

"This is absurd. It's just idle gossip."

"Is it? As you say, you should have a full report at your next Board Meeting. I would imagine that will be quite an interesting one!"

CHAPTER 40

"They dress her in the finest skins. Around her neck is the necklace I make for her. The 'pieces of the moon' I give her. By her side is a pot filled with the food she takes to the 'next life'. Elalie arranges her hair in the way she wears for special ceremonies. She is washed and soft skin moccasins are on her feet. In the pit with her the People place flowers and sweet herbs. Some sing for her spirit.

"I cannot sing. I cannot move. I stand and look at my Anasan. I feel my own spirit in the pit with her! I long to lie down next to her and be her 'little toad' forever. I cry my eyes dry. There are no tears. My heart is a stone pulling me toward the earth.

"Father...are you angry with me?' Elalie stands next to me. She speaks without looking into my face so that the others do not know we speak.

"'No...I...feel nothing. No anger...no pain...'

"'Have you...no love for me as well. I go with you to care for the Dark One. If I stay, I fight with Mother. The English dies before he takes us! It is my fault!'

"'It is not you! I am the one who went to him. I am the one to blame. She does not like him in our lodge, and I do not listen!'

"'It is done, Father.'

"'I am done!'

"'No, Father! What of me? If you are done, so am I! I lose my

270

Mother and my Father too?'

"'You are a woman, now. You are of the Wolf Clan. I am...not. I am other than you. I have no place now.'

"'I am your place! I am my Mother's daughter, yes...but you are in me too. I think deeper than you know. What you do...what I see—'

"'That was not for you to see! Do not speak of that!'

"'Nevertheless I see it. I...feel it. I feel it is right...'

"'You do not know what you speak of! I cannot speak of this with you!'

"'Why? Why can you not tell me of your people? Why can I not know about the half of what I am?'

"'I cannot! I am forbidden! I disobeyed the Gods once, and now I am cursed! Look at your Mother! The Gods do this! I do not know how to stop their anger. I do not want you to pay as well!'

"The singing stops. The women come and cover her with skins, then they pour the earth over her until she is gone. The People go away. Elalie leaves me alone to my sadness. There I stay.

"It is days. Many days I sit by Anasan. There is rain. There is sun. At night the wind blows. I feel nothing.

"Elalie comes. She builds a fire at night. She leaves food, but I do not eat. Water I take but only a little. I cannot bring myself to leave her. I cannot move myself. I can see no life for me anymore.

"Finally Oratamin comes to me. He says, 'It is time for us to leave here. The English are too dangerous to be around. I See that we must cross the river and go away from them. It is our best chance to live well.'

"'I cannot leave here.'

"'This I See as well. I do not ask you to come with us because of

what you do. You are not a man like us! We cannot have you with us, or you destroy us. Your Gods...are not the Gods we follow. Our Gods to not drink blood...do not...bid us eat the flesh of men. This ends our bond with you.'

"'I know this. It is well. Go well, Oratamin. What I teach you is good. Forget what you see me do. Remember only what is good, and I think of you as part of my spirit.'

"'Elalie does not go with us.'

"'You must take her! She is Wolf Clan. She belongs with her people.'

"'No. She is not of the People. She is the image of my sister, but that is only a cover. Inside she is you. She carries you. This I See. This I know. She does not come with us.'

"'You leave her here to starve with me?'

"'She is a good hunter. She does not starve. She has a Father who cares for her. It is also her will. She does not wish to go with us'

"'You make her go!'

"'I don't make her go. She is a woman. She follows her Father. If he does not rise up from the grave of her Mother, she dies there as well.'

"'You are not a good man! You are not a Shaman if you do this!'

"'Talk to your daughter. She is here.' Elalie comes from the bushes. She stands in front of me.

"'Go with your tribe!' I shout at her.

"'I do. I am here with you. I am your tribe; you are mine.'

"'There is no tribe here! I sink into the earth with your Mother.'

"'Then I sink too, Father. Make room for me next to you. I wait with you until we both join my Mother in the earth.'

"'I leave you both. I cannot see where your paths lead. It is too far ahead for me. Tlaloc, make peace with your Gods. I know they are not done with you. Keep this one well. She is what you have left of our Anasan. I think of you both. Part of my heart stays here with you. Goodbye.'

"He leaves us. Elalie makes a fire, and she hunts. She builds a lodge by the place where Anasan lies. A long time it is the two of us. I see she is much of Anasan. She stays, and little by little she drags me back to life."

CHAPTER 41

"Mrs. Olsen, Brad Holliman. I'm the Headmaster at Crayden. I'm very sorry for your loss."

The body had washed ashore in Rockaway...what there was of it. After weeks in the water, there wasn't much left. The pathologists couldn't find any evidence that would suggest foul play. Suicide was suspected, but with so little to go on...there was nothing to do but have the funeral and bury him. All of the Spencer and Chase people had come. There was a smattering of 'civilians' but not many. It seemed as though Olsen didn't have much of a personal life. He kept to himself. He worked obsessively. Had very few friends.

"It's very good of you to come Dr.—"

"Holliman. I met your son only a couple of times, but I wanted to extend my sympathies. Your son had made some excellent plans for the improvement of our school. He was very dedicated."

"Martin was devoted to his job! Just devoted! That's all he cared about. Oh, Dr. Holliman, it used to make me crazy how he would spend hours—days going over plans and drawings. I wanted him to get out! Experience Life! You know? A Mother wants her son to...have 'interests'."

She was still pushing him even at the funeral it seemed.

One by one, the Spencer and Chase crowd paid their respects. A few of them were Board members. These I singled out when I could. I made a few respectful comments, and then I would bring the discussion around to the current plans at Crayden. As soon as I did so, I notice the "curtain" drop behind their eyes. I got comments like, "Yes, yes! Very exciting.

You'll be very pleased with the results!" But I got no particulars.

I finally cornered John Beeman, a Second Vice-President or something in charge of "Strategic Supply". With him I tried a different approach.

"Mr. Beeman! Nice to see you. Brad Holliman—Headmaster at Crayden?"

"Yes, I recognize you, Dr. Holliman. Sad occasion. Mrs. Olsen is holding up well under the circumstances. They had to close the coffin, of course. The body was terribly decomposed! God!"

"Did you know him well?"

"Martin? Well, yes, as a colleague. He wasn't exactly the backslapping type, if you know what I mean, but I worked with him quite a lot. I was working on your project with him when he disappeared."

"Really? He seems to have made a good plan for us."

"Oh, yes! Martin was very thorough. His plan—as far as it went—was excellent! The building would be quite useable."

"Yes. I'm sure. Was he very knowledgeable about the building and its original design?"

"Martin? That's the first thing he would do. He was our 'Restoration Specialist', you know. If course, now with the new plan, all that is a drop in the bucket."

"Mm...right. So the new plan is completed?"

That's when he "caught himself."

"Uh...well no. Not really. The...uh...new *study* is nearly completed, is what I should have said. All that will be laid out soon. You know, I'm not much for this type of gathering. I'm meeting my family in..." He hastily looked at his watch. "My God! I'm late. Nice to talk to you, Dr. Holliman. I'm sure I'll see you at the Board Meeting."

He made a quick get-away, but I knew that Delaney was right. Something *was* up! They were under orders obviously not to discuss the project with me. I could smell Julian behind this. I was sure it couldn't be the drastic thing Delaney had suggested, but I knew something was being done that Julian didn't want me to know about. At least not now.

I was about ready to pay my last respects, and I was waiting to say goodbye to Mrs. Olsen when I spotted a young man hanging back from the rest of the Spencer and Chase crowd. He was subdued. He didn't seem to be part of any particular group. In fact he seemed to be alone. I stood behind him in the rather disorganized line of people getting ready to leave.

"It's hard, isn't it?" He nearly jumped when I spoke.

"Hm? I'm sorry?"

"To know when to leave."

"Oh....yeah...it's always awkward." He was holding a 'remembrance card', the kind with the deceased's picture on it and prayer on the back. He was turning it over and over waiting for his turn to say goodbye.

"Did you know him well? Martin, I mean?"

"Yes...very well. We worked together. He was a good friend!"

"Really? I'm glad to hear it! Mrs. Olsen was quite forthcoming about Martin's lack of a social life earlier. I'm glad to hear that he had his own life—even if she didn't know about it."

"She didn't know him at all. Marty has....had a whole side to him that nobody knew!" With that the young man hitched back an involuntary sob, which he quickly stifled.

"...You all right?"

"I will be. It's just knowing it's all over. When he was missing, I thought maybe...maybe he...went somewhere. Got away."

"Got away? Away from what?"

"Really? You met his mother! How would you like to have that on your case twenty-four/seven? Marty was pretty...well...exhausted! He thought about moving out. Relocating maybe...I don't know...anything but staying with his mother! Then he disappeared..."

"Sounds like you knew him better than anyone! Brad Holliman. I'm the

Headmaster—"

"At Crayden. Yeah, I know who you are, Dr. Holliman. We all know who you are. The whole Goddamn office is working on your project!"

"...So, how well did you know him?"

"We...were close." He focused on the card as he said this.

"...I see."

"If you say anything, I'll deny it! Spencer and Chase is not a place where the Twenty-First Century operates. It's hard enough to get a decent job in architecture...Spencer and Chase does not appreciate the ideas of 'tolerance and equality'."

"You mean they don't hire a 'diverse' staff?'

"It's the fucking 'old boy network' on steroids! No women, no Blacks...no queers! If they thought Martin and I were anything but straight-up, all-American boys...we'd be out on our asses!"

"How do they get away with it?"

"C'mon. Look around. Corporate America still works in a vacuum. Small old firms like Spencer and Chase just keep chugging along like it's 1955! Martin and I got our positions through family connections. If it got out, we'd not only lose our jobs—"

"Family disgrace? Really? In this day and age?"

"...I don't care—but Martin did. He couldn't stand her, but he loved his Mom. Sorry, I don't mean to dump on you like this. You aren't going to—"

"Naw! I'm just sorry you have to...go through this alone. It's got to be pretty lonely."

"...Yeah...it is what it is..."

"...So the whole firm is working on Crayden?"

"It's pretty big. Reynolds is putting out the money, and Spencer and Chase are happy to take it!"

"How do we look...on paper?"

"You tell me. They don't let us juniors in on many details. It's all some kind of state secret! When Marty was your lead...it was a straight-up renovation. Now...What are you planning to do, a space launch?"

"...Uh...no. Not really."

"Well, you got all the 'old boys' jumping! Look, Dr. Holliman—what I said—I do need my job."

"I don't remember a thing about this conversation!"

CHAPTER 42

I got back from the wake in time for a faculty "tea". A "tea" was our way of serving coffee and pastries and talking shop after the school day. This was lobbying time for the teaching staff. It was my job to be "open", encouraging and "agreeable" without "agreeing" to spend any money.

"Watch out for Brother William. He wants new uniforms for the basketball team. Remember he still works for St. Barnabus—he doesn't have a stake in our budget!" Sally always kept an eye on our expenses. Crayden was in the black, but just. The projected changes in the building did nothing for our operating budget.

"Can't we give him something for that? He's the reason we have a basketball team!"

"If he left St. Barnabus...and the Church, I'd give him me! But he's still theirs, and we're just crawling to the end of the year with the budget. By the way, don't have seconds. I only ordered half the pastries...we can both do without the calories."

"Gotcha. Did anyone from the Reynolds Foundation call today?"

"The Reynolds Foundation? They never call. Why would somebody call?"

"...Just wondering. I talked to a lot of Spencer and Chase people at the wake—new members of the Board. I thought someone might have called."

"Nope. Nobody. How was it? Imagine washing up like that in Rockaway!"

"...It was...interesting. I think I might owe Mr. Delaney an apology."

"What? What's going on?"

"I don't know, but something is happening, and no one is telling me squat!" Just then Dr. Nichols found me, and I was off to an hour of new curriculum "possibilities" for the fall. Nick wasn't at the tea. I was disappointed. Aside from Sally, he was the only "adult" I could speak to.

Once the "tea" was over, Sally managed to herd the faculty out of our offices. It was the last "tea" of the year, and I was grateful.

"You need me to do anything?' Sally always asked before she left. I know she meant it, but I tried never to take her up on the offer. I figured I couldn't offer much in the way of a raise, but at least I could respect her "own time".

"Thanks Sally, I'm fine. I'm just going to make a few notes for myself, and then I'm going home too."

After she left, I sat there thinking about Delaney's warning and listening to the bells going off in my head. Had I maneuvered us into a blind alley? Did I really screw this up big time?

"...You are not good." Santiago was standing there with the cup in his hand. He put it down on my desk. "You have worry."

"...I went to a wake today. A young man."

"I know this...."

"The casket was closed. The body washed up on shore far from here."

"...That is not what makes you worry."

"No. I think perhaps I made a mistake."

"...You think maybe you wake up a bear, yes?"

"How did you—"

"I See this. You think maybe it is you who makes all this go away! ...It does not go away."

"The Jewish people have a saying, 'From your mouth to God's ear!'—You know the Jewish people?"

"Tlaloc knows. They do not believe in Jesus."

"Ah, but his Gods abandoned him...or he abandoned them."

"They see him. They hear him. But he Sees only what the Gods allow. They give him only a little—when they choose:

> *"For a long time Elalie waits with me. A long time we keep our lodge. The English town grows big and bigger. All Anasan's people are gone. Game is harder to find near us, and we must go farther and farther away to hunt and fish each day. The English kill all the game, catch all the fish. There are farms now where there were none before. The English are many.*
>
> *"Elalie grows lonely for people. She says, 'Father, the English are here. We can learn from them.'*
>
> *"'No! It is not safe. I do not lose you to them! I do not let them take you like your Mother!'*
>
> *"'I know their words.' She looks at me like one that does wrong. 'I go sometimes to the town and listen. No one sees me. I am as a shadow. I listen. I know many of their words. They are not so clean, but they are not so different either.'*
>
> *"'They are no different from the Spanish! They hate any different from themselves. They burn and torture the world to their will. They take whatever they want and break anyone who stands in front of them.'*
>
> *"'I see them! They have big lodges! And there are ships and many people. I see all kinds of English. Dark Ones working everywhere. People I never see before! So many!'*
>
> *"'All they do, they do for power! Power and Gold those are their two Gods. They do not see the land. The plants and animals are only something to take. The People like us are no different from the animals to them. We stay away from them!'*
>
> *"'Do you tell me that all of them—all the English are this way? There are not good ones among them? Father, here there are*

just the two of us. We are alone. No one of the tribe comes. Only more English. If we do not go to our people—'

"'I do not leave your Mother!'

"'I know, Father! If we stay here, the English will come to us. It is better that we go to them first. Learn to live with them. Find the good English.'

"So it is between us. Every day she says the same. More and more she longs for people. It is a way she is like her mother. She can't be like me. Alone. A shadow. I see her grow silent and sad. She talks little to me now, and she walks away to the woods with her eyes empty.

"She is my only life. I cannot tell her all that I have seen. All that I know. I am forbidden. I know I can't keep her like this. I know I must listen."

I realized that he had begun again. I reached into the drawer and pulled out the recorder again, but I don't think he even noticed. He had that look on his face he always got when he was deep into his story. It was a look I remembered when he told those stories to me as a child. It was mesmerizing then, and it still was. Of course, I couldn't have known then how...much more he wanted to tell:

"One night when she is sleeping, I leave Elalie in the lodge, and I go near the town. She is right! So many houses! I did not know this place from the time I am there before. Few are awake. I see some Dark Ones working before the sun rises. They make themselves small and quiet. They do not see me, but I see them.

"I walk long, moving through darkness...looking. Some places I see, I know. I start by the water. There are more ships now. Many more, and more houses around where they tie up, but some places I remember. I am looking for the tree with two trunks. It is not far from here, but which direction? What if it is no longer there?

"I move slowly past the places I know and try to see the town as it is when I am here before. I see the fort. This I know! There is a well. The tree with two trunks is near that! I run to see. It is there! The tree with two trunks is still there. It is much bigger

now, but it is there!

"*Quietly I take a flat stone, and I scrape at the earth near the tree. I remember the gold I take from the ship, from the Mixed-Blood I kill. He tells me it is more than one like me has. If it is here, it helps me with Elalie. We need gold if we come to the English Town. We need food...a way to live. I know these men! Gold is God to them. It gives us something to protect us from these.*

"*I find it! The skin I wrap it in is stiff and rotted, but inside I see the coins! Quickly I take them up. There are not so many, but it is something for this new life I must make for her.*

"*I come back as the sun is halfway up. Elalie is by the fire. She grabs a knife when she hears me, and she is ready to attack. I call her name.*

"'*Father? Where are you? I look for you, and you are nowhere!*'

"'*I go to the town.*'

"'*You—-go to the town? You? Father, what do you mean?*'

"'*You do not sing. You do not speak as you do before. I see that you are sad. There is only me, and I am ugly.*' *I spill the coins on the ground in front of her.*'

"*She is silent. He eyes are big, and she reaches slowly touching the gold.*

"'*How do you get gold? How do you have this?*'

"'*When I first come...this is given to me...for the healing of the Dark Ones in the water-houses—ships. It is mine. Now it is yours too.*'

"'*What do we do with this?*'

"'*We use it...go to the town. Find out the English.*'

"*She does not speak but holds me. There are tears on her face, and I think maybe I do not please her.*

"'Why do you cry? I go to the town to find this. It is for you!'

"'It is more than I can dream. Father, we find a life there; I know it! We are with people. They are not our people, but we find a way to be among them. It is good. Mother is not alone. We come back always to see her; to speak with her spirit.'

"'I do not think so, Elalie, but it is what you wish. I can't keep you alone any longer. I know this.'

"We plan our way. Elalie says we must not go in our skins and with our knives showing or our weapons. We creep close to the town. She shows me what the women wear and the men.

"'We wear their clothes and make a place not in the town but near for us to stay. A small lodge. We go in and watch and listen. Soon we know what we must do to be in the town, so that they do not look at us as strange. Father, there are so many, they do not see us.'

"'You think of this before, my daughter.'

"'I have thought of nothing else this long time! Father, we have a good way here, and, look, we have gold!'

"'If the English see the gold, they kill us for it! This I see; this I know!'

"'They do not see it! We do not show them this. This gold we keep hidden. No one knows we have it. We use it only when we must, and then we do it so that the English do not see.'

"'Gold has a way of being seen, Elalie. It has a way of being heard.'

"I do not like this thing, but I know it pleases Elalie. We make a camp far enough away in a place no one goes. It is close enough to be in the town when we wish, but far enough away that no one sees us for now.

"I go at night and steal clothes for myself. For Elalie, I cannot do this. The English women wear things not so easy to steal. By day I look and listen while Elalie must stay in camp. She *waits...impatiently.   Every night she asks when she will have clothes so that she goes into town too.*

"Finally, I have enough words to ask if there is work.   I know from before, that one works to get money to live among these people.   I see a woman who seems rich.   She is big.   Her 'house' is big, and she dresses very big, and I ask.   She looks at me like a storm.   'You ain't Black—what are you besides ugly?'

"'I am poor, but I work hard.   I am strong.   I have a daughter who works as well.   We work for you?'

"'What can ya do?'

"'What you say, I do.   My daughter as well.   We are strong, smart.   You give us work?'

"'I don't own no Blacks!   Those'll kill ya in yer sleep!   I need help in the Inn.   Can you clean, 'n fetch, 'n carry?'

"'I do not know this 'fetch 'n carry', but I say 'Yes!''

"'What about the girl?   Can she cook 'n serve?'

"'We do whatever you ask.'

"'Bring the girl.   I'll look at her.   Come back tomorrow.   I'll see what ya kin do!'

"I am not sure if I do the right thing, but I tell what happens to Elalie, and she is excited.   Now we must have clothes for Elalie. I go to town that night.   I find a 'Black' woman.   This woman is as tall as Elalie.   She wears clothes that are not good, but are English.   I tell her I give a gold coin for what she wears.   She gives me all the clothes for the coin.   She is very excited by the gold, and I tell her she does not know where it comes from, and she does not say.   I tell her this in a way that she knows I will come back to her, if she does.   I go back to Elalie with the clothes.   She takes them and hangs them on a bush to sweeten them.

"The next day we are at the big woman's big house.'

"'She's a tall 'un, ain't she!   Pretty, too.   How'd an ugly little runt

like you get this pretty thing? Girl—kin ya cook and clean?'

"Elalie nods. 'You'll work—I'll tell ya that. Got no time for shirkers.' She looks at us and says, 'I'll try ya for three days. No pay. If ya last 'n I decide, ya kin stay. Ya can both sleep in the barn loft...up there. Ya ain't White, so you stay in the kitchen. We get a rough bunch from the wharfs. They get drunk. They grab. Kin ya stand that?'

"I see Elalie does not know all the words, but she knows enough to say, 'Yes.'

"'Right! Well, git then! Wait! What are your names?'

"'I am Elalie—This is my Father, Tlaloc.'

"'Ellie and Lock!' You'd better prove out, or yer'll be out on yer asses! Lock, you go fetch the wood. Ellie, I got tankards need scrubbin' and floors that need sweepin' and straw to be put down. Chickens need feedin' 'n you gotta fetch up the flour from the cellar.'

"We understand only some. We look at each other with questions.

"'C'mon! Don't make me fire ya before I even take ya on!'

"In the three days I see what we do. The big house is a place where men come to drink and eat. They are loud, angry men. They fight sometimes. They stink! Some stay in rooms 'upstairs' for pay. Women come in too. These are not good women. These women sleep with the men. I learn they do this for money. The big woman is 'Annie'. She is loud too and often angry, but she does not sleep with these men. She takes their money. They give her money for drinks and food and rooms. The women give her money too, sometimes. This I do not understand for a long time.

"Elalie and I work hard! We clean. I keep the horse for Annie, and I go with a cart to 'fetch' whatever is needed. Elalie washes and cleans the rooms, and soon she cooks. At first, Annie says she must go because she does not know cooking. Elalie tells her that she knows the cooking of her people but not the English.

Annie shows her, and soon Elalie cooks English. I do not like it. For me she still cooks as we always do. Annie, I think, grows used to us. We are good workers.

"In summer we stay in the loft. We sleep in the hay. We make a place that we can keep for ourselves. In winter, we must stay in the cellar. The floor is dirt, but it is warm. Annie pays us small, but we get food, and this is a place to stay. In the cellar I bury the gold we keep, so that no one finds it.

"I learn these English are not only English. The ships bring in many from everywhere. There are even some from my old world. There are few Mixed-Bloods with the Spanish in their mouths. Sometimes I hear a word or two of my own tongue—it is only that, a word. It goes away, and it makes me feel more alone.

"Elalie is content. The People and the noise and the smell do not trouble her. She likes them! She moves about her work happy. I do not hear her complain, and so I am content.

"Once, though, I see her come out of the kitchen. She carries a pot of stew that Annie calls for. This she places on a table. As she turns to leave, a man comes up behind her. I am putting wood by the fire for burning. It is getting colder now. I see this man put his hands on her.

"'Here, Annie!' he calls out. 'Yer've been keepin' the best piece in the kitchen the whole time! Come, lass, I'll pay yer real good!'

"I take a log, and I am ready to spring on him, but Annie steps between and calls out in a loud voice, 'Keep yer bloody hands to yerself, ya son-of-a-whore. That there's my servant girl. She ain't no skivvy for hire! You touch her again, and I'll skin ya with me carvin' knife!'

"The man moves off laughing, but I stand with the log still ready. Annie looks at me with a warning, and I slowly put down the wood. Elalie quickly goes back to the kitchen, and the night goes on, but I have a lizard in my stomach. I don't like this place.

"Soon I think it is time to chew the plant again. I have waited *long enough. I pray to the Gods. I give the blood in our old lodge where Anasan's Spirit lies. I wish to know if the Gods let me See; do they see me; do they hear Tlaloc again? This time I dream a small dream. It is night. No one is around but Elalie and me. She is dressed in good English clothes. She is almost an English. She walks in the street...away from me. I call to her and she turns and waves, but she cries! As she passes from my sight, I see the Great Cat moving in the shadows. It follows her! It looks back at me with its green eyes glowing in the dark. It makes the whirring sound in its throat. Then it growls long and low and slips through the night to follow Elalie.*

"It was all They gave me. I wake with sweat, and my heart pounds. What is the meaning? The Great Cat follows her, but he does not strike! Then she is safe. Why does he follow? She is dressed in good English clothes. Is this good fortune? Why does she cry? I understand more before. I do not know the true meaning, but They let me See something. I am not lost to them! This I know, but I also know they do not let me See all. Only small things. They do not forgive all I do.

"I tell Elalie, we must be invisible. These English destroy whatever they see. They must not see us. We must keep to ourselves in their Town. We must not let them know us!

"She is angry for me saying these things. She does not want to hear this.

"'Father, we are with the English. We speak their language now. We know many of their ways. These men at the Inn are not decent. The Women here are not the Good English. They sell themselves for a few coins! To these dirty men. I know this! I am not a child anymore. We save what Annie pays. We have the gold. Soon we leave his place and do what Annie says— 'better ourselves'.

"'What is this 'better ourselves'? What does it mean?'

"'It means that there are some English who are not like these we see every day. They are the low ones fit only for being drunk and sinking into the earth from their own vices! Annie tells me she knows one, a man of quality who sees me. He has been at* *the Inn and he...looks at me.'*

"'No! What is this man if he comes here? How can he be any better than these that stink and shout and have no honor?'*

"'He is not a "regular". He is one with a fine house, and he is known in the town. Annie says he has horses and land and everything he needs. He is almost a chief among them. She says he brings gifts to you, if you say.'*

"'I do not say! Elalie, you do not know this man. This is not like our village—like your mother's people. Everyone there is known to everyone. If a man looks at a woman and her parents agree, he can bring the gifts. The man is known to all!'*

"'You are not known to the People! I know this! You are a stranger to them when you come. It is only because Oratamin accepts you, but no one knows you. Mother does not know you! I do not know you! You never tell me about where you come from. All that is known is that you are a traveler. What is that, "traveler"? What does that mean? Mother tells me that you give the healing to Oratamin, but I do not see this! The People do not know this. Mother knows nothing of who you are or who your people are. All she knows is that you are not of us, and now you say this one cannot give the gifts because you do not know him!'*

"'Anasan loves me. That is how she knows me. She is the only one. She gives me the knowledge of life. She gives me you! I do not give you away so lightly!'*

"'...I am not yours to give or to hold back, Father...I am my own...'*

"'In this I know she is her mother all over again! It is her mother who decides I am her man. I do not. I follow the ways of her people, but I do not decide. Elalie is the same. She is deciding.*

"'You...know this man? You speak with him?...'*

"'...Yes, Father...I speak with him...'*

"'How can this be? I am here always near you. How can you

speak with this man?'

"'...When Annie sends you to fetch things. She tells me of this man. He talks with me. He is kind. What the English call a "gentleman". He says he looks at me. He wants me.'

"'It is easy for a man to want a woman!'

"'No, it is not like that! He gives gifts to Annie to speak with me.'

"'She is not your Mother! She does not accept the gifts! That is not the way!'

"'I speak with him! He is not like these others. His clothes are good. He is clean. He speaks with soft words. He tells me that he comes to ask if I can think of him as husband...I see him many times now...'

"'You...would have this man?'

"'Yes.' She does not look at me now. I know she is cut in two. She feels for this—one who comes without my knowing, and me. She knows I live for her.

"'He is like the others! His words are soft, but he looks to take you like those that pay for women!'

"'He does not touch me! Never! He lives alone in his house. His mother and father are dead. It is me he wants as a wife.'

"'And you believe him! He is English! Why is it that he does not take an English girl?'

"'He finds me beautiful, Father! Is that so hard to understand?'

"I am silent. What can I say to this? She does not listen. I leave her, and I go to the barn to do my work with the horse and think. While I am there, Annie comes to me.

"'I see the girl's told ya, then?'

"'She tells me.' I am brushing the horse, but my mind is dark and angry.

'"Well, don't rub his skin off! Now, Lock...She's a fine, handsome girl. You know the men are goin' ta try!'

'"You see what I do if they touch her!'

'"An' yer'll git yerself killed. You know that, Lock! Yer both Nigger-Injuns! Ya don't have much choice 'round here. Work yerself ta death fer whatcha kin git or...give her a chance with this 'un. Leastwise he's rich!'

'"Why do you care for this? If we go, you have none to do the work!'

'"Hell, dontcha think I know that!'

'"You think this is a good man?'

'"How the hell would I know! His money's good. He paid me right smart to talk to Ellie.'

'"You sell Elalie!' I turn on her, but she stands not afraid.'

'"Yer want her like this? Moppin' ale and puke off my floors? Watchin' those louts eyein' her? It's only a matter 'o time—ya know that, dontcha? Ain't nobody—not me, not you, nor nobody's gonna stop her havin' a man! Hell, you oughta know! You done it with her Mother! You want to wait 'til one 'o these arses jumps on her? Sure you'll kill 'im, an' the whole town'll kill you! That what yer want? This dandy's taken a fancy to her! She's got one thing—why not let her profit from what she's got before one 'o them drunken tars steals it from her! I got feelin's for the girl! You too...ugly and bad tempered as ya are! I feel like a Mother ta her, and that's the God's honest truth!'

'"You lie.'

'"Lord, Lock! Ya do me a hurt, talkin' like that! You do! The two of ya been a fine good hard-workin' pair! I ain't anxious to have ya go. I get right emotional when I think it!' Now she tries to cry. She sniffs and puts her apron to her big red face.

'"The lies slide from your mouth like snakes. Each one is filled with poison. I am not a fool! Do not believe because I do low *work, I do not think! I see you and what you do. I know you for a liar and a cheater and a woman who worships only gold! You keep us because we are cheap! You pay us less than we are worth and think we do not understand! You water the drinks these men buy, and you steal from them when they are too drunk to know. You take your portion of the sleeping-money from the women who come to your house.'*

'"An' what if I do! I don't do nothin' everbody else ain't done before me! They get as fair a shake in my place as they'll git anywheres else, and that's a fact! You lookee here, you ugly Nigger-Injun, I'm tellin' you this here gent wants your Ellie. He's a cousin or somethin' to the Governor hisself! Got land, a fine house and a rich contract supplyin' pelts to the trade! If you got any sense at all, yer'll jump at it! I don't know what the hell he wants with a squaw—exceptin' she's a looker. Lord knows a man's ruled by his cock!— ya better git on it right quick before that fool goes and changes his mind! Ain't likely she's gonna git another offer better than him!'

'"You take money from this man to talk to Elalie!'

'"An' why the hell shouldn't I! She works for me! There ain't no harm in it!'

'"He only pays you to have her?'

'I know my business better'n that! He ain't never touched her! I swear it to ever' God there is! That young dandy's plum stupid about her! He wants a pure girl, an' I told him Ellie was a virgin guaranteed—a tribal princess is what I told him. Fallen on hard times—in need of a protector! Oh, he liked that all right!'

'"He cannot make the gifts. I do now allow it!'

'"I don't think you can stop 'em, Lock. Your Ellie's just as stupefied over him. You don't make somethin' outa this fer yerself an' her—it's gonna happen anyways! I can promise you that! Suit yerself...' She is walking away, and I know about this she does not lie.

'"Tell him...I talk with him. Only that.'

"She turns back to me, her big, red face smiling full of rotten teeth. 'Now yer gettin' smart! Now, don't talk no money less ya come to me! I'll set you right. You hear? A' course, I'll expect ya to do right by me, Lock!'

"'I do right by you...'

"'That's done then! A bargain good and proper! You'll see. This'll be the makin' o' you two. Yessiree, the good and proper makin' o' yez!'

"This is how it goes. Elalie is happy that I speak with him. She is ready to make the cakes for him, but I say no. I agree only to speak with this young English, nothing more. Two days pass, and he comes to me. He rides to the inn-yard on a fine horse, like the horses I first see the Silver Men ride. He wears a coat with shiny buttons. His boots are clean, and he does not smell like the other English. He comes down from his horse, and he comes to me with his hand out.

"'Mr. Lock, I am William Schuyler. A pleasure, sir!'

"I am carrying sacks from the barn. I do not take his hand. I do not want this one to think I care about who he is, so I look at him and continue carrying the sacks toward the Inn door.'

"'May I help you, sir? This is a heavy burden for one man!'

"I stop. I say nothing. I wait...He comes toward me with his arms held out, and I drop the two sacks into them. He falls into the dust struggling to get up under the weight. Finally I help him. My belly laughs but my face doesn't change. He gets to his feet, and I see him struggle to the door.

"'There!' I say. He puts the sacks down. He is not so clean now as when he comes. 'Come to the barn. We can talk there.' He follows me.

"In the barn we sit. I look at him. He looks at me.

"'You're very strong for a man of your size and age, Mr. Lock!'

"'Why do you want Elalie?'

293

"'I see...Well, I-I...that is we have developed feelings for one another. I'm sure your daughter has told you.'

"'She says this. Why do you want her?'

"'I am a man alone, Mr. Lock. I don't care much for the society of the town. My parents left me with some resources. A fur trade business. Don't let these clothes fool you; I am often in the wilderness, and I am desirous of a wife and a family.'

"'There are many English girls.'

"'Yes. There are many young eligible ladies, but they...are not Elalie! None of them has her bearing or her honesty, and none of them could stand the time out on the trail! I don't want a decoration for my home. I want a woman to be with me—share my life. What would these delicate town wenches do on horseback for days? Outside in rough weather? I know Elalie, and I have shown myself to her. She is the woman I seek. The woman I would have.'

"'What happens when you tire of her?'

"'That would never happen. I wish Elalie to be my wife.'

"'You pay Annie to talk to her behind my back.'

"'A bride-gift only. I did not know Elalie's circumstance. I thought that Annie might serve as a mother, until I learned you were her father.'

"'The big woman is no mother! She cares only about gold!'

"'I know Annie well, Mr. Lock. Everyone knows her appetite for money.'

"'Bride-gift?...How do you know about this?'

"'I know the Algonquin ways. I have lived among them. I am prepared to bring the roasted deer, if you accept me. Elalie will make the cakes, and I will join the Wolf Clan, if this pleases you both....Or, if she...you both prefer...I will arrange a Christian wedding.'

"'No Jesus. I do not like this God. He is weak! He brings nothing but sorrow to his followers!'

"'There are more than a few Englishmen who would agree with you, sir!'

"His face was real. He was...young. I do not have the wisdom of a father. I am a Warrior-Priest and Healer. I am far away from my time, my people. I am too long away from Anasan. Perhaps this is the good fortune from the dream."

CHAPTER 43

"All those in favor?" Julian was pushing the meeting.

"Aye!"

All hands were raised. The new Board members were well trained, and they knew which side of their bread was buttered. They had just voted to approve the coming year's budget. There would be no increase unless enrollment was up by more than twenty percent. I felt that was reasonable. I also knew that we would make it come fall. We had a healthy increase in applications for the lower grades and more than a few transfers. We were turning it around as I had hoped.

"Good! Who has the poop on the Feasibility study? I'm sure Dr. Holliman wants to know when work will start on the building! So do I, Goddammit it."

The Board members managed a politely unified chuckle.

"Jack, what's the scoop?" Julian directed his glare in the direction of John Beeman, the man I had spoken to at Olsen's funeral. Beeman was already opening up the folder he had brought, as if on cue. The rest of the Board shuffled, coughed...transferred its attention to the man at the end of the table.

"Um...yes. The current study is still in process. In view of the age of the building, Spencer and Chase recommends we defer action pending the conclusion of the study."

"Wait I minute!" I stood up. "Spencer and Chase have been all over that building twice! Olsen's first recommendations were prepared and ready to go. Why is it taking so long for this 'Feasibility' study? Why are we still waiting? The upgrades were to be done during the summer in time for fall classes!"

"Fair question! What's the damn hold up?" Julian's challenging tone seemed to ruffle Beeman a bit. Quickly he turned a page in his folder and continued...

"Um...yes...well the building's age as well as its Landmark status has forced us to access additional government permits and allowances to accommodate the re-purposing of the building in accordance with the plans submitted by the Foundation."

"Jesus Christ, you guys can talk circles around a wheel! What the hell are you waitin' for!" Julian banged his pudgy fist on the table for emphasis.

"Well...City Hall, Mr. Reynolds. We can't proceed until they approve the plan, and they have been...well...slow." Beeman was too relaxed in this exchange. In view of what I had seen of him the previous week at the wake, he was not a relaxed person. Confronting Julian should have made them all very uncomfortable. Instead, I heard the other Spencer and Chase members murmuring their agreement on the point without a single defensive comment.

"Umhm! So I 'spose I gotta spread some more money around those bums downtown to get what I want, huh?"

"I'm afraid so, Mr. Reynolds!"

"Fucking whores! That's what they are. Bleeding this city to death. New York politicians! Hell, I own a dozen of 'em! You'd think at least one of those bums would step up and make sure I'm happy! Don't worry, Holliman, I'm on this! I'm gonna call a couple of Assistant Mayors and share a few choice Goddamn words! We'll see what the Goddamn delay is!"

I looked at Julian and at the appreciative faces of the Board members who were again muttering their agreement to his outrage, and I got the distinct impression of a little play being put on solely for my benefit! Everything was all just a little too pat, too...orchestrated.

"Is there a motion to file a formal letter of protest regarding the delays of Crayden's approval papers by City Hall?" Julian threw a look at Matthew Thornton.

On cue Thornton raised his hand, "I so move!"

"All in favor!"

"Aye!"

Once again Unanimity.

"All right, gents. If there's no other business, I recommend—"

"What 're-purpose'? I managed to throw this out before Julian was able to bring the gavel down on the meeting.

"Huh? Holliman, we just said we were sending a formal letter. I'm gonna call those scum-suckers tomorrow! I'm gonna get some answers!" Julian was still blazing with self-righteousness.

"And I know you'll get the answers, Julian. You always do. What I want to know before we close this meeting is...what 're-purposing' are we talking about? Crayden was to receive a re-fitting of its aging mechanical systems and a new roof. There was nothing in our plan for a 're-purposing' of the building. Crayden is a school. That's its purpose. Nothing's changed in that...has it? Mr. Beeman?"

Beeman looked uncomfortable for a split second, but then he seemed to find his composure and look me in the eye.

"Um...nothing has changed in the Foundation's original plan for the building. The delays reflect nothing more than bureaucratic red tape."

"All right, can we get on with this now? You young fellas can schmooze all night, if you want, but I'm throwin' this old carcass into bed. Dr.'s orders! Who moves to adjourn?" Julian was maneuvering to close the meeting, but I wasn't letting go!

"So moved!"—Thornton again.

"What was the Foundation plan?" I threw it in there again. I felt the entire Board tighten up.

"Holliman, we can detail all this crap at our next Board meeting!"

"With all due respect, Mr. Reynolds, we were supposed to 'detail' everything at *this* meeting. That's what this meeting was for. I believe as

Headmaster I have final approval of all changes proposed by the Board, according to the Charter by-laws. Every day we wait jeopardizes the resumption of classes in the fall!"

"Nobody's gonna hurt your Goddamn school, Holliman! We're trying to help you, dammit!"

"That's very encouraging, Mr. Reynolds. Now suppose you apprise me of the 'Foundation Plan' submitted 'at the beginning' which requires so much red tape." I looked Julian squarely in the eye, and he glared at me. Finally he nodded to Beeman.

"Go ahead, Jack. Tell him the whole story!"

Beeman looked nervous now. His script was gone. This was something he clearly had not expected. "Uh...Well...Mr. Reynolds..uh."

"For Christ's sakes, spit it out, Beeman! He's not gonna let it drop, so tell him the main part of the plan!"

Beeman hesitated, closed his folder and took a deep breath.

"Well...in view of Crayden's financial difficulties in the past and its unique geographic position, in addition to the extensive footprint of the building—"

"We're gonna build a Goddamn tower over Crayden's current structure. Thirty-five Stories, residences and offices. The sale or rental of the additional space will fund the school...fucking forever. Unless you get stupid about it! You wouldn't let it go, would you, Sonny-Jim? You wouldn't just let it wait another week!"

It was out. I could feel the Board members holding their breath.

Finally Julian broke the silence, "Anyone move to adjourn the meeting?'

"So moved!"—Thornton.

"All in favor?"

"Aye!" It was a silent stampede as the Board members tucked away their papers and left the meeting room leaving Julian and me on opposite sides of the table. I waited until they had all left.

"You can't do this!"

"Sure I can! I can, and I have!"

"The building is Landmarked!"

"You think I didn't think about that. I spread a little money around— greased the right palms. I'm just waiting for the Mayor himself to approve the plan! Lighten up, Sonny-Jim. Crayden's sitting pretty! You'll be 'Crayden at the Reynolds Tower'."

"It'll completely change the character of the school! What we have, what Crayden's got going is Old World Tradition! We're the oldest continuing private school on the West Side!"

"And you'll fucking continue on, Goddamnit! Because of me! I'm setting you up, so you can't fail! No more worrying about enrollments, or endowments. The income from the building will keep you going, no matter who comes to the Goddamn place!"

"Julian, I know that building a thirty-five-story on top of Crayden can't happen without practically destroying the building!"

"The façade will survive. It'll look like Crayden on the outside!"

"But on the inside—"

"It'll be new! Sleek! Ready for the coming century! It'll be a testament to your Goddamn foresight, ya schmuck! You'll be the Headmaster who saved Crayden, not by inches, but by miles!"

"And destroyed it! What are we supposed to do while all this is going on? This isn't just a swimming pool, Julian. This is total destruction of the inside of Crayden. Where do we go while that's going on? How do we function?"

"I set you up in one of my other buildings downtown. I give you three floors; you hold your classes, then in a year or two, you move into your new digs. My PR guys have a whole campaign pumping up the changes. Letting people know all about the brand new Reynolds Tower and Crayden's new facilities! Done deal!"

"What was wrong with a simple renovation? Refitting the building with new systems and installing the new roof? That would cost you far less!"

"You think small, Sonny-Jim! That's why you're a fucking 'Headmaster' of a fucking dying old school! What the hell kind of a legacy is that...renovating that old pile of bricks? Installing a pool in a crummy basement? Who's gonna see that? That's no legacy! Hell—steel and chrome—something that'll last two-hundred years—that's a Goddamn legacy!"

"So, you don't really care about saving Crayden. You want a monument— to yourself."

"I've got other buildings..."

"But this one means something. What? Why do you need this building? You could build a tower anywhere and slap your name on it. Why are you doing this?"

"Because I fucking can! All those exclusive, patrician...Gentiles! Goddamn patronizing, smug sons-'o-bitches thinking they ruled the world. Well, let 'em roll around in their graves! Their precious 'alma-mater' was had by a Jew!"

"They're dead, Julian! It doesn't matter anymore!"

"The hell it doesn't! I don't care if they're all gone. *I'm* still here. *I* know it! I get the last laugh, and I'm going to laugh my ass off all the way to eternity!"

"I can't approve this plan. It doesn't save Crayden. It makes it into something...entirely different."

"You'll approve it!"

"No, Julian, I won't approve it! You can go ahead and fire me from the Foundation. I don't care about that. If you thought that bought me off, you were wrong."

"I know about your ethics, Holliman. I'm not talking about your Directing position in the foundation. I'm talking about being Headmaster of Crayden. I own that Board! We can replace you with someone with a different vision for Crayden altogether! Hell, I could have the Board vote to shut the damn school down! How about that? The fucking end of Crayden! We could vote to sell the building to the Foundation. I think it's time to shake it up a little, don't you?"

"I have a contract."

"Ha, ha, Sonny-Jim, you go right ahead and hire a lawyer. Hire two! Hire a whole staff! I can have you out on the street come lunch if I fucking choose!"

"You're really this...bitter."

"Keeps me warm, Sonny-Jim! All these years. Keeps me warm!...Now I suggest you take this little conversation home with you and sleep on it. You think hard before you decide what you want to do, and if you think it's going to be anything but 'I approve,' well, just close the door and don't look back because Crayden will be nothing but a pile of dust!"

I walked home from the meeting. I knew I had no choices here. Julian had both the power and the money to swat me like a fly. He had set his sights on making Crayden's transformation his personal vendetta against a world that died decades ago. He wasn't going to give up, and I had successfully put Crayden squarely in his sights. I had accomplished the opposite of my goal. I went from being Crayden's savior to being Crayden's Judas!

CHAPTER 44

"Elalie and William are good. Months they spend out trading, trapping. Elalie finds a tribe of her People. She makes good talk with them, and William has many skins! They stay out long and come to the town only when the snow flies.

"I care for the 'big house' when they are gone. It is the house of William's mother and father. It has many rooms and fine things inside. I do not live in it. I do not like being in such a great place alone. There is a 'cottage' in the back. It is a room with a fireplace and a place above for sleeping. The floor is dirt. It is there I move and bury the small gold I hold for Elalie and me. William says it is the cabin his father builds when first he comes and begins the 'fur trade'. It is bigger than the lodge I make with Anasan, but it is small enough that I am not lost. No one sees me. I watch. Wait. When they come back, I sit with them and listen.

"'William is like one of the People! They take him as their own, like you, father!'

"'That's Elalie's doing, sir. She speaks with them, and we have great friends among them. They come to us before all the other traders. Bring us the richest and finest pelts!'

"'It is because William is fair and kind and stays with the People! He learns more of our ways, Father. I tell them that he makes me his woman in the way of our People, not in the way of the English. They trade only with him!' Elalie's eyes are shining, and I see that she is happier than I ever see her.

"Now in the cold months, William fills the house with others.

One cooks, another cleans as Elalie and I did for Annie; others 'tend' to things...Work is always happening. I stay quiet in my place. None disturb me.

"This one day Elalie comes to me. She comes wearing an English dress the color of the sun. I think she is more beautiful than any English girl I see in the town, but she is ...worried.

"'Father,' she says, 'Am I a good wife?'

"'Why do you ask? Is William unhappy with you?'

"'No...when we are out on the trail, I am part of everything William does. I hunt, trap, cook for him. At night we lie together, and I know he is content.'

"'Then you are a good wife.'

"'Look at me, Father. One of the house women tells me "Go away! I know my job! I don't need no "Nigger-Injun" in a gown telling me what to do.'

"'Do you take your knife to her?'

"'No! If I kill her, I know it will not be good with William.'

"'She is jealous. You are the wife of a top man! He has a place, your William.'

"'William has a place—not me. I am only his squaw to them. I know this. I do not know the ways of the ladies in town. I do not understand this big house! In the woods, I have a place. I know how to please him. But here he is always with "business". I cannot be with him. In this place I am in the way of all these that do the work of the house. I have nothing to do. I am worthless!'

"'What is it the ladies of the town do? Surely they must have work.'

"'I know only that they keep their houses. I know how to work like these in the house, but it is their work. How can I be a good wife, if I don't have work?'

"'Do you say this to William? A husband should know the heart of his wife.'

"'If I tell him...he thinks I am worthless too! I cannot go to him with this! I must find a way to know these things.'

"'I see books in the big house. These may have something in them to tell you what work you can do.'

"Elalie brightens at the idea, but then grows dark again instantly. 'How do I listen to them, Father? I cannot read the marks!'

"I think about my time with Padre. I learn much from him about the Spanish. He teaches me Jesus, but I learn what I need about the Spanish from him. 'Elalie,' I say, 'Go to a church! Find a Priest. He will teach you the words in the books!'

"'A Priest?' she says looking at me confused. 'I do not want the English faith! I follow the ways of our People.'

"'Sometimes, my daughter, one must follow other ways to find one's own way. Go to a Priest, and ask to learn the reading of books....I think he helps you.'

"Elalie does as I tell her. There is a Priest in a church not far from the great house. To him she goes and asks for the reading. She tells me that he is greatly pleased! He takes her hands and tells her that he brings her to God. I know that he brings her only to reading, but it is well that he thinks so.

"She is quick. The Priest teaches her the Bible. There are many words, but Elalie is happy to learn. I tell her what I know of Jesus. I warn her not to be taken in by the Priest even though he is kind. Jesus is a weak God who makes no one happy, but I tell her to learn the words and use them to read things not about Jesus.

"She wishes to make William proud in the Town as well as out on the trail. By spring she is reading...everything.

"'There are worlds in these books, Father! Great and wonderful things I did not know. And languages! Did you know that other languages besides English have words? Why is it my People have no written words?'

"'Your people have deeds. The words are only the memories of deeds.'

"'And there are numbers, Father! Ways to count and understand the weight and value and amount of everything!'

"It is like a fire in her! She reads and learns. She asks questions I cannot answer. Soon she is telling the women and men who work in the house what they are to do and how they are to do it. At first they are angry. The one who calls her 'Nigger-Injun' is first to leave. Elalie tells this one what she is to do that day. Again she calls Elalie 'Nigger-Injun'. Elalie beats her and throws her from the house screaming while the others watch, but she does not care. Many leave, but none say words to Elalie. They slip away in silence. Elalie finds another and another until the house is full again, and it is her lodge, and she is the chief!

"William does not see this at first. He is in business. Selling the pelts from their trip and making ready to go back on the trail. At last, it is time to go out again. Elalie puts on the skins and carries her knife, but in one hand she holds a small pile of books.

"'What are those?' I hear him ask.

"'Books...to read when I am on the trail,' she answers proudly.

"'How do you read?' he asks. 'I don't teach you this?'

"'I go to the Priest and ask to learn. I want to be a good wife, and so he teaches me to read for you.'

"He looks at the books she takes and says, 'Women do not need to read these! These are books for men. They are books about mathematics and philosophy—much too difficult for a woman! Leave those, Elalie! You will be too busy hunting and trading with me for books.'

"'I wish to know what is in them!'

"'Leave them, I say! A woman is not built for books. Soon enough there will be children. You will have no time for books!'

"I see her put the books down with a cloud in her face. She looks to me with a question I cannot answer and embraces me. I say goodbye to them until the snow flies again. It will be a summer with the big house locked and quiet. I will go to the lodge I have with Anasan and stay with her spirit for a time and think about Elalie and William...and books."

CHAPTER 45

"No room for compromise?"

"I blew it! I pushed it in front of the whole Board. Forced his hand. It confirmed Delaney's whole suspicion. Reynolds is just about wiping out old Crayden. He's re-making it in his own image. It's to be a memorial to himself and his sixty-year resentment of events that took place almost three generations ago! A glass and chrome tower springing out of the shell of Crayden! My God, I've destroyed everything! How am I going to face people?"

Nick listened carefully. He was the first person I told about my failure. We sat in a booth in Maffei's, and he listened while I detailed the entire meeting.

"Well, it sounds at least that he wants the school to go on." I knew he was trying to be hopeful.

"As what? It won't be a Crayden anyone recognizes. He's determined to pretty much delete anything that resembles Crayden's tradition or the Old World caché it had built up over the years. That's his target. You should've seen how intent he was when he talked about having the 'last laugh'! It was sickening!"

"As you said, you don't have to approve the changes."

"He'll have the Board fire me. Steamroll right over me! He's got unlimited money, Nick. At least with Delaney, I could push back. With Julian...he planned the whole damn thing. He set me up, and I fell right into the trap. I handed him everything he needed to take over and have his way with it."

"Why was he delaying telling you? If he had everything set up, why would he need to do that?"

"He's just waiting for the Mayor's approval. Once he has that, Crayden's toast!"

"Well, maybe not! If he was waiting for the Mayor's approval, that means he doesn't have it yet! The Mayor is a political animal. Deals like this— they don't thrive out in the open in the sunlight! We can invite the press into this! The Mayor's already under fire for his crony real estate deals for the new stadium and the train station. If enough people make enough noise about the damage such a change would make in the neighborhood, not to mention the destruction of a renowned institution like Crayden....well, that's a lot of votes! This might just be one more project he doesn't want to defend right now!"

"Maybe...there should be an environmental study?!..."

"Oh yeah...and my buddies at the EPA could probably find the need to do some geological surveys to check on the viability of such a large structure at that location....Soil studies....impact studies...could take time!"

"Barbara belongs to several neighborhood organizations..."

"Don't leave Delaney out of this. He came to you—to warn you! The old boy might still have some useable clout. He might make a pretty good ally."

"Maybe Julian doesn't have quite the slam-dunk he's expecting!"

"...Good. Nice to see you back on your feet!"

"We could still lose this..."

"And we could win! It's worth a fight!"

"Damn right! If I'm going down, I'm going down swinging!"

"By the way, what's up with Santiago? Is he still finding you? Spinning his yarn for you?"

CHAPTER 46

'"You have what you have because of me! No one else could have given you the contact I have. No one else could make you the single most trusted trader in the territory!'

'"I do not need you to conduct my business! Woman, it is not meet for you to flaunt yourself before traders and men of business like a common whore!'

'"Whore! You call me this? Am I a whore flaunting myself when we are on the trail, living on the land with the People, wearing skins, and sleeping on the ground?'

'"Then you are my wife! Giving support to your husband!'

'"And is it not "support" when I prevent you from giving our wares to those thieves!'

'"Dammit, woman, it is a debt I owe!'

'"It is a gambling debt! One that can be paid at our leisure. I will not let you ruin yourself—ruin us with this weakness, William. These wolves can wait for their money. They will not go hungry, I can assure you!'

'"I cannot go out in decent society with my debts unpaid!'

'"Decent Society? Gamblers, drunkards and layabouts? This is your decent society?'

'"What else have I got! I can't have genteel folk in my house. Not with a—an arrangement like this.'

'"A Squaw—that's what you mean, isn't it, William? That's how

310

those "genteel folk" see me. A "Nigger-Injun"! You wanted me! You wanted a woman who could take the trail with you. One who could be with you. Well, I have been! And I can match you in the town as well. I can calculate the proceeds of our trade better than you! I can speak French, English, and Spanish, and I can set a table to rival the daintiest dame in the town—if they care to come and see! Would you care to discourse on the Greeks? Philosophy...mathematics...politics—or would you prefer I skin a deer for you!'

"'Make a child, Woman. It is all I ask! You're accomplished, all right! I give you that! You're a damned she-devil for learning. You do everything...but you can't give me a child! You're not a woman...and you're no wife to me!'

"It is how the years go with them. I see it happening. Each year goes by. Elalie grows more and more in her books. She buys them. Takes them into her spirit! As she grows strong, Williams grows small. This time I hear them. We sit at dinner, and they speak so. William leaves the big house. I know he goes to places like Annie's—although she is now gone. Dead from a drunk man's knife. Another is there. Like her.

"Elalie weeps. She cannot understand what she does to make this happen. I know I must tell her things I begin to see. Things I know.

"'He is hurt by a woman too strong for him to hold.'

"'I cannot give him children! I have tried, Father. None come! What am I to do?'

"'How long are you with William, my daughter?'

"'Uh...some time...fifteen years.'

"'How old are you now, my daughter?'

"'Thirty-five...I think. We were never certain.'

"'I am...You are forty-five, Elalie.'

"'No, Father! I was fifteen when Mother was killed!'

"'And we are staying in the lodge by her...a long time. You grow tired and lonely. Your spirit longs for people. Someone besides your ugly father. You want to go to the town. By then you are nearly thirty...'

"'No...it wasn't that long...'

"'It is. Come here, my daughter, and look in the glass.'

"She comes to me, and we stand in front of the glass. For a moment we look inside to see the faces that we have. In a moment she begins to see what before she never thinks about.

"'...I...I am one of the People! We are strong. We do not age like the English.'

"'Are you ever sick or weak?'

"'I have always been well! So have you! What does that mean? Many people stay well their entire lives!'

"'Like this? A face that changes little. A body that remains strong—that heals?'

"'That's nonsense! Superstition! I have read about these things, Father. Our People have many things they believe which are not true!'

"'It is not the People who think this...I live these things, my child. I live them...a long time. You are older than William, but he is getting fat and weaker than he was.'

"'He drinks!'

"'He grows older! You do not. Not like him.'

"'Why are you saying this? What do you hope to do by telling me these ridiculous things?'

"'I must tell her! I tell her how I am changed. I cannot tell her about my journey—that is forbidden, but I can tell her how the Gods change me through the plants the Priest-Father gives me. I tell her I think she is changed also because she is my daughter. I think that this is why she does not make children. The Gods *give her life, but not the way to make life.*

"'You had a child. I am that child. Your Gods allowed you that!'

"'What I do—I do this against them. I think for a man it is different. He does not carry a child; he only plants it.'

"'I am my mother's daughter! I will have a child, I know it!'

"But she does not. Time moves past her, taking William farther and farther away. He is gone most times now. Some bring him back foul and drunk and screaming at Elalie. He calls her 'witch' and whore and 'Nigger-Injun'. He is never without drinking. On the trail he is worthless. It is Elalie who pushes him along. She talks to the People and tells them that William is ill in spirit. They must forgive him his ways, and she makes sure that they have the trade goods they need. On these trips I go with her. I keep William safe and quiet. I help the ways I can, but I do not speak to her again about how we are changed. We do not speak of it.

"This one trip William drinks by the fire. In the night he rolls over into the flames. He does not scream; he does not wake; he dies.

"For Elalie the People make a burial place for him. He is given the honors of a loved one, and he is placed in the earth. Elalie does not weep. She does not talk with any. She sits by herself in a lodge, and she stares at the fire as if she can bring William's spirit out of it and make him come back.

"Finally a young chief comes to me.

"'She is a fine woman! A Woman should not be alone. I will take her to my lodge. I am in need of a wife. Will you accept the bride gifts?'

"I tell him, 'If she accepts you, it is well with me,' but I know she does not hear him. He is a strong, young man. He does not know that she is older than the age of his mother. I feel the lizards in my belly. I do not know how this will end.

"Each night the young chief goes to her and asks to make the *bride gifts. Each night Elalie tells him that that the spirit of her husband still sleeps by her, but I see her look at this young man. He comes. No matter how many times she tells him this. He speaks like a man, but he is a man possessed by her. He cannot do other than ask her.*

"Finally she tells him that she cannot live as a wife with him. She tells him not about the curse she bears from me, but that she cannot make children. She tells him that it withers the spirit of her husband who haunts her now and will not let her rest. She would not bring that curse to him.

"It does not discourage the young chief. He says to her that to have such a one as her, strong, honest, and knowing the ways of the English is an honor to him. 'I am not afraid of the ghost of your husband. He does not come between us. I will take you for the time you are with us. When you come, you are my wife. When you go, I am no worse than I am now. I can take another one to give me children and make a lodge. I am Chief.'

"It is not the way of the People. Elalie knows this. It is a dishonor for a man to accept such a thing. Elalie sees that the Young Chief cannot think of another. She tells him not to come again, or he will lose honor with his people. This he does, but I know that she meets him when none can see. I know this because the young chief comes to me. He is uneasy in his mind that he does me dishonor in this way. I tell him he is a good man. If my daughter takes him only in this way, it is because it is all she can give. I do not ask for bride gifts, and I do not shame him with the People.

"He is a proud young man, and he gives Elalie respect that William takes away. I know that she still feels for William, but she is content with the young chief. And for a time she can forget the strangeness of her journey and the pain of her losses.

"On the trail she is one woman; in the town she is another.

"When we return, there are questions about William, about what has become of him. Elalie sees that the English think we have killed him. She has an English who travels with us. She pays him much and has him talk for us. He tells the other

English how William dies of the drink and in a fire.

"Elalie as his wife is to be the owner of the big house and the fur business, but a Cousin comes. He says that Elalie is not William's wife. He says she must prove she is his wife, or she must give over the big house and the business to him.

"She does not have a piece of paper to show they are married. There is no priest or church to show this as well. We must go before a judge who says to Elalie that she must give up the property that William left. She has no rights to William's property. Nothing of his can be hers now. She must go. I must go with her.

"I dig up the gold from the floor of my cottage and keep it close in my clothes. Men come with muskets, and they take us out of the house. We are on the street. I have my knife, and I am ready to cut out their hearts, but Elalie says, 'No.'

"'Father, I do not need William's house or his property to make a way for us. You do not kill these men. It would go badly for us.'

"I tell her to go to the young chief and live where she is wanted. She tells me that she will not bring that sadness to him. She must go forward. Then I show her the gold I take with me—our own gold.

"'Father, with this, I can make a world for us.'

"Even though it is late in the hunting season, she buys knives and pots and iron things and we go back to the trail. She goes to this young chief, and she tells him that enemies seek to destroy her. They take her lodge and her skins, and she must continue the trading if she is to survive the winter.

"The young chief is full of her in his heart. He tells her he will go to war and kill these English that do this, but Elalie says he must not risk the People fighting so many English. It is not the way to win this fight. She tells him that she can fight the English way, but she needs the help of the People to get more skins that the English cannot take away. He tells his tribe to hunt with Elalie to help her. There are more pelts than ever I

see in so short a time, and Elalie goes back to the town with the richest furs to trade.

"We find a place, a small, poor house that will keep us warm enough. It is in a place where no one sees us. Here we are to stay for the cold months, but we must have money for food. 'We have the best pelts anyone has ever seen, Father. I have the help of the People! We will crush them!' she says to me.

"She knows the ways of the English. She plans to make her own business. She goes to the Cousin and tells him that she takes the pelts of the People away from him and makes that trail her own. The People will not trade with him because he is not a true man. They will drive him out if he comes. He takes her to court, but the judge can find no way stop her. She does nothing but to tell him what she can do. The Cousin must make his own trail if he is to make a business.

"This one is angry and dangerous. He seeks to frighten Elalie. One night he finds us, and he puts his musket to her saying, 'Indian bitch! You can't ruin me! I'll kill you now, and no one will care! What's one more dead nigger in the street?'

"'I will beggar you!' Elalie spits in his face. 'You greedy, grabbing bastard, you will lose everything you stole from me! Everything William and I built! You'll lose it all! I will see you in the dirt!'

"He pulls the trigger but the musket does not fire. Elalie is on him before I can draw my knife. She has her own at his throat, and his eyes are wide with the sight of death coming to him. I take my knife out to finish him, but she stops me.

"'No, Father, this one is not worth the trouble of killing. We will kill him in a way which hurts him more—we will take his money from him!'

"'You'll take nothing. No one will trade with you, nigger-bitch! I'll see to that. Just try and unload them pelts! They'll rot before anyone will touch them!'

"The Cousin is right. The traders will not talk to her, so she pays the same English from the court to be her voice. He

pretends to be the owner. She sends him to the traders with the pelts and tells him what he must get for them.

"They are greedy for the rich pelts Elalie has. The English makes much money, but when he is done, he does not come back. Elalie goes to him and tells him that she must have the money, but he does not give it up. He says that the pelts are his by right of law unless she can prove they are hers. Elalie knows it is the Cousin who does this. The Cousin promises this English one-half the money if he does this. This she learns from a slave of the Cousin. Too many know about this business. She cannot kill either man. She cannot take back her money, or they lock her away. The slave says the two men laugh about this. They know they have beaten her!

"I know what I must do. At night I go to the Cousin. I give him a chance to save himself. 'Tell this English to give the money he takes from Elalie. It is what he owes,' I say this to him, but he laughs and tells me that he knows nothing of what the man does. He says, 'If your squaw-bitch can't trade, it is her own fault for trying to take what is mine. Now she knows who is the man here!' I do not listen long; I know what is in his mind. I take his heart. It is a long time since I felt a beating heart in my hand. I give his blood to the Gods to drink. I take the heart still warm to the English and I show him. If he does not give the money, I will have his as well. 'Do not think you can scare me, nigger! I can have you hanged with the raising of my hand.' But he does not raise his hand fast enough. I am on him with my knife. The bodies I carry beyond the town where I know wolves and animals will take them. I bring Elalie this money, and she does not ask me how I get it. She knows."

CHAPTER 47

"I'm surprised you came to me."

Delaney sat in his leather easy chair like a king on his throne. Our little delegation stood awkwardly in his book-lined study overlooking Fifth Avenue. It was Barbara, Nick, Sally and me. There was a fine view of the park. Everything about the room and the rest of his apartment was classic and redolent of "old money". It was a little like something out of an old movie set—brass lamps softly shining, leather bound tomes on the shelves, and even a huge globe sitting on a mahogany stand in one corner. It was all perfect.

"Look, Mr. Delaney, don't blame Dr. Holliman for—for all your trouble! That was me! I told him about our money problems. I had to. If he was gonna do anything about 'em, he had to know! When this is all over, I'll quit, if that's what you want!" Sally insisted on throwing herself under the bus. I alerted her to Julian's intentions, and she rose up like a lioness defending her cubs. She wouldn't let us go to Delaney without her. "We've come so damn far! We're in the black, Mr. Delaney. I know you don't want to hear that, but Dr. Holliman stopped us from slowly bleeding to death. You've got to see the importance of that! OK, you two don't see eye-to-eye, I get that! But you both want Crayden to survive! Mr. Delaney, Dr. Holliman has worked night and day to save Crayden! You can't just let him get torpedoed by Julian Reynolds!"

"What makes the four of you think I can do anything about Julian? It seems to me Dr. Holliman has done...everything possible in that direction."

"We don't! We don't think you can do anything about Julian!" Nick was always good at coming through the back door of an argument. "But you do know the Mayor and, I think, a fair number of his cronies at City Hall."

"We're acquainted. He's a businessman. He gravitates toward money. That would tend to make him more an ally of Julian's than mine." Delaney was being coy.

"But he's also a politician! One whose current 'projects' have been under scrutiny lately. If an 'acquaintance' were to point out that a project such as Julian has proposed at Crayden might be socially and politically 'unfeasible' and a danger to his other, more lucrative concerns, he might be less interested in giving the plan his approval." I could see that Delaney appreciated Nick's thinking.

"'Socially and politically unfeasible, huh?' In what way?"

"Crayden is an historic building. It was built even before the Dakota! Generations of New Yorker's have sent their children to Crayden. I believe a number of very important people, including yourself...count themselves as Crayden alumni." Barbara was determined to break down Delaney's resentment of me, at least for the duration.

"Two Secretaries of War, a brace of federal congressmen, four governors, One Vice President and more captains of industry than you would care to count, Mrs. Holliman! Crayden has been very productive!"

"Certainly among that distinguished group there is a small army of sympathetic souls who would not want to see Crayden bastardized! Of course, that would take the insight and organization of someone well-connected and concerned about Crayden's future...like you." Barbara wanted to make sure to make our mission plain to Delaney.

"So you want me to help you put right what your husband has managed to make very wrong!"

"And right away, if you please, Mr. Delaney. I don't think we have time for you to gloat. Julian Reynolds' plan launches as soon as he gets the Mayor's nod. That could be even as we speak." That was it. Barbara was challenging him, and I saw a gleam in Delaney's eye."

"I think I may have hired the wrong Holliman! You seem to have a more practical approach than your husband!"

"And I don't have time for your flattery, Mr. Delaney. You got the right Holliman when you hired Brad. If you want to help save Crayden, you need to get on that phone, and call the Mayor, and stop him from giving that approval until he's talked to you."

"And then, what do I tell him, Mrs. Holliman?"

"That if he gives approval, there will be a huge community protest that will bring down a media storm on the rest of his 'public projects', possibly derailing all of them."

I chimed in. "It's what you hate the most, Mr. Delaney. Publicity...Negative Publicity! Crayden in the public eye. Everything you think of as destructive and wrong. And we need to use it if we're going to try to be effective!"

Delaney blinked a few times and looked at the four of us standing there. Suddenly he stood up and went to the phone and pressed a number into the keypad....

"Hello...Rachel?...Cameron Delaney. I need to speak to him. Yes, now, please. It's urgent. Yes, I'll hold..."

CHAPTER 48

"Bad times come. Between the English and the French. Many of the People join with one or the other. Many die. It is the English and the French who want to hold the trading and the land and the People only for themselves. Elalie goes on the trail even though I beg her to stay in the town. She knows how to talk with the French and the English, and she is also close to the People. She says it is a time for her to make much of all this confusion. I see men, many men from every side looking at her, but she stays with her young chief. With him only she is quiet and soft as I see her as a girl.

"Many of these men kill each other in the fighting. The Young chief also is one who is killed. Elalie bears his death with no tears. She makes the burial gifts and helps with his grave. She does this with all the duty of a wife, but she tells me that for her all feeling is dying. Soon she will feel nothing at all.

"Many of the young chief's tribe die. Some of the People think this happens because of Elalie. Because she is a wife but not a wife, she is of The People—but not of The People. For a while they move away from her. Elalie is patient and clever. She waits until things are hard, and she comes with the things they need to live. These she gives to the People as a sign of good will. She tells them of her loyalty to them and their nation. Soon the trapping and the hunting go on.

"She makes a great house. It is bigger than the one she had with William. She has many who work for her now. Two or three talk for us as though it is their business, but they are paid by Elalie. We are always away from the business, but Elalie

knows everything that happens. She has those who see for her; tell her everything that goes on. None dare to do what the Cousin or the English does. Not anymore.

"The trouble finally passes. We have a time of peace. Elalie tries to be one of the town. She gives money for the things the town needs. It is taken. She helps those that are hungry. They eat but have no thanks in their hearts. She makes a great feast in her great house to celebrate...none come. She is not greeted by any. We are invisible to all. Not to be seen. There is no one I can kill for this. I know I cannot kill all in the town. We are still the two of us.

"Then there is news that the English make war on us. This I do not understand. I ask Elalie, 'If we are part of the English, how is it that we make war on ourselves?'

"'Father, these that live here think of themselves as different from the English. Yes, they began as Englishmen, but now they see themselves as a different tribe. The English want to control them, and they will not be controlled. So there is to be a war!'

"'We must go to our old lodge and stay safe then. I keep it good. It stands there for us. We do not need to be in this war. Or we can go to the People and stay. They still see you as theirs.'

"'I cannot go to the People, Father. Not anymore...'

"'Why can you not go? They always take you before.'

"'...Have you forgotten, Father?'

"'They do not take me. I am never one of them, not without your mother. But you they hold to themselves!'

"'You showed me, Father...in the glass. Look, I do not change...not much. Neither do you. We are still strong and we have been here...80 years! I should be old, toothless...a husk. You...far older than me. I have seen for some time. I share this curse of yours. I live but I don't know why or how long...'

"'It is the will of the Gods. I am the Memory.'

"'And what am I, Father? Your Gods don't know me, yet I am cursed by them! I have no children! They will not even grant me that. What am I here for? I walk the earth but I make no footprint to show I have been here. I live in this great house with you. I live with the memory of William who died cursing me! What do I have to show I am alive?'

"'You...are the love of your mother and me! You are my daughter! I see you! I know you are alive!' I do not know what to say to her but this. In her eyes is a great emptiness. These are the tears from the dream! I See this! I know now what the dream is.

"'...That is not enough, Father. I have learned about the world, but I have lived so little in it. If I stay, I'll go mad! I must leave....'

"I do not know what to say, to think. 'Where do you go?'

"'Far, I think...'

"'Why do I not go with you?'

"'You are on your own journey, Father. That much you have told me. I don't know where it is from or where it goes, but it is not my journey...not any longer.'

"She tells me this and then she is quiet. No more words. I see she thinks. I do not know what I can say, what I can do. It is my doing, this curse. I take a woman. I make a child even though I am told it is wrong!

"I leave her. I must pray! I must talk to the Gods! That night I go to the old lodge. I make the signs. I dance. I weep. I give the blood and pray to the Gods to give me a sign what I can do. I chew the plant, but the dreams do not come. I wake in sweat and blood upon the ground. The fire is out, and I am cold. The Gods do not tell me.

"I stay there days, praying to know what the Gods want of me. I pray to know how I help Elalie. The time is heavy, but I do not leave. I give much blood, so much I have a dark fever.

"This one night I cut deep. I think, 'Take this blood, and give me a way to help her. This is my curse! Do not make it hers!' But there is no answer. In the night I am cold! Colder than I am ever. I sweat much, and I feel pain over all my body. I think inside myself that this is finally my death. I am to answer for my sin to the Gods themselves! Maybe they let me take the curse from Elalie! But finally the blackness comes, and I know nothing for a long time.

"When I begin to wake...I have a dream! It is Anasan! She comes running to me. 'Tlaloc, wake! Go back! Go back, now! You must stop her! She cannot leave this way! Wake up! See what you do! Do not let her go!'

"I jump awake! I can still hear Anasan's voice in my ears. I call her name, but she is not there. I am weak, but I know I must go back.

"It is slow to go back. I have given too much blood. I never feel like this before, but I know that this is the reason. Along the way I find plants that help make the blood come faster. These are common. I eat them as I walk. Halfway I find a stream, and I put myself in the cold water to wake up my body. The cold water makes me draw in great breaths of air. I shiver and feel the pain, but I stay in the water long enough to bring my mind back.

"Finally I am in the town. It is early morning. I turn to a place near the great house where I see there are new houses being built. All is quiet, but there is a smell in the air. It is strong. It is a burning, but I do not see a fire.

"Then when I get to the great house, I see what I do not want to see. The Great House is gone! There are people, talking and excited. They are dirty and smell of smoke. I come closer and I hear one say, 'Told us all to go! Paid us and just said, "Go"'. I ask, 'Where is she? Where is Elalie? Where is she?'

"'That's him?' one says.

"'I guess. Never seen much of him. Must be the Injun that worked for her!'

"Another takes me by the shoulders and looks at my face, 'It's gone, friend! Burned in the night. The lady burned with it. We tried to get her out, but nobody could! You're out of job, I guess. There'll be nobody here to pay you!'

"I cannot understand them. I cannot understand any of it. There is nothing but burnt wood and pieces of the great house everywhere. There is no Elalie. There is no sense to anything. I fall, and everything is black...

"When I wake, I am in a dark place. It is damp, but I am warm. I can smell the earth and the faint smell of rot. There is something binding my arms to my sides. I cannot see what it is. I struggle, and soon I free myself. Then I see it is a blanket that is wrapped tight around me. I am on a narrow stiff cloth bed. When I sit my feet are in the hard dirt of a floor.

"Slowly my eyes begin to see a little light above me. There are stairs! I am in a cellar. Someone has put me here and put a blanket around me. There is water in a pitcher on a wooden box by this bed. I drink. I drink it all, and it is not enough. I take the pitcher, and I climb the stairs. I hear voices on the other side of the door. I push on this door, and it opens.

"'Ah! He's alive! He's alive, Elder! Look!'

"'Quiet thee, Prudence!...Good even', Friend. I am glad to see thee still with us. We had some doubt about it, but a Provident God has given you back to us! I am Elder Praise, this is Sister Prudence. We brought you here when you collapsed at the site of the fire.

"'I do not die.'

"'Thank God, Friend! Thank God! You were badly cut. We though perhaps you had been attacked somewhere, your arms were...my word, look at your arms! It's a miracle! You are nearly healed!'

"'It is so. I heal.' I could not think of anything but Elalie. I know now what she means that she leaves. It holds my heart to the ground.

"'But, Friend, the wounds were deep. Sister Prudence sewed you as best she could. We could not find a doctor...not one who would tend...an Indian.'

"'Water...please.' I have a great thirst! Thirst and Elalie are the only things I think about. I do not feel pain. I do not hear this man or this woman. I think only that I lose her. She is gone...forever. And still my body cries out for water. It is a joke of the Gods! Elalie—Anasan the only ones who love me...gone, and I do not die. My body continues living...wanting water! The Gods laugh at me! I can do no more but drink the water they give me and weep.

"'There, now, Friend. It is a good thing! You live! God has worked a miracle! You have your life!'

"'I lose...my daughter! She is gone from me! I cannot stop her! She goes, and I am alone! I am always alone!'

"'God is with you! He is always with you! He sent us to you, and now you live! You must give Him thanks.'

"'The Gods take her! I do not thank them! They punish me! I do not obey them. I do what I must not. They take...everything. They take my Elalie...my Anasan! What do I do that is so bad? I am a man! For a small time, I am a man! They do not let me! They make me as I am, and they do not let me go!'

"'What is he saying, Elder? What does he mean?' The woman is afraid of my words. I can feel this. I cannot stop myself.

"'She is gone! I do not ask for this. It is put on me! I am made this way by my Priest-Father! He says I am the Memory! I do not want to remember! I do not want this life! I want to slip into the earth and be as nothing!...I cannot be this thing anymore!" The tears come as a flood. I remember all. The Fall of my people, The Silver Men, the pain, the ones who look to me to tell them who we are, and the time I am alone...the time, the long time I am always running, hiding, watching...waiting. It shakes from my body. I weep and weep, and I slip into blackness again."

***

This time Santiago did not lose control as he told the story. He voice was almost flat as he described the events leading to Elalie's death and Talloc's frantic return to town to try to save her. He seemed to be feeling a sense of inevitability about it, or perhaps he was growing tired of telling me the story.

I waited as he stopped talking. His eyes were downcast, but his breathing was regular and constant. He seemed to be lost in deep thought.

"Santiago, I have to tell you that there is a good chance I may not be here much longer."

He didn't respond or move, for that matter.

"I...have been very foolish. I have asked someone very rich and powerful to help me with the school, and he wants to make changes that may force me to leave."

"Sí. Our time is shorter now."

"I'm sorry I can't do much more for you."

"You do much. When I tell you, I am free. I tell you everything. It is what I must do."

"I wanted to help you. Give you something to retire on...but now I'm not sure I'll even have a job in a few more days!"

"You have the picture?"

"...Hm?...What picture?"

"The picture. I give you a picture. You have this?"

"Oh, you mean this?" I reached into my drawer and pulled out the small, old leather case with the miniature."

"Sí. You see this face?'

"Yes. She's very lovely. Anasan, isn't it?"

"Not Anasan! Elalie! It is my daughter, Elalie..."

"Santiago—"

"It is a Bride Present...William gives it...to me. I keep, but it is part of what I must give. I see it once more?"

I handed him the miniature, and he took it out of its case lovingly, looking at the face of the girl who stared sadly back at him.

"'Far,' she says. It is far! I do not see her, talk with her long, long time! She waits for me with Anasan. She knows now what my journey is. She sees from the side of the Gods. She knows what I cannot tell her."

He handed the artifact back to me and sighed deeply. He looked at me for a moment.

"You give me much. More than you can think. You are the only one I can say all to. The only one... I tell you, you do not lose. I See now. I See since the day I find you as a boy. That is how I know you are the Angry Young Lord. That night I dream. The Gods See me, hear me. I chew the plant, and the dreams come again. I am forgiven because I wait for you. I do not know why they do this, but it is what They do! They give me to you. You do not lose."

"All right, Santiago, I don't lose! I'm certainly going to try not to!"

"I tell you. The time grows short that I can speak. Tlaloc must finish..."

"His journey has been a long one."

"Sí, there is still a journey to come..."

CHAPTER 49

It was a war council. Barbara, Sally, Nick, Mona and me. Nick had not told Mona much about the political struggle at Crayden. She got a quick fill in from Barbara, and she insisted on helping. She was in our kitchen cooking more food than I had ever seen come out of that particular room! She was one of those women who saw food as an answer to most struggles in life, and it was a way she knew she could contribute.

Delaney's contact with the Mayor had bought us some time. The Mayor had agreed to meet with him and us to discuss the "Crayden issue". I didn't know the substance of Delaney's conversation with His Honor, but it was serious enough that we were now an *issue* on his agenda. What we were trying to iron out was an approach that would make it clear to him that Julian's expanded plans for Crayden would actually jeopardize the stability of the surrounding community and compromise the existing character of a fine old school that had contributed so much to New York City. It sounded good, but how were we going to make an act of incredible philanthropy, which seemingly should benefit Crayden, look like what it really was—the revenge of a bitter old man on a world who had rejected him in youth. It sounded ridiculous to *me*, and I was trying to make that argument!

"We have to point out the environmental impact on the neighborhood," Nick was arguing. "Screw the generosity of the building; it'll overwhelm the whole area! The city will have to add infrastructure, and most of the existing services are pretty old. Once you open that can of worms, it'll cost hundreds of millions to rebuild the sewer lines, water supply, gas delivery, electrical. It'll tie up the whole neighborhood for months, perhaps years!"

"Hey, aren't we screwing ourselves?" Sally was good at keeping us grounded. "If we stop Reynolds from building this tower, what's he going to do? He's not going to want to give us anything. We still have an old building that needs a lot of repair! What do we do about that? Sure, we're in the black, but we don't have the bucks to take care of the kind of renovation that old hulk really needs."

"...We go to Delaney," Barbara offered.

"He doesn't have that kind of money, Barbara. He's well off, but he doesn't have the kind of money Julian has. He couldn't finance the refit of the building. Besides, he's not going to do anything to help me outside of trying to fix this little mess I've created with Julian." I knew Delaney would hold this whole fiasco against me if we were lucky enough to stop Julian.

"Don't underestimate him, Brad. If he can pick up the phone to the Mayor and get us a meeting, who else can he call? How much money could he raise if he were pressed? And I don't think he dislikes you as much as you believe. In fact, I got the impression he enjoyed fencing with you. He's an old man. I think this whole battle has him pretty juiced!"

"You think he's enjoying this?"

"I think it gives him a mission in life. I think that's what Crayden has been for him for a long time. Let's just say, you've added a little sauce to the meal."

"There you go, Brad, " Nick chimed in a little too cheerfully, "Think of yourself as a condiment!"

"Dinner's ready!" Mona was right on cue. Everyone had a good laugh at my expense, and we went to the table to eat.

The phone rang, and I answered. It was Delaney for me.

"Mr. Delaney, we were just planning for our meeting with the Mayor. We want to be sure of our appro—What? Yes...Yes! I understand—Barbara, turn on the local news station! Something's happened to Julian!"

Everyone rose from the table and crowded into the living room. Local CBS was just broadcasting a "breaking news" story...

"...The body of real-estate mogul Julian Reynolds was found in his home in Turtle Bay this morning. Although police are not revealing any details, Reynold's death has been listed as a homicide. Police are investigating...."

The camera switched to the Chief of Police being interviewed outside of Julian's building. Reporters were everywhere, and there were microphones jammed up to the Chief's face waiting for his statement.

"Good morning. This morning at approximately 7:00 a.m. the body of Julian Reynolds was discovered by one of his staff. We are investigating the circumstances of his death, and I can't discuss any details until the investigation has been completed. What I can say at this time is that Mr. Reynolds was the victim of foul play. When we have more information, we will release it at an appropriate time."

At that, the Chief walked off camera, and a CBS news reporter stepped in front of the camera.

"Julian Reynolds was one of the most influential men in the city. His real estate holdings represent billions of dollars in high-rise structures throughout the city, and his Reynolds Foundation funds a great many charitable institutions around the city. Mr. Reynolds had no heirs. The question remains who will marshal the vast real estate empire Reynolds amassed in his more than sixty years, shaping and influencing the real estate market in the City. John, back to you..."

I was still on the line with Delaney, but I hadn't said a word while the report was airing. Finally, I heard Delaney on the other end calling my name.

"I'm sorry, Mr. Delaney, I was just listening to the report. Yes...yes, it's a shock! I understand. Yes, we can be at your apartment this afternoon, if that's convenient. Fine. Thank you for calling..."

"Oh, my God, Brad! He's dead. What does this mean for...everything?"

I looked at Barbara just as stunned as she was. "I don't know, Barbara, I don't know..."

***

"The body hasn't been released from the morgue. It probably won't be until they've analyzed...whatever they need to..." Delaney's voice trailed off, and his gaze was lost in the glass of brandy he was holding.

We had gone to his house at his request—the whole team including Mona. Delaney was able to discover certain details that nobody in the public was supposed to know. His back channels were still strong in city government, and we were being sworn to secrecy. If anything about Julian's murder got out to the press it would compromise the entire investigation.

"I don't know why, but Julian named me as his Executor...the lawyers called me shortly before you arrived. We haven't been in touch, not really, in...years. I don't know if I want to take that on...At my age...it might be too much..."

"I'm sorry, Mr. Delaney. This must be quite a shock for you! You knew Mr. Reynolds a long time, didn't you?" Sally was trying to offer the old man some show of sympathy. It was clear that he was holding down some emotional charge.

"It's always...difficult to see pieces of your youth...vanish. Julian was the last person I knew who knew the world in which we grew up. I didn't call you here to be maudlin..." Delaney pulled himself out of his reverie, and his eyes flashed at me signaling that he was about to throw something unpleasant my way. "Julian was mutilated by his murderer."

"What? What do you mean, 'mutilated'?" I couldn't believe I heard him correctly.

"His heart was cut out."

All of us gasped almost in unison. I felt the floor disappear under my feet, and I exchanged a glance with Nick and Barbara. This was impossible! This was too bizarre to believe. That couldn't have happened.

"My source wouldn't give me any details beyond that, but he did let me know that the police have connected this to another murder that happened some months ago. They think it might be the work of a serial killer"

On the way home in the cab, the three of us were silent. Sally sat up front with the driver and flirted with him. Mona was the only one who talked. After expressing her horror about the whole event, she couldn't resist appreciating Delaney's apartment. Her quick eye had taken in every detail it seemed. Her description actually filled the space left in the cab by our absent worrying over the news we had just shared. Nick, Barbara and I were the only ones who knew about "Tlaloc" and the bloody ways he worshipped and dispatched enemies. We were all circling the same screaming, ugly suspicion—the same impossible possibility. We couldn't look at each other.

CHAPTER 50

"The war is long. English ships come. The town is closed from the sea to any but the English. Those in the town are divided. There are some that would be English. Some say they are their own! It is a bad time.

"Before the English come, those that say they are their own, they drive the English ones from the town. Then when the English come, those come back and drive the others away. There is hatred everywhere in the town.

"English come in red coats and silver buttons. They carry more muskets. 'Regulars' the town people call them. Elder Praise is not part of this fight. His tribe does not think that war is good. They do not fight with any. They spend their time helping any who need their help and keeping themselves away from those who want to fight, but it is not enough. The English say he is a rebel and throw him from his house. They give it to an English captain. Many of his people are thrown from their houses. They say nothing. They just go. They live with others of their group who take them in. I am given a place in a stable in the house Elder Praise goes to. I work, but it is hard for Elder Praise and his people to find enough to eat.

"I think it is strange such a young man is called 'Elder' and that he does not fight. He tells me he is a follower of Jesus— 'Friends' is what his tribe calls themselves—and that war is something the Friends do not do. But the Silver Men bring this Jesus to us, and they burn my world and kill more than any I know. I know he is wrong! The followers of Jesus are the worst of all, and yet he does not fight. None of his tribe I see fight! It is strange to me. I fight. If someone throws me from my house—I fight! Men will do what they can if no one stops them. War is the way of all men. I know this; I see it!

"When he first asks me my name, I do not say 'Tlaloc.' It is my Warrior-Priest name. I do not think it is right to tell him this name. I tell him my 'Spanish' names 'Epifanio' and 'Santiago,'— the name Padre gives me from before. 'Epiphany' he calls me, and he gives me work. I stay with him. There is nowhere else for me to go. When I can, I go to the old Lodge, and I talk with Anasan's spirit. Many times I say I am sorry I lose Elalie. I weep for her with Anasan. I make the prayers and the signs and give the blood. I am never sorry enough!

"When I come back, Elder Praise does not ask me. He lets me stay, and I work hard for him! I know he is a good man. He never tells me of Jesus. This he keeps for his own people. I do not ask, but I keep quiet about their ways. I watch and learn them, and I am what they need of me. This I know to do. This I have always done.

"One night I am sent by Elder Praise to a house to bring papers. I do not know what they are, but he says they are important. It is late. When I go, I see men. They are not Regulars. They are dressed like everyone, and they are quiet. I stand back and make myself invisible. They begin to set fire to the houses. Quickly they move from one house to the next. Soon many houses are on fire, and the men go away. The town is on fire! People come from the houses and try to make the fire stop, but it is too late. The fire spreads from one house to another on the wooden roofs. English soldiers come out and try to stop it, but none can do this. There is much wind, and the fire grows to the west. It burns many houses—many. I stay and watch. There is much shouting and people trying to bring things from the houses. The house I am to go burns as well. I know I must go back. I must not be found here. They think it is me if they see me. I move in shadows and find my way back to Elder Praise. I tell him what I see and give him back the papers. His face is clouded.

"So much is burned. The English throw many from their houses to the street. They take the houses for themselves, and the *people are left outside. They must make their own way. Many make lodges of cloth in the open spaces. There some stay in these for a long time. The English are angry and blame the people of the town for the fire. They do not help them. It is Elder Praise and his tribe who try to help the people of the town. I work with them making the lodges and finding food. Some who are sick or hurt I heal. I save some, but I do this quietly. I do not want any to see that I know much of healing, but Elder Praise sees me. I am healing a man with a chancre that is very bad. I find the plants needed and make a paste. In a few days he is much better, and Elder Praise sees this. He asks me, and I tell him I know the medicine of my people—small things. Nothing as good as the English. He is silent, but I know he watches me now. I am careful not to do all I know. I do not want him to think I am more than he needs me to be.*

"Many stay in the cloth lodges. There is sickness. Water is filthy. Houses are not built back. The town is in misery. I do not see much fighting. There are many 'Regulars', but I do not see any battles. We hear of many all around us. For a long time we think that the English win. These Regulars are strong warriors. They have strong leaders. In time the war is over, and one day the Regulars leave. The say that 'we' win, but the town is bad to see. Men argue and drink, and steal, and kill even without these English in the town. It is this that Elder Praise talks most about. He talks of this to his 'Friends' and others who will listen. He says men must return to the ways of Jesus. He worries for the 'souls' of men, but I know the 'souls' of men. These are the things they love. It is always thus..."

Santiago broke off his narrative and turned off the recording device. It surprised me that he knew how to do this.

It had been two days since Julian's murder. The school year was winding down. Classes happened. I buried myself in the school's routine—anything but entertaining my nagging fears. I was contacted by the Reynolds Foundation almost immediately. Sheaves of papers were messengered to me concerning the Foundation projects and budgets. With Julian gone, all of his "flunkies", as he called them, were looking to me for guidance. I had called a "strategic meeting" the following day at Crayden because I didn't want to be away from the school at this time. This extra work had actually helped me push things away, but at the end of the school day, Santiago had found me. I listened to him without comment recording his story. He was looking at me.

"You are not good. You have questions you do not want to know. Do not ask them, and you do not know."

I looked at him for a long moment, "Did you kill Julian Reynolds?"

He shook his head, and he wheezed his strange laugh. "Santiago is an old man. He cleans. He fixes. You know this man does not kill."

"Santiago, you're my friend. I don't want to think this, but everything you've told me...everything you have said..."

"It is a story, sí? It is something I give you to remember. It is something I do for my Gods, and you do for me. You keep these things for me; I am free of them."

"You've told me this is your own story. You've been angry with me for not believing you."

"Do you believe me now?" He was waiting...

***

"I'm afraid we have to treat this visit with a little more formality, Dr. Holliman..."

Lieutenant Rifkin and his partner Gergan were back again in my office. They were the same two Police investigators who had come to me when Soldani's body was found. Alarm bells were clanging in my skull.

"I don't know if you are aware of it, but in the past nine months three people have died who have had some connection to this school."

"...Well...yes. I think I was, but...are you saying that there's some direct connection to Crayden?"

"We can't say with any certainty, Dr. Holliman, and I don't want to alarm you, but two of these three deaths have more in common than the connection to Crayden. There are certain elements of the deaths of Dr. Emilio Soldani and Julian Reynolds that...require a closer look."

"What 'elements'?" I couldn't reveal what I knew about Julian's murder, but I could feel my palms sweat. Julian had his heart cut out of his body. What else could it be, but that Soldani had the same thing happen to him? My head was beginning to spin.

"I can't say right now. It may be that Crayden has nothing to do with either of them, but we have to explore every possibility. You understand that, don't you?"

"Uh...yes, of course. But I hope you understand that I wouldn't want any of this to be made public. Crayden is very vulnerable right now. I've spent this entire year restructuring the school to save it from bankruptcy. Something like a police investigation could compromise everything."

"You're the Director of the Reynolds Foundation, aren't you?"

"Yes. I was hired by Julian Reynolds to run the Foundation. It was strictly a rubber-stamp position. I signed off on whatever Julian wanted to do. He was really running the organization."

"Quite a large salary for a 'rubber stamp' isn't it?"

"Yes. It is. Mr. Reynolds wanted me to advise him regarding the tone of his philanthropy. He was concerned that his charitable activity be viewed in a positive light."

"Why would he need that? He's giving his money away to all kinds of good causes. Why would he worry about his 'tone'?"

"Julian had an...outspoken style. He liked things his way. Sometimes he tended to...bully the organizations to which he donated."

"And your job was to...'rein him in'?"

"In a manner of speaking. I don't think anyone could rein Julian in. He was a very...volatile individual."

"Well, not now, is he? With his death, I guess you'll be pretty much free to run the Foundation as you see fit."

"...Wait a minute! If you're suggesting that I—"

"I'm not. Sorry, Dr. Holliman, but we already checked you out. In both cases we know where you were and what you were doing. You couldn't have had anything to do with either murder."

I had started to panic in my head, but this last bit of news allowed me to breathe again. "I don't know whether to be insulted or relieved."

"Nothing personal, Dr. Holliman. It's our job to check out anyone who might have a motive. We also know that everyone closest to you is accounted for, so please don't feel that we're here to try to connect you to a crime. We're simply trying to find out if there might be someone— directly or indirectly—connected to the school who might have a reason to kill these men."

What could I say to this? My brain was screaming out, "Tlaloc! Tlaloc! A five-hundred-year old Aztec Warrior-Priest! It was him! He did it!" If I did, they'd send me to Bellevue! I could see the headlines, "Headmaster of Private School Cracks Under Pressure!" If I told them about Santiago, an eighty-plus-year-old janitor who has worked at the school for decades, they'd still think I was crazy. How could a man that age commit such a crime? What? What could I say?

"...I assume the third death was Martin Olsen, the architect?"

"Yes."

"His death doesn't show the same...'common elements' as the other two?"

"The remains were badly degraded. We couldn't determine any cause of death. Right now, it's listed as a suicide."

"That must be hard on his mother."

"So, you have no idea who might have a reason to kill these men?"

"I'm sure Julian had a lot of enemies. Soldani?—I didn't know him well enough to say, but he didn't strike me as someone noticeable enough to want to kill. He was an academic. Socially awkward, but non-threatening. I can't see anyone wanting to do him harm."

"I see...." He closed his notebook. Gergan, who had been silent through the entire interview, just stared at me. "We'll be back in touch if we need anything from you. You are going to be around for a while, I take it?"

"Yes. Oh, yes, I have a great deal to do! Between the school and my new responsibilities for the Foundation...I...uh, this is all so overwhelming..." It was occurring to me that Hell was just opening its gates to me.

***

"What do we say? We have to say something!" Nick had come over without Mona. He had purposely kept her out of the loop about Santiago. He and Barbara and I sat in our living room trying to determine what was right.

"We don't know anything. We suspect, but we don't know. Those files of Santiago telling you stories of Tlaloc are just that—stories! It's impossible...we know that!" Nick was reaching for some logic in the situation, something his scientific mind could hang onto.

"OK, Nick, they're stories—just stories, but they're stories about ripping out hearts and making blood sacrifices! Whatever they are, they have a striking similarity to two very real murders on our doorstep."

"One! We don't know for sure about Soldani. That's only a conjecture on your part."

"We can't ignore the possibility that Santiago may have done these killings. I can't stay silent about this!"

"Oh, Brad, I'm sorry I minimized this whole experience! I thought he was just dramatizing, making the story real for a new generation. I never thought he would...do...anything." Barbara was searching too. We all were.

"What are you going to say? We're not even supposed to know about Reynolds having his heart cut out. Delaney was very clear on that point. If you tell the police what you know, you'll only incriminate yourself. They'll think you're the killer! If you try to explain...well, how far into the story do you think you might get before you get thrown into the Criminal Psych Ward never to return?"

"Brad, Nick is right! There's no way they'll believe any of this. They'll take you for the murderer. Even with the audio files...they'll say you listened to his story, lost touch with reality due to stress, and committed the crimes. No one is going to believe an elderly Janitor could have committed such vicious attacks. If it comes out, you had a believable motive for killing both men! My God, you can't say anything!"

"...Christ!... I'm the logical suspect. *But* the reason they didn't arrest me was because they knew my whereabouts when both murders were committed—they know I'm innocent!"

"If you walk in there with this story, they'll find a way to *make* you the killer. They need a suspect. Their job is to find one and to 'solve' these murders! You'll give them exactly what they need, and they'll railroad you right onto the gurney for a lethal injection!" I had to listen to Nick.

"So...that's it? We just...say nothing? Do nothing? Is that the kind of people we are?"

"No. We go to Santiago. We tell him that we know what he's done, and *you* tell him that he must never kill again."

"Me?"

"Brad, he believes he belongs to you. Didn't you say he said that?" Barbara was holding my arm and searching my eyes. Pleading for me to see this way.

"...I don't know. We're dealing with a primitive sensibility. He believes that killing is right. He sees it as a solution, as an indelible part of human nature!"

"I'd have to agree with him there...Brad, anything else will get you in so deep you'll never get out! Do this! This is what you can do!"

I knew Nick was trying, along with Barbara, to reach past my guilt with common sense, but I was miserable. Every way I looked, I was conflicted.

There was no way back and no way out....

***

We went to Crayden and headed for Santiago's basement room. When we got there, he was nowhere to be found. We searched the school, but we couldn't find him.

"He does this. Then he shows up like a ghost when you don't expect him. He may not come with the both of you here." We were standing at the staircase, and Nick and Barbara looked around uncertainly.

"It's creepy here at night!" I recalled that Barbara had never seen Crayden after it was put to bed.

"Maybe we should go. If we're gone, he might come to you."

"Good idea. Nick, you and Barbara go back to our apartment. I'll wait for him in my office. That's where he usually pops up. I don't really need you here to do this. He's not dangerous to me."

They agreed. I promised them I'd return in two hours if Santiago didn't materialize in that time.

After they had left, I went to the office. There on my desk was the maté! Moreover, the recorder was already out and the record light was on. I quickly turned it off. I felt the cup and it was still hot. He was just here!

"Santiago?...Santiago, are you here?" I waited, but the only sounds were the creaks and whispers the old building always made. "Santiago, please! I need to talk to you!...." Nothing. No response. No sudden appearance.

I waited another few minutes. I sipped the maté hoping he'd arrive. Finally I backed up the recorder out of curiosity and listened...

> *"Soon people return to the town that were made to leave. They build, and the town comes alive again. Those in the town that wanted the English are pushed out!*
>
> *"It grows, the town! Wherever it goes, the game flees, the trees die, and the stink and noise of people come. The water grows dirty. Everywhere there are more people of every kind. I hear speaking in words I do not know exist. Elalie tells me that there are 'worlds in books.' I do not know they can get out and come to this world, but then I think how the Spanish come to us and burn our world, and I know it is always the same with this too.*
>
> *"In Time, Elder Praise takes a wife. He and his "Friends" make farms north of the town. The farms move much more north now than I think they can. It is Elder Praise's farm that holds the old lodge! When I see this, I tell him this is where I go some times. I say to him that his place is sacred to me. It is where my Anasan's spirit lies. He tells me that it remains so. He does not plant or change anything there. This, he says is a promise he gives me!*
>
> *"He has three sons. He has a farm, but he is a poor farmer. He spends too much time leading his tribe. In time two of Elder*

Praise's sons do the farming of the land. The other is not a farmer. This one loves books. He is Samuel.

"This one I watch. He is like Elalie for learning! Everything he reads, he takes into his spirit! He knows much, and he talks always! I listen as I do with Elalie. He is alone too much, and he is with me much as a child. This one also sees the worlds in books. I teach him about plants and animals. Not the healing but the uses of plants and what game is good to eat in what seasons. He learns this happily, but he always has his books with him. I know he is never a man of work, but he is a chief like Elder Praise.

"When they are older, Elder Praise must divide his land. To his two farmer sons he gives the best land. To Samuel he gives the land that holds the lodge. It is poor land. Not good enough for a farm, but it does not matter. None of this land is very good for a farm. The two other sons soon sell their land and leave to 'go West' to find better land.

"Now Elder Praise has only one son near him. The time is hard for him. The farm is poor. There is a sickness among many. It brings fever. It is much like the sickness that kills so many of my people. I am afraid for them. I do not know how to stop it. Some I make well. Elder Praise and his wife take the sickness. For days I see a bear circling the house, waiting for them. I use the plants I know—all the knowledge given to me by my Priest-Father. I do not rest. I think for a time that the bear leaves them, but one night it comes for them both even though they are not old.

"It is Samuel and I left. I worry for him. He is only become a man. He is not yet seasoned in the world. I stay by him, and he grieves, but he does not sink. He shows much strength even in one so young.

"Elder Praise is a leader of his people. Samuel is young, but he knows much. He stands up and takes the place his father has. He talks, and the people listen. Soon he leads as his father does, but the farms are poor, and his farm is the poorest. A few pigs he has and not much more. He does not have enough to live on even with me to help. It is the tribe of Friends that keeps him.

"He is not so stiff as Elder Praise. He forgives much and tries to teach his tribe how to help each other and understand what cannot be changed. He is much loved by them, and some send their children to him to learn. Elder Praise's old house becomes a school. It is a few children at first, but the money he makes keeps us.

"In time there is another war. This one they say is brother to brother. Samuel says it is because some keep the Dark Ones as slaves in a distant place. He says it is a great wrong, and those of our town and others go to free them. He and his tribe of 'Friends' are strong against this making of slaves.

"In our school there are several barns. He tells me to fix one.

"'Make a place for ten to stay. Put in beds and a stove for warmth. Soon some will come, and we will help them.'

"They come...Dark Ones. These have come from the distant place where they are slaves. Samuel feeds them, sends them to places for work...helps them move on. In their faces I see Lele and his mother and father. I see the hold of the ship where I healed the sick and dying. This I do for Samuel. I do it in small ways. Many are sick or hurt. I find the plants I need. I make them well, but I am careful to do this when Samuel is not around. I do not want him to see more than he must.

"They come and come. Samuel and his tribe help them. I heal them. They go. Before long, the war is over. The river of Dark Ones slows and stops. We are only a school again.

"Soon more children come. Some of these are not children of the tribe now, but children of people in the town. They wish their children to learn from Samuel. They see him as a good and learned man. It is good. I keep the pigs and do the work around the house so that Samuel can be with the children. He is good like Elder Praise, and kind as well. He must hire more to teach the children. Like the town the school grows too. Without thinking about it, much money comes to him. It is not long that he has something he never dreams before.

"We make more houses on the land. These are only for

learning. First there are two, then four, then these are taken down and larger ones are built. Before long this poor piece of ground is like a village. Samuel finds others like himself who love books and who teach the children. The people hold him very high. This place is where many want their children to come.

"The town is like a beast running. It comes closer and closer. There are more people now than I think are in the world.

"He comes to me and says, 'Epiphany, I know what I must do. God calls me to lead these children and many more. I am to build a great place of learning. I must plan for it.' He asks me to stay with him and help. This I know I do. He is for me another child. A son. I can do no other than stay with him. He has no wife, no children. He says the children of the school are his children. He needs no others. I think this is wrong. I want a man such as this to make children and teach his own, but it is not his way.

"It is this Samuel who makes this place that you come to. You, the Angry Young Lord. He makes this place, but he does not see it. He works like one held by a demon. As it is building, Samuel is fading from me. He is growing older, weaker. I do all I can, but I cannot stop the time in his body. I would not curse him in that way.

"One day he says to me, 'Epiphany, when I leave, this place is to go on. The other men who teach here keep it. I ask these men to keep you. To give you work as long as you wish and a place to live. If I ask it, they do this. Is this what you wish?'

"I say that I wish him to be well, to stay, and see his work finish. But he cannot. He slips into the earth as everyone who shares my spirit does. Only I stay on the earth. The Gods make me stay. I am here, and I wait. I see the town grow bigger than anything I ever see. After Samuel I stay. I work. I pray. Wars come. Men fight and kill as they always do. They are driven by the same demons I see long ago. The time is all the same. It is only the few who care for us that make Life. The little of this I steal from the Gods teaches me this.

"Then there is the day I see you. The dreams come back. The Gods see me, hear me. I See again. I tell you they give me to you. It is true. I am with you. When you need me, I am there. It is well..."

The recorder was clicked off. I knew that was all of the story. As he always did, Santiago appeared and disappeared when he knew the time was right. I knew instinctively that I would not see him again. I would not find him. I knew that he would slip into the anonymity of the city and become invisible. The subsequent months proved me right. He was gone...

EPILOGUE

The sounds of construction were all around me.

I couldn't believe that it had been only a little more than a year that I had started as headmaster at Crayden. The new semester was about to begin. So much had happened, and yet, to the outside world, nothing had really changed. That was New York. What we saw as a titanic struggle between altruism and revenge, between the rationality of the modern world and the chaotic forces of ancient gods, was lost in the din of humanity. I wonder how many epic struggles occur next to us every day without our even being aware of them. We remain invisible to each other.

Julian had never fired me as Director of the Reynolds Foundation. He hadn't had time. In spite of his age, Delaney did take on the executorship of Julian's estate. He also returned as head of Crayden's Board of Governors when most of Julian's flunkies quit. He was joined by most of the original members. Being Julian's executor gave him status and money without too much responsibility. Most of the business transition had been worked out by Julian himself. The Real Estate Group that held the bulk of Julian's assets was to continue under the current management. All the proceeds were to be donated to the Foundation to continue its "good works" in Julian's name.

That was my job. With Julian gone, I was truly the Director of the Reynolds Foundation. It was more than I bargained for, but it allowed me to fund Crayden. I was able to increase faculty salaries and hire on more staff. There was a new "Director of Maintenance." He had three men to keep the building running. Three men...I thought about that dilapidated old chair by the boiler where I sat with Santiago years ago, but I shook off the image. It was truly a new Crayden. The Foundation money had attracted a swarm of new applications. It seemed Crayden was once again the place to go!

I hired Nick and Sally to assist me in the day-to-day running of the school. Sally had her own assistant. She loved being in charge. Nick filled in for me when I had to attend to the business of the Foundation, but he made it clear he wanted to be in the classroom, not the office.

I instructed Spencer and Chase to scrap the tower. They were to proceed with the renovation of Crayden's physical plant as indicated by Martin Olsen's plans. They threatened to sue, but since Julian had never signed the plans, there wasn't much they could do. They were paid for the structural analysis, and during the spring and summer Crayden got a new roof, new mechanical systems, new windows, and I even ordered that the neglected old courtyard be re-landscaped and made useable.

Nick and I were reviewing the class schedule for the New Year when the construction foreman entered the office.

"Dr. Holliman?"

"Yeah, George, what can I do for you?"

"We hit a snag out in the courtyard. I need to know what you want done."

"What is it?"

"Well...it's hard to describe. You wanna come out, and I'll show you."

He led us into the courtyard. The old slate walks were jackhammered up, and the bobcats were digging up most of the space for the new plantings. Over in the corner near the west side of the yard, workmen were standing around looking into a hole.

As we approached they moved aside, and George stepped down to explain...

"I stopped 'em from doing anything else when we found it. There was this stuff all over it—soft as wet paper towels. I threw a tarp over it and came to get you. Uh...we were opening up this side for installation of footings for stone benches when we came across it." He pulled back the tarp— "I think it's an Indian burial."

There in the shallow pit was a skeleton lying on its side in the fetal position facing east. Around it were a few clay pots, carefully arranged.

"I thought you might want to call someone, you know, to check it out. Some archeologist or something."

Nick and I saw them right away...

In the loosened dirt around the skull there were a number of small iridescent disks...of cut oyster shell—the "pieces of the moon"! I couldn't quite absorb it at first, but then I was sure. It was the necklace Tlaloc had made for Anason. This was Anasan! Her grave! I felt my stomach turn slightly. This was Anasan's grave! This was the location of Tlaloc's lodge with her! Nick and I looked at each other dumbfounded. It couldn't be, —but there it was. We couldn't rationalize it away; we couldn't find any neat explanation that changed its reality. It was proof, undeniable proof! If this was Anasan, then everything...the Fall of his people, the passage on the slave ship, the time with the local tribe—everything he told us...was true! It was not just a tribal memory; it was *his* memory.

"You want to take a better look, Dr. Holliman?" George was offering to help me down into the hole"

"...No...thank you, George..."

I couldn't bring myself to step into the burial. I felt like we were intruding into something so...intimate and personal...like walking in on two people making love. I didn't want to look more closely. I touched the soft covering that had been tossed to the side of the grave. I could tell that the covering was actually animal skin. It was just as Tlaloc had described it. This was his sacred site, and we had violated it.

"So...What do you want us to do?" He was waiting. I had to say something.

"...Put the covering back over the body gently and rebury it. Don't touch anything. You can locate the benches further over. This site is to remain empty and...respected."

"...Ok. If that's what you want. It's going to mean changing the landscape architect's design, though."

"That's OK, George. It's a small change. But it's important. No one is to disturb this grave again. Keep all the heavy equipment away from here."

"Sure. We'll get right on it. Hey, guys! We put it back the way it was! Move that cat outa here!..."

We left the courtyard silently and went back to the office. I remembered what Tlaloc had said to me:

> *"What is 'real'? Only what you know? Only what you see? Is this the only 'real' you know? That is a small life!"*

He was right.

By mutual agreement, Nick and I don't talk about it. We can't. Nick was in unchartered territory. He found himself on the "Yellow Brick Road", and he couldn't find his way back through the science on which he had always relied. I found myself in a world with more dark corners than I had ever imagined. It was a much, much bigger world, and it was scarier than I wanted to admit.

I didn't tell Barbara about the grave. She already felt guilty about persuading me not to reveal what we believed about Santiago; something like this would only wrack her conscience more. We all felt guilty about not going to the police with what we suspected, but they never would have understood.

I had the files. I had transferred them to a thumb drive and transcribed them adding everything I could remember about this impossible experience. I shrouded it all in an envelope in my safe next to the morion and the leather case holding the miniature of Elalie. It all sits there in my safe. I have the memory, Tlaloc's memory. He is free...and somehow I'm held by it....I probably always will be.

The End

ABOUT THE AUTHOR

Mike Champagne is a playwright and teacher who lives and works in New York City. His plays and musicals have been produced and critically acclaimed in New York, Los Angeles, San Francisco, Chicago and many smaller cities around the country and in Europe. *Brother to the Blood* is his first work of prose fiction.

www.ingramcontent.com/pod-product-compliance
Lightning Source LLC
Chambersburg PA
CBHW020242200626
46816CB00001BA/89